The Hell of Heaven

The Hell of Heaven

Shanta Kumar

Translated by

Sushil Kumar Phull

Ocean Books
DIVE IN THE OCEAN OF KNOWLEDGE

Ocean Books Pvt. Ltd.

ISO 9001:2015 Publishers

Published by
Ocean Books (P) Ltd.
4/19 Asaf Ali Road,
New Delhi-110 002 (INDIA)
e-mail: prabhatbooks@gmail.com

ISBN 978-81-8430-327-8
THE HELL OF HEAVEN
by Shri Shanta Kumar

Edition
2025

Price
₹ 600.00 (Rupees Six Hundred only)

Printed at
Shree Sai Printers, Sahibabad

PREFACE

'The Hell of Heaven' is the description of sublime human feelings. I have witnessed the political scenario in India for more than four decades but I have felt the tragic impact of the same on the Indian society with a feeling of helplessness.

I underwent very bitter experiences when I became the Chief Minister of Himachal Pradesh after the national emergency in 1975. After relinquishing chief minister ship in 1980 I thought of writing my memoirs. The manuscript was ready which contained the under currents of discontent of the Janta Party spreading over the period from 1977-1980. I discussed about its publication with my friends. They suggested that I had a long way to go in politics. If such a book is published, your future is going to be bleak definitely. They also advised that such memoirs are normally written after saying good-bye to politics.

My soul did not agree to the advice. I felt I was basically a writer and not a compulsive politician. I thought my writings were the heritage of the society which should reach them without any fear or fuss. So my book 'Rajneeti Ki Shatranj' was published which presented a truthful history of the conspiratorial events of two and a half years. I still am feeling the anger of my friends and co-workers till today.

There was much more let to be described other than what had been presented in 'Ratneeti Ki Shatranj'. I wanted to share those experiences with my readers. My of the experiences could not be narrated in the memoirs. I was itching to communicate those experiences to my readers. That made me write 'The Hell of Heaven'.

Politics has completely engulfed the social life, which does not augurs well. Politics should be a component of life but today life has become a constituent of politics. I don't relish this form of society. The hero and the heroine, Promod and Savitri, they prick my conscience when I have a pen in my hand to scribble their adventures on paper. And I proudly feel that the hovering depicted in 'The Hell of Heaven' are relevant even today.

There have been ample dissertations on politics but not many political novels exist in the realms of Hindi Literature. I feel satisfied on this count also in dedicating 'The Hell of Heaven' to my readers.

1

She found Delhi, the capital of India, flagrantly different this time. She had been to Delhi frequently. Then, it was a joyous place. There, she had not always participated in the mirthful atmosphere but the atmosphere was totally bleak today. Ah; Delhi was almost lifeless. She felt as if she was not in the metropolis but wading through a cremation ground.

She was on the threshold; rather fag end of her life. She had enjoyed many a happy summer of her life and was now a middle-aged woman, who still possessed the charm and beauty of days gone by. She was graceful in her gait. Even the growing wrinkles on her face could not diminish her loveliness. She carried the glimmer of a setting sun and the rising moon harmoniously.

She marched out from her room in the Birla Mandir. It was shining briskly and the Nature was all smiles. Visitors were making it to the temple. She saw a couple coming from the opposite direction. The husband accompanied her bride dressed in red with a tiny basket of flowers. She wore wedding *chuda* with vermillion powder on her *maang*, and the vibrant husband walked in pride.

Standing at the entrance, she watched the bride's husband. He put his hand on her shoulder. She looked into his eyes. Both of them felt close to each other's heart. He signalled to his wife. They went aside, took off their shoes and entered the temple.

She could not help herself and was reminded of her own early days of marriage. She followed them to the temple.

She had reached Delhi last evening, with something unique in her mind; but she was at a loss to understand how to translate that into reality. So, she wandered aimlessly here and there. She would glance at persons blankly, unaware of her destination. What to look for, she did not know! She would stand silently and be lost in herself. Then she would take out her handkerchief and wipe her tears. When confronted, she would move in the other direction. She had come to Delhi by a morning train yesterday. The entire day passed away without any business. She could not sleep at night. She came out of her room and went to the temple. She joined the prayers and sat before the statue of God for a stretch of time. The onlookers thought her to be a serious devotee. But she was trying to navigate the storm inside.

She came up the stairs and found the couple taking a round of the temple. They were walking close to each other. They would look at each other occasionally. When they caught each other's eye, their feet would stagger. They would smile. They were beginning on a long journey of life. All people normally start their lives the same way. Every step spoke of their promises to move together, and keep the warmth of love alive. But how many succeed in this venture? Many a time, love is lost before reaching the destination. The intoxication loses its impact like liquor that fades away with the passage of time.

Lost in her thoughts, she moved in another direction.

Though she had not seen the couple from close quarters, yet she was moving closer to them. The couple was unaware of anyone else except themselves. They did not look at the surroundings. They kept on walking round the sacrosanct deity. Then they turned to the temple and recieved the *bhog* (*Prasad*). They started reading the writings on the wall. Talking to each other happily, they were moving here and there and she saw them intently from a close distance.

She was reminded of her visit as a newly-wed bride to a temple on a hill top. It was the first day of her married life. She was with her husband. Similar joyful moments and the same intensity of feeling for each other. There was no one in the old temple on the hills. No crowds like the present scenario. They were all alone. Not even a priest. The old temple nestled in the lap of Deodar trees was still fresh in her memory. She was walking around the temple with her hand in her husband's hand. It was evening time. Birds were chirping melodiously. The sun had already set, but its reddening glimmer made the scene beautiful.

She was reminded of the incident instinctively. While they were going round the temple, her husband had caught her near the loneliness of the Deodars. Looking into her eyes, he had said,

'You are mine and mine only.' 'Yes, yours for ever,' she had blurted out, 'we shall take every step of life together.'

'I promise to arrange all comforts of life for you. I shall hold your hand warmly till we reach our destination,' her husband had promised.

'You are with me, this is the greatest comfort to me. I had never imagined about any other comfort. I wish it remains with me what I have got in you. Not only in this life, but in life after life...' She kept her hand on her husband's chest. And then, her husband had given her such a hug of life that she could never forget.

She was entranced in her nostalgia. She felt a chill in her spinal chord. Now there was anger in her eyes instead of love. She flew into a rage that spoke of extreme hatred. She felt as if she was on fire. The volcano was erupting again.

She blinked her eyes. Saw here and there and moved in a direction. Many devotees passed by her. The same couple followed her. She confronted them for the first time. She looked at the couple. She viewed the beauty of the lady. She saw her own image of a bride of yore in her. The couple came close to her. As soon as she saw the man, she was surprised. She stopped and then turned back.

She disappeared swiftly. Went downstairs and made her way to her room. She closed the door and fell on the bed. Her heart-beat had fastened. Tears were rolling down. She wiped her tears with the bed-sheet as the handkerchief was not sufficient.

Her past was mirrored in the tears that flowed unabatedly. She had started her life joyfully like a murmuring stream but the end result was not encouraging. She had reached a volcano instead of finding the depth of sea.

This youngman? My Pramod was also like him! And I too... She tried to sleep but to no avail. She was tossing in the bed, reminded of her past.

The day was on its wane. She felt hungry. She got up, cleaned her eyes but the redness in her eyes stopped her from going out. She washed her face. Closed the room and went outside. She wandered in the temple. Then came out on the road. She viewed the cars and buses plying on the road. All activities were going on. Nothing was stand and still. Nothing spectacular but she had fallen apart from the life's path.

After a great deal of contemplation, she reached the main gate of the Prime Minister's residence. There was a great hustle-bustle and the vehicles were moving in and about.

'This way please,' she was stopped by a stern voice.

'Who are you? Come here,' a soldier rushed to her.

'I want to meet the Prime Minister,' she said summoning her courage.

'Oh, you would like to meet the Prime Minister?' The soldier said in a thoughtful voice.

'As if the Prime Minister does not have anything else to do. The ignorant people from the village converge here of their own,' another fellow commented laughingly.

'Go away. The Prime Minister won't meet any one at this time,' the policeman pointed out.

'Sir, I have come from a far off place. I am in distress. I did not get justice any where. There is darkness and darkness everywhere.'

'We don't have a magic lamp here to dispel the darkness,' the policeman retorted flauntingly.

'You might have come here to complain against some officer. People become restive these days for nothing. If any one does not act according to their dictates, they feel annoyed. Why come straight to the Prime Minister's residence? There are so many channels. Go to the Tehsildar, D.C., Minister or Chief Minister for redressal of your grievances. Why have you come here?'

Fed up with the advice of the policeman, she stood in one corner. Frustration was now writ large on her face. She remembered the old times, when the policemen would behave respectfully and dance to her tones. Today, the same breed was flouting her.

She was in Delhi but she never wanted to be there. She felt no one could deliver justice to her now. It was useless to go from door to door. She was so tired and exhausted. She did not want to plead with anyone. However, she felt that she must once meet the lady Prime Minister—the supremo of the country. She is a compassionate mother. May be she comes to her rescue.

The crowd was swelling before the Prime Minister's residence. The Ministers were making their way to it. She was thinking what to do and what not to do. She felt like running away but as a last bid of effort, she wanted to meet the Prime Minister, with a glimmer of hope.

'Who is that woman?' An officer asked the policeman to enquire.

'Sir, we have already told her to leave this place.'

'What does she say?'

'She wants to meet the Prime Minister.'

'Why?'

'She says she has been denied justice everywhere. And hence, she is here.'

'What did you say to her?'

'I have not said any thing but she said there is darkness all around.'

'What?'

'We have not lit a lamp here to dispel the darkness.'

'What a fine answer.' The officer laughed heartily.

The officer called the other policeman and patted him.

'The foolish women came here for justice and create problems for us,' he blurted out.

'Sir, democracy is great. People come to the Prime Minister for petty things. If she gets an appointment and lodges a complaint against some officers, they would certainly be taken to task.' The policeman said after getting a pat.

'That is why I don't allow anyone to go in. Why put a colleague in difficulty!' The other policeman commented.

'Sir, she is still standing there. Please ask her to go away, or we push her out.'

'All right. We shall be in trouble if any one witnesses it. Call her.'

The policeman called her!

'Hello, who are you? Why are you still standing here despite being advised to leave this place? Don't you obey the orders....' The officer said while shaking the baton in his hand.

'I want to see the Prime Minister,' she said boldly.

'You have been already told that the Prime Minister cannot meet you,' the policeman said.

'You have not confirmed from inside? You have refused yourself.' She said in a complaining tone and waited for the reaction of the officer.

'Why do you argue like a lawyer when you have been told that you cannot meet the Prime Minister! Did you hear it? Go away at once.' The officer said agitatingly.

She looked at him, in disbelief.

The police officer was reminded of a similar character that had come across him years ago.

She was now nostalgic. How the things started and how they all ended up?

Three cars arrived in front of the Prime Minister's residence. There was stir all around. The officers on duty were alert.

'Why don't you go away? Some special guests are expected today?'

She listened silently.

'The foolish woman. Won't you go?' The police officer headed towards her in a true police-like manner.

'I won't go!'

He stopped hearing her loud voice.

'I have come to see the Prime Minister of my country. Who are you to stop me?,' she shouted.

Hearing her harsh voice, some of the workers rushed to the spot. Some more people moved to her. It was becoming quite crowdy. A senior officer reached there. He made his way to her. She was wiping her tears.

'Tell me what do you want?' The officer's politeness astonished her.

'Thank God! You consider me as a human being at last.' She raised her eyes and looked at him.

'Why? What's the matter?'

'Ask them. They neither know how to talk nor they understand the feelings.' She pointed out towards those policemen.

After listening her version, he scolded the two policemen and directed them to go. Looking at the third one, he said, 'You are an officer! You have been posted at such an important place. This is the residence of the Prime Minister of India. People from all over the country visit this place. Why can't you behave like normal human beings. And moreover, why can't you behave decently with a lady? I am sorry. Go away from this place. See me in my office tomorrow.'

'Sorry... Sir. Please forgive me,' he pleaded.

'Get away from my sight.'

He disappeared from there.

'Yes, tell me why do you want to meet the Prime Minister?'

'I am grateful to you. People like you are rare, no doubt. But it restores my faith in the goodness of man. I can't believe. You are also a policeman.'

'Why?'

'Yes, it is like that.'

'How can you make your opinion about the entire department after just meeting three persons. All are not alike.'

'Leave it please. Not only these three, I have seen many such persons in my life,' she said it with a sigh.

'Tell me what can I do for you?'

'I have come from a far off place. Kindly arrange my meeting with the Prime Minister.' She implored.

'A meeting with the Prime Minister can only be possible if it is pre-fixed. She is awefully busy these days as she is planning to reshuffle the Cabinet and to expand it. Many leaders are arriving to meet her.'

'I am a small fry. Please make me see her for only five minutes. I shall present my case.'

'Please try to understand my problem. Two Chief Ministers are here for the last two days but they have not been able to meet the Prime Minister. There is only one Prime Minister but she has plenty of engagements and appointments. Yes, if you can wait for a few days. I can try for your appointment with the Prime Minister.'

'Wait?' She felt helpless.

'Yes, you will have to wait.'

'I have already waited for a long time. It has been a wait for life time. Everything has been plunged in darkness. I can't wait any more.'

'What did you say?'

'I don't know if God is there. May be He is, may be He is not. I don't know if He wants to set the things right or not. He has done no favour to me. Nor I even asked for it. He could never deliver justice. The Prime Minister is a woman. I hope she will do justice to me. That is why I have come here. Please arrange my meeting with her only once.' Tears rolled down her eyes. She made all efforts to hold herself but in vain. She was feeling embarrassed.

'I can understand your problem. I assure you that I shall try my best to arrange your meeting with the Prime Minister. Please come tomorrow morning at 10.00 in the Prime Minister's office in the South Block. Please hold yourself.'

She wiped her tears.

'If you don't take it otherwise, will you kindly tell me where from you come? And what kind of justice you are seeking for?'

'Please excuse me. I shall not be able to repeat it before you. I feel tired. I shall reveal it to the Prime Minister only or to God if I even come across him....'

'O.K.'

I shall come to the South Block tomorrow ... I shall never forget your favour.

'Namastay ... I shall see you there.'

'Oh, what's your kind name?'

'I am R.K. Kapoor, Special Security officer.'

'Thanks. Bye.'

She boarded a three wheeler for Birla Mandir and was soon in her room in the Sarai. She felt a bit relieved today. All is not bad everywhere, she thought. She had a ray of hope now. She enjoyed sound sleep after a sumptuous food.

She reached the Prime Minister's office in time the next day. There was strict security. Many eyes watched the visitors. She went forward. When stopped by one, she told she had an appointment with the Prime Minister. When she was further interrogated, she told about Mr. R.K. Kapoor. She was allowed to go ahead.

'I have been called by Mr. Kapoor to arrange my meeting with the Prime Minister.' She told someone standing guard to the Prime Minister's office.

'Mr. Kapoor? Please wait here, I'll enquire from inside.' He went in.

'She has come again to meet the Prime Minister,' a known voice from inside caught her attention.

'The foolish woman. She got reprimanded yesterday. Our duty has been changed.' Another voice was heard.

'We shall see who Mr. Kapoor is to facilitate your meeting with the Prime Minister. No one can surpass us?'

She could recognise the face who had confronted her the previous day.

'Get lost. There is no Kapoor-Vapoor. You may be arrested under doubt,' he said disrespectfully.

'I am not addressing you. Nor I want anything from you,' she said boldly.

'I have enquired from inside. Mr. Kapoor has been sent to Assam for some emergency. He went by a morning flight today,' he told her.

'Kapoor Sahib?' They spoke contemptuously.

'What's the matter? Why do you laugh sarcastically,' he asked those policemen.

'You don't know. She had come at the Prime Minister's residence yesterday. She complained against us and Mr. Kapoor scolded us for nothing.'

'I don't have to say anything about these people. I just want to see the Prime Minister, as promised by Mr. Kapoor. Please help me in meeting the Prime Minister. I shall be obliged,' she said politely.

'Go away. It is not the way to arrange appointment with the Prime Minister.' One of the policemen said angrily.

'She appears to be a lunatic. She has been wandering here under suspicious circumstances. She can be a danger to the life of the Prime Minister. I think we must arrest her,' the second policeman said to the man who was talking to the woman.

The man on duty said to her, 'It's not that easy to arrange a meeting with the Prime Minister. One has to register one's request a number of days in advance. The Prime Minister is awefully busy these day. There is a stir in Assam. A few senior officers have been sent to Assam today morning. Some of the Ministers are being dropped and a few others are being inducted. You seem to be from a respectable family. Please don't stay put here.'

She could read the sympathetic attitude and simultaneously she could understand the mischief in the eyes of the two policemen. She heaved a sigh of relief and looked towards the sky.

'I thought it was impossible to meet the Almightly. I would have asked him why justice was not delivered to me? How paradoxical that we cannot meet the Prime Minister even, who has been elected by us? How could I expect to see the God. Anyway.'

'Please understand our problem also. A few senior leaders and members of Parliament have been able to meet the Prime Minister today after a week's wait. You tell me your name. You will be allowed to see the Prime Minister when your turn comes.'

'No, my turn is over,' she said in despair.

'Please get aside. Ministers, leaders and M.P.s are coming.' This announcement interrupted their conversation.

All of them got aside. The policemen also disappeared from there. The man on duty stood alert.

Talking to each other, the leaders in white came out. One of the leaders saw the lady intently. One of the leaders said, 'Walk straight. I know you are an expert in duping women but....'

'But this is the Prime Minister's office. It is not a hunting ground. And moreover, new birds do not flutter here,' the other fellow commented sarcastically.

'Let me find out. She may be in distress.'

All others laughed heartily at his comments.

'All right. May be God has entrusted you with solving the problem of all beautiful women. You are great. You are discussed everywhere.'

'You should be awarded Tamra Patra.'

'Please wait.' He went towards the woman. He had not seen her complete face but he was surprised at her sight. His enthusiasm was gone. He was trembling now.

'So you have come here too?,' the leader said to her in a frightened tone.

He was Gurcharan, the young leader from a rich family, who had come to Delhi after being elected. He hoped to find a ministerial birth.

'Yes. I have come here now,' she said confidently.

'What for?'

'For justice.'

'You have'nt got justice yet?,' he said scornfully.

'No. I have got atrocities as yet. I have not come across a person who could deliver justice.'

'Do you know the consequences of making me a target?' He tried to look normal but said in a threatening voice.

'I know it well. I have borne the brunt of it.'

'Why don't you sit peacefully at home?'

'I wish I could?'

'Now be at rest.'

'Once bitten twice be shy.'

'You want money? I can oblige you with any amount. I can provide you with land and a house. I pity you. But what has passed is passed. Leave it all. Tell me how much do you want to have?' He asked her, moving closer to her.

She was full of venom. She viewed him from top to toe. He was feeling perturbed and upset. He wanted to be sure that no one saw him in conversation with her.

'Speak out. I certainly want to help you. Tell me where are you staying. I shall come there and deliver the amount today itself.'

She stood silent. She would look at him occasionally or stare downwards.

'Listen. I am in a hurry. The Cabinet is likely to be expanded.'

'And you are trying to be inducted into the Cabinet?'

'How do you know?'

'I had read it in a newspaper while I was on my way to Delhi.'

'I need your help. Forget all about the past. Pardon me.' He folded his hands in respect.

'How simple? You have stated it so naturally.'

'I am in a hurry. They are all waiting for me.'

'A wolf could be so civilized even after slaughtering hundreds of lambs, I cannot believe.'

'Please pardon me. One lakh, two, three or five lakhs. Kindly do not reveal anything ever. Tell me your address. I shall come at 4.00 p.m.,' he said.

'Get away, scoundrel. What do you think. I am not a politician. I am neither an MLA, nor an M.P. who would indulge in horse trading. I am an ordinary woman, a mother,' she tried to push the politician away from her.

'Do you know the consequences?,' he said angrily.

'I shall be crushed to death, that is what you frighten me with. I am a handful of ashes of the graveyard. I simply want to expose the bloody hands. Anyhow...' She tried to wipe her tears.

The young politician retraced his steps and said something to an officer. She also went there and said, 'I know what you are hob-nobhing. You want he should not allow me to see the Prime Minister rather he should arrest me. Since you now are here. So I know my meeting with the Prime Minister cannot materialize. Don't you worry. No one has delivered justice to me. Not even God. Nor the Prime Minister. I have never bowed before the God for seeking justice. But I have been hankering here for the last two days to make it to the Prime Minister but sorry it has not been possible. I can assure you that you will not find me anywhere anymore.'

She disappeared hurriedly. The politician joined his colleagues.

Next day, there was crowd all around in one corner of the Prime Minister's residence. People were watching something lying on the road. The police arrived on the scene. A senior officer from Prime Minister's residence rushed out to the scene.

'Sir, a dead body of a woman.' A policeman informed the officer.

'And Sir, an envelope containing a letter...on her body,' another policeman said.

'And this small bottle lying beside her. May be she has committed suicide,' said the third policeman.

The crowd swelled. More police reached the spot.

'Oh, she is the same woman who had come a day before yesterday to meet the Prime Minister,' one of the officers said after looking at the dead body.

The crowd dispersed. The dead body was removed from the road side. The police was very careful in keeping the letter safe as it was quite crucial to the incident.

□

2

'Come here my son. I am very happy today,' Pramod's father said to him blessingly. He called him and made him sit close to him. He hugged him warmly.

'My dear father. It is all because of you,' Pramod retorted.

His father felt satisfied and elated. Pramod could hear his father's heart-beat.

'Pratibha, Sunita and Praneeta come here all of you.' The father called his three daughters, overflowing with joy.

Two of them were in the kitchen and the third one was in her room. All three of them went to their father.

Looking at Pratibha, the elder daughter, her father said, 'Call Sheela also.'

'She must be asleep.'

'Wake her up. Go yourself and bring her. Yes, take care that you wake her up lovingly.'

Pratibha went upstairs to Sheela, the youngest sister. Pramod was still in his father's lap. He raised his head when her sisters had come. But father's affection did not allow him to get up.

'Dear brother, it is already morning time. It's not night time that you like to hear lullaby.' Suneeta said sarcastically.

'It is an age of equal rights. But what is happening here.' Praneeta said.

'What is going on, my dear daughter?,' the father said smilingly.

'The daughters are standing at a distance of three feet from the father whereas the son is in his lap for more than one hour. It is a clear case of discrimination, my dear father!'

'I shall not talk to you even!' Sheela said grudgingly.

'Why? Why will you not talk to me?' Her father said affectionately.

'You did not ask me to sleep with you last night. You went to Pramod's bed.' Sheela commented while cleaning her eyes.

'Another witness corroborates our accusation of discrimination,' said Praneeta.

'Come all my kids. I am very happy today.' He made all of them sit around him.

'Get up brother. Our father's lap belongs to all the children and is not your exclusive right,' Suneeta roared.

Pramod got up.

'I wish your mother was alive tody.' There were tears in his eyes. Sheela was sad at the mention of her deceased mother. She was sighing.

'She could not see all this. It all depends on luck.' Their father was sad now.

'Father dear, tell us everything. Where and as what has been our brother appointed?'

'My dear ones, Pramod has successfully qualified for the Indian Police Services. I learn from Mr. Khanna that Pramod has been posted in a hilly area.'

'Congratulations, dear brother.' Suneeta said.

'And where are the sweets?,' Sheela inquired.

'And a film too today.' Pratibha said gleefully.

'Just wait. I shall bring sweets. Pramod, you will take your sisters to the movie. You have to move tomorrow. And make your arrangements also in time,' His father said.

'No, my father. You will also accompany us to the cinema. Why should you remain all alone at home?,' Pratibha asserted.

'Yes, father will also go with us. He will not bring sweets here but we shall eat together in the restaurant.' Sheela was very happy.

'We all want to go together, dear father,' Pramod declared.

'Let me be at home, my dear son.'

'Why at home?' All of them said simultaneously.

'I am reminded of Rekha whenever there is a moment of happiness. I can tolerate everything but not her reference. Why did she leave us suddenly?' All joy of life has ceased. There is everything but it looks as if there is only hollowness. I am alive but feel as if I am no more. The father heaved a deep sigh.

They all were listening to him seriously. Sheela was sitting in her father's lap. Others had tears rolling down.

'We all remember her. She is no more. But it is the way of the world. Life must go on. We have lost the light of our home. We do not say anything about her. But, in fact, we are like branches broken from the mother tree.' Pratibha sat beside her father making effort to console him.

'You had rightly said that we are all travellers in this world. We must quit after completing our excursion here. We have a specific role to play in this world. No one stays back after playing his role,' Suneeta said to her father.

'I remember how my aunt wept bitterly at the demise of Parnesh. You had consoled her saying that no one has any control over life and death. Man is simply a silent spectator. I remember another of your saying, if there is life, death is imminent too. Even when God took an incarnation, He had also to pass through death.' Pramod said while clinging to his father.

'Yes my son. It is easier to console others. She had given me lots of comforts. So I remember her. Anyhow, leave it. You are all with me. She lives in you. I don't lack anything. Let us go.' He said pretending to be all comfortable.

'Father, when has our brother to go?'

'He will leave by tomorrow morning bus.'

'I am happy, Pramod. You have become an officer. You should work honestly and carefully. You will not forget that you have four sisters. Whatever I had, I invested in you. Pension is only sufficient to run the domestic expenses. Moreover, I am almost broken and cannot do anything. You all have to take care of the family collectively. I am already looking for a bride-groom for Pratibha. Her marriage should be solemnized this year. I can find out a suitable match for her but I don't have the requisite money for the purpose. Yes, I have Rekha's ornaments. You can use them as you all decide.'

Hearing about herself, Pratibha went to the other room. All others were intently listening to their father.

Wiping his tears, Pramod said, 'My dear father, I understand your concern. They are not only your daughters but my dear sisters too. All right your wife is no more to share your responsibilities but I am here to share the burden. You should not worry now. I have a good posting. You just find out a suitable match for my sister, leave rest of the arrangements to me. I am fully aware of your sentiments and my duties. As long as all my sisters are not married off, I shall not think about myself.'

'Well done brother. You want us to say goodbye to this home. What an excellent police officer you are?,' Suneeta said in a lighter vein.

'We want a bride for our brother first of all.' Sheela said in a joyful mind.

'O.K. everything will happen at its appropriate time. Be ready to enjoy the movie together. We shall also dine outside.'

All of them were very happy to know it from their father. Sheela was almost dancing.

The whole day passed in a festive mood. Pramod was busy in making arrangements for his movement. He reached Dharamshala the next day for reporting at the headquaters of Kangra District. He was told that he had been posted at Kullu.

□

3

Pramod had to catch a bus for Mandi at 5.00 a.m. It was his first visit to Dharamshala. His education and training had been completed in Punjab and Delhi. It was his first visit to the hilly areas. He was very happy to be with Nature. He got up at 4.00 a.m. The last day's journey was afresh in his memory.

After alighting at Pathankot Railway Station, he had caught a bus for Dharamshala. It was an old mini bus. The seats were hard and the road was rough. There was nothing special till Nurpur. It was like the plains. The fields were also like the ones in the plains. But as soon as the bus reached Nurpur, it followed a serpentine road uphill. There were snow clad mountains in sight. Some peaks were without snow also. It appeared as if a newly wed dark complexioned bride was trying to hide its face in a white veil.

'What's that beyond,' Pramod asked his unknown fellow passenger.

'These are the remnants of an old fort. Have you come here for the first time?' The fellow passenger looked at him inquisitively.

'Yes. I have come here for the first time.'

'Right. That is why you are so moved.'

'I am experiencing a hilly area for the first time in life. It's a wonderful land. The Nature seems to be dancing and singing. How lucky are the people who live here?' Pramod was ecstatic with joy.

'Where are you going?'

I have been appointed a police officer in Kangra District and am going to Dharamshala.

'So you belong to the Police Department.' The fellow passenger was a bit scared now.

'Not yet but I shall be. What's the matter? Why are you so astonished?'

'No, nothing. You appear to be a gentleman.'

'Are'nt the policemen?' Pramod tried to laugh.

'No, not all are alike.' The passenger was cautious now.

'Leave it all. What kind of fort is it? How many centuries old are these remnants. Time has elapsed. People came, built it and were no more. Then more people came, witnessed it and went away. Our bus will also pass by but it stands as it was on the high hill.' Pramod stared at the walls of the fort and was making a running commentary on it.

'But Sir, it is not the same as it was built. Then it was a fort, later on it was an old fort and now the remnants. Neither the builders nor the onlookers are any more. Gradually, it will also vanish. This is the way of the world.'

'You have said it rightly. My attention was on its one side. You have shown me the other side of the coin also. What is there in this fort?,' Pramod asked curiously.

'It is Nurpur fort. Jahangir's queen Nurjahan had come here once. She was fascinated by this spot. She asked her husband to make a palace for her at this place. It is said the work for construction of the palace had been started. Foundations had been laid. A few walls had also been erected but for unknown reasons, the work was stopped. Some say that there was no provision for water here. Others are of the view that the place was not considered appropriate for administrative purposes. There is a temple in this fort. It contains a historical statue.'

Pramod was listening to the passenger raptly. The bus stopped for a few minutes at the Nurpur Bus Stand. The driver and conductor took tea in a nearby shop. But both of them were absorbed in conversation. The bus started again. Crossing the Nurpur fort, the bus was moving ahead leaving behind the splashing waters of the Chakki river.

'Sir, Wazir Singh of Nurpur had challenged the British army here. His bravery is sung in the songs. He did not bow his head and fought to the last for Independence.'

'So, it is not only a land of beauty but also a land of bravery.'

'What do you call those mountains?'

'Behind those mountains, Chamba, the land of beauty is located. There is Bharmour, a place at a distance of some hundred miles. It is said Bharmour was the capital of Chamba. There are 84 temples at one point.'

'Eighty-four?' Pramod asked surprisingly.

'Exactly, eighty-four—! There are many legends. The size of the temples is small but they are at one place. A path from there leads to Mani Mahesh, the famous religious place of Shiva. A tough terrian. Takes a number of days to reach there. But thousands of people visit the place every year.'

The bus was on its way to its destination. Pramod was ecstatic with the beauty of Nature. He viewed outside constantly. The fellow passanger was also very talkative. Pramod would ask him question after question and he would answer it in detail. Neither he was exhausted in asking nor he was irritated in replying to the queries.

The bus was sometimes on a zig-zag way and at other times it was a straight passage. At times, the vehicle moved on the road close to the hill-side and at times, it crossed small bridges to go in another direction. It would stop to pick up the passengers wherever any one was standing to board it.

At moments, Pramod would forget about the current journey and would flash back about his home. He was reminded of his lively sisters and the affection of his father. His classmates of school and college flashed in his eyes like a film.

'This journey is symbolic of the life's entire journey,' Pramod spoke after a brief pause.

'How?' The passenger felt tired after sitting silent for sometime now.

'Life is like that. There are difficult turns at times and sometimes it is quite straight. At places the murmur of a rivulet and at other places the dense forest. Ascent and then the descent.'

'It appears you have been a problem?'

'How?'

'There, lived a professor as a tenant in our house. He was fond of conversation. He would call me. Many of his comments passed off my head. Listening to you has reminded me of him.'

'Don't you understand my talk also?'

'I understand a few of your views.'

'Life contains happiness and sorrow alike. Sometimes it is all joy and at other times, it is darkness around. Time is never the same always in one's life. Similarly, this bus is going on its path, sometimes it is hazardous and at other times, it is quite smooth.'

'Now I understand. I had no time in life to think about all these things. To say the truth, I never had a smooth going in my life. My life started on a turn and it has never been without more and more complications.'

'They say hilly people are always very simple.' Pramod wanted to change the topic.

'What can you expect of people belonging to a poor and backward area?'

'No, that is not true. There are poor people in Punjab villages also but they are not so simple.'

'That's true.'

'Not the people alone but this bus is also so simple as it stops at every turn to pick up the passengers waiting for it. It drops the passengers where they want to get down.'

'So, the hilly ascent is over. We are in a beautiful Kangra village. No more hillocks for miles together. On its left is Dharamshala where you have to go.' The fellow passenger said pointing in that direction.

'And those snow clad mountains?'

'That is Dhauladhar range. When you go to Kullu, you will pass by those mountains.'

They reached Dharamshala and got down from the bus.

'Oh, you have not disclosed your name please?' Pramod asked him after getting down.

'Did you ask for it?'

Both of them laughed.

'Anyhow, I have asked it now. Your area is so beautiful that I am forgetting my name even. How could I ask you.' Pramod said with a smile.

'I am a small shopkeeper of this small town. I am Vinod.' The passenger told hesitatingly.

'And I am Pramod.'

Pramod extended his hand to say good-bye.

Both of them smiled and parted ways.

Pramod recapitulated all that had happened yesterday. The bus travel was fresh in his mind. It was just like a film running before his eyes.

He took a cup of tea. A policeman came to him. To help Pramod board the bus, he accompanied him to the bus stand.

It was February and the weather was quite cold. Pramod had worn the available warm clothes. Even then his teeth would stutter.

It was darkness all around. It was not even 5.00 a.m. Some street lights were on. The misty light appeared to be dull and dim. He saw dogs shivering in the veranda of some home. The cock was crowing at a distance.

'Sir, here itself...' The policeman who was carrying his buggage said.

'Will the bus come here?'

'Yes, sir. The bus will start from the Kotwali Bazar and will stop here.'

The luggage was kept on one side. Pramod stood on one side of the road. He felt the chill of the cool breeze. He felt as if he was not wearing any clothes. He at moments felt that his clothes were drenched. As he was moving on the road, he felt lesser cold. But as soon as he stopped at a point he felt his blood freezing. He was shivering. He felt he would not be able to stand after sometime.

'I can't. I can't darling, I can't forget you.' Pramod heard a thin voice from closely. He saw shadows of two persons.

'Do write a letter on reaching there.'

'I shall certainly write it.'

'And you will keep my letter safe from him.'

'Don't you worry.'

'And listen.' He went close to her and whispered in her ears. So Pramod could not hear anything. But the warmth of conversation made Pramod feel a bit relieved. And more passengers had come. But no one was standing in the direction from where the voice was heard. There was darkness and darkness around.

As soon as the bus arrived, the passengers boarded it. The employee accompanying Pramod kept his luggage on the roof of the bus. He stood relaxed as the conductor told him that a front seat had been reserved for him. The police officer at Dharamshala had asked for reservation yesterday evening.

'Sir, I have kept your baggage carefully.' The employee accompanying Pramod said.

'Please do not worry. I am here to serve you.' The bus conductor said to him. He had come to know that Pramod was a police officer.

'Please have it, you have come in such a cold weather to help me.' Pramod took out a 2 rupee note for him.

'Sir, it is our duty.' The employee said with folded hands.

'Keep it please.' Pramod insisited.

He took two rupees with trembling hands and put it in his inner pocket.

There was rush in the bus. Passengers vied with each other to find a seat. Some of them found seats, other were trying for the same. A few of them were quarelling for a seat. The front seat was vacant. Its cushion was kept upside down meaning thereby that it was reserved for some one. All had an eye on it but no one tried to occupy the same.

'Sir, the front seat is for you.' The conductor pointed out to Pramod.

Pramod occupied the seat.

'Why? Is he some big officer?' Sitting in the back seat. A passenger asked the conductor.

'A police officer.' The conductor said authoritatively.

'You or he?' The passenger asked on finding the conductor speak aggressively.

All the passengers laughed.

'Police officer? Really.' Another passenger said in a whisper.

'Why? what's strange in it.'

'I do feel surprised at what I saw outside.'

'What did you see?'

'I had always seen policemen receiving money but here I saw a policeman giving it. I have seen it for the first time.' The passenger was all smiles.

'What do you mean?' Another passenger asked.

'The police officer gave two rupees to someone.'

All could now understand the whole episode. They laughed at it.

The conductor moved towards the front seats.

'Please.' Someone spoke in a melodious voice close to Pramod. There was only a dim light in the bus. It was misty outside. There was a thin smoke wall in the bus as well. A few passengers were smoking in a relaxed manner after having got seats for themselves.

'Is that seat vacant,' someone asked moving close to him. Pramod raised his hand in response. The bus was packed badly. A few passengers were standing and trying to get seats. Pramod's adjoining seat was still vacant. No one had occupied it so far.

'Only conductor can tell it, madam,' Pramod replied.

'He can only ask about the ticket. Only you can tell if there is anyone else with you.' An attractive young woman said bursting into laughter.

Pramod was a bit surprised at the comments.

'I sit for the time-being. I don't feel you will ask any one to have the seat. You appear to be nice.' She occupied the seat and sat in proximity to Pramod.

Pramod felt awkward at first. Was a little bit angry also. Then he felt astonished and finally he was feeling quite good.

'There is great rush today. But for your benevolence, I would have travelled the long distance in a standing posture. I have no words to thank you for your kind gesture,' she continued. Pramod felt the fragrance of a scent emanating from the young woman. He felt he was now free from the pungent smell of smoke.

Someone has rightly said, 'There are all kinds of people in the world, good and bad. Your behaviour has strengthened my conviction that the world still has good people. Truly speaking, I would have found it impossible to travel today but for your kindness. So many people are still standing. I really am thankful to you.'

'Please take it easy,' Pramod said. She went on talking, caring little for any response. Pramod had never imagined to come across such a talkative girl that too in a backward hilly area.

She was wearing a costly but charming saree and warm coat. She sat tightly close to him. She had a black scarf on her head. The coat was brownish in colour. She looked all the more beautiful. She was imposing with her sharp features. The foggy morning made her figure very attractive. Nature had blessed her with beauty but her upkeep was also meticulous. Her reddened lips and her snowy white teeth added to her charm.

'Why no thanks? You have really obliged me. Look others are still standing. I was one of them a few moments ago. And now I am sitting comfortably beside you.'

'But this seat was really vacant. I did not have any one with me.'

'Don't say it now.'

'What do you mean?'

'Now I am with you, sitting by your side.' She retorted with a mischievous smile. Pramod felt uneasy and did not respond with laughter.

'You appear to be very interesting.' Pramod tried to save the situation.

'Lesser than you,' she said.

Unaware about the fact of the bus journey, they completed it in no time.

'I had a little sleep last night. I was tired also. I wanted to get a seat reserved but there is no provision for reservation here. It would have been tortuous if I had to travel standing till Mandi.'

'So you are also going to Mandi?'

'Yes, and you?'

'Yes to Mandi as of now and then I shall catch a bus for Kullu.'

'Oh!' She almost jumped with joy and caught his hand impulsively. Then immediately she let his hand go and said, 'what a coincidence? Our destination is the same.'

'Are you also going to Kullu?'

'Even if I was not going to Kullu, I would not have resisted the temptation to go with you.' She looked into his eyes.

'May I know your name please?'

'Rita.'

'What a lovely name! Exactly modern.'

'Thanks.' Rita posed to be shy.

'And what's you name please?'

'Old type or stereotype name...Pramod;' Pramod felt inferiority complex.

'What is old about it? It appears fresh and novel.'

'Leave it please. I am from a poor village family.'

'You also leave it. Pramod dear, see it with my eyes.'

'Lend me your eyes then.'

'What will you do with them?'

'What do you mean?'

'You have won my heart.' Rita said going closer to him. She wanted to read his eyes. Underneath the coat, she held Pramod's hand. A few minutes passed. She fondled his hand.

The bus was moving to Palampur after crossing a small town called Nagrota. A few passengers were feeling sleepy and a few others were enjoying smoking. Some were talking. All windows were closed. The chilly wind entered the bus through crevices. The cigarette smoke gathered inside the bus as there was no outlet or exhaust for the hot air.

Both of them were silent. Pramod felt excited at the touch of Rita's hand. The experience of an electric current. The maiden touch of a woman made him feel intoxicated.

Rita's image shattered all his opinions about the hill society. Hill society must be backward, orthodox and wedded to old traditions he had thought. Hill women live in veil, even at home, they used purdah, he had learnt. A daughter-in-law does not talk to elders. She cannot talk to strangers. He was reminded of his old concepts. At this juncture, Rita pressed his hand hard.

'When had you come from Kullu?' Pramod initiated the dialogue.

'Day before yesterday.'

'Who lives in Dharamshala?'

'One of my friends. I came for my friend.'

'Friend?' Pramod could not make it out. Male or female friend? Pramod was eager to know it.

'Friend means a friend.'

'Oh, I see.'

'He is a lovely friend of mine. I often come to Dharamshala to see him. He had come to see me off at the bus stand at that early hour.' She was ecstatic talking about her friend.

The bus halted. Some passengers had to get down. Some had to fetch down their luggage from the bus roof.

Pramod was reminded of the conversation. While he was waiting for the bus, he had heard the voice of a young woman. He had heard. 'I can't...I can't darling...never, never I can forget you. ... Write a letter to me on reaching there. And look, you will keep the letters in safe custody...away from his reach.'

Pramod could now understand that that was Rita's voice. Rita had herself told now that her friend had come to see her off. Pramod surveyed the passengers in the bus. A few of the village women were sitting on the rear seats. They were middle-aged women. He thought they could not use the expression 'darling'. He was now sure that the voice that he heard emerging from the darkness was surely of Rita. He wanted to sit at a distance from Rita but she again moved closer to him. He had failed in his attempt.

She had called him her darling, only a while ago. She had promised him never to forget. She insisted that he should write letters to her and also had warned him to keep her letters hidden. And now sitting beside me, she says I have captured her heart.

Either she was befooling him or she is making a fool of me. There can be love only once and for one person only. May be I am not known to the world of love. I have not watched the intricasies of life so far. I have simply been trained in policing. Love does not recognise the Indian Penal Code provisions. Oh, why do I think so badly about all this. I have simply to travel for the day to reach my destination. Why should I bother about all this. Pramod was still in thoughts. The bus started with a jerk. Rita moved closer to him.

'Pramod, you are lost in thoughts,' Rita spoke taking his hand into her hand. Pramod was shocked but he felt easy after the initial shock. Her hands were soothing. As if he was pushed on a cushion after a hard fall. He kept silent. When called, he looked towards Rita. She looked into his eyes with amorous designs. She would laugh intermittently. Her eyes and hands were busy overpowering Pramod.

'She is so beautiful.' Her eyes are captivating. They say the eyes of a hind are always imposing but Rita's eyes are bewitching. And her long magistic neck...round like a SURAHI...red blood lips and matching shade of lipstick...soft hands.... He felt as if the petals of rose had touched him," Pramod thought.

'Pramod! Life is not meant for thinking and thinking. It is for action also.' Rita intruded upon Pramod's thinking posture.

Pramod sat cautiously.

'What for?' Pramod looked at her intently.

'For the moment, it is time to chit-chat.' Pramod could not contain his laughter.

'Just to chit-chat, for the moment.' Pramod repeated her dialogue.

'Yes, just now in the bus. We can talk only. Nothing else can be done. Please do talk.' Rita implored.

'Only Pramod? That flatters me. Thanks.' He now felt happy when he was called Pramod only by Rita.

'And I...'

'You... you ... Rita.'

'Thank you,' Rita said jovially.

'Oh, look there. How beautiful is the mountain, covered with snow and the charming reflection of morning sun rays. Rita it is a wonderful sight,' Pramod commented.

'Pramod, it's Dhauladhar range. The entire Kangra valley is situated in its lap. Snowfall transforms it into a wonder land.'

'The mountains look so close that if I extend my hand out of the window, it will have a feel of the mountains.'

'This is the place where we find ourselves so close to the mountains. I have travelled extensively. I have visited the entire India and almost half of the world also. Truly speaking, Pramod the view of Dhauladhar from Palampur excels all other places. I wish I had a small room here to live for the whole of my life.'

'That's a good idea. You will arrange one room for me also adjacent to yours. This white Dhauladhar has captured me also. I shall also have my abode here. You will be present here and...'

'Then what? Why have you stopped in between?'

'I have said what I wanted to say.'

'Don't pose riddles. Do speak what you mean.'

'Rita, Do you understand only the spoken word. Silence also speaks, so do the eyes.'

'Pramod, you are marvellous. I now get you.'

The bus had reached Palampur. There were so many buses at the bus stand. There was great hustle and bustle. The tea shops close by were packed to capacity. There were people in the tea shops enjoying tea. The seating space was tight. So some of the folks were sipping tea standing outside the shops. A few others carried tea to their female companions sitting in the buses. Some others took their small children for toilets in the open space. The children shivered because of cold.

Men were wearing rough woollen coats. Some wore woollen trousers also. Some were in coat-pants. A few of them had blankets around themselves. The colourful Himachal caps were attractive. Some had wrapped the mufflers round their heads. It was the bright season after the rains and the snowfall. There was the chill of the snow and the warmth of sun rays. It had been raining for the last two days. It was a bright brisk day today.

Women were in salwar kameez, only a few were in saree. Very few had worn long coats. Hill women wore thick clothes. They had warm scarfs on their heads. Most of them had shawls round them.

Pramod and Rita loitered in the compound of the bus stand. Just then, the conductor came and told that the road was closed because of heavy rains during the last two days.

So all the buses will wait here till the road is opened for movement. He told that it could take three to four hours before the road is cleared for traffic. Pramod was worried to hear the announcement but Rita felt mischievous.

'Come on, sir, have tea,' the conductor said and moved to the tea shop.

'Do come please. You will feel uncomfortable. We would have reached Mandi in time but for the closure of the road.' The bus driver said while coming close to Pramod.

'Sir, we shall have to wait. Let us have a cup of tea,' the driver said. Pramod was a young police officer. He was tough and simple at the same time.

'Thanks for your courtesy. Will it take such a long time,' Pramod asked.

'Yes, sir. It has just been known that debris of a hillock has come down on the road at a distance of 10 km from here. The labour is engaged in clearing it. But it will take time.' A bus inspector said.

'The debris has fallen today but it rained day before yesterday.' Rita said surprisingly.

'It generally happens that way here,' the driver said.

'Why?'

'The rain makes the mountain friable. It had rained slowly but continuously day before yesterday. The water entered the soil slowly. It made the earth wet. And consequently it gave way.'

'Pramod, every impact takes time.' Rita said moving closer to him.

'Well said.' Rita was happy at the comment made by Pramod.

'Listen to me please.' Pramod called the driver close to him and asked: 'Is there a police station here?'

'Yes sir, it is there. Just close to this place. We had passed by the police station before stopping at this point.'

'Will you send a message there? Someone will come from there.'

'Please be seated in the bus. We shall drop you there. When the road opens, we shall pick you from there.' Saying this, the driver moved towards the bus.

'That will be all right. It may be difficult for you to spend three hours here.' The conductor said.

'Moreover, you are not alone. She is also with you. She will be bored and exhausted if she is made to stand here for three hours.' The bus inspector did not want to lag behind in pleasing the police officer.

'She is with you,' these words excited Pramod. Suppose someone asked, what is she to you? How will he answer the query. He has not joined his new posting but is being discussed like that. It won't be in good stead. It would not be nice to take her along and at the same time, she cannot be left behind now. He rocked between the decision to go or not to go for sometime. It would not be right not to go once he had expressed his desire.

'All right let us go.' He crossed over to the other side of the road.

'Not on foot, sir. What for is this bus? We shall take you there you stay there. We shall pick you from there when the road opens.' The driver moved towards the bus. The conductor and the inspector also boarded the bus. Pramod and Rita sat in their seats in the bus.

Many people watched Pramod and Rita being meted out a special favour. To add to it, a young police officer was with them. A few people were happy to be at his beck and call. They had now a subject for discussion.

Pramod was silent as long as the bus did not start. Rita went on talking. As soon as there was noise of the bus, Pramod whispered to Rita. 'Rita, if anyone asked what you are to me, what should I say?' He said in a low voice.

'Tell me first of all. I ask you the same question. Tell me who is she sitting beside you?' She laughed.

'This is no time for joking. We must decide it before reaching there.' Pramod showed his anxiety.

'Pramod, the decision is very serious. But such important decisions of life cannot be taken in haste. What is your opinion?' Rita was playing mischief now.

'You don't understand. The policemen are a strange lot. If they have any doubt, the subject will be discussed here and there. This story will travel to my place of posting before I reached there.'

'It's O.K. First of all we should reach there and then let the story follow.'

'Tell me what should I say there?'

'As you think right.'

'Even then?'

'I am what I am. Neither you have told about yourself nor I have spelled it out. God knows if we know about each other or not. You may say whatever you feel right for the sake of saying.'

'Maternal or a paternal sister.'

'No, no. I don't believe in orthodox beliefs.' Rita was irritated.

'You tell me, then?'

'Just say that I am your sister-in-law.'

'Wife's sister?'

'I am not married yet.'

'How does it matter? Nobody knows it here.'

'Rita, you are being unfair. When I am not married, how can there be a sister-in-law?'

'Why are you so scared? You just say I am your friend.'

'Friend?' Pramod was in a thoughtful gesture.

'No, it cannot be. A girl friend of a new police officer. It will lead to adverse propaganda. No, not that way.' Pramod asserted.

Many buses were parked at the bus stand. The driver drove the bus out with difficulty. He brought the bus on the road leading to Pathankot. It took less time in reaching the police station and more time in turning the bus back. Even during this time, they could not finalise their relationship. It was at the end of the market. The hospital was on the right side. The conductor who was sitting behind said. 'Sir, the police station is next to the hospital. It is visible from here.'

'You are niece of my father's friend. Your father and my father were class-fellows. You met me in the bus after a long gap. Understand?' Pramod said in an authoritative manner.

'I follow you, Sir.'

The bus stopped in front of the police station. The conductor went inside. Two policemen came out. They saluted Pramod respectfully and took them both inside the thana. They were seated comfortably in a room. The bus returned to the bus stand.

'What was the name of your father's friend?'

'What do you mean?'

'You mean my uncle's name. Pramod tell me the whole role if we have to enact a drama lest we are ridiculed by the onlookers.'

'Rita, you have met me for the first time. Only a few hours acquaintance has made you play such a mischief. I feel enraged and...'

'What more?'

'And I love you too.'

'That's the finest part.' She spoke vibrantly.

'Sir, we have sent a message to the S.H.O. He has gone

somewhere closeby. You have your tea. Please ask freely if you want something else,' a policeman said. They kept a fire-stove in the room. Pramod and Rita were warming their hands now.

'No, it is O.K. I shall appreciate if we get hot tea. It is very cold here.'

'Yes, sir. It has been snowing on the Dhauladhar ranges for two-three days. Otherwise too, it is winter season now. May be you have come for the first time, Sir.'

'That is why cold is intolerable for him,' Rita intercepted.

'O.K. please arrange to send tea.' Pramod did not went to indulge in excessive talk with him.

They took tea which was refreshing. Pramod used to take tea extensively during the last days of his exam so that he could avoid sleep. But it was a special tea. The breath oozing out of mouth looked like smoke. It appeared as if clouds emerged from his mouth. The teeth gave a striking sound. He felt a shiver. The cool breeze almost froze his body. Hot tea came as a respite. He had never felt tea so useful.

'Sir, welcome to Palampur. I am sorry I had to go out on some urgent work early in the morning,' the SHO said respectfully on entering the room.

'It's perfectly all right. We are being looked after well. We got the heater to warm up, and hot tea. You are here these days.'

'I came on posting here this year.'

'I am also going on first posting to Kullu. I was at Dharamshala yesterday. I learnt from there that I had to report at Kullu. Rita met me in the bus. We have met after many years. She is niece of one of my father's close friends. She lives in Kullu these days.' Pramod stopped suddenly as a vehicle stops on finding an animal before.

'Please ask for whatever you require,' the SHO said.

'Could you find out how much time will it take to clear the road.'

'All right, Sir.' He went away.

'Rita, do you know why I suddenly stopped talking. I only know that you are going to Kullu. I do not know what you do, where do you live or with whom do you live or what is your job, etc. If he had asked any of the details, I would have stuck in there.'

'You would have been punished?' Rita took her hands close to the heater.

'Punishment? For what?'

'For keeping incomplete details about the niece of your father's friend.'

'But that you are not.'

'Then for accompanying an unknown girl.'

'Now you are not the unknown even.'

'What do you mean?'

'Rita, you are not a stranger to me any more.'

'I hope you remember your saying.'

'But you have not told anything to me about yourself.'

'You never asked for it.'

'I had not even invited you to sit beside me.'

'Then?'

'You had occupied the seat of your own will. As if the seat had been reserved for you.'

'And if I had not occupied that seat?'

'Then some person with rough woolen clothes would have sat in the seat. He would have choked me with his cigarette smoke. It would have spoiled my joy of being in the paradise of Nature. You have given a new dimension to my travel. Really, I am grateful to you.'

'Pramod, leave aside all this. In fact, I should feel obliged to you.'

The Sun was quite bright now. It was no more freezing cold. One could hear the sound of buses moving on the road. The chirping of the birds was also audible now.

'Sir, it will take three hours before the road is cleared for traffic. I have personally enquired. I have made arrangements for your breakfast. You will have your lunch here before leaving. A big boulder has fallen on the road. The labour is busy dismantling it,' the Thanedar reported.

'What shall we do here for so long?'

'Sir, if you wish you can go around.'

'That's a nice idea. We can visit Palampur. May be the road is blocked for this purpose.' They all laughed at Rita's comment.

They used the washroom before taking their breakfast. Thereafter a constable accompanied them to the Palampur Bazar. There was hustle-bustle in the shops. The town had witnessed it after rain for two days. The mountains were heavily loaded with snow. Palampur had also received a little snow fall. But the snow melted because it was followed by rain.

From the police station, they started upwards in the bazar. The Civil Hospital was on their left. The shops on both sides were opening to business. It was bright sun shine. The sky looked like deep blue sea. Pramod and Rita evinced keen interest.

'How wonderful! Rita, come here.' Pramod almost jumped with joy. He held Rita's hand. The constable was moving ahead of them.

'What a divine sight that is! Extremely wonderful. How beautiful the Nature is?,' Pramod went on.

'Really, Pramod!'

They viewed the Dhauladhar range from the Palampur Bazar. The small shops of Palampur on one side and the snow clad high peaks of Dhauladhar beyond. Some peaks were low in height. The sun rays reflected in the snow and presented a charming sight. Some portions of the mountains looked plain also. At places, the snow had melted. A portion of the mountain looked like a thin line. It appeared like a bride sitting unaware with some exposed part of her body. The sun shine made those thin lines all the more conspicuous.

The enchanting scenery was at an approximate distance of 3 to 4 miles but it seemed to be very close. The artistic peaks laden with snow looked marvellous and formed different shapes to different people. Imagination can play wonders. It also appeared as if the newly weds were in each other's arms.

'Pramod, will you not move on? The constable is waiting for us.' Rita almost pushed Pramod.

'I have also been waiting for it for long.' Pramod had fixed his gaze on the scene. He had forgotten that he was a police officer and was in the bazar with a young woman.

'Will you please move or not?' Rita's voice was left unheard. Her voice did enter his ears but he was lost in watching the snow-clad mountains.

'Pramod, shall we spend the night here on the road today?' Rita said in an irritated tone.

'Rita, let me enjoy the wonderful scene. Who knows we may or may not get a chance to see it again!'

'You are getting very emotional.'

'Really, I am undone.'

'You seem to be haunted by Nature.'

'Yes, Rita. Come here.'

Rita went closer to Pramod. He whispered into her ears...

Once
I had thought.
The abode of Shiva
Is just a mountain
Of dry soil and boulders
Just a heap, a dum
But
Today I realize as if
Lord Shiva stands
Holding Parvati in her hands.

'Well, Pramod, you are a poet too. Did you write verses earlier also or you have been inspired to write poetry by the extraordinary scene today alone?'

'Yes, I do write poetry but it has been prompted spantaneously.'

Pramod, Nature is extremely charming here. Everything looks fresh after two days' rain followed by sun shine.'

'As if a young woman stands in a new sari after a bath.'

'You are a great poet, Sir.'

They moved forward. They reached the end of the bazar in a few moments. There was a Kachcha road. They followed through a tea garden. Pramod had seen a tea garden for the first time in life. The small tea bushes grown in lines with tiny leaves looked like dancers moving in harmony. And the tall trees in between posed as security sensitively.

'Rita, I take tea daily but I had not seen tea plants earlier. I wish I am lost here.'

'You will not be lost. Yes, you will scribble another poem.'

'Poetry flows only when one is lost. Poetry is creation. It is Nature's rule that you write something by contributing a part of your being.'

'But Pramod, the poem, the Nature and your police job? Is there any coherence among them?'

'You are right. I never wanted to join police department. I wanted to be a Professor in a college. But if wishes were horses, beggars would ride. I wanted to pursue my post-graduate degree but I had to quit after graduation. Life has its own ways. It is not bound by our desires.'

'I feel either your love for Nature will make you leave your police job or the police will imprison your love for Nature permanently.'

'No, I feel I can carry on with both simultaneously.'

'Pramod, it is very difficult.'

'All is not easy in life.'

'My best wishes.'

'So, you are leaving me.'

'When did I catch you yet? How can I leave what I have not caught?'

They reached the Bundla village after walking on foot. It was surrounded by tea gardens. Tall big trees in between. A small rivulet flowed murmuring abutting the tea garden. The water flowed from some height. It was flowing sharply and making a sound also.

They went to the upper ridge of Bundla village. Pramod sat on a boulder. Rita sat on another boulder. They were two kms away from Palampur. The high peaks of Dhauladhar were now close to them. The huge Neugal river flowed magestically between Bundla and the Dhauladhar ranges. Neugal was so deep that it looked frightening if one saw downwards. The Neugal originated from the high mountain. It flowed engulfing the colourful boulder. The river looked like a lining in the centre. There was less water this time. During rainy season, one cannot see the bouder. There is water and water all around. The rustling murmur of the water flowing down is always intoxicating and rhythmic.

The sun rays provided warmth to the body and a cool breeze from the mountains sent a shiver down the body. There was a dense forest below the snow-clad mountains. The wild wind created a melodious sound of its own, as if someone was playing on a flute.

They sat there for a while. The constable then took them to a shop where tea was arranged for them. It was a small village shop. The shopkeeper sold pulses, flour, rice, spices, etc. There were bangles in one corner and tea stall in the other corner.

Both of them started back after taking tea. Rita was not accustomed to walk on foot. She was feeling tired also. By the time they reached the police station, it was mid day. The SHO had arranged lunch for them. When they were taking lunch, a constable came and informed that the road was open for traffic now. They hurriedly finished their lunch. Just then the bus came and stopped in front of the police station to pick them up. Pramod thanked the Thanedar for his hospitality and care. They boarded the bus. Rita sat beside him. The passengers in the bus watched them curiously as they were being meted out a special treatment.

The bus turned back from the police station and was now on its way to Mandi.

The journey upto Baijnath was of similar nature. The bus stopped there for some time. From there, the bus was moving on a higher road and then the Mandi region started. Now the turns were sharp and zig-zag. Every spot was charming for Pramod. He watched the surroundings eagerly. He found Rita sitting silent.

'I think you are also enjoying Nature now silently. But conversation will not disturb your enjoyment.' Pramod tried to break her silence.

'I thought you were bored with my talk.'

'How could you think that way? I have got all these things for the first time in life.'

'First time in life?'

'Yes, first time.'

'What does it mean?'

'I mean...I mean that I have come to the hills for the first time.' Pramod said hesitatingly with a view to avoid the issue.

'You were discussing about myself.' Wherefrom the hills propped up?'

'You are also a beautiful creation of this wonderful Nature, decorating hills, mountains for the first time, and you have also been seen for the first time.'

'I am not from the hills. I have been brought to the hills?'

'Oh, Rita. You have not introduced yourself. We have been together for so long now.'

Rita looked outside. The bus was crossing a dry rivulet.

There was little water at some spots. The road was covered with stones, small and big. The driver was driving at a low speed. There was steep ascent and a circular turn. As the bus negotiated the turn, Pramod and Rita almost fell aside. Rita sat by the window. Pramod was dislodged from his seat. He was out of his seat on the next turn. He caught the seat with his hands. Rita held his hand and said, 'You are sitting on the edge of the seat. Are you annoyed with me or you are hesitant.'

'No, nothing of that sort.' Pramod tried to hide his hesitation.

'The travel cannot be comfortable if you sit on the edge in a journey that is zig-zag.'

'You have said it right. One needs a companion in life throughout and not only at the turns. Such a companion who can save you from falling.'

'You will embark upon your journey of life now. Please sit closer to me in this hazardous travel.

'Since you are inviting me, I shall have to oblige you.'

'I am just inviting you at the moment. May be I have to pick you up also.'

'What do you mean?'

'You may not fall from your seat. When the bus takes a turn. In that case, I shall have to lift you.'

Both of them laughed.

'You talk about the whole world but you do not tell anything about yourself.' Pramod tried to pick up the earlier chord of conversation.

'You are talking about what I wish to forget.' Rita was serious. Pramod found Rita serious for the first time.

'I am asking for any such thing. I want to know where do you live? And wish to know about you and your family. Just that.'

Rita kept silent.

'Do you want to forget your existence?'

'Yes, Pramod. I do not want to be conscious about myself. I hate myself for what I am. As long as I throw it into oblivion, I am happy. And the moment I am reminded of it, my happiness disappears. And when I am there, don't ask what I am. Yes, I do exist.'

'Because man cannot easily undo what already exists.'

'Exactly.'

They were silent for a while. Pramod felt that Rita was somewhat frustrated. 'What kind of woman Rita is,' he asked himself. How she talked to her friend in the early hours of the morning, when it was dark. She enjoyed her conversation with him. Now she is lost in frustration Pramod had never been so close to any of the girls. He had never talked so freely with a girl. No girl also had even chatted with him so frankly. He was a little surprised. But the man in him was excited finding a young woman in proximity.

He felt disturbed when he thought of the comments made by a friend about Rita at Dharamshala. He wanted to stay away from Rita. 'I should keep away from Rita-like women,' he thought.

He was a changed man when Rita talked to him and behaved in an uncontrolled manner. When she laughed, her teeth bristled like pearls. He looked at her instently. A touch of her fingers made him feel an electric current. Her deep eyes bewitched him. A stare at her bosom made him shy away. But his mind was always fixed on her.

His intellect warned him of his status as a police officer. Moreover, he was going on his first posting. He must be conscious of his status and popularity at the place of his posting. Who is Rita? What stuff she is made of? What reputation she enjoys in Kullu? He felt that he should stay away from Rita.

He could not resist the temptation of being close to Rita, who smiled while in conversation with him. He felt as if the man in him was going out of control. As if the man in him had an independent existence who refused to dance tunes to his command. He felt the rebel within.

He had to compromise at last. He made himself adaptable. He decided that he would leave behind the experiences of the bus travel. He will not maintain special relation with Rita at Kullu and brushed aside the travel adventures. You come across many people during journey. And there is no harm in being conversation with all. If someone comes closer on the way, what's the harm in being nice to him or her. One may enjoy its feel and fragrance. I am not going to tie myself with her. Yes, only a few hours connection in the bus and afterwards no relationship.

Pramod now sat confidentally. He was able to shun his worries aside. He felt lightened.

'Am I deceiving myself?' Pramod said to himself and he was shaken for a moment.

'No deceiving. Who can deceive me? I have been educated in a college. It was co-education there. There were so many girls. We met each other daily. But I never deviated. And here, it is just a co-travel in the bus.'

The bus negotiated a sharp turn and to save himself from falling, Pramod's hand clung to Rita's knee. Rita helped him by holding his hand and dragged him closer to herself. Pramod looked at her carefully. Their eyes met and it was a moment of joy for both of them.

'Thanks.' Pramod said with a smile.

'For what?' She was extremely happy.

'For holding me.'

'You extended your hand and I held it.'

'May be many people extend their hands to you but I am the lucky one.'

'Well said.'

'Rita tell me one thing.'

'Ask please.'

'Why don't you tell anything about yourself?'

'I shall tell it also if anyone asks me with love. Why should I tell it if it has not been aksed for.'

Both of them laughed. Pramod moved closer to Rita. He sat down. Rita kept watching him.

'Rita, tell me where do you live in Kullu?'

'Pramod, I do not belong to the hills. My parents live in Ludhiana. I had been brought up there.'

'I had judged that you did not belong to the hills. Your dress and conversation made me conclude that you are a Punjabi.'

'Your judgement is not right. I am not even a Punjabi.'

'My guess is wrong?'

'It appears you don't have the complete qualities of a police officer. They say police can read anybody's face from a distance.'

'You mean that I could not discern the facts, though I sat very close to you. But remember I did not look at you with the eyes of a policeman.'

'With what kind of eyes you have seen me then?'

'I have seen you with confidence, friendship and love.'

'What kind of police eyes are?'

'Police eyes are full of doubt and always eager to unearth something new. Let us leave it all. I have not asked what you are not. You are not a Punjabi, not a Bengali or a German...you are not...this...nor that...what does it all mean? I had asked what you are but you started telling me about what you are not.'

They both laughed heartily.

'My father belongs to Uttar Pradesh. He came to Ludhiana for service long back. A family lived close to our house. They became friends with my father. He had an industrial unit in Ludhiana and he an Apple Orchard in Kullu. My father had an eye on his son and vice versa, he had an eye on me. We also used to meet each other. But before we advanced in love, the elders of both the families decided about us and performed our marriage.'

'You were married into a rich prosperous family. You must be very happy. Yes, you said you wanted to forget yourself. Why?'

'Pramod, you have only seen the blossoming rose flower. But the rose has a thorn close to it and when it pricks, it not only pricks but it makes me bleed.' Rita heaved a deep sigh.' She continued, 'One year after marriage was all great fun. I changed myself all together. Ours was an orthodox family. We did not use even onion in the kitchen. And there was a tradition of purdah also. But there were no such bindings in my husband's family. And moreover my husband was a modern man from all angles. I also enjoyed full freedom. Just after marriage we went for honeymoon. In our family, the girl was not sent immediately to her in-laws after marriage. Next year, my father earned a huge profit. He sent us abroad on holidays. We really enjoyed those days.'

'What happened then?' Pramod asked. Rita was silent.

'But those days passed off quickly. The industry suffered a loss after two years. My father-in-law passed away. The brothers divided the assets. Apple orchard fell to us. So we came to Kullu. I had gone to see my sick mother at Ludhiana. My husband was all alone. God knows how he was trapped by a hill girl. He indulged in excessive drinking. I was shocked to find all this on my return. But he could not avoid anything. He perhaps found something that I could not give. Once it started, he did not stop. I learnt that he was in the trap of another girl after a few days. He was being looted and he wasted money himself. I spent days weeping and shrieking. He was cold to me. The family members tried to advise him to be fair to me but to no use. I thought of committing suicide many a time. One year elapsed. I also came in contact of a young boy. He asked me not to be frustrated. He was the lone person those days who sympathised with me. My life was like an empty pitcher. He made efforts to fill it. Pramod, it was a painful time for me.'

'Rita, I am unable to understand why a happy life turned adverse. Why did your husband fall a prey to another woman when both of you loved each other so intensely?' I cannot believe it.

'All right. I also felt like that in the beginning but that all happened before me. I was a witness to it.'

'Then what happened to that young boy?'

'Gradually, his sympathy for me turned into love for me. I did not accept his love to start with. My traditional beliefs revolted against it. But what could I do? My husband was a habitual drunkard who ran after new butterflies. He found friends with similar temperament. I was drowned in loneliness. Not only loneliness, but the way he ignored me I felt offended. One day, the young boy gave me unique advice which changed my life.'

'What did he say?' Pramod was listening to her intently.

'One day, I was very sad. The sky was overcast with clouds. It was raining a bit. My husband was busy with his friends consuming liquor in the adjoining room. After sometime, they went away and did not return till night. The clouds were thundering, the lightening frightened. The servant went to his bed. The young boy lived nearby. I summoned courage. I woke the servant and sent him for the young boy. He came in no time. Finding me sad, he said. 'Rita, I know you live in a blind alley. You had lit a lamp. Agreed, that has also gone out but tell me who stops you from lighting another lamp in your life?'

'He must have been a poet?'

'Yes, just like you.'

'Do only poets charm you?'

'You may say that. It was the moment when I decided not to live a desolate life all alone. Why suffer for no fault. So I kindled a new lamp in my life. It once started, it never stopped.'

'Like your husband?'

'No, I excelled him.'

'Now, what?'

'Now, we both had our own ways I did not question him and he did not intervene in my way of life. We were free of each other and indulged in our ways differently and openly.

'Where do you live?'

'I live in the same home.'

'Do you call it a home?'

'Yes, not home but under the same roof.'

'But how both of you can live under the same roof? How do you carry on with the daily routine.'

'It is difficult to explain. We felt the discord in the beginning. Gradually, I became attached to my friends. I felt at home. Pramod, what for are we in the world? God has created us to live our life vigorously. Why complain? And how is it going to help. As long as I kept weeping, no one accompanied me. Not even my husband. And once I started laughing, the entire world laughs with me. I enjoy life to the brim.'

'How long has it been going on?'

'Almost four years.'

'That is why....'

'What do you mean?'

'Rita, one can have flights of imagination for sometime but one must live one's, life wedded to the ground realities.'

'Poets say like that.'

'Not only poets. You can enjoy a boat ride in a lake but ultimately you must find a shore. You cannot be on the waves for ever.'

'Oh, you are still an orthodox man. Life is not like boulders. It is like the sonorous flow of water. Once you enjoy the jump, you will forget the shores.'

'Anyhow, its your life. You may live as you like.'

'You are also related to me now in one way or the other.'

'What?'

'A friend.'

'Yes, Yes. I am one of your friends. That's why I wish that you find a shore of your life.'

'You have seen the shores yet. Have a dip in waters of life. Life exists in flow. It does not waste time on shores. I have enjoyed both the forms.'

'Rita, then you...'

'Yes, yes, ask whatever you want to ask.'

'A few moments ago you said you wanted to forget yourself. You got sad when I asked something. Did that speak of a shore or the flow of water.'

'About the shore.'

'Meaning thereby?'

'When I was tied to the spot, I was commodity to someone. The commodity must live at home, the husband may go anywhere and do whatever he liked. I did not compromise. I rebelled and liberated myself. You wanted to know that I have left it behind and have marched ahead. I do not want to look back.'

'You may not look behind but you must make it sure that you don't have obstructions ahead.'

'I have left the hell to be in the heaven.'

'There may be many people in heaven who love you.'

'As for now, you are the only one.'

Rita kept her hand on Pramod's and moved closer to him.

'Just now...'

'Yes, Pramod. Just now. I live in the present. Only the present. I want to forget my past, and I have no control on future.'

'But you cannot live in the present without the past.'

'How?'

'Whatever you said just now is past. Every moment of the present turns into past. It is a continuous process. Whatever you thought of me and said about me, has gone into the past. Will you like to forget that too? Your friend whom you met at Dharamshala stands consigned to the past. The moments you spent with him are not with you in the present. Can you imagine of future by throwing your past into oblivion?'

'What I wish to retain with me, that exists in the present.'

'No, Rita. I understand you have suffered a shock in life but just one jolt is not sufficient to change the meaning of life.'

'Meaning of life has not changed but now I know the real meaning of life.'

'What kind of meaning?'

'Life is not a bond, it is freedom. God has not assigned anyone to anyone. Man and woman are the equal actors in the drama of Nature. There is a slight difference in role but the rights are equal.'

'I have not followed the philosophy of bond and freedom.'

'Is it necessary that a woman should be tied to one man throughout her life. It is an insult to womanhood. That's the reason that woman in India has remained backward. And the man grew in stature.'

'Rita, you are sitting on this seat at the moment. If you are asked to move to another seat...'

'I shall like to sit with you here itself.'

'What is your wish to sit beside me in this loaded bus? Is it not an act of bond of fondness.'

Rita kept silent.

'And if two persons decide to live together for the life, will you call it binding?'

'Not binding but slavery...slaves of one another.'

'Rita, either you do not understand or you do not want to understand or you are deceiving yourself. What is love? It is to be one with one's beloved. It exchanges feelings of love freely, unbound. If you are not attached to one another, you cannot love each other. It is not conclusion but an extension of warm feelings. An attraction that accepts no bounds.'

'You appear to be a college Professor of Philosophy and not a police officer.'

'I wish I were. I am a teacher by nature. It is by chance that I am in police.'

'Please stop all this. It will make me feel dizzy. Change the topic please.'

'Rita, you are very interesting. I have seen this facet of a woman for the first time.'

'You find me interesting?'

'No, attractive too. You are very beautiful really. You look good.' They sat touching each other. Pramod tried to read her eyes.

Rita smiled.

The bus reached Mandi by the evening. There was a bus for Kullu the next morning. Where should he stay, Pramod thought. Where shall Rita stay? It would not be right to let her stay with himself. And in case he stays as per police arrangements, he could not allow Rita to be with him. Where will she remain all alone, he thought. It is not good to leave her alone. And why does he fear? If someone meets you during journey, you must help him or her. Behind all these arguments was his attraction for Rita. The bus stopped at the bus stand while he was thinking of stay arrangements. The passengers got down. The conductor came to Pramod.

'Sir, you might have been put to discomfort because of delay,' the conductor said.

'No, it's all right. You took special care of me.'

'Sir, any service for me?'

'No, thanks.'

Pramod alighted from the bus. Rita also got down. I asked a coolie to unload my luggage.

'Now, Rita?' Pramod asked hesitatingly.

'What now? The bus will not go beyond Mandi.'

'So we shall have to live in the present.' Pramod said in a lively mood. Rita returned the smile.

'Only the present is true. Rest is imagination. Dreams are a reflection of hope,' Rita said authoritatively.

'We must live in the present with memories of just passed moments. And if we are a bit away, we must live with the hang over of the bygone moments.'

'Yes, that's right.'

'And with a hope of future.'

'That's also right.'

'So Rita, we do not live in the present with the experiences of the present alone but with memories of the past and determination for the future. Exactly like the Dharamshala to Mandi travel and Mandi to Kullu travel is connected.'

'My dear philosopher, let us take care of the time first that is left at our disposal at present. Everything else afterwards.'

'Yes, you have reminded me of the present. I had asked you what now?'

'As you decide. I shall also like to live in the present.'

'But I am also worried about my and yours tomorrow.'

'Should I call it wisdom or cowardice?'

'You may say whatever you like. I don't have any of my acquaintance in Mandi. I do not know the stay facilities available here. May be police at Dharamshala has sent a message here. It might have made some arrangements. If that's the arrangement, your stay with me will not be justified. So ...'

'So, I shall have to make my own arrangements.'

'No, I can get your stay arrangement made.'

'I shall not put you to an awkward situation.'

'Are you angry with me?'

'No, I am trying to understand the decorum of a newly appointed police officer.'

'You do not understand. You are simply trying to understand.'

'Yes.'

'Please don't take it ill. You are welcome to meet me at Kullu.'

'That belongs to future.' Rita forced a smile.

'But when you meet me, that moment will be the present of that time.'

'At the moment, we are concerned with the present not about the 'then' of future.'

'Please check your luggage. Please tell me where do we go.' The coolie asked. He had tied Rita's small attache also with Pramod's belongings. The coolie kept waiting after tying the luggage for carrying. Then he asked Pramod about the place.

'You have tied the entire luggage in one bundle?' Pramod asked surprisingly.

'This coolie seems more courageous than you.' Rita laughed mischieveously.

'So tell me where should your stay arrangements be made?' Pramod was in haste. Some policeman may come to receive him if the Dharamshala police had informed them. He wanted to get rid of Rita before anyone from the police saw her with him.

'You need not worry. I have my comfortable stay arrangement here. If you wish, you can also come along with me. I just wanted to test you.'

'You were testing me or making a fool of me?'

'You were also making a fool of me?'

Rita got her attache separated and called another coolie. In the meantime, a police officer came and enquired about Pramod from the conductor.

'O.K. Pramod, I take your leave. Your present has come.'

'Thanks for a happy co-travel. We shall definitely meet in Kullu, in today's future and present of that time.'

Rita went away with a smile. The police officer had come to Pramod by that time. Both of them introduced each other and shook their hands warmly. Pramod went with the police officer.

Where will Rita stay? May be she has a friend in Mandi also as the one in Dharamshala. She left with confidence as if someone was waiting for her. She is a strange woman. She wants to live only in the present. May be her husband's behaviour offended her. But she is very charming. Her palms are silky. Her body must be soft like a rose. She is marble white. Her touch had made him felt a current in his body. A shiver went down his spinal chord when she touched him. Once I had touched a fan. It sent a light shock in my body.' I felt the same shock today when she held my hand. The touch was inspiring and not a killer shock of electricity.

'Sir, you have not taken your tea. I bring another cup for you.' The attendant said to Pramod, who sat lost in his thoughts.

'Yes, do bring a hot cup of tea. It's very cold here.'

'Sir, the Beas river flows near by. There are high hills on three sides. Sir, Mandi is very hot and very cold too.' The attendant went away. The police officer made Pramod's stay arrangements in a very old looking rest house. Pramod was eager to join his duty at Kullu next day but he was reliving the moments he had spent with

Rita in the bus. Rita flashed in his memory when he sat in the room. He wanted to change the charm of his thoughts but Rita popped up again and again.

The servant knocked at his door. Pramod opened the door. He had closed the door to avoid cold. The servant came in with a cup of tea.

'Sir, I have brought very hot tea. Kindly take it this time. You were in deep thoughts. May be you are remembering someone. But don't forget to take tea.' Pramod was surprised at his comment. He also felt a little raged. Why should a servant make such comments. And that too before a police officer. The Mandi police officer had told Pramod that the old cook was a talkative man. He had advised that Pramod should not mind his comments but must enjoy them instead.

'Yes, it is human nature that we remember someone or the other. Don't you remember someone?' Pramod wanted to release the tension.

'Remember? Whom shall I remember at this age?' He said while pouring tea in the cup.

'Rememberance of youth days. You don't look old. Hill people do not get old early. You are beautiful too.' Pramod said looking into his eyes while enjoying tea. He felt a bit shy.

'No, sir. I am not that beautiful now what I was in my youth. All people praised me. Wherever I went, I got married.

Neither I have children with me nor my wife. And my brother is enjoying a happy married life.'

'You have your son in the village?'

'Yes, he is there but he cannot be attached to me. I had deserted him and his mother. I married thrice after that. I did not bother about them. He is settled with his family. He does accept me as his father in public but he has no love for me. And Sir, it cannot be. I went on and on and did not look behind.'

'Is it common in your area to go for more than one marriage?'

'Sir, it was like that earlier. We belong to low castes. All our men and women followed the tradition but now it is on the decrease. In higher castes, men go for more than one marriage but not the women.'

'Even after so many marriages, you are all alone.'

'Yes, Sir. And my brother who married only once, lives happily with his family.'

'But you had four different women...' Pramod was joking.

'Sir, I beg your leave now. I forgot that. I have to cook food for you. This is a bad habit with me. I forget myself once I start talking.'

'What a man he is! Marriages and marriages. May be it was the flush of youth. He had no time to stop and look back. Must have been a healthy youngman. He is quite healthy even at this age,' Pramod thought lying in his bed. He had covered himself with the quilt. There was a room-heater also in the room. He would warm his hands on it. When a cool breeze entered the room, he shivered.

'Where would Rita have stayed? How free she is? She was talking like an uninhibited woman. She met me for the first time and that too in a bus and she talked of love. Is she really in love with me? But she had gone to Dharamshala to meet her friend. One can be in love with one person only. But why should it be binding? Gone are the days of love sticking to one and only one. Woman is betraying herself. She does not want to be tied to one man. Rita heralds the new age, so handsome and so lively. She said only conversation could take place at that point of time. She also told about falling in love, offering oneself. I also felt attracted to her. I am a coward. I sent her alone. I should have brought her here with me. I felt hesitation unnecessarily. She has other friends, how does it affect me? There could be one more in me.'

He heard the voice of a person from another room. His chain of thought was disrupted. He took his hands out from the cover and tried to warm them.

"My upbringing is orthodox. I am not an illiterate village boy who may go on practicing the old tradition blindly. Rita rightly said that one should live in the present. Past is gone. Why worry about it? Future is yet unborn.

Moreover, future is not in our hands. So it is useless to worry about that. We live in the present. Then why burden ourselves with the past and the future.'

Pramod thought but he wanted to deviate from his line of thinking. Either about his family or about his job. But he could not think of anything else except Rita.

'You are an idiot Pramod. What will Rita be thinking of you? She was so sarcastic in her comments. When the coolie had put their luggage together, she had said 'the coolie is braver than me.'

She wanted to come along. I was reluctant. And when the police officer enquired from the conductor, I had heard it. I had lost my wits at that moment. I took leave of Rita in a manner as if she was nothing to me. Had I shown some skill and courage, I would not have faltered in my first encounter with a woman. It would have been much better if I had taken her along.'

'Sir, I have brought food for you.' The servant entered the room.

'So early?'

'Sir, I have a message from an officer who lives closeby. I have to go and cook for him.' He kept the plates on a small table and also a glass of water.

'There is no one to cook food in his family?'

'No, sir. His family lives in the village. He is here for the last three years. He has never brought his family. He is alone here. Lives boisterously.'

'Who cooks food for him daily?'

'His servant.'

'Why you have been called today?'

'When his particular guest comes, he calls me for cooking once. He relished my preparations. So he said that whenever he would come to Mandi, I should cook food. Sir, you had not pointed out. I cook meat of various types. If you stay tomorrow, I shall serve it to you also.'

'No, I must reach Kullu tomorrow. I shall be coming to Mandi many a time. I am also fond of meat. I learn that hill people consume meat extensively.'

'Yes, Sir. Only a little percentage is vegetarian. Here mutton is served in marriages too.'

'Your preparations are indeed delicious. The ordinary dishes are also very good. If you had served such food to any of your wives, she would not have deserted you.'

'Sir, they did not leave me, instead I deserted them. All my wives were faithful to me. It was I who did not bother. I did not care for anyone. That is why no one is there today to look after me. The blunders of youth hang heavy in old age. Just wait, I bring a loaf for you.' The servant went to bring a chapati. Pramod warmed his hands on the heater. He was feeling very hungry today.

'Hurry up! Your guest may be waiting for you.'

'Take it easy, Sir. They take food very late at night.'

'What do they do sitting?'

'They just.'

'Even then.'

'Sir, they are high class people. I am a rustic. What can I say.'

'The guest is also a govt. officer?'

'No, Sir.'

'And what is the Mandi officer? He appears to be a big boss.'

'Yes, Sir. There are four or five top officers in Mandi. He is one of them. He is from a very rich family. Quite prosperous. I cook food at their place every Sunday. Many of his friends come to him. All of them play cards and intermittently indulge in gossip. Sometimes, they go on drinking till late at night. I also enjoy the party that day. I also get whisky as otherwise it is beyond my reach.'

'You have not told who is the guest today and from where? And what does he do? Pramod had finished his meals. After washing his hands he sat close to the heater.

'Why should he serve? He is...' The servant stopped in between.

'What?'

'Why a woman from a rich family will join service?'

'So, that is the story. That is why you were a bit hesitant. Who is she? Is she a relation of that officer?'

'No, Sir.'

'He is all alone at home today?'

'He is always alone at home.'

'So, will the woman stay with him tonight?'

'Yes, Sir. She lives there whenever she comes.'

'From where does she come?'

'Sir, she belongs to Kullu. But stays at Mandi when she comes or goes, and comes only to this officer.'

'She is from Kullu!' Pramod was alarmed. 'Kullu and Kullu woman,' these words alerted him.

'They live together in that building?'

'Yes, Sir.'

'What do they do late at night?'

'They talk extensively. Then they take drinks. Then I serve food to them. Then I come to my place.'

'What is her name?'

'I do not know her full name but the officer call her Rita lovingly.'

'Rita? Pramod's fingers touched the heater. He got aside. One of his fingers got red by burning. His heart burning was manifold.

'Sir, what happened?'

'No, nothing of the sort. My hand touched the heater. I was lost in your comments. Yes, you can go now. You have to cook food there.'

The servant went away. Pramod was now walking to and fro in the room. He kept the heater aside. He was no more feeling cold. He was restless now. He loitered in the room for some time before moving out. It had a small compound. But he enjoyed moving in the dark. The sky was clear. Stars were shining in the sky. He watched the stars. He sat in the veranda because he was tired. He felt cold soon after. He got up and moved into the room. He bolted the door and put off the light before going to bed.

'May be she is another Rita,' Pramod tried to console himself. 'There can be two women with the same name in a town. Such coincidences often happen. But a voice came from the inner recesses of his mind—'Pramod, you are unnecessarily trying to hide it. You have already played an idiot. You are trying to escape the reality. She belongs to Kullu. Her name is Rita. She has come today. She has her friends. She had stayed with a friend at Dharamshala. She is none else but the same Rita.' What a strange woman! How many friends she has? Did she really want to stay with me or she was just making a fool of me. How can she be in love with so many people at the same time? She stayed with a friend at Dharamshala. She swore love in darkness of the morning while taking leave. Then I met her in the bus, she kept talking to me throughout the day as if she was ready to live with me in life after life.

I could not say anything as I felt shy but she was so happy so free. She went to another friend leaving me alone. I am alone here and she is with her friend there. She must be gossipping at the moment. She consumes liquor. Oh God, if women take to drinking, what will men take?

Pramod tossed in the bed. He could not sleep. The bed sheet was in disarray because of his tossing in the bed. He had covered himself with the quilt cover as he was feeling the chill of the weather. He would cover his mouth also but soon he felt the suffocation. He was feeling about the woman in his thoughts. He was upset to find that Rita stayed with her friend. He was tossing in the bed to safeguard the cold onslaught.

Pramod could safeguard himself against the chill but he could not free himself of Rita's image. Both these experiences were the maiden experience in his life. He had met so closely and so truly any woman in life for the first time and he had experienced the cold of the hills also for the first time. Both the experiences in one day were heavy on him. It was a bit difficult for him to absorb the same. He felt as if he had been cut off from his family. Only Rita haunted him.

"What has happened to me? After all what is she to me. Why should I go on thinking about her. I have so beautiful sisters. I have an affectionate father. Who is Rita? Just a co-passenger in a bus. If she had not occupied the seat next to me, we would not have been acquaintances even. I am caught in my gentlemanly web. I thought she had reserved the seat. She had to sit there. I was fed up with her. I am a fool. She had plainly told that she lived only in the present. The moments she enjoyed with me have already been turned into past. She has no relation with the past. Whenever she goes, the present welcomes her. When she leaves that place, the present bids her farewell. She swears love. But as soon as she leaves, the present is over. She jumps back into her present and the game of present and past goes on. How warmly she bade adieu to her friend in the darkness of the morning. The words were magical. He might not have reached his home with sweet memories of love but the same had turned into past for her. I met him in the present. She lived in the present for the whole day. She was ready to live in the present during night also. I was frightened. No, no, I escaped the trap. My wisdom came to my rescue. The moment she reached Mandi. I turned into past for her. She has reached in another present.'

Pramod turned side in his bed. He removed the quilt from his face and felt the chill again. He tried to protect his body from cold. Pramod felt pain in his body.

'It's not good to meet such a girl. I should not have introduced myself to her. I met someone for the first time in life. Her touch was unwanted. Oh, what is my fate? Whatever type she may be but the electric current of her touch is still fresh in my body. How could it matter if I had also lived the present moment today. Is it necessary to carry the burden of the past and the future on my head? It's right that the temple of life cannot be built without the base of the past and future's tomb. But here only present was concerned. Occasionally, one can think of the present day. I was misled for nothing. Since I was confronted with the present, I should have faced it. I sent her there and now I feel repentent. I spoiled my sleep. I have to get up early in the morning to go to Kullu. That is a new place. And my posting is also new. No,...but I did the right thing. If it was leaked, my future would have been destroyed in the present itself. What is all this? Why should one go with a stranger...just for the fun of it. It is prostitution. Shun these thoughts...,' he wavered.

He heard the sound of ringing bells from a distance. Pramod again turned side in his bed. He was soon asleep.

'Sir you were sleeping deeply. I knocked the door twice and went back. I had brought tea. I have brought it for the third time now,' Pramod heard the knock and opened the door. The servant presented the cup of tea and stood aside.

'Yes, you served me very nice food last night, so I slept deeply.' Pramod said while rubbing his eyes.

'Please have tea.'

'Thanks. You might have also slept well late last night?'

'Sir, they are different people. I am a rustic.'

'Please do tell me. Your food is very tasty and your gossip is also spicy.' Pramod wanted to read him.

'When I went from here, the door was closed and the curtains were on. I kept knocking at the door. No one responded. I thought of going back. But he is a big officer. I am afraid of him. I stood long in the cold weather. The door opened after a gap.'

'What were they doing inside?'

'The same thing. They sat on the bed and were talking. She had come after a long interval this time. So they were busy.'

'Then you cooked food for them?'

'The dinner was ready but they were not in a mood to take it as yet. They were lost in talks. Both of them were sitting in the same quilt.'

'How did you feel?'

'May I tell you the truth?'

'Yes, only truth.'

'Very bad. This is not good. It is called bad character. If people belonging to the higher strata will have illicit relation with other women, how will it affect the ordinary man. It is very bad. The times are no good.'

'But you have also been changing women throughout your life?' Pramod commented while taking tea.

'You are right. But I had married them. The society was a witness to it. As long as my wife lived with me, I was bound to her. Once I deserted her, I married another one as for rituals. But I have never met any woman in a closed room under the cover of darkness.'

'You are a man of character, better than the officer.' The servant felt flattered to hear Pramod.

'Then what happened?' Pramod wanted to know the entire story.

'Even after cooking the meals, I kept writing. They were on talking and laughing. Thereafter, they started drinking. I kept waiting in the kitchen.

'Tell me if Rita belongs to Kullu?'

'No, Sir, her parents live in Ludhiana in Punjab. She is married in Kullu.'

'Where did she come from yesterday?'

'From Dharamshala.'

'How did you know?'

'I could make out from their talks.'

'Has she no family of her?'

'She has.'

'Then why here?'

'She is not happy there, here she is.'

'Why had she gone to Dharamshala?'

'She said she had some job there. But he said she might have gone to meet one of her paramours.'

'Does the officer know it?'

'May be'.

'Does he not feel bad?'

'What?'

'That his beloved has another lover.'

'He should not feel it.'

'Why?'

'Because his own wife lives in village. He has three or four other beloveds. Then why should his beloved stick only to one?'

'Please serve me breakfast. So that I move on.' Pramod knew that it was time to catch the bus.

A policeman came there. He waited outside. Pramod was packing up. He took his breakfast and went to the bus stand with that policeman. Pramod was alarmed to think of an incident. He stood there where he had departed from Rita. He could not decide if Rita flashed in his mind because of love or because of neglect.

'If she meets me again in the bus today?,' he asked himself. And if she again sits beside me and engage me in love chat?'

'I won't care. I shall not talk to her. I am neither a lover who was with her in darkness nor I am the one like the officer in Mandi. Neither I have deserted my wife nor I believe in misadventures.' He said to himself.

'If you are so brave why are you haunted by Rita?' A voice came from within.

I do not remember her. Moreover, the time spent by me is already past time. I also want to live in the present. I have to take charge of my new responsibility. Rita met me and has taught me a lesson. I must tread in life carefully... It is a closed chapter.

In the meanwhile, the bus arrived.

Pramod reached Kullu in the afternoon.

□

4

The historic Kullu Dussehra was in full swing. It was a mega show after many years. There had been obstructions during the past few years. Heavy rains often spoiled the show because of bad roads, the buses would not ply. And at other times failure of crops restrained people from coming to the festival. But it was a commendable show this time.

Kullu Dussehra is unique in India. Dussehra begins here when it ends in other parts of the country. And it continues for full seven days.

The Dhalpur Maidan of Kullu was full to capacity. All sorts of shops had come up. The shopkeepers had come from outside. The local people looked attractive in their colourful attires. They were roaming in the *mela* with their families and friends. A few were busy shopping. The melodious drum beat was audible. Songs were played on loudspeakers. A sea of crowd was moving jovially in the ground.

There was a tent at the centre of Dhalpur Maidan. Raghu Nath's statue was placed there. The Kullu Raja sat there in his traditional dress. The incense was burning in the tent. Prayers were also being offered.

With an attractive baton in his hand, Pramod roamed in Khaki. The policemen on duty saluted him smartly. Pramod talked to them and then would go further. The police had to work hard to maintain law and order.

It was Pramod's first year at Kullu. The entire hilly region was something new to him but the Kullu Dussehra was all the more peculiar to him. He was watching the different activities very minutely.

Pramod stopped for a moment near the tent where Raghu Nath's statue had been kept. He witnessed the proceedings intently. His excitement was on the increase. Just then, the District Police Officer, Mr. Prakash Verma arrived on the spot.

'Hello Pramod, you are watching all this with great intent.' He said moving closer to Pramod.

'Sir, it is all new to me. I am experiencing it for the first time,' Pramod replied.

'Pramod, it is the peculiarity of this place. It does not happen this way anywhere else.'

'Wherefrom are those deities coming? So many deities in such a small valley?' Pramod expressed his curiosity.

'Pramod, there are 365 deities in this valley. Almost every village has its deity. Look, the big statue is kept on the strong carrier made of two parallel bamboos. The devotees carry the deity on their shoulders.

'Are all the deities brought here today?'

'Yes, all the deities register their presence before Raghu Nathji on this day of Dussehra. The village devotees carry them to this place. Some villages are far off. Some of the devotees take two to three days to reach the point.

'And Sir, these instrument players?'

'Almost every deity has his musical instrument. A few deities have instruments of silver and some have gold plated ones. These deities own property worth crores in the valley.'

'They carry their deities on foot? Such a long journey?'

'Yes, Pramod, it is religious fervour. It is their faith in their deity. They cover the distance singing and dancing. They do not feel tired. They make the presence of their deity felt before Raghu Nathji. The king as representative of Raghunath acknowledges their presence in a traditional manner.'

'So many people come with every deity. How do they manage their food and stay?,' Pramod asked. 'They spend the night dancing and singing with their deity. Otherwise too, singing and dancing is an integral part of life here.'

'How?'

'The festival starts with dancing and singing. Men and women dance together. They have their specific folk dances and folk songs. The dances have a mountain-like seriousness and decency. It is not noisy like Punjab's Bhangra. They even dance while coming from and going to the fair. If some famous leader comes, they welcome him dancing and singing. The deities are worshipped by dancing and singing.'

'Sir, they seem to be illiterate and backward people.'

'Yes, in modern vocabulary you cannot term them as completely civilized but...'

'But what Sir? Man has scaled the unprecedented heights and has established new parameters of success. He has reached the Moon even and these people are so away from the glimmer of modernism. I am sorry to say they believe in superstitions.'

Prakash was serious on hearing the comments of Pramod. Both of them stood apart from the crowd and were busy talking.

'Yes Pramod, this is one way of looking at them. But where does the modernism of science take us. Is the atomic program not dragging us towards destruction? Man is losing his sense of balance and he is growing uncivilized. Why the maximum percentage of suicides occur in USA which is the richest country? Most of the people live in America use sleeping pills. The youth of rich Western countries seems to hanker after mental peace. We call it civilization, modernization that has driven mankind to unrest and has pushed it on the verge of atomic war.'

'Your opinion also carries weight, sir,' Pramod said.

'Look there. How happily the people are coming, dancing and singing with their deity. They work hard throughout the year. They sweat working in their fields. They grow gold in the form of grains. And during Dussehra, they come with their diety to Raghu Nathji. Content and fully happy, they come to Raghu Nath in a festive mood. Perhaps you don't know that very few crimes are committed in this area. There are many such villages where people even do not lock their houses. There is entirely a different world of Lahaul and Spiti beyond Rohtang Pass. People were not aware of locks till recently.'

'They did not know about the lock?' Pramod asked with a surprise.

'Yes, they did not know about the locks. They would go away from homes for days together but never locked their homes.' Prakash said,

'But why?' Pramod was curious to know in detail.

'Because they had not become civilized as yet.' Prakash made this comment and laughed. Pramod also burst into laughter.

'And this is the reason why crimes are less?' Pramod wanted to know more.

'Yes, this is the reason. Pramod, one thing is strange about the humans. Where modern civilization has not intruded upon as yet, people are poor, illiterate and backward but they are happy and content. They are not aware of suicides. Crimes are very rare. They do not take sleeping pills. Look at them, how absorbed they are, how devotional they are, Will you find even such contented and happy people in and around Cannaught Place? When modern life invades this part of the country, they will also lose the content and mirth. Whatever new civilization gives to these people, it will snatch their festivity and contentment.'

'It means man should be left as he is and where he is?'

'Not the least. It is good to shun the superstitions but at what cost?'

'Can we leave man to destiny?'

'No, Pramod, I do not mean it. But the theory of fate and destiny is not that bad too. Everything has two aspects. It has a good aspect also which I always notice.'

The crowd had gathered for a view of Raghu Nathji. Some of the deities had came forward. When it was noisy, Prakash asked Pramod to go in one side. Pramod moved that side. More policemen arrived. People stood outside as advised by Pramod. The crowd receded. The way was cleared. The deities were brought forward one by one. Pramod came to Prakash after posting the policemen there.

'How gentle the poeple are! It was such a big crowd. Just at my call they cleared the passage. If it were Ludhiana or Amritsar, the crowd would have had to be pushed with force. May be lathi charge had to be used to disperse the young men,' Pramod said coming closer to Prakash.

'That too because these people are not civilized as yet.' Both of them laughed.

'Yes, Sir, narrate that incident. Your observations are interesting. And moreover, what is police's job here. Law and order is being maintained here by indication and instructions only.' Pramod was eager to listen.

'I was talking about destiny. I do not know how much right or wrong it is. There is no doubt that for hundreds of years this way of life has made people live satisfied without tension. A helpless, hungry man would go to his hut without grumbling. He would think that he might have done something wrong in his past life. He was suffering in this life because of his bad deeds in the previous life. This thought would give him consolation despite he being poor. He would enjoy sound sleep. Now the things are changing. Now the person living in a hut thinks that the rich neighbour is an exploiter. The pedestrians call a cycle owner an exploiter, the cycle owner terms a car owner as the exploiter and a person who owns a single car calls the person with two cars a blood-sucker. It is the cause for dissatisfaction, tension and the crime.'

'It means you want status quo where the poor continues to live poor. As long as he does not revolt against the status quo, how can he progress? Fate means fetters.'

'Pramod, you are right. I am not in favour of status quo. But consider this point. Civilization has snatched the support of fate from the poor. Belief in fate allowed him sound sleep but did not give him anything new in lieu. The poor remains poor but his sleep has been snatched. The result is struggleful tense life.'

'But what does it mean?' Pramod expressed his curiosity.

'I can't say exactly. It's a difficult question. Is it not possible that we retain the old faiths in the light of modern civilization? Let the new civilization usher in. It should enlighten the world. Education should expand. But it should not snatch gentleman's peace, the satisfaction, the joy etc. of life.'

'Do you mean harmonious blend of the old and the new?'

'Yes, something of the sort. You may construct something new on the old foundation.' Prakash said.

'But this Dussehra is new for me. Your comment has given a new light to me. It is a new turn in your ideology. But I am surprised at one point.'

'What is your surprise, Pramod?'

'To be in police department and to have such ideas?'

'Yes, you are right. I was born in a religious family. I studied philosophy in college. And the influence still flows in me. Pramod, your tastes also do not match with the police services.'

'At least, my tastes are somewhat similar to yours.' Pramod smiled.

'Please forgive me, I forgot to thank you yesterday.' A young lady intruded upon their conversation with her remarks. A few other young women accompanied her. Talking loudly they walked towards them near Raghu Nath's tent. They stood there for some time. One of them suddenly sighted Mr. Pramod. Leaving her friends, she immediately rushed to Pramod to thank him. Pramod observed her seriously and in turn Prakash was watching Pramod.

'Thanks to me? You have wrongly recognised me. I am in police...' Pramod said astonishingly.

'No, Pramod, you should not feel shy. And when she expresses her obligation, you should accept it.' Prakash said laughingly.

'But, Sir, I do not know anything.' Pramod said without pretension.

'Very strange. Those who do not do anything, even they boast of their doings. And you do not remember after doing the good. You are really selfless,' she said.

Pramod once watched her, was lost in her magic.

'If all policemen were of this kind...' another young woman came closer to him. She added her comment to support her friend.

'Are you asking me to solve the riddle or you are just making a fool of me?,' Pramod said controlling himself.

'There is something definitely, Pramod. After all both of them are saying.' Prakash again laughed.

'You have forgotten perhaps. We were walking all alone on the road yesterday. We had watched the cultural show till late at night. It started raining at night. We were being drenched in the rain. You were in a jeep. You asked the driver to stop the vehicle. You gave us a lift and dropped us near our village.' The first young lady made him remember.

'Oh, yes. I recollect now. It relates to the last night. In fact, I had not seen you. It was dark at night. You boarded the jeep and then got down. It was raining too. Pardon me, I could not recognise you,' Pramod said recollecting the meet.

'Kindly accept it now. 'The second girl said jovially.

'What?' Pramod asked.

'The thanks.'

All of them laughed.

'There is nothing special in it. It was just a human duty. And, moreover, I am a police officer. I simply performed my duty. In fact, you are being liberal as you are expressing thanks,' Pramod said hesitatingly.

'So you also thank us.' The other girl said happily.

'Very nice, thank them for their thanks. Pramod is a new but very able police officer. I am happy he helped you. I am all the more happy to know that you kept it in mind and have come to say thanks. O.K., Pramod, I take your leave. See me in the evening. The Minister is coming tomorrow. We shall review the arrangements once again.' Prakash kept his hand on Pramod's shoulder, pressed it and then left.

'All right, Sir.'

'If you had not met us yesterday night, God knows what could have happened and when would we have reached our home in the rains and the darkness of night.' The first girl once again expressed her thanks.

'Many people passed by in their cars but only you helped us.' The other girl spoke.

'It was a human act. Moreover, I was going the same way. The jeep had to go in that direction. If I invited you to board the jeep, what new I did? After all human beings help each other. I am happy I helped you.'

'But you did not remember it.'

'I am sorry for that. I shall not forget now.' Both of them felt shy at Pramod's comment.

'O.K., Sir. I thank you once again, Namaskar.' With her hands folded, the first girl said Namastey. Pramod also folded his hands in response. Both the girls joined their other fellows. Pramod stood there for a few moments. His eyes were searching someone all around but he was looking at them. The first girl stopped after covering a few yards. Pramod also looked at them but he could not face them. They moved away from there.

'How simple, all these girls are? They have come to convey thanks for a small act. They are simplicity and beauty incarnate. Not only Nature has created beautiful trees and birds but the girls are also very pretty. Thinking all this Pramod had reached the other corner of the ground. He was walking slowly.

His feet were on the ground but his mind was busy with the girls. The girls watched him for a few moments. Then they disappeared in the crowd.

'How foolish I am? They thanked me so lovingly. They stayed here for sometime and talked but I did not ask them their names. They were in the jeep yesterday. I did not see them. I did not talk to them either. Yes, the driver did look at them and tried to talk. I could not do anything. Leave it I am not a driver. And if they meant to show superficial behaviour, they would not have come here today. But I did not ask their name even. The first young lady was quite impressive. Smart like the towering mountains with beautiful sparkling eyes. Her eyes had a depth of a lake. She appeared vibrant and youthful even in an ordinary attire. And the second one, she frolicked like a sparrow. But I did not ask them their names even. Where do they belong to? But why should I bother about their whereabouts? They may be from any place, how does it matter? I just gave them a lift and they thanked me for the same. The scales are balanced. But I should have asked their identity for the sake of decorum.'

'Sir...' A policeman saluted him with police etiquettes. 'Pramod's chain of thoughts was broken. He was taken by surprise but soon he controlled himself. He accepted the salute presented to him by the policeman.

'All is well in the fair?' He asked the policeman.

'Sir, there was a scuffle on that side.'

'Scuffle? Why did you not inform me? Come on, let us go.' Pramod started in haste.

'No, Sir. You need not go. We have settled it at our level. A few people were drunk. They had consumed excessive liquor. They picked up a quarrel with a shopkeeper but as soon as we reached there everything was in order. We have made them disperse. I just came to inform you.'

'But why do these people drink in the fair? That is the root cause of disturbance in the fairs.'

'Sir, liquor is an integral part of their life. It cannot be separated. There is extreme cold on higher mountains, where it becomes a necessity.'

"But there is a way to consume liquor. They should take it at their homes. Or they should take it with friends in a closed room. It creates a law and order problem if they take it in public. And it causes inconvenience to others as well. The worst part of it is that it affects the children negatively.' Pramod said while moving to and fro.

'Sir, you have put it rightly.'

'Where do you come from?'

'Sir, I belong to a village nearby.'

'Do you drink?'

'Yes, Sir.' The policeman felt shy.

'Do all the people drink in your village?'

'Almost all.'

'How many do not drink? And who are they?'

'Sir, the number of non-drinkers is very small, there are four only. A few of them do not consume alcohol because they are sick. But Sir, no disturbance occurs in the village.'

'Drinking promotes crime?'

'No, Sir. Not here. Crimes are very rare here.'

'Where do you drink?' Pramod looked at the policeman.

'Sir, at home. Never while on duty.'

'You were among those policemen who yesterday...?'

'No, Sir. I was not among them. That's a typical group. They drink even while on duty. They bring bad name to all. They have been caught many a time but...,'

'But what?'

'Sir, they are never penalised. They are caught every time and are let off unpunished invariably. Mr. Verma wants to punish them harshly but the issue is hushed up every time.'

'Why, why does it happen so?'

'Sir, he is connected to a famous local leader.'

'What do you mean? Are discipline rules not applicable to persons related to leaders?'

'Yes, Sir, not here. Now he says openly that no officer can harm him.'

'Is that? I shall see him. Is it all well there. You please go there.' Pramod was fuming. Yesterday's event once again haunted him. He was pressing his teeth. Waving his baton, he moved to and fro.

The Dussehra festival was going on at one pace. People carrying gods and deities were coming to the tent. The king would get up and receive them. The musical instruments were being played on. Children were moving from one place to the other whistling around sweetly. A *halwai* was busy preparing hot 'jalebis'. Another shopkeeper was frying hot *pakoras*. There was hustle and bustle all around.

Pramod reached his office after sometime. Prakash Verma called him in his office. They kept talking for long. The main assignment before them was the visit of the Minister. The Minister was scheduled to address a public meeting also. They discussed the arrangements for the public meeting. At the end, Prakash Verma stood up to go.

'Sir, what about the yesterday's incident? You have not said anything about that.' Pramod pointed out.

'Yes, I forgot that. What should we do, Pramod?'

'What should be done?' Pramod was astonished.

'Yes, you advise me.' Prakash said scratching his head.

'Sir, what is to be done? We cannot tolerate indiscipline and misbehaviour in the police department.'

Prakash kept silent. He looked at Pramod.

'Sir, Khushal consumed liquor while on duty. Moreover, he made three other constables to drink in his company. And then he started a scuffle in the police station itself. When the SHO tried to make him understand and behave, he started abusing him. He roams unbridled because he thinks no one can harm him. If we cannot maintain discipline in the police station, how will the police manage it in public?,' Pramod said in anger.

'You are right and it is not a new idea even. We all know this aspect.' Prakash said giving a serious thought to it.

'If police acts this way and that too within the precincts of police station, how will the police manage law and order in public? Sir, it is a very serious matter.'

'I told you that your comments are not new,' Prakash said in an irritated voice.

'Then, what Sir?' Pramod was scared a bit.

'Your comments are not novel, Pramod but you are new. Every new officer thinks the same way as you do but gradually...'

'Gradually? What, Sir?'

'Gradually, he is moulded as I am.'

'I don't follow you, Sir.'

'You will understand it but gradually.'

'Gradually...' Pramod muttered.

'Listen, Pramod. I thought twice the same way. I tried to punish Khushal. All evidences were available. You are right when you say that it's a sin to tolerate such kind of behaviour. But Khushal is Thakur's real nephew. He acts as his right hand during elections. Thakur asked me not to initiate any action against Khushal. When I did not listen to him, my senior officers ordered me not to take any action. I was told plainly that we could not even touch Khushal. Now tell me, what can we do?' Prakash said while having a deep puff of cigarette. 'Sir, it is very strange. So much outside interference. Then how shall you and me maintain discipline?'

'The discipline is going down since that day. Following Khushal, a few other policemen have also started taking liquor. If we cannot punish Khushal, we cannot punish others also for the same crime. I also remained very restless in the beginning. My soul cramped me. I felt myself disgraced before Khushal. But Pramod, what can we do?'

'But Sir, we have to run the police administration. And if we punish him, who can intervene?'

'Should we act against the orders of the senior officer?'

'Verbal orders are no authorized orders. The authorized provision as per rule says such a person should be punished.'

'No, Pramod, we cannot go against the verbal orders also.'

'Even if the order is against law and illegal?' Pramod was enraged.

Prakash had probably no answer for his queries. He lit another cigarette. He had a deep puff. But he remained silent. Both of them looked at each other. Prakash put the ash in the ashtray and relaxed in the chair.

'Sir, if a senior officer orders us to kill someone, shall we comply with his orders?' Pramod put another problem.

'It is a different issue. There is no relation between the two.'

'There is a relation, Sir.'

'How?'

'Murder of one man amounts to the loss of one man. But such kind of orders will murder the entire law and order. Indiscipline will ultimately destroy the entire administration... If the administration fumbles, the entire society will suffer.'

'You are having a far-fetched conclusion. Even if I accept your argument, what can we do?'

'We should implement discipline strictly. And the punishment should be exemplary.'

'And what about the orders from high up?'

'We should ask them to give in writing that punishment for indiscipline exists no more.'

'Look Pramod. You are new, your excitement is high. I have bowed before that pressure. I had also thought a lot about it. I wanted to act also but after a prolonged thought to it, I decided to let happen the things they are happening. Why take it on ourself unnecessarily.'

'Sir, if everyone thinks like that and bows before wrong things, how will the things get right and lawful?'

'O.K. I entrust this case to you for independent action. You try it once.'

'Agreed, Sir. I accept the challenge.' Pramod was excited.

'But listen. You will not do anything till Dussehra is over. Ministers will come here. A few of them are very close to Thakur. He will lodge a complaint against us. And we shall be put to trouble unnecessarily.'

'Sir, if you have handed over the matter to me, let me do it my own way. Either I do something in this case or I shall accept your line.'

'It's all right. I hand over this case to you in writing right today. I am impressed with your ideas. Your enthusiasm is commendable. My best wishes.'

Both of them got up. They came out of the office. Prakash was loitering. He went inside again. Pramod went his way.

□

5

Pramod had his mind stuck up with the day's incidents, when he reached his home in the evening. Prakash had entrusted him with Khushal's case. He wanted to have a specific plan for Khushal but the first young lady who had met him near Raghu Nathji's tent intruded upon his imagination. She stood live and expressive before him. He wanted to avoid her thought but could not.

He sat on his bed. He closed his eyes and was lost in her memory. In the process, sleep overpowered him. He was awakened by noise outside. He rubbed his eyes and saw hither-thither. He felt the atmosphere in his room gloomy. The show pieces he had arranged in the room fondly appeared pensive today. He got up and sat in his chair with the newspaper in his hands. He read a few lines but there was no intent. He was reading news but his mind was not there. He had turned to the same memory.

Pramod got up and started to walk around. He opened all the windows and the door also. He sat when he felt exhausted trying to console himself. I should not be so emotional. I am a police officer. Who knows who is she? A casual meeting with her, who was stranger to me and now this problem. I don't know how many more will come across me in life. She saw me and came to thank me. If she had not sighted me, I would have never met her. I should not be so sentimental.

With all this going on in his mind, he again went to bed and was soon asleep.

There was a knock at the door. Pramod got up and opened the door. An exhausted policeman entered the room.

'Sir, you will have to go immediately.' The frightened policeman said.

'Why, what's the matter?'

'Sir, Khushal...'

'What has he done?'

'Sir, he has created a scuffle. A large crowd has surrounded the police station. A few anti-social elements have also joined the crowd. They have started pelting stones also.'

Pramod immediately dressed up and moved out with the policeman.

'Yes, now tell what has happened?' He asked the constable after sitting in the jeep.

'Sir, Khushal was badly drunk. He did not attend to his duty. When the SHO came to know that Khushal was heavily drunk, he ordered to send Khushal to his room instead of posting him on his duty. But he did not retire to his room. He was asked not to go to the fair but he went. He created a scene and started hurling abuses at us all. At the sametime, he picked a scuffle with some youths in the fair. He beat one of the boys who was injured on the head and was bleeding. At this point, a few boys caught Khushal. They brought him to the police station. They are sitting in the police station and raising slogans. They are making noise. Sir, it is not good for the police department. It is bringing bad name to all of us.'

'Yes, I'll do something,' he said enraged.

As soon as the jeep reached near the police station, he heard a noise. The young men had gheraoed the thana. They were shouting slogans and pelting stones on the thana intermittently. A few youngmen were trying to dissuade them from throwing stones. No sooner the jeep reached the thana, enraged youngmen rushed towards it.

'Sir, just wait. Let me get down first. The crowd is going out of control.' The constable said while getting down hurriedly.

'You need not worry.' Pramod said and he proceeded towards the crowd. Some of the youngmen were furious. They headed towards Pramod. Pointing at Pramod, they were shouting slogans adding to the din and bustle.

'Listen, I have come to hear you. I assure you that you will get justice.' The youngmen in the forward line were now peaceful but their followers were still raising slogans.

The main door of the police station had been closed. The SHO once came out to advise the crowd to be peaceful but since he did not accept their demand, no one was prepared to listen to him. He went inside and shut the door. When a constable found the situation worse, he had gone to Pramod of his own.

'No one has got us justice till today. Our patience has been exhausted. He have crossed the tolerance limit.' A serious but furious youngman pronounced.

'If it has happened with you, I fully agree with you. But my young fellows, all are not the same stuff. You can try me also once.' Pramod said while touching the youngman's cheek affectionately. Finding the affectionate touch of a policeman, the youngman felt remorseful. He turned back and started to mollify the mob.

'We cannot initiate any dialogue with you until you become peaceful. As long as you don't tell me anything, I shall not be able to do anything,' Pramod said in a raised voice.

'Excesses will not be tolerated.'

'Hell with the police.'

'If the guards turn rascals, what will be the fate of the country?'

The persons in the hind part of the crowd were still raising such slogans. Some of them were trying to ask the public to be silent. Others were provoking slogans. There were many leaders. All of them did not listen to a single leader.

Attention please, if slogan raising and noise making could solve your problem, I would also join you in the venture. If denouncement of police can get you justice, it would ease the job of the police. So please sit down. I join you in slogan raising. And when you are all tired, you will go home.' Pramod was calm. Even the provocative slogan showed no impact on him.

The main gate of the police station opened. A few constables with lathis in their hands came out. Two of them had rifles with them. The crowd was infuriated at this sight. High pitch slogans rented the skies. Those who had sat down on the advice of Pramod again got up. Now they raised slogans against the police, the SHO, Thakur and Khushal.

'Listen, you all go in and close the door.' Pramod pointed out looking at the Station House Officer.

'But Sir, you are lonely here among the uncontrollable crowd? They had misbehaved with us today.' The SHO said in an angry tone.

'Excuse me, Sir. Your Khushal has been misbehaving with people for over one month now. You are protecting him. Even being in police, he indulges in vandalism. If we have come to protest against it in a peaceful manner, you call it misbehaviour.' An elderly person retorted.

'Sir, you come inside. We invite some of them for talks. We shall talk to them.' Thanedar suggested looking at Pramod.

'No talks. We have been exhausted. We want clear-cut decision. We want justice. We shall not budge from here without getting justice,' A voice was heard.

'We shall continue to sit here as long as we do not get justice.' Another young voice was floating in the air. Some of the persons started raising slogans again.

It all started in the evening but it was dark now. A few lights were glimmering.

'You all go in. You will not come out until I call you.' Pramod directed the Thanedar and the constables.

'But sir, you are all alone here?' Thanedar showed his anxiety.

'Not all alone. Don't you see this crowd.' Pramod said smilingly.

'But they? They are big crowd?,' Thanedar said again.

'They are not from China or Pakistan. They are Indians. I am standing among the youth of India. Completely safe.' The crowd was calm to hear Pramod's comment.

'Listen.' Thanedar stopped to hear from Pramod.

'Go inside and take it also with you.' Pramod handed over his pistol to him. Thanedar looked at Pramod with astonished eyes. He wanted to say something but Pramod asked him to go inside the police station.

'But, Sir, Khushal...'

'Where is Khushal?' Pramod was alarmed at his name.

'Khushal is with us. We shall hand him over to you. We have full faith in you.' Someone from behind shouted. Pramod again signalled to the Thanedar. He went inside with the constables.

'Pramod zindabad,' the crowd shouted.

'Yes, now tell me, what do you want?' Pramod asked.

'Here is your Khushal.' Some youngmen brought Khushal to Pramod. He was stinking with liquor, completely intoxicated. He was tottering and eyes were red. He was not able to walk. He was in police dress. He felt relieved when he found himself close to Pramod.

'Such a constable is a curse for Kullu,' an enraged youngman shouted.

'Not only for Kullu but he is a black spot on the police fraternity, which even the Beas waters cannot wash,' Pramod said.

The mob clapped and shouted. Pramod zindabad. Khushal was sorry to hear it. He thought that he would escape the wrath of the mob as Pramod was there. The police officer will help the policeman. And this has been the practice till today. But hearing Pramod's comments, he was all the more furious. He raised his head slowly and looked at Pramod.

'Khushal, if you are not bothered about yourself, you should not have insulted the police dress. I learn you have done it many a time,' Pramod said staring at him.

'He has injured a youngman on his head and has abused all of us. The Kullu policeman has turned into the greatest goonda of Kullu.' A youngman said while coming forward.

'I know it all.' Pramod pacified him.

'But probably you do not know it. It is the medical certificate of the boy. We are witnesses of the occasion. And we want justice from you.'

'You will get justice, complete justice.' Pramod answered in a confident voice.

Pramod saw the certificate intently. Then he called the Thanedar. He whispered in his ears and handed over the certificate to him.

Faltering Khushal tried to get up but fell down.

'Let me go home.' He uttered these words.

'I just send you to your real home.' Pramod said angrily. He pulled Pramod's ears.

'I just call Mr. Thakur. What do you think of yourself?' Khushal said in an irritated voice.

'Sir, just one minute.' Thanedar was trembling.

'I know why you are frightened. You don't worry. I shall handle the situation. Do whatever I have asked you to do. I shall listen to your advice later.' Pramod ordered.

The Thanedar came out after sometime. He was accompanied by a few constables. A policeman came forward and handcuffed Khushal. Khushal hurled abuses but the public lauded the action by clapping.

'It has not been done just to show you. He has been arrested formally. He will be penalised. The eye witnesses will now get their statements recorded in the Thana. Rest of the people can go home.'

Khushal was sent to the lock up. The public kept watching Khushal with handcuffs as long as he was visible to them. The crowd dispersed thereafter. The Thanedar was recording statements of the witnesses. Pramod sat in the adjoining room.

'A seasoned officer like Prakash has been tolerating Khushal. He had advised me also not to touch Khushal. How strange? Prakash was talking so ideally as if he is the only storehouse of knowledge. No doubt there was substance in what he said. His thinking is deep. I was impressed with his comments. But finding him afraid in respect of Khushal, all his influence on me was gone. To talk high and to behave like cowards. Let me leave the police discussion. I have severe headache. She met me out of the tent. Her smile during thanks giving had made the atmosphere lively and festive.'

Lost in these ideas, Pramod reached the tent once again. Her thanks and chit-chat resounded in his ears. He closed his eyes and was living those moments.

'Sir, you have not done good.' The worried Thanedar said to him.

'I have not done anything...she thanked...' Pramod was awake now. He said what he was living in imagination. He got up to find the Thanedar before him.

'Oh, sorry, I have not done good.' He said staring at the Thanedar.

'Sir, Khushal is Thakur's favourite. Thakur is the local MLA. There are rumours that the Cabinet is being expanded. He is sure to be inducted as a Minister. No one has committed such a mistake so far. Verma Sir had also become cautious. You have made me do a wrong thing.'

'You mean police is not for restraining crimes but it is for committing crime.'

'Sir, the Minister is coming tomorrow. Thakur belongs to his camp and is special to him. We shall have hard time.'

'You are frightened for it. What will happen to you if you have to confront the robbers with guns? Do not worry. You did what I ordered for. If it is a crime, I shall undergo the punishment. Be at peace. I shall handle it all.'

Pramod came out of the Thana and went straight to his home.

□

6

Khushal's arrest was a hot news in Kullu. It was talk of the town next morning. People narrated the story to each other with exceptional interest. Persons sitting in tea shops were enjoying the same topic. The hair dressers were narrating the same incident to their clients. They were all praise for Pramod. People waited eagerly for the next movements to happen.

Pramod was in his office. He was reviewing yesterday's events to guard himself against any untoward incident. He was aware of the opposition and the confrontation. He might have to fight against so many fronts simultaneously.

'Sir, someone has come to meet you.' The peon informed Pramod after entering his office.

'Is it she or he?' Pramod asked.

'Sir, a lady has come.'

'She wants to meet me or Mr. Verma? Please ask her specifically. What has she to do with me? She must have come to see Mr. Verma.'

The peon came out of the office. Pramod was examining a file. The moment he opened the file, he found that there was some mention of Raghu Nath temple. It reminded him of Raghu Nath's tent and the young lady who had met him there. He got up with a jerk. And came out of his office hastily. He looked at the lady standing at some distance. His anger was gone and he returned to his office.

'Sir, the young lady wants to meet you,' the peon said while entering the office.

'Me? But I do not know her.'

'But Sir. She is waiting outside. You have not seen her.'

'Yes, yes. Send her in.'

'Namasteyji'.

'Please come and have a seat.' He said finding the girl shy.

'Yes, please sit in the chair,' Pramod said. She looked ordinary but was attractive in local dress of Kullu. She occupied the chair hesitantly. Pramod had never seen a lady in Kullu attire from so close a range. If at all he had seen such a lady, it was in a group. Moreover, such a raw young girl had come in his sight for the first time. She was wearing a woollen lehnga. It was covered with another cloth. There was a colourful scarf on her head. She was fair in colour and had deep black eyes. She was lean and thin. Pramod viewed her from head to toe. May be she had come to the police office for the first time. She was feeling very shy. She sat in the chair but did not speak anything. She was looking downwards.

'Yes, please tell me what brings you here?'

'Sir, no. I have not come for myself.' She said raising her eyes up a little bit.

'Nothing concerning you? But you are here before me?'

'Yes, I have come.' She said smiling a little bit. Pramod liked her shyness and her attractive figure.

'Tell me what I can do for you.' Pramod asked looking into her eyes.

'Sir, you know her?' She said with her eyes downward.

'Whom?' Pramod could not restrain his laughter. He thought perhaps she wanted to say something about her husband. A hill woman does not speak her husband's name.

'Your's he? You should have brought him here. Was there any scuffle between both of you. But it's a common thing.'

'No, no, Sir, I am not married as yet,' She interrupted.

'Excuse me. How does it matter if you are not married. My best wishes to you for early marriage.'

She again felt shy at Pramod's comments.

'Please. Ms. Rita has sent me here.' She summoned courage to say it. Pramod tried to be himself now. He thought for a moment, called the peon and asked him to bring tea.

'All right. How is Rita?'

'She is perfectly all right. She remembers you.'

'You also live with her?'

'Yes, my house is close to her house.'

'You are related to Rita? How?'

'She loves me immensely.'

'So, she has sent you here.'

'Yes, I carry her important messages. She trusts me very much.'

'How is her husband?'

'He is perfectly all right.'

Pramod controlled himself and was a bit cautious. He wanted to have more information about Rita. He prepared himself to ask many things from that girl. Then he thought, it would not be proper to ask her so many questions who had met him only for the first time.

Both of them were sipping tea. She was sitting like a statue and would only shake her head when she wanted to respond. She was extremely shy. Pramod liked her simplicity.

'Please sit comfortably..You are being very hesitant. It is your own town.'

She kept silent.

'I understand you go to different places to deliver Rita's messages?'

'The word 'Police' frightens me. I was reluctant to come. But she insisted on me. But you don't look like a 'police-wala.'

'Then what do I look like?'

'Very nice.' She became all the more shy.

Pramod was pleased with her comments but was surprised also. Initially, she was so shy but now she dared to tell me that she liked me. He said to himself, after all she lives with Rita.

Rita had met him once or twice since Pramod had come to Kullu. He was in a fix. At times he felt like meeting Rita. He was reminded of his talks with Rita during his bus journey. He had tried to meet her but he could not meet her exclusively. And when he met her, he could not talk anything specific.

He felt Rita had the same kind of feelings for him as she had earlier. But he was surprised to think that Rita had not made any attempt to meet him.

On the other hand, when Pramod got information about Rita from various sources, he made his mind to forget her. He was of the view that his interaction with Rita would downgrade his position in society. But despite all this, he still had a fascination for her.

The day he met the girl who had come to thank him near Raghu Nath's tent he had fallen in love with her. He had lesser attraction for Rita now.

They had finished tea. She sat silent before him. She was in a thoughtful mood.

'Yes, what's the message from Rita?'

She suddenly woke up to the situation. She was earlier lost in her thoughts.

'Sir, she wants you to know that Khushal is close to a very dear friend of hers. Since you are here, no harm should be done to him.'

'Khushal?' Pramod was astonished to hear it. He could never imagine that Rita could send a handsome girl to convey her message regarding Khushal. He flew into a rage in the first instance. He was surprised to know that Khushal could approach even Rita.

'Ritaji has also expressed her desire to meet you. Can you come to her residence for dinner today? If you agree, I can come to escort you? I am greatly impressed by you in the first meeting itself.' She was smiling now.

Pramod saw her intently. She was so shy moments ago, he thought. She is quite open now, no hesitation. She is impressed with me. I appear good to her. She is prepared to escort me to Rita's residence. What is all this?

'So what do you want?' He looked in her eyes.

'Simply, that you let Khushal off.'

'Do you know where is Khushal at this time?'

'Yes, I know. That is why Rita has sent me.'

'Where is he?'

'In your lock up.'

'What do you want?'

'Please leave it. It is easy for you. Talk something else. I shall love to talk to you.' She said while trying to look attractive.

'Do you know, it is police office?'

'Yes, I do know. You tell me, where should I meet you?'

'Here and here only and that too for the last time.'

Pramod got up fuming with anger.

'Listen you and tell Rita also that Khushal has been arrested for a serious crime. The case has been registered and it cannot be cancelled. Moreover, it should not be.'

'But Rita has promised her friend that it would be settled through you. What will happen? What shall I say to her?'

'The same asnwer that I have said.' Pramod was rough in his gesture.

'But...'

'What but...you,' Pramod wanted to ask her to leave but controlled himself.

'Do you also know Khushal?'

'Yes, I do know him.'

'That's the story.'

'Yes.'

'Have you any relationship with him?'

'I don't have any relation. But I often go with Rita to her friend's place. I have seen him there many a time.'

'Excuse me, I cannot do anything.' Even at these comments of Pramod, the girl did not get up. Pramod moved towards the door. Finding him leave his office, she also got up to leave.

□

7

'Pramod, what did you do yesterday?,' Prakash Verma said while entering the room. Prakash called him to his chamber. He was smoking profusely and was lost in thoughts. Neither did he ask Pramod to sit nor he said anything else.

'I did not do anything. It is what he did,' Pramod sat in a chair and said.

'Listen. The Minister is coming today. You should have waited for a day a two. Mr. Thakur is very angry. He will talk to the Minister and we shall be in soup.'

'May be the details have not reached you.'

'It is not the question of details. But it is the question of saving ourselves from the wrath of the Minister and Mr. Thakur. Why don't you understand my point?,' Prakash said in a confused tone.

'You know what Khushal did. The mob had caught him. He was drunk at that time too. The mob had surrounded the police station. The SHO and all the policemen were locked up in the Thana. The crowd was uncontrollable. They brought drunken Khushal before me. Tell me what could I have done? If I had not taken action to appease the crowd, they would have created law and order problem. The crowd was pelting stones. The police would have lathi charged, which could result in public strike on arrival of the Minister today. It would have turned Dussehra festivity into a sad situation. I thought you would appreciate me for controlling such a situation but you appear to be angry.' Pramod said all this in rage.

Prakash appeared all the more worried. He lit up his cigarette with the earlier one and had a puff. He left rings of smoke. He was non-plussed at hearing Pramod.

'Sir, why have you gone silent?'

'Yes,' Prakash had a puff.

'Are you angry with me?'

'No.'

'I have explained the entire situation. You tell me what should I have done."

'You should have asked me before taking action. It was necessary to consult me in such a delicate matter and that could have been useful too.'

'But where was the time? I had been called from home and made to face the crowd straightaway.'

'You could have managed time. You should have gone to the police station after listening to the crowd. You could have called me. It appears you did not need my help.'

'Sir, truly speaking, you had handed over this case to me.'

'I had handed it over to you for solving it, and not for complicating it.' Prakash spoke angrily.

'You sent Khushal to the lock up to appease the mob but you actually arrested him. You completed all the papers at night. What prompted you for it? The crowd would have dispersed to hear that you had sent him to lock up. He could have been sent out sometime in the morning. He could have avoided himself from public appearance for a few days. People would have thought he was behind the bars. The case could have been disposed of just after Dussehra. People would have forgotten. But you filed an FIR then and there. And you registered a few witnesses. You prepared all the papers required for his arrest and you handcuffed him publically.' Prakash was smoking after every word. His anger was reflected in the high rising smoke.

'You mean I should have told a lie to the public? I should have deceived the public to save a scoundrel, you mean. No one has ever taught me such a lesson neither in the college nor in the police training college.' There was red rage in the eyes of Pramod as well.

'Pramod, we learn many things from experience.' Prakash was now softened.

'I have just performed my duty, Sir. Kindly excuse me for saying one thing. After all, why do you fear so much. What harm the Minister or Thakur can do to us? And moreover we have not committed any crime. Khushal is making merrry in the jail even after committing a crime whereas anxiety has gripped us, although we have committed no crime. You do not worry, Sir. You put all the responsibility on me. I shall face it.'

'It cannot happen that way. You are my subordinate. I am answerable for all that happens here.'

'Sir, you were discussing excellent things yesterday. I was influenced by your knowledge and depth in thought. I find you all different today. There is drastic difference between Prakash Verma who stood beside Raghu Nath's tent yesterday and Prakash Verma who sits in his office. These are two poles apart. Difficult to recognise!'

After listening to Pramod, Prakash looked at him harshly but remained silent.

'I am sorry for my aggression,' Pramod was a bit frightened.

'You are being arrogant repeatedly. How many times will you tender apology.' Prakash again started smoking.

'You have pushed me into dangerous waters,' Prakash said, 'I shall have to get myself transferred to some other place.'

The peon came in, saluted and said, 'Sir.' 'Sir, Rita has come to meet you.'

'Yes?' Prakash raised his head and said.

'Ms. Rita?' Alarmed Prakash got up from his chair. He rubbed his cigarette in the ashtray. He set his coat and tie in order. Pramod was also surprised to hear Rita's name but he was not as worried as Prakash Verma was.

'Tell me now, what shall I say to her.' Prakash said looking at Pramod.

'So police is answerable to these people also?' Pramod was being mischievous.

'You do not know Rita.'

'Not completely, but a little bit.'

'Your time has come to know her fully.'

'I do not follow, Sir.'

'You will come to know when you are transferred to some other place at the instance of Rita.'

'It means she is a big boss.'

'May I come in?' Rita could not wait any longer. Prakash was ready to let her in. Pramod stood there. The peon waited for the order but Rita was not accustomed to wait outside so long. So she entered the office.

'Oh, you are here? Why did you take the trouble. You should have called me.' Prakash stood with folded hands.

'Namastey Ritaji.' Pramod said and looked at her.

'Namastey. How do you do?' Rita was now fully focused on Pramod.

'Perfectly all right. All is well in your town.'

'But I wanted to know about you.'

'God is kind to me.'

'I had a keen desire to meet you. I tried a number of times but it appears you are awefully busy here.' Rita had moved closer to Pramod.

'You may interpret it this way.'

'So as long as the landslides do not stop the buses on the roads, our meeting will not be possible.' Pramod laughed to hear Rita's comment.

Prakash was surprised to note that Rita had moved closer to Pramod for a dialogue. He had not expected that they knew each other so closely. He felt bad that Rita had ignored him. He was angry with her but at the same time he was happy at heart. He thought Rita would handle Khushal's case herself.

'Please have a seat Ritaji. I am fortunate to have you here in my office. You are welcome.' Prakash offered a chair and she occupied it.

'Excuse me, I have not come but I have been made to come here.' Rita said in a serious mood.

'Whatever the motivation, it is our good luck to have you here.' Prakash laughed in a flattering tone.

'Look Mr. Prakash, you have not done anything good by arresting Khushal.' Prakash looked at Pramod with his eyes downwards.

'You know it well. He is Thakur's special favourite. How dare you touch him? I have restrained Thakur so far. He was sending his messenger direct to the Minister. The honourable Minister is coming here today. And if Thakur complains to the Minister, what will be your fate?' Rita went on saying and they both listened silently.

'If there was anything, you should have disposed of the case after advising him. If it was a bigger problem, you could have told me or Thakur. We would have settled it. But you neither told any one nor informed us but you simply arrested him and put him behind the bars. You should know that it is not the Britisher's rule. Now the democratic govt. governs it. His favourite was handcuffed in his area without his permission. Prakash I never expected it from a seasoned man like you. I have sympathy with you because you had helped me once. That is why I have asked Thakur not to take any action. I have come here to help you,' Rita said. After saying all this, she sat comfortably in the chair.

Pramod had observed Rita from so close a range today since he met her last. She was wearing warm coat over sari at that time. But it was sunny today and Rita wore sari and blouse only. She was vibrant. A large part of her body was exposed which appeared as a patch of ground covered with snow in the given mountains. Pramod watched her beauty intently. Prakash sat subdued. He tried to read Pramod's mind.

'Why don't you speak Prakashji?' Rita thundered.

'I have always abided by your instruction.' Prakash said in a flattering voice.

'You have been doing but what about today. What should I say to Thakur?'

'It will be done as you desire but...'

'No ifs and buts. Just be straight forward.'

'I mean. The case had been entrusted to Pramod.'

'Oh, No worry then. We can get anything done from Pramod. I was afraid of your obstruction.'

'How dare I?'

'You can go please. I talk to Pramod.' Prakash was annoyed when she uttered these words but at the same time he felt relieved also. He felt he was being ignored. He has been in Kullu for a longer period. Rita is her old acquaintance. He has done a lot for Rita. And in turn, Rita has got his transfer cancelled twice but he never took anything from her. Pramod had just recently joined at Kullu. Prakash did not know that Rita and Pramod were known to each other. Rita talked to Pramod so closely. Prakash felt jealous. Now she has asked him to go out. He was happy to be rid of Khushal's case. He came out of the room.

'You had sent that girl?' Pramod asked her.

'But you turned out to be stone-hearted. You have broken her heart. I could understand your behaviour but you should have kept her word too.'

'What did you understand?'

'That if I wanted some favours from you, I should visit you personally. But listen, I had sent the best one. You liked her or not but she is one of the most beautiful girls of the area. It would have been nice on your part if you had talked love to her.' Rita said with a smile and kept her hand on Pramod's hand.

'Love chat and that too in the police office?' Pramod made a concious effort to rid himself of Rita's impact.

'Lovers do not shun it even on gallows.'

'How wonderful is your comment?'

'Rita, you look very beautiful when you are angry. You appear beautiful when you talk love on meeting but you are exceptionally charming when you frown.' Now Pramod kept his hand on Rita's hand.

'You never cared to meet me since you came to Kullu,' she said in a complaining manner.

'Listen, I shall introduce you to Thakur and the Minister today. The Minister will be at Thakur's place for dinner today. You also come there. I shall get an invitation card for you.'

'Rita, why Thakur and the Minister between us? Nothing else, not even the invitation for dinner at the moment. You wore a heavy coat that day that I could not see you properly even. But today, you are so beautiful, fantastic. God has been kind to you.' Pramod was a bit derailed. Rita laughed at his comments.

'And how were you manufactured by Him?'

'The likes of me were manufactured in a group.'

'Alas! You could see Pramod with my eyes.'

'What could happen then?'

'You could know how beautiful Pramod is.' Rita looked at Pramod with intoxicating eyes. Pramod was also lost in Rita's eyes. 'I just come after using the wash room.' Rita went to the adjoining small room.

Pramod was serious now. He said to himself, what am I doing all this. What shall I do when she asks me to release Khushal? Ignoring the seriousness of the case, I talked love with her. What has gone wrong with me? I had resolved not to have any truck with Rita-like women but the moment she came before me, I forgot my commitment. I behaved like a 'Majnoo'. I don't know why this weakness in me for women. Is it the case with me or it exists in all men? What shall I do, when she comes now?'

Pramod was in a thoughtful mood when she came and occupied her seat.

'Let us talk about the present.' Rita said.

'Present cannot be talked about. It has to be lived, Rita.'

'Pramod, you have grown wiser.'

'It is all your blessings.'

'Only because of that little contact.'

'Yes,' Pramod tried to control himself. He wanted not to talk frankly to Rita but actually he was involved in the chat quite deeply.

'So, Pramod, I take your leave now. You must come to the dinner in the evening. You will release Khushal, of course. And kindly take care in future. Thakur is an influential local leader. He should not be offended under any circumstances. And he is my close friend too.'

'Your friend?' Pramod asked curiously.

'Yes, very close friend.'

'Rita!' Pramod could not say what he wanted to convey.

'Please speak out.'

'Look, the Khushal case.' Pramod was in a fix. He wanted to refuse it flatly but he was helpless before Rita.

'What is Khushal issue? Release that policeman. What is he? You cannot waste time in petty things. Listen, just after dinner...there is a rest house nearly. We shall talk to our heart. I have lots of things to say to you.'

Pramod kept silent. He was a bit downcast.

'Thakur will be very happy. I had assured him on your behalf. I had also told him that Pramod is my friend and I can get anything done from him. If Thakur is pleased, the Minister will also be happy.'

Pramod wanted to say something but he could not.

'You were talking nice things just now. But you have gone silent suddenly. Please do speak.'

'Rita...'

'Yes, speak out. What's the problem?'

'Khushal's arrest has been entered in the Register. All relevant papers have been filed. A few evidences have been recorded. It is difficult to release him.'

'Pramod, how simple you are. You look so beautiful in this simplicity. May be as beautiful as I appeared to you when I showed my danger to Prakash.' Rita got up and came close to Pramod. She held his hand lovingly.

'You are a police officer. And a man. What cannot a police officer do? Thakur wants it, the Minister will also desire it. Why worry if the entire government wants it. Instal a new Register. Who can question you? They who matter want it.'

Pramod was lost in deep thoughts. He did not want to release Khushal at all. He felt he would belittle himself before the police administration and the public if he let him off. Moreover, he will fall in his own esteem. But he could not summon courage to refuse Rita. He made attempts but could not utter anything.

'I shall try to do something after consulting others.' He evaded the issue.

'Whom do you want to consult? Prakash is the top police officer here. He cannot even budge before us. You can do whatever you want.'

'All right.'

'May I go now?'

'Yes.'

'And you remember, today's night...' Rita looked into his eyes mysteriously.

'On getting an invitation.'

'That you will get. But that will be from Thakur for dinner only. My invitation is after dinner.' Rita went out of the room smiling.

Pramod loitered there for sometime. Then he came to his office. He called for Khushal's file. He reviewed it. He started thinking. He had a nap.

'Sir, the Minister is reaching Kullu within ten minutes.' A policeman informed him.

'Thank you, I am going.'

Pramod came out of his room.

□

8

There was festivity at Thakur's residence today. The Minister was scheduled to dine there. Many officers and prominent citizens had also been invited. The roads to Thakur's place had been closed right in the morning. The PWD labour was busy there. The road was being cleared. Repair work was in progress. They were lining lime on both sides of the road. Some departmental labour was working at Thakur's residence also.

Cooking was in progress. A goat had been slaughtered. Meat was being cooked besides other dishes. The cooks had come from the Govt. Dak Bungalow. A government officer was supervising the preparations.

Thakur lived in a village at some distance from the town. The village was alive to the scheduled visit of the Minister.

When the Minister's car with a flag on it reached the village, there was noise all around. The villagers came out of their houses and lined up to welcome the Minister. Thakur had asked all the villagers to come to welcome the Minister. The entire village regarded Thakur in great esteem.

The Minister was loaded with garlands. He was welcomed whole-heartedly. The artists played on the musical instruments at the welcome door. It appeared as if marriage ceremony is being solemnized. All top govt. officers and eminent persons of the town were present. Many had been invited but many had come there uninvited even. Among those were people who had worked in elections for Thakur. Thakur's home was their home and they had the right to dinner also.

'You have invited so many people, Mr. Thakur,' the Minister said while entering Thakur's bungalow.

'Sharmaji, it's your arrival that has made so many people came spontaneously. Moreover, you are at my residence for the first time after being sworn in as a Minister. You are my friend, in addition to being a Cabinet Minister; and that too on maiden visit to my place.' Thakur had a long puff of cigarette.

Shri Dhanwant Ram Sharma was a veteran Congress leader. He had participated in the freedom struggle also. He had never been to jail but he had arranged a certificate from a jail.

One of his friends and relative was a member of Lok Sabha. He had obtained a fake certificate with his help. On that basis he declared himself a freedom fighter. He had become a pensioner. No one called him by his full name. He was called only Sharmaji. He had become a Minister for the first time a few months ago.

Sh. Budh Singh Thakur hailed from a respectable family of Kullu. Neither he nor his family members had anything to do with the freedom struggle. In fact, the entire family had been loyal to the British rulers. They were from among those clever people who had hoisted Congress flag on their houses on the morning of 15th August 1947. Congress flags were hoisted on the houses of Congress men of Kullu after Thakur family had already hoisted it in the morning.

'Shall we have to dine in this crowded atmosphere?' Sharma whispered in Thakur's ears.

'Yes, dinner together but drinking...' Thakur smiled and whispered back.

'Kindly see to it. It will spoil the dinner. Moreover, it is party at Thakur's place. It cannot be dry.'

'I get the arrangements made. Let the public dine first and we can follow.' Thakur puffed his cigarette and left the smoke in air.

'Yes, this can also work. We are not in a hurry.' Sharma sat clamly.

Thakur came out. He called the organisers. He discussed it with them. Dinner was now being laid in the compound.

"I have told them. The dinner is ready. All the guests have come. We serve it to the public first. You will have to sit there. You take a little bit. We shall eat later otherwise it will be difficult." Thakur told the Minister.

"It's all right. Our dinner will be an extended one. Thakur, I have not seen her. Where is she? The dinner will be tasteless without her".

'Who? Sharmaji?'

'The same... I forget her name. Last time she had come with you when the assembly was in session.' Sharma wanted Thakur to recollect.

'You mean, Rita. Well done Sharmaji. She is stuck in your memory. Thakur said in a low voice.

'Is that for Thakur only?'

'Earlier it was, but now...'

'What now?'

'Sharma is an equal runner in the race now.'

Both of them laughed.

'Thakur, it is a time of equality. Why should you bear the entire burden?'

'Sharmaji, flowers don't weigh heavy.'

'Well said, Thakur.'

'So Verma is not wrong when he comments about you.' Thakur was satirical.

'Thakur, he talks loud and wants to belittle me.' You know individual life is different. If I have become a Minister, I don't cease to be a man. And the tension increases after becoming a Minister. There should be something to release it.

'What is that something?'

'Women and wine.'

'Sharmaji, you are great.'

'No Thakur. I am telling the truth. All big leaders release their tension this way. We are busy day and night in the service of the country. Such a hard labour, and so much tension. We may die if we don't have anything to ease our tension. It happens in the world the same way. Leaders have always their beloveds.

'You have asked it right. Very little was heard at that time.' Sharma did not say anything further. He was silent now.

'Did the earlier leaders had no tension at that time?' Thakur asked.

'They must also have had tension.'

'Then...'

'They did not have the responsibility of running the government. The real tension lies in the working of the government. Where was the tension then?,' Sharma pleaded vehementally.

'Tension might have existed then too. The freedom fighters suffered a lot during the freedom struggle. Movements, jail many a time, tear-shells, lathi charge, etc. followed by legal implications and hanging. Sharmaji, it is no tension as compared to those times. The real tension might have existed when the Freedom call used to confront death penalty.'

'Your logic is right, Mr. Thakur. But those were the days of war. One has a different kind of feeling in war. There is always a difference between peaceful and struggleful days. A warrior cannot think during war the way he thinks in the post-war times. Moreover, the level of tension varies very much,' Sharma argued.

'Mr. Sharma, you have experience of both the kinds. You have been in jail for long. And you are a Minister now. You had experienced that tension and now you are going through the present times.'

'Those were different days, Mr. Thakur. Let us stop this topic. Yes, you are very clever. Hurrah to your wisdom.'

'Where did I play clever?'

'You made me busy with the conversation.'

'Why?'

'Thakur, I had asked you about her. She was not there probably. And you dragged me into history.'

'So you want to be lost in women and wine.'

'Yes, why not? You know I dedicated my childhood and half of the youth to the freedom struggle. Only a part of youth, that too on the decline, is left. I want to enjoy this period to the full.'

'Sharmaji, where did you stay in jail and for what period? You might have been in prison for a long time. That is why you are getting freedom fighter's pension.' Thakur was being mischievous.

'Leave it Thakur. You are avoiding her. Don't you want to tell anything about her or you have kept her exclusively for yourself. I am your friend. If such is the case, say it frankly.' Sharma tried to evade the issue of his journey to jail.

'Sharmaji, don't worry. She has come. She will act as Saki today and will appear on the stage only when all of them have left. She is in a room that side.'

'Well done, Thakur. More fantastic the feast, more efforts shall I put in to recommend you as a Minister to the Chief Minister.'

'There will be no let up in the feast. Your favour is my luck.'

They were invited to attend the dinner. Thakur and Sharma both came out of the room and went to the site of dinner. There were *daris* spread on both sides of the veranda. The veranda was sufficiently lengthy. On one side, people with buckets full of lukewarm water stood to help the guests wash their hands before taking dinner. All the guests were called. Prominent persons from the town, senior government officers and party workers had been invited to dinner. All of them washed their hands and sat on the daris.

'Thakurji, this style of dinner is excellent. It's a new method all together.' Sharma said looking at the 'Pattal' (a plate made of green leaves).

'You are experiencing it for the first time?,' Thakur asked.

'I did come to Kullu area but I did not get a chance to eat this way.'

'And in your area...'

'They all use dining tables.'

'That is the style in Punjab. The style in the hills is quite different."

'The hilly areas of Punjab have their typical cultural identity."

'That's the reason that the demand for merging these areas into Greater Himachal has often been raised.'

'No, Thakur. Such a demand is dangerous. If these areas are separated from Punjab, the Hindu population in Punjab will decrease making it a Punjabi Suba automatically,' Sharma said in a worried voice.

'Sharmaji, we shall carve out states later on. Relish it, it is a special dish of Kangra. It is called 'Madhra,' Thakur said while mixing 'Madhra' in the hot rice.

'It's aroma is wonderful.'

'Our dishes not only have aroma charming but they taste delicious also.'

'Thakur, I shall say after tasting it.'

'Exactly.'

'How wonderful? It's matchless. I have not eaten such a dish even before. But tell me if it is a vegetable or a dal?'

'Neither vegetable nor dal.'

'Then what is it?'

'Madhra.'

'Madira?' (Whiskey?)

'That later on, Sharmaji, just now Madhra.' Both of them laughed.

'How is it prepared, Thakur?'

'First of all curd is fried. Then roasted potatoes are put into it. Cauliflower can also be used in place of potatoes. But everyone cannot cook it.'

'Yes, it is very delicious.'

Sharma asked for Madhra for the second time. Thakur called the man in *dhoti*, who was serving more. Rice was also given to Sharmaji.' Mr. Sharma enjoyed the food and was at it.

'It is only Madhra. Don't fill you tummy with it. There is Madira also after it.' Thakur whispered into Sharma's ears.

'And the person who will serve...' Sharma also spoke whisperingly.

'She is also there, don't worry,' Thakur said.

The dinner was over. They all were washing their hands. Thakur then introduced his main workers to the Minister. He introduced each and every one. The Minister shook hands with them. Some of the officers also introduced themselves to the Minister. All were eager to talk to the Minister. Some of the guests instructed the photographer also. They would shake hands with the Minister or stood closer to him. And the photographer would click the camera to capture their photographs.

By and by the guests left the place. Prakash Verma was also among those officers who was present just close to the Minister and Mr. Thakur. But Pramod was much behind. In fact, Prakash had asked him to remain behind. He feared that in case Thakur saw Pramod, he would start talking about Khushal's case.

'Pramod, you may go if you want. I shall come later.' Prakash said with an eye on his watch.

'I stayed on here just because of you Sir, otherwise.' Pramod said indifferently.

'What otherwise?'

'I had no business here. It was a private function. It is not binding for all govt. officers to be present here.'

'Pramod, a Minister is a Minister always. And the officers are required to be around him.'

'All right. That is why I am here with you,' Pramod was exhausted.

'You are the only officer who remained in the background. You neither talked to Mr. Thakur nor to Sharma. Pramod, there are occasions when you can extend your acquaintances. Introduction can help you in life at one or the other moment.'

'But you had asked me to remain behind.'

'Yes, I had advised you. You have made me recollect it. And if he calls me and asks about you, what shall I say? After Rita's assurance Thakur seems to have forgotten the issue. He cannot believe it that you did not release Khushal despite Rita's request. Pramod, you have put me in an odd position.' Prakash expressed his dissatisfaction.

'Sir, there is still a way out,' Pramod said.

'What is that?' Prakash was a bit relieved.

'Yes, but...'

'What but...'

'Yes.'

'What?'

'You will have to give me in writing. I shall execute it.'

'Pramod, how can this happen? Nothing can be given in writing in such a case. In fact, we shall have to destroy what you have written.'

'It cannot happen.'

'Can't you do it for me?'

'No, Sir.'

'Why?'

'My soul does not approve of it.'

Prakash was disappointed. Pramod stood apart.

'Pramod, have you to go to the town? Our jeep is going.' The local PWD officer Gupta asked him.

'Yes, I shall like to avail your offer, Guptaji,' Pramod said.

'And Prakash, Vermaji? You will be with the Minister...'

'Yes, I shall have to stay.'

'Good night, Sir,' Pramod said and boarded the jeep. The jeep started for the town.

'Guptaji, why did you stay for so long? I had to wait for Mr. Verma.

'Pramod, we do not know what we had to do. There is no answer to these questions.'

'What do you mean?'

'We have to make efforts to arrange such big community dinners, etc.'

'But the dinner was on behalf of Mr. Thakur. How are you concerned with it?,' Pramod smiled.

'How I am concerned? The party was arranged by us.'

'It was arranged by you!' Pramod was surprised.

'Yes, we had arranged it.'

'But the invitation card showed Mr. Thakur as the host. And it was at his residence. All his friends, relatives and party workers were invited to the dinner. And you say it was...'

'Pramod, do you see cinema?'

'How does cinema come into the party?'

'An actor does live movements but someone else sings it in the background. The singers do not come before the spectators and the actor does not sing.'

'Mr. Gupta, say it plainly. What is all this about?'

'Sir, how long you have been in the police department?,' an employee sitting in the back seats asked.

'Why?' Pramod tried to look behind.

'Because you do not know it all as yet.'

'Pramod, the party was on behalf of Mr. Thakur. All know that he has spent all the money on it. But in fact it is his name only, the entire amount has been spent by us.'

'That means Mr. Gupta has spent?'

'No. The PWD has spent the money.'

'Departmental!'

'Yes.'

'Under which head do you arrange this money?'

'From Four Hundred Twenty head.'. All of them laughed at this answer of Mr, Gupta. After crossing a hilly rivulet the jeep was now on the metalled road. It was late at night but there was hustle and bustle on the road. People were sitting in groups because of Dussehra festival. Some of them were singing, and some others were dancing.

'Mr. Gupta, are you making a fool of me?, Pramod asked.

'Pramod, whatever expenses have been incurred on this party, the entire money has had to be arranged from our department. Thakur has not spent a single penny. Very rare are such leaders, who spend on such parties from their own pockets. In most of the cases, they are the hosts on paper only, the amount is arranged by our department.'

Pramod was shocked to hear it. He tried to put his hand on his forehead but the jerks of the jeep made it slip.

'It is strange Mr. Gupta. It is beyond my imagination. It happens that way in free India?'

'Sir, what does not happen in India?'

'But Mr. Gupta. Wherefrom your department arranges such huge amounts?'

'By manipulations. We collect it from contractors. That meets the expenditure. The contractors get some relaxations in turn.

'And they mix sand in cement?', Pramod was enraged.

'And newly built bridges and buildings collapse killing innocent people.' The employee sitting in the rear seat said.

'How much has been spent on this party?' Pramod inquired of Mr. Gupta.

'One thousand.'

'And how much has been raised?'

Pramod was cautious now. The employee sitting in the rear seat said, 'That's like a policeman.'

'Pramod, you have got the point now.'

'Tell me, how much money you collected?'

'Three thousand.'

'What will you do with Two thousand?'

'We four shall share one thousand. And one thousand will remain in balance for expenses at other occasions.'

'What expenses?'

'When the Ministers comes on tour, we have to bear their bills of the rest houses, food, etc. Very few make payments from their pockets. It is difficult to collect money repeatedly? So we keep this one thousand as reserve money.'

'Thanks Mr. Gupta.' Pramod said while getting down the jeep.

'Thanks for what? Sir, the jeep is yours.'

'Not for the lift but for the knowledge about Head No. Four Hundred and Twenty.' They all laughed. The jeep went away. Pramod went to his residence.

□

9

The party was over. All the guests had left for their homes. Thakur took Sharma to the upper storey. Servants had also gone to their abodes now. The utensils were being arranged in the kitchen. Thakur's family had retired to their rooms.

'Mr. Sharma, do you recognise her?,' Thakur said signalling towards Rita.

'Namasteyji!' Rita said with folded hands.

'Yes, why not. She had met me along with you once.'

'You have rightly remembered.'

'Mr. Thakur, there are some events which cannot be forgotten in life. You have met me after a long gap, Ritaji.'

'You never came to Kullu,' Rita said.

'Yes, I did not come but you also did not make it to me.'

'That's true.' Rita appeared to be hesitant.

Thakur went to the outside room. One of his servants was still there for service. He asked him to bring something. Then Mr. Thakur went downstairs for a few minutes.

'You did not come with Mr. Thakur after your first visit.'

'No.'

'So you did not go out of Kullu for so many days?'

'No one invited me?'

'Kindly note my permanent invitation. I was very much impressed by you that day.'

'Impressed by me?'

'Rita, I had never met a woman like you.'

Rita felt flattered. She got up and then sat again. She looked into Sharma's eyes. She did not find anything special in Sharma's comment. She had met many a persons in life. She was accustomed to such dialogues.

Rita wanted to raise her importance by coming closer to Sharma in govt. She had come in contact with various persons. She was living a free life and was now interested in politics. She had cultivated her friendship with Thakur quite recently but now the friendship had grown into warm relationship. Thakur also promoted her ambition. It was he who had suggested that an educated, thoughtful woman of her stature should join politics. Since then, Rita had thought of trying her luck in politics. She thought the blessings of a Minister could help her in politics.

'I am surprised, where were you all these days?' Sharma said breaking the silence.

'Sir, I have not followed you.' Rita was again shy.

'An educated, beautiful woman like you must enter public life. You should come forward to serve the people. There are not many educated women in India.'

'But this area is reserved for men only?'

'No Rita. Our party believes in equal rights of women. Women had also contributed in the freedom struggle. We wish that women like you join our party and work actively.'

'Everything is ready, Mr. Sharma. May I bring the drinks.' Thakur asked on entering the room.

'Come Mr. Thakur. Be seated.' Rita got up from her chair. She sat in a chair lying close to Mr. Sharma. She vacated her chair and requested Mr. Thakur to sit.

'Yes, bring it please,' Sharma said.

'Which one should I bring, Sharmaji. I am fond of stocking all kinds of liquor. Whatever brand you desire, I shall bring it. There is a famous liquor of Lahaul-Spiti called Aara. One of my friends is there. He had 50-year old liquor in his house. He has presented it to me. If you wish, I can bring that.'

'You are asking the consumer. Why don't you ask her who will serve it.' Sharma said pointing towards Rita. Rita felt shy.

'Yes, Rita, You decide.'

'Whatever you bring, I shall serve it.'

'No, Rita whichever you decide, we shall enjoy the brand.'

'I do not know all the brands.'

'That we know.'

'What?'

'That you know all the brands.'

'How?'

'Thakur is my friend. He knows you. So I also know you.'

'You try to know each other. I bring whiskey of my own choice,' Thakur said and went out.

'Rita, why don't you join our party?,' Sharma asked her.

'You have ousted me from the chair close to you and now you ask me to join your party.' Rita said in a complaining voice.

'I did not notice it. You got up of your own. The chair is yet far off but I wish to keep you closer to me.'

'It will be kind of you.'

'No, no kindness. I was greatly impressed by you in the first meeting and had a keen desire to see you. I talked to Thakur twice or thrice but he did not show any enthusiasm. May be he does not want that I should also...' Sharma laughed. Rita joined the laughter.

'No, it may not be like that.'

'Rita, sometimes, it happens that way. Delayed it may be but you have met at last. Come sit in the chair here. I desire to see you from a close range.'

Rita now occupied the chair lying close to Mr. Sharma.

'Can I really find some work in your party?'

'It is not the question whether you can work in our party. You have to be in the party and work for it.'

'But I do not know the ABC of politics. What shall I do?'

'I shall train you in politics. Now it is my responsibility to promote you in politics. You will not remain an ordinary worker. We must utilize your wisdom and experience to the advantage of the party.'

'I shall be obliged to you. You know my family life is not happy. I remain upset. May be my involvement in public life releases my tension.'

'What obligation?' Do you consider me a stranger? Rita, my family life is also not very good. My wife is old fashioned and is not sufficiently educated. By God's grace, I occupy a coveted place. With my elevation my responsibilities have also increased. I am always tense. But there is no one whom I can talk heart to heart. There is no way out to release the tension. I propose let us be friends.'

'Really. Am I so lucky to be your close friend?'

'Why not? Rather I shall be lucky to have you as a friend. You do not know how competent you are? No one has recognised your talent so far.'

'But I shall be dependent upon you in politics. I do not know anything. I shall require your guidance.'

'Rita, just wait. I shall help you achieve heights. No one has recognised the pearl of hills.'

'You can start now, Mr. Sharma.' Thakur entered the room with a servant. Rita once again got up from her seat. Thakur asked her to sit but she sat in another chair. The servant was with a tray in his hands. These were some plates and glasses along with two bottles of whiskey.

'Keep it here.' Thakur asked the servant. The servant kept it on the tripod.

On Thakur's signal, the servant went out. Thakur arranged the glasses.

He opened one of the bottles.

'Do the Thakurs play Saki in Kullu?,' Sharma laughed.

'No no, Sir. I do it.' Rita got up and laid the glasses.

'Yes, Rita. What about Khushal's case? I forgot to ask you. You also did not tell.

'No progress, sir.'

'No progress.' Thakur got up from the chair.

'I requested Pramod repeatedly but he did not agree.'

'Did he refuse you plainly?'

'No. On my persistence, he said he would find a way out. Later on I enquired about it but came to know that he did not do anything. I sent someone but he refused. Khushal is still in the lock up.'

'The bastard is so daring?'

'Thakur, how does this topic crop up at this moment?,'' Sharma said after having a sip from the glass.

'No, Mr. Sharma, I cannot tolerate it. If such an officer continues, me and my party will be gone.'

'Please leave this topic at this moment. Tell me in the morning, I shall set him right. We shall take morning tea only after your man is set free.' Sharma consolded Thakur.

'No, it will not be sufficient.'

'Tell what do you want. I shall do that also.'

'The officer.'

'If you wish, I shall hang him. Thakur, nothing will stir in Kullu without Thakur's or Rita's wish. Is that right Rita. Why don't you speak Ri...ta?'

'Yes, it is all right now. I shall teach him a lesson in the morning. Now, Rita, give me my peg. Let it overflow now.' Thakur extended his hand for the glass.

The lights had gone off in all other rooms. There was peace in the kitchen too. A small child was weeping in one of the rooms a few minutes ago. Now he was also asleep. The murmur of a rivulet near the house was audible now.

Sharma did not believe in restricting himself to a limit while drinking. He not only took liquor, he enjoyed it also. Both of them drank excessively. Thakur asked Rita also to drink but she declined. Thakur knew that she occasionally took liquor but Rita did not went to be that free with Sharma in her first meeting. Sharma was now drunk and talking irrelevantly. Thakur was used to excessive drinking but he never lost the control over himself. Sharma was now trying to hold Rita's hand. He would keep his hand on her shoulder. Rita tried to escape him at times and at other times she herself made proximity to him.

It was late night now. They went on drinking endlessly. Rita felt tired after serving them for so long. If she had no ambitious to join politics and if she did not need Sharma's help, she would have left the party much earlier. She used to consume liquor also in the company of her friends. But she was not accustomed to hear long conversation of drunkards. She was feeling bored but she did not express her feelings and kept on serving them and she tolerated all of their actions.

'Sharma, you please sleep here today.' Thakur was fumbling in saying it.

'No, not at all Mr. Thakur, I shall go to the rest house. It's always better to be at one's place. Is that right? Rita let us go and let Thakur take rest.' Sharma said in a broken voice.

'And Rita you?,' Thakur asked.

'Why do you worry? I shall make arrangements to send her home.' Thakur looked at Sharma with doubts in his mind. His eyes were already red under the influence of liquor. There was more redness now. Rita had a mixed feeling of romance, astonishment and joy to hear Sharma's comments.

"All right." Intoxicated, Thakur retorted.

'I enjoyed your party. Rita's company was wonderful. I shall straightaway talk to the Chief Minister to induct you as a Minister. Thakur will be a Minister, Rita.' He walked tottering and kept his hand on Rita's shoulder.

'Thakur, you will remember. Rita will also join our party. We have to arrange a ticket for her from somewhere. She is so nice. She will be a leader in our party.'

Rita was now fresh to hear such comments. Sleep and exhaustion bade her adieu. She was very happy to hear about a ticket for her. Her ambition was now taking shape. She felt Sharma will shower that comfort on her which no one had given to her. Her face was aglow with expectation. She had not consumed alcohol but she had been serving it. Her cheeks were more red as compared to those who were drunk. She felt awkward when Sharma said he would send her to her home. Not because of the fact that Sharma wanted a pretext to take her along but because he had said it in the face of Thakur.

Rita knew it well that the Minister was not all alone. It is so late in night. His personal staff would be with him. The Minister was fully intoxicated. No body knows what he may say or how he may behave. She was preparing herself to avoid the Minister on one pretext or the other but the probability of a ticket to her haunted her at the moment. She was ready to dance tunes to Sharma. She was afraid of Thakur's reaction. She noticed that Thakur was now feeling jealous. Whatever the stature of Rita and Sharma, Thakur was the king of Kullu. Rita can't Carve a niche in Kullu politics without Thakur's blessings.

The cars were waiting outside Thakur's residence. The Minister's personal staff was alert. Prakash Verma stood before the Minister along with a few constables.

'Thakur, Sir. May I go with him.' She asked in a hesitant voice. Thakur's ego was satisfied. At least she had sought his permission.

'Yes, yes. If the Minister wants it, you...'

'But I shall straightaway go home now. You direct your driver to leave me at my residence.'

'You are not going with the driver? You are going with the Minister.' Thakur smiled. But Rita did not like this comment.

'All right.'

'Who is waiting for you at home?,' Thakur was sarcartic.

'Come on Rita. Thakur is Kullu's leader. He lives here. Let us take you to your home.'

'Namastey.'

'Namasteyji.'

'Good night, Sir.'

The cars and jeeps raised dust and the party ended. Thakur kept watching the car in which Rita went with the Minister. The Minister asked Rita to sit in the back seat. He placed his hand at Rita's shoulder and it went down to her waist while they were taking their seats. He asked his personal staff to use the other vehicle. With faltering steps, he entered the car.

'Sir, whither?' The driver asked the Minister when the car was on metalled road after covering the Kaccha road.

'My residence is on that side.' Rita pointed her finger.

'Why trouble the family members at this time?' The Minister once again kept his hand on her shoulder. He dragged Rita closer to himself. Rita felt the stink of liquor.

'Is it O.K. Rita, darling?' Sharma said. Rita was in a fix. If the ticket chat had not made her so eager, she would never have come all alone with the Minister. And even if she had to come, she would have requested him to leave her at her place first. Rita was a liberated woman but she kept a posture in Kullu. She used to go out of Kullu to her friends for open interaction.

'Sir, tell me, where have we to go?' The driver slowed down the car at the crossing.

'Straight to the rest house.' The driver and the car felt a jerk. The driver turned to the right. Rita saw towards Sharmaji. Sharma dragged Rita in a manly manner.

The Dussehra festivity was still on when the car reached the Dhalpur Maidan. It was 1 a.m. at night. People had slept in their homes but Dhalpur Maidan was still awake. Some of the shops in the fair were still open. There was music going on and some were playing on the instruments. The policemen were patrolling the area.

There were dogs busy scanning the dustbins near hotels. Barking of dogs from other places was also audible. There was fight among the dogs for crumbs of food. Their barking added to the noise of the fair.

It was very cold at night. At places, people sat on the ground around bonfire. Others were busy in gossips. A few were busy singing. All those who were awake at night had a glimmer of divinity whether consuming liquor or dancing before their deities, they were all very contented.

At places ladies also joined men. They accompanied men in dancing and singing. Such a huge mela. So many people drinking and dancing in the open but there were no clashes and quarrels. The police was simply performing its duty.

The lights were still on in the rest house. The employees sat waiting for the Minister in the veranda. As soon as the car stopped, a few of them got up. They were shocked to find Rita with the Minister. The attendant who had to open the door of the car retreated.

Sharma went straight into the room with Rita. Rest of the vehicles also arrived. The members of the personal staff got down. Prakash Verma was with a few policemen. They kept talking in the veranda for some time. They were whispering in small groups. Then they all retired to their places.

□

10

Pramod came direct to his residence after the dinner at Thakur's place. He went to sleep after changing but sleep was nowhere in sight. He was surprised at the revelation that the mega party had been arranged by the PWD department on behalf of Mr. Thakur. This fact disturbed him. The officers of the department collect money from contractors who in turn do bunglings in contracts. Pramod tossed in his bed. He was lost in the manner of arrangement of party and Mr. Gupta's comments.

He had learnt during police training that the job of the police was to nab the culprit. He was upset to think that in case the officers collect money by unfair means, how will the police be successful in catching the culprits. I and all other police officers have also took the dinner in the same party. May be the contractors were also present in the party who had spent on it. No body can spend so much from one's pocket. They will adopt unfair means to recover it. The party and the festivity is just symbolic of corruption. And we all, the govt. is a party to it. Under such circumstances who will apprehend the culprit? All that training in the police training college was wastage of time. That stands nowhere in real life. I have come to a wrong job. I wish I were a teacher in a school or a college.

It was mid night but sleep still eluded him. Sleep once delayed was endlessly delayed. He tried to sleep but could not. He closed his eyes to invite sleep but thoughts made him awake. Rita, Khushal and Prakash Verma all danced before his eyes.

Lost in the cloud of these thoughts, his mind struck on one figure. All his restlessness was gone now. He felt relieved. He stopped tossing in the bed. Now his thoughts were floating over a colourful valley.

He was now engrossed in the imagination of the girl who had come to thank him near Raghu Nath's temple. He remembered her face vividly. Her arrival, her folded hands to convey her thanks innocently rolled before his eyes like a scene in a film. He was reliving the entire scene.

'How foolish I am? I did not even ask her name. What she might have thought of me! Decency required that I should have talked to her for a few minutes. Seeing me from a distance a village girl came to me to say thank you but as police officer I did not behave properly to accept her thanks. God knows what she thought of me... But how could I ask? Verma was sermonising to me. In his presence... no, he had gone then... even then I did not talk to her. But why I am so enamoured of her now? Neither I know her name, nor her village but I am spoiling my sleep for her. Why?'

Pramod turned sides in his bed. He had felt relieved at the thought of that girl but now it turned into restlessness. There was moisture in his eyes now. His intellect pointed out, neither you know her name nor the name of her village. Moreover, what is she to you? Who knows to whom she is related? Whether married or unmarried...? We come across so many people at various places...' But his heart did not surrender before his intellect. He was sorry that he had not even enquired about her name.

'Cannot she be traced now? After all I am a police officer. If I make efforts, I can meet her once.' He was happy to have thought like that. But no one saw her in the dark. His eyes were wet no more.

It was the fag end of the night. Pramod got up to hear a knock at the door. He noted time. It was seven in the morning. He does not know when did he sleep at night. He wanted to rise late in the morning but had to get up early. He looked around with lazy eyes. He kept the quilt aside and noticed the wrinkled bed sheet. He set his dress in order and opened the door.

'Good morning, Sir.'

'Yes, you, so early. Good morning.'

'Sir, Sir has asked you to reach the office at 8.00 a.m.'

'At eight?' He looked at his watch.

'Yes, Sir. He will also reach office at 8.00 a.m.'

'All right.'

'Thank you, Sir.' And he went away.

'To be at eight in the office? God knows what's the problem. Prakash Verma has nothing else to do. He might have been in the attendance of the Minister late last night. He is a good officer but he likes to be around the Minister like a peon. Yes, it may be Khushal's case.' Pramod stopped while roaming in the room as if he was stuck in a place. He walked slowly and sat on his bed. He was in a serious thinking mood.

'Rita might have talked to Thakur and in turn Thakur must have discussed it with the Minister. Now Prakash Verma will discuss it with me. Why should I oppose when all of them want it to be done as per their dictates. Is it my duty alone to run the police department smoothly? The Minister, the MLA and the police officer Prakash Verma want him to be released. So why should I obstruct? I made Rita unhappy. She had sent so beautiful a girl, I did not accede to her request also. I shall be an irritant in Thakur's eyes. The Minister may harm me.' Having all these ideas going in his mind, Pramod got up from his bed and stood close to the window.

The lofty mountains were visible from there. There was a small plain peace of land also where small houses had come up. And an apple orchard looked charming. The lined apple trees looked like school children in the morning assembly.

There was a beautiful house in the orchard.

'I wish I had a similar orchard with a small house in it. I would have enjoyed the tranquility of the atmosphere and would have written poems. That could have saved me from the intricacies of job I am holding now. It would have relieved me of mental tension. Prakash Verma and Khushal on one side and the girl who came to thank me... all are torturing me.'

Pramod left the window and was again loitering in the room. It was 7.30 a.m. He was now busy in getting ready for the office.

□

11

'Is Mr. Verma in the office?'

'Yes, Sir. He has been waiting for you for long.'

'I coming just within five minutes. Please inform him.' Pramod said to an employee standing outside the office and moved to his office.

'Now tell me Pramod, what do you say? He might have called me for the same issue. The problem is Khushal. Pramod, you are the stay of an ordinary family. The old father and young sisters...and you are away from home. Weigh all these things. The entire govt. is on one side. They all want Khushal to be released. I am the only obstruction. Moreover, how does it matter if a Khushal is let off? Will this act damage the entire administration? I am wrongly stuck in this case. Should I agree to what all of them say. Should I cultivate friendship with Rita? Should I call that girl? May I tell her that I have released Khushal because you wanted it. The Minister and Thakur both of them will be happy at this act. Rita and that girl will also feel elated. And Mr. Verma too.' He thought. He got up from his chair and stood by the window. We could see the lofty peaks of the mountain. A small Deodar stood on one side all by itself. It had a few branches only. It gave the resemblance of a young lady from a distance. His imagination again took him to Raghu Nath's tent where she had met him.

I should avoid all this hassle and must concentrate on locating that girl. Nevertheless, she hails from Kullu. I must find her. The spot where she had got down from the jeep can be traced. May be there is a village nearby. May be my driver can identify that place. But how shall I ask the driver? What would be his reaction? And even if we identify that village, how shall we find her? How shall we enquire about her? Her name is not known. Even the name of the village is not known. Pramod, what information do you have of her? You are getting mad unnecessarily. Stop this nonsense. Where will you search her in this vast world?

'Sir, Mr. Verma is waiting for you. He has called you?' An employee informed Pramod.

'Oh, yes. I am coming.' Pramod was alarmed.

'Pramod, decide yourself. Confrontation with the government or surrender. Am I a robber, a culprit that I should surrender. And before these useless persons? Before them who arrange parties with money collected from the contractors by unfair means. No, I cannot do like that. The educated youngmen cannot do it in free India.'

'Good morning, Sir.'

'Pramod, you have taken a lot of time.'

'Sir, pardon me.'

'I had sent a message to you much earlier. You should have immediately responded.'

'Sorry, Sir. Excuse me please.'

'Listen, Khushal's matter has taken alarming proportions. I knew it all. I made you read the situation but you did not. Now the situation is worse. But I can try to help you if you...' Mr. Verma stopped at this juncture.

'But what, Sir?'

'If you agree to my advice...' Verma picked up a file. He put off the cover and started examining the papers inside. Pramod was silent lost in his thoughts. Verma was looking at the papers but he tried to read Pramod's face also.

'Give a thought to it, Pramod. I am helpless. I don't know why I have affection and sympathy for you. You are a faithful, dutiful young officer. You have just started your career. You have to go a long way. Your capability and your virtues can take you to heights. But you are emotional and not practical. Life is not run by emotions alone. You must understand the realities as well.'

'But Sir, I cannot understand what have I done. I have just caught a mischievous scoundrel only. Will the police not take such action even in Independent India?'

'Pramod, there is no time for logic now. I have to reported the case to the Minister.'

'Sir, what does the Minister want?'

'Pramod, please agree even at this juncture.'

'Please tell me'.

'Please destroy all the papers related to Khushal's case. Change the entries in the Register. Tender an apology before the Minister and Mr. Thakur.'

'What more?'

'You will have to apologise to Rita also. She is also very angry with you.'

'And from that girl also?'

'Which girl?'

'Who had been sent to me by Rita with the message.'

'No, Pramod. You need not talk to her. She is only a messenger of Rita.'

'But, Sir. She must also have been annoyed. She had come dressed up beautifully and I did not concede to her request.'

'Anyhow, forget about her.'

Pramod looked towards the woods through the window.

'Pramod, the world goes on its own way. Everthing does not go the way we want. And we are not bound to set every thing right.'

Pramod maintained his silence.

'Administration today is run by politics. There is certain impact of politicians on it. We must act according to their wishes. They have their henchmen, in villages as well as in administration. Leaders need votes in elections. These people help them in getting votes. The leaders are ineffective without votes. In turn, they want open patronage. You will be told about them all. You just avoid them...'

'Sir, in case Khushal is released, the papers are torn, the Register is changed, the promise I made to the restless crowd in front of the police station will be falsified. Khushal will be free after committing such a big crime.'

'You are being emotional again, Pramod.'

'Sir, I can't imagine a man without emotions.'

'A human being is guided by reality.'

'Sir, reality is also a feeling.'

'Your thinking is totally irrelevant.'

'Khushal will be released. He will come out triumphant and what about me. I shall have to beg pardon from the Minister, Mr. Thakur and Rita? No, Sir I cannot stoop so down. I am thankful to you for your affection and sympathy but no Sir. I can't stoop down.'

Pramod got up. He was furious. He stood near the chair for a few minutes and then slowly walked out.

'Pramod, just stop. Come here.' Verma was now harsh in voice. 'Here it is for you.'

'What is it, Sir?'

'The result of your foolishness, which I tried to avoid.'

'What is it, Sir? My eyes are burning. Kindly tell it yourself.'

'You have been suspended. And you stand transferred to Keylong in Lahaul-Spiti. You have to hand over your charge today itself and to move to Keylong. Receive this order, sign it here and go away from my sight.'

'Sir, is there no place beyond Lahaul-Spiti?'

'What do you mean?'

'You may transfer me to any far-off place.'

Mr. Verma looked askance.

'But Sir, it cannot happen because it is Tibet beyond Lahaul-Spiti. And you cannot transfer me to Tibet. Anyhow...'

Pramod laughed sarcastically. He continued laughing for a few seconds. Verma could not make out if the laughter meant Pramod's madness or anxiety or sarcasm.

Pramod signed the paper. Put a paper in his pocket without reading it and kept one copy on Verma's table.

'Pramod, this is arrogance...' Verma got up in anger.

'It is not more than what has been done to me.' Pramod said and went out.

□

12

Prakash Verma heaved a sigh of relief when Pramod left his office. He felt his tension released. He placed his feet on a small stool and tried to relax in his chair in a sleeping posture. He closed his eyes and was busy thinking. He kept lying for some time. Then he straightened a bit. He felt backache. He took out a cigarette from his pocket and watched it for a few seconds. Then tapped the cigarette on one end. He lit the cigarette and was having deep puffs. He appeared to be mechanical in action. His mind was wandering somewhere else.

Verma suddenly rang the bell.

'Yes, Sir.' An attendant immediately responded.

'Call Prem.'

'Yes, Sir.'

The room was filled with smoke. He was smoking like a chimney.

'Yes, Sir.' Prem stood before him.

'Prem, you know all the happenings.'

'Yes, Sir.'

'As it was discussed with you yesterday, it has been decided the same way after clearance from the Minister. You take the charge immediately. Let the issue be settled promptly. Destroy all the papers. Release Khushal. Tell him to behave himself.'

'Sir, he must be offended and disturbed after having spent some time in the prison.'

'I had asked him to apply for bail. Neither he agreed nor Mr. Thakur. We could not let him go without destroying the papers. Please advise him to be peaceful. And tell him that Pramod has been suspended for the same.'

'Sir, you need not worry. I have made all the preparations. You need not worry as long as I am here.'

'Prem, I know that. Pramod unnecessarily put me into trouble. I have been tense for the last four days... He not only created problems for himself but put me also in a precarious situation.' Verma put his hand on his head as if to cool the heat in it.

'Sir, it is police deparment. If we do not act as per orders of the seniors, how can the discipline be maintained. Pramod was obstinate in action.'

'Yes, this was the only drawback in him. Otherwise he is a nice, honest and efficient police officer. If one defect is ignored, he is an excellent officer.'

'Sir, may I go?'

'Yes. The Minister and Mr. Thakur have to attend a public meeting today. All this should be done before that.'

'Yes, Sir. I shall make Khushal meet Mr. Thakur before that public meeting.'

'Right. Excellent.'

'Sir, you need not worry once you have entrusted the job to me.'

'That is nice. Take care that you destroy the papers wisely. No evidence of his arrest or of FIR should be left.'

'O.K. Sir.'

Prem went away.

Verma was busy with the files. He signed a few papers. He read the yesterday's newspaper. He smoked at short intervals. Time went on.

'Sir, everything is done.'

'Very good.'

'Khushal must have gone to see Mr. Thakur by this time after his release. I have sent one of my confidants with him. I have arranged a jeep also. I myself met him in the lock up. He is very happy to learn about Pramod's suspension and transfer. He was happy to know that Pramod had been penalised for his action. He will not say anything to Mr. Thakur now.'

'O.K. It is all settled. I was afraid that he might be angry even after all this action. He may not backbite with Mr. Thakur. It is good that you met Khushal in the jail. Prem, I am rid of a nonsense.'

'O.K. Sir.'

Prem came out of the room.

A jeep halted outside. Some employees got down. One of them came inside.

'Sir, everything is all right but.'

'But?'

'The news of Khushal's release has spread in the town. Someone came to the police station to enquire about the news. A few youngmen are broadcasting the news in shops. It is talk of the town. A few youngmen belonging to a party are planning to disturb the public meeting,' one of the employees expressed his concern.

'So, the matter is not yet over.' Verma said.

'It is almost over. You need not worry.' Prem announced while entering the room.

'Sir, the city president of Congress has come.' An employee informed Mr. Verma, who immediately got up in his seat.

'Welcome Panditji, please have a seat.' A middle-aged man in warm coat and Kullu cap occupied his seat.

'Look Mr. Verma, Mr. Thakur has sent me to you. It is good that you have freed Khushal. Pramod has been transferred. But. Thakur has learnt from his sources that there is some stir in the town on this issue. I have had a round of the town just now. A few boys belonging to Jan Sangh are holding a meeting in a shop. They are planning to disturb today's public meeting. Mr. Thakur wants that since it is Sharma's first public meeting in Kullu, there should not be any disturbance.'

'Panditji, you tell Mr. Thakur that no one can create nuisance in the meeting.' Prem bursted before Verma could speak.

'Prem, what arrangements have you made?'

'Everything is in order.'

'Just tell me.'

'Sir, I have sent one Inspector. He will make fake challan's of a few shopkeepers. The shopkeepers will be told that if the public meeting passed off peacefully, their challans would be cancelled. I have called some hardliner Jan Sanghis to the police station. I have opened up some old cases. And I have arranged false complaints against a few. I shall make all of them sit in the police station till the public meeting is over. You do not worry a bit. Everything will go smoothly.'

'Well done, Mr. Verma. We want officers like you so that the government functions properly. ' Panditji laughed heartily. All others also smiled.

'Very good, Prem. I am pleased with you.' Verma felt relieved.

There was anger in the town against Khushal's release. A meeting was held. All but the hardliner Congressmen attended it. Some of the Congressmen belonging to Thakur's opposite camp also attended the meeting. It was decided that one of their representatives will stand up in the gathering and ask a question from the Minister. If the Minister does not answer rightly, they will boycott the meeting.

The enthusiastic youngmen were called in the police station one by one. Some of them were challaned. The policemen were patrolling the bazar. They called a few persons and advised them to behave themselves. A few were frightened. The younmen sitting in the police station continued their noise. They raised slogans also. The noise of slogans echoed in the Thana.

A large public meeting passed off peacefully.

After the meeting, Thakur escorted Mr. Sharma to his car. And Khushal walked by the side of Thakur. Thakur introduced Khushal to the Minister. The Minister smiled.

The crowd saw the Minister and Mr. Thakur walking together but their actual focus was on Khushal. People talked about Khushal and some of them showed Khushal to their friends. The small groups of people did not discuss the speeches delivered in the public meeting. All of them discussed the release of Khushal and suspension and transfer of Pramod.

The Minister had to leave straight after the conference. He stood with folded hands before entering his car. The leaders and officers also folded their hands to bid him adieu. Mr. Verma opened the door of the car. The Minister occupied his seat. The car left the place.

The Minister shook his hand from inside and bade them good bye.

All the people present also waived their hands.

A departmental jeep arrived.

'Thakur Sahib, please come here. I drop you at your residence.' An officer said.

'Yes, you also come.'

Thakur boarded the jeep.

The officer wanted to sit with Mr. Thakur but he called Khushal also. So Khushal sat beside Thakur in the front seat. The officer sat in the rear seat.

The crowd saw Khushal sitting happily with Thakur.

□

13

After receiving his suspension and transfer orders, Pramod went straight to his home. He stopped when he aproached his house. He turned back and went to his office with a heavy heart. His anxiety was reflected on his face. There was anger also in his mind.

'Come in please.' An employee opened the door for him.

'Call him.' Pramod said it so angrily that the peon at once went out even without asking who had to be called.

'Yes, Sir.'

'Whosoever has to take charge from me, should take it immediately...' Pramod was in rage.'

'Charge? What do you mean, Sir?'

'Yes, charge.'

'But Sir, we...'

'Don't you know anything?'

'No, Sir.'

'Here it is. I have been suspended and transferred too. These are the orders.'

'It is sheer injustice, Sir. They wanted to release Khushal. So they have done it. Agreed that he is a favourite of Thakur but why punish you?' Shankar reacted. Pramod felt relieved. There was someone at least who sympathised with him.

'Police exists to deliver justice to all?' Pramod said.

'But sir, is it the way of delivering justice?'

'Shankar, I have no regrets. I am happy that I performed my duty honestly. I did not bow down.'

'What do you mean, Sir?'

'I was being pressurised to free Khushal. And that I should destroy all the papers related to the arrest of Khushal. That I should change the Register as well. But I did not do that.'

'Who pressurised you?'

'From the Minister down to Rita.'

'So she had come that day for this purpose?'

'Not she, but that girl also.'

'And Mr. Thakur?'

'He was the actual force behind.'

'What a change in times. Police is meant to nab the culprits. And now the police officer who arrests the culprit is suspended.

'And at the same time he is transferred to a far-off place also.'

'Where Sir?'

'To Keylong in Lahaul-Spiti.' Pramod laughed.

'How can it happen?'

'Why?'

'Sir, if you have been suspended, you cannot be transferred. You are required to be at your station till the enquiry is completed and decision announced.'

'Is it the rule?'

'As far as my knowledge goes, this is the practice.'

'Shankar, is it all happening as per rules? When they do not follow rules in suspending me, it is useless to expect rules in transfer. I accept the punishment that has been awarded to me for my dutifulness. I am proud of my action.'

'You are very daring.'

'Shankar, please find out if Prem is there on the other side of office. I understand he might have been instructed to take charge from me. Kindly tell him to take charge from me.'

Prem entered the room a short while later.

'Hellow Pramod, I am sorry.'

'It's O.K.'

'You have not been treated well.'

'Why? Crime must be punished...' Pramod was a little sarcastic.

'No, no, you have not committed any crime.'

'I have. I have broken the traditional rules prevalent here. I have thrown a challenge. I have not acceded to the request of seniors. Such a huge crime was liable to be punished.'

Hearing their conversation, a few more employees gathered on the spot. Pramod stood up and shook hands with two of them and said, 'Meet Mr. Pramod, who has been suspended and transferred.' Pramod took his chair.

'Is it true or a joke?'

'True, it is and a joke also.'

'I do not understand.' Vinod said.

'Here is the truth.' Pramod showed the orders.

'And joke?'

'The police officer has been punished because he arrested a culprit in police uniform. That is Khushal. The accused has been let off from the lock up. All the papers related to his arrest have been destroyed and the Register changed. His meeting was arranged with the Minister. He was taken in a jeep by the local MLA. And I was suspended. As if the punishment was less, I have been transferred to Keylong. The government has made a mockery of its own rules.' Pramod tried to laugh.

'Prem, is it not injustice?'

'Yes, injustice it is.' Prem said disinterestedly.

'It has happened to Pramod today, the same treatment may be meted out to us tomorrow.'

'Why not, Sir? If it can happen in your case, the similar treatment can be meted out to us, the petty employees.'

'It has happened because of the junior employees,' Vinod said with his eyes on Prem.

'But he is not a small fry.'

'He is very big. All are dwarfs before him.'

'But there were Mr. Thakur and Rita also in between.'

'What is special about Rita?'

'She is very powerful.'

'What does it mean?'

'She is matchless.'

'She is very clever. She shines like a star. She gets it done whatever she wants. She was present in the Minister's dinner also.'

'No, not at all. She was not present there.' Pramod was surprised.

'Pramod, you did not see her with police eyes.'

'What do you mean?'

'She was very much present there. She had come first of all. Mr. Thakur had made arrangement for her in the upper room. When all the guests had left, the actual party of the Minister and Mr. Thakur started. Rita acted as the Saki. And then she went with the Minister in his car to the rest house also.' Vinod told all the details promptly.

'Then?' Pramod asked.

'Then the same... The Ministers deliver sermons on morality. Sharma spoke on religion yesterday at length. He gave a lecture on character building to the school children. And we saw him exposed at night.' Vinod was fuming with rage.

'And Pramod is punished.'

'But I had learnt that Pramod was also friendly with Rita.' Prem said in a low tone.

'No friendship, Prem. I came to know her when I was travelling in a bus from Dharamshala to Mandi.' After that she met me twice in Kullu.' Pramod wanted to explain the actual position.

'They say you and Rita lived together at Mandi.' Prem said to persuade Pramod to reveal more.

'No, it is not true. I stayed all alone as per police arrangements. Who the fool has told you?' Pramod spoke in anger.

'All keep a track of Rita's movements.'

'False diary?'

'Sometimes it may be wrong. But Pramod, no one can doubt you.'

'And if there was any doubt, it will be removed now.'

'How?'

'Because of your suspension and transfer.'

'That means?'

'That you did not accede even Rita's request. If you were friends with her, you could not refuse her. She could not get such a small favour even from you.'

'It was just a normal thing.'

'Pramod, nothing is bigger or smaller in love. People do strange things when they are asked for by their beloveds.'

'Please leave Rita's story. Now you all enjoy these things. I look to Keylong now.'

'We are sorry, Pramod.'

'Thank you for your sympathy.' He thought for a moment and asked, 'Who has to relieve me? I want to leave this office immediately.'

'May be Prem has to take the charge from you.'

'He is their blue-eyed boy.' Prem was upset at Vinod's comment but he did not say anything. There was a momentary reaction on his face but it soon faded away.

'Does not matter if I am their blue-eyed boy. Everyone is a tool in someone's hands.' Prem tried to shun his hesitation.

'But sir. It is injustice. It is also injustice to tolerate it silently.' Shankar said.

'If I were in Pramod's place, I would have kicked the job. It is tyranny.'

"I wish I had an apple orchard as big as you have and I had not the responsibility of my old father and three young sisters.'

'Pramod, we all have family responsibilities. But there is a limit to every thing. Culprit is someone else and someone else has been punished. Look here. Earlier Thakur and Rita's relationship was confined to their personal life only. No one was concerned with it. Especially, we the government employees were least affected. But now Rita directly interferes with the administration. Thakur is her henchman. It appears it is Rita who runs the government here. Now either you play tunes to what Rita says whether right or wrong or become their Yes men and if you cannot do it, be prepared for a transfer to Keylong like Pramod.' Vinod said in a serious tone.

'Sir, what kind of era is this? Was the great freedom struggle launched for all these things. Such an injustice could not be done during British rule. Sir, I am a very small employee. But remember it sir, what has been done to Pramod will repeat itself in your cases also. And our department is to catch the culprits and not to hide their crimes or to cover them up. It is also not wise to accept the punishment like dumb animals. Khushal has become all the more arrogant since he has been released. He does not salute even his senior officers. He misbehaves with his equals. He does not attend the office. He wanders along with Thakur and his party workers. Sir, once Pramod is gone, he will make our existence tough.' There was anxiety visible on Shankar's face.

'Shankar is right. We all must raise our united voice against this injustice. Prem, what is your opinion?' Vinod looked at Prem with inquisitive eyes. Prem was shaking his foot. His eyes were downcast.

'Pramod, you are not alone. We are all with you. Don't hand over the charge. We talk to the higher officers. Our officers and leaders should come to know that we are not dumb-driven animals but human beings who can think and act.' Vinod said thumping the table with his hand.

'Give a serious thought to it. It is the police department and not an ordinary section of the government. Unions, strikes, struggle such things are not tolerated here.' Prem expressed his opinion.

'Gone are those days Prem, when it was a police department. It has become a place of political interference. After all we are also human beings. We shall not violate discipline. We shall not go on strike but we can meet the higher officers to apprise them of our feelings. What's the problem if we tell them our feelings. We can at least ask them why Pramod has been punished and what for Khushal has been rewarded?' Vinod's anger was visible now.

'Dear friends, you will not do any such thing. I am a disciplined police officer. I learn that Lahaul-Spiti is a wonder land of its own kind. I shall not do anything now. You will also not talk to anyone for me. I am obliged to you for your sympathy for me. We are bound to obey the orders of the seniors but we don't have the responsibility to change or rectify the administration. We should act within our limits. Prem, you take the charge without hesitation. I want to be rid of all things.' Pramod said all this. He was silent now. He was playing with the papers on the talk. All others were also silent.

'I have thought on this aspect. When Khushal has been freed and all papers related to his case have been destroyed, it is no good for me to continue here. It is not only good for the administration but to my advantage also to transfer me to another place.'

'But what was the necessity to suspend you?'

'And Khushal has been let off. They could send him to another place.'

'No that could not happen because it was now concerned with the ego of Thanker and Rita.'

'What ego?'

'The person who apprehended their man could not escape punishment. It is punishment to Pramod and warning to all of us.' Vinod thumped the table again.

'You may say anything Vinod. But I am not prepared for any resistance in the matter. I want to tolerate it silently.

They have committed a mistake. We should not sow seeds of dissension and indiscipline in the services. It will be a blunder.' Pramod said calmly.

'Pramod's analysis is right.' Prem said enthusiastically.

'I know you will like this attitude.' Vinod said angrily.

'Prem, you take the charge.'

Vinod called for tea. They all took tea. They bade farewell to Pramod. Pramod and Prem signed a few papers. Pramod shook hands with all of them and left.

□

14

Pramod came to his residence and changed his clothes. He had demonstrated control and balance in behaviour while he was in office but now he felt very aggressive. His hands were putting off his clothes as if mechanically but his mind was wandering elsewhere. His eyes were red. And he was murmuring at intervals. He looked absent minded. However, he put on his pyjama kurta and sat on his bed.

He was thinking and thinking. He felt as if every article in the room was revolving and were lying in disorder.

Pramod felt hurt by the events. His ideals had been shattered. Inferiority complex had rendered him frustrated. Pramod was boiling with the thought that the government had worked in favour of Khushal, the drunkard who created scenes in comparison to Pramod who was a disciplined soldier. Pramod had the consolation of his colleagues only who had expressed sympathy for Pramod. He was sore over the behaviour met out to him.

Now he had to go to a far-off place. To a more desolate and lonely place. He was not going of his own but he was being sent there. He had been insulted and was being pushed to that corner.

He never wanted to join police services. Instead he wanted to be a professor in a college. But when the compulsions of life brought him to the police department, he had happily accepted it. He underwent the police training enthusiastically. He had many ideals before him. As a dutiful police officer, he had endless zeal to serve the country. He was happy to be posted in this backward area and wanted to serve and help the poor illiterate people. He wanted to deliver justice in the beautiful valley. But all his dreams were shattered to the ground.

He kept tossing in his bed but could not sleep. He was lying with his eyes closed. He had no desire to see this world.

Pramod got up. He saw around. He again returned to his thoughts.

'Alas! There is none to whom I could talk. Rita...oh...she is the prime reason of my troubles. I am a fool. Only if I had agreed to her proposal. When all the seniors wanted that way, why did I not concede. I could have been friendly with Rita. No. no...I could not. I can't stoop down so low. I shall prefer to die rather than bow at the feet of Khushal. And Rita. She is beautiful in body but rest is...who knows how many people had relations with her.'

In the meanwhile, the deodar trees standing on far-off hills attracted his attention through the window. He saw the shaking leaves. His eyes were riveted on a tiny deodar. When its leaves swung, he found the image of a young damsel drying her hair in the sun. When the small tree started shaking because of harsh winds, Pramod thought it was the slim waist of a young lady showing her flexibility. He kept on watching the tree. He was enjoying nature outwardly but in fact, he was drawing a figure in his imagination.

'Alas! I had her address known to me.' Pramod suddenly got up and moved to and fro. Then stood by the window and started looking at the deodar tree.

'It would have been a consolation to me if she had met me. Here I don't have any of my own but she was also nothing to me. Who is she? To which family does she belong? Why I am so bewitched by her. Why I feel so much attracted just after one sight of her. There must be something different in her. But Pramod had felt attracted to Rita also. You had cultivated friendship with her also. In Mandi, you repented throughout the night your act. Why had you sent her away? Man's attraction towards woman is but natural but to be attracted to each and everyone in the world is a hoax.' Pramod again started loitering. He kept walking from side to side.

'No, no, it is not a superficial feeling for the girl who met me near Raghu Nath's temple. There must be something special about it. I have come across hundreds of girls in life. And come in contact with more girls daily. My pang is on the rise. It is not an attraction between ordinary man and woman. But who is she? Where does she live? Simply, I am attracted to her. I remember her, feel pangs of separation. Nothing else. What a fool I am?

'Shankar and Vinod have their sympathy for me. I can seek their help. May be I can trace her address. I shall like to meet her once before going to Keylong.'

'But what shall I tell to both of them. How will they react?' 'Who was the driver that day? The spot can be located where the girls had been dropped. May be the driver can tell something. But why should the driver help me now? I am suspended and transferred. If I had tried a few days ago, all would have helped me. I was an officer at that time. Now I am an accused, under punishment.

Pramod was quite worried and tense. Tears rolled down from his eyes many a time. He felt headache and was restless. He could neither sit nor walk. The moment he tried to sit, his feet started walking and when he attempted to be walking, his feet would stop.

'Come what may, I shall try to trace her. I do not want to leave Kullu with this hanging on my mind.' He came to the door, wiped his eyes with a hanky.

He opened the door and came out. He called a boy from a nearby home. He said something to him and returned to his room.

Pramod entered his small kitchen. He lit the stove and kept an utensil on it for preparing tea. Tea was ready in no time. He came to the window with a glass in his hands. He looked at the deodar on the high hills while enjoying tea. When the leaves shook, he imagined that the girl who had met near Raghu Nath's tent was dancing merrily. He felt as if the girl was looking at him. Now he felt a concern for the girl. He felt a prick.

'There was a knock at the door. Pramod opened the door.

'Come Shankar, come. Be seated please.'

'You have called me?'

'Yes Shankar. I need your help.'

'Please do tell me. It will be my pleasure to be of any use.' Shankar sat in a chair and Pramod on his bed.

'Oh, I forgot. I had made tea for you.' Pramod went to the kitchen.

'Sir, why did you take the trouble?'

'No trouble at all.' Pramod came with a cup of tea. Shankar took it. They started sipping tea. Pramod looked at Shankar twice or thrice. He wanted to say something but soon changed his gaze. Shankar also viewed him inquisitively but kept silent and continued with his tea.

Shankar emptied the cup and asked, 'Please tell me what I can do for you?'

'Shankar, you are one of my confidants.' Pramod said while having the last sip from his glass.

'Sir, you can trust me. I have sympathy with you. You are so capable and so honest. And they have punished you for no fault of yours. I wanted to raise a voice against this injustice but you restrained me. It is your greatness that you have decided to tolerate the injustice without resistance.'

'It was destined that way. I had to be in Kullu only for a short time.'

'That's O.K. Sir. Man may think the way he likes or he may plan as he likes but it does not all happen the way he desires.'

'That's why it is said man proposes, God disposes.'

'But not all the proposals.'

'All my plans have failed, Shankar, I wish one of them was fulfilled.'

'I do not follow you.'

'You have been called for it.'

'Let me know it, Sir.'

'Shankar, I have been your officer. You have always respected me. You have expressed your sympathy also. But you know basically I am a human being.'

'Sir, you are being enigmatic. It is right what you say. You are not a human being but you are an angel.'

'No, only a human being.'

'Right, Sir.'

'Every human being has a heart and sometimes it...'

Pramod was silent. He looked towards the window. Shankar was trying to read Pramod's face.

'Yes, Sir.'

'Shankar, I think...'

'What Sir?'

'That...'

'What?'

'That whether I should share my secret with you or not.'

'Don't be unjust to me. You have called me to discuss something. I don't know why are you reticent. May be you don't trust me.'

'Shankar, that's not the reason.'

'Then why do you hesitate so much?'

'Really speaking, I am a bit hesitant. You may find my problem strange. You may even dislike it or you may not like it. You may not refuse to help me.'

'So you don't have faith in Shankar.'

'If I had no confidence in you. I would not have sent for you.'

'Then why do you delay the revelation.'

Pramod raised his eyes and found Shankar also looking at him. He now smiled.

'Sir, you are not saying anything to any of your subordinates. You have one of your friends with you. Shankar can sacrifice even his life for his friends. You can test me once.'

'Shankar, my friend.' Pramod got up and hugged him. Friendship was live in his eyes.

'Shankar, I am going to Keylong without resistance. I don't have any regrets. I can tolerate the injustice but...'

'Please say it without reservation.'

'I cannot leave Kullu without one thing.'

'Tell me. Now Shankar will do it instead of Pramod.'

'Come what may?'

'Yes, come what may.'

'Shankar, I had met a girl during Dussehra. Only once. But the maiden meeting has made me enamoured of her. I cannot leave Kullu without meeting her.'

'She met you only once?'

'Only once.'

'Only one meeting with her has made you so fond of her, it is strange. And if she meets you repeatedly, what will be your fate?' Shankar laughed. Pramod's anxiety was now gone. He also tried to laugh.

'Pramod, so this is the story. You are love torn. All right, you need not worry. I shall help you to the maximum. I know the impact of love.

'You have also experienced it?' Pramod asked.

'I have also gone through it.'

'How?'

'First tell me your story. I shall narrate mine later on.'

'Shankar, arrange my meeting with her once.'

'Definitely. Where does she live?'

'I don't know.'

'What is her name?'

'I don't know.'

'Whose daughter she is?'

'I do not know.'

'With whom she met you?'

'I do not know that even.'

'Then? What do you know Pramod? Did you meet her in a dream? Dreams cannot be translated into reality.'

'No, Shankar, I did not meet her in a dream. I met her in Kullu.'

'My dear friend, you do not know her name. Neither you know her father's name nor the name of her village. You do not either know any of them with whom she met you. You are asking me to solve a riddle.'

'That is the real problem.'

'Did she meet you really?'

'She did meet me.'

'Thank God, you have answered one question in the affirmative.' Shankar said.

He continued, 'Where did she meet you?'

'Near Raghu Nath's tent,' Pramod said. 'Then she went away,' he added.

'Let her go if she has gone. You move to Keylong.'

'So, you have also accepted the defeat.'

'How shall we trace her? Neither her name, nor her village is known. Who is she? Has she any feelings for you or not? May be she is married. Pramod, narrate the story in detail.'

'Shankar, I was going to Manali from Kullu on the eve of Kullu Dussehra. It was late in the evening. We were only two in the jeep, i.e. my driver and myself. It started raining. I saw some men going to their homes. A few girls were also returning to their homes after visiting Kullu Dussehra. It was a desolate place. They had bags in their hands but they were without umbrellas. The driver halted the jeep at once. They boarded the jeep. The jeep was open from the rear. They got in. They were almost wet with rain. I was lost in my thoughts. So I did not see any one of them. After we had covered some distance, a girl sitting in the back seat asked the driver to stop. They all got down and went their way. I had not seen anyone of them. I did not talk to them. When I was in conversation with Mr. Verma the next day near Raghu Nath's tent, one of those girls came to me. I did not recognise her. She thanked me. I was surprised what for she thanked me. She narrated the last night's happening. She said I helped them a lot by giving them a lift when it was dark and raining. She thanked and left. I could not ask anything. I did not even talk. And since that day, he has haunted me. I thought I would be in Kullu. She would meet me one day or the other. I was hopeful and confident to meet her but now I have to leave Kullu for Keylong. My all hopes are dashed to the ground. And my confidence is shaken.' Pramod was silent after the narration. There was anxiety apparent on his face. He was again drowned in thoughts.

Shankar listened to him calmly. He looked outside through the window.

'Jeep driver...' Shankar uttered these words.

'They got down on road side on Mandi road.' Shankar again spoke.

'And she came to thank me the next day.'

'Pramod, was it Ranjit driver with you that day?'

'Yes, it was he.'

'All the more difficult.'

'Why?'

'He is a friend of Khushal.' Shankar revealed with a note of dissatisfaction.

'She met you once only, Pramod. How long was that meeting.'

'Just five to ten minutes.'

'Do you remember her face?'

'Yes, I remember it well. I would have drawn her sketch if I were a painter.'

'Tell me one thing.'

'Ask.'

'Was there a 'bindi' on her forehead and vermilion powder in her hair?'

'No, nothing of the sort.'

'She must be unmarried then.'

'Yes. She is not married.'

'How do you know it?'

'You yourself said it just now.'

'Right, Mr. Pramod. You relax. I give a thought to it. It is a ticklish issue but I belong to police department and that too to C.D. Moreover here friendship is at stake. Let me think over it calmly. I shall come tomorrow. You worry not. I shall do whatever I can. I am confident that I shall trace her.'

'Thank you, Shankar.' Pramod held his hand fondly.

Shankar went away. Pramod felt relieved.

□

15

'Sharma has close ties with the Chief Minister.'

'Now, they are at loggerheads these days.'

'Did you not tell it to me?'

'It was not the latest.'

'You used to fondly discuss their friendship. And you also hoped to become a Minister with his help.'

'That turned out to be false. So I lost the chance.'

'What do you mean?'

'Someone else has been inducted as a Minister instead of me.'

'Why?'

'Because the Chief Minister wants to weaken Mr. Sharma.'

'Why did they fall apart?'

'The Chief Minister felt that Sharma was growing stronger. And the number of MLAs supporting Sharma was increasing. He apprehended that Sharma had his eye on the Chief Minister's post.'

'They were really very close friends earlier.'

'They were friends?'

'Then what happened suddenly.'

There were only a few passengers in the bus. There was some defect in the bus also. The driver was a middle-aged man. So he was driving the bus at a low speed. The passengers enjoyed the scene of hilly fields and the springs. Some were talking to each other. Seating behind the driver seat, they were also busy in conversation.

'Politics is a strange field. Nothing is permanent in it.'

'Not even friendship?'

'Yes.'

'My dream will also be dashed to the ground then.'

'No, not yours... You are my...' He said keeping his hand on his shoulder.

'If political frienship is like a wall of sand, it can come to an end any moment. Who can trust whom?' He said in a dejected mood.

'Yes, it is like that but not at all places. All are not of the same kind.'

'May be they are chips of the same block.'

'No, no, it is not like that. Our frienship is not political, it is lifelong. You remember we were friends before we entered politics.'

'I agree.'

'It is generally said there are no permanent friends in politics. Only selfish motives are permanent.'

'I do not follow you.'

'Every leader has his own motives in politics. Every one has his own ambition. To achieve all that, he has his own leanings. Whosoever helps him in achieving his target, he is his friend. When his demands are not fulfilled by someone, the friendship ceases. So people move from one side to the other and vice versa.'

'And what about the loyalty of Ministers and party MLAs towards the Chief Minister?'

'It is nothing. He who finds his motives attained satisfactorily is loyal to the Chief Minister.'

'Is that the way?'

'And that loyalty is as long as his selfish motives are achieved. As soon as he learns that his interests are not being protected in the Chief Minister's group, he crosses over to the other camp.'

'But you belong to the same party.'

'But there are many groups within.'

'Not all members of our party accept the Chief Minister as their leader.'

'They accept him leader only with their selfish motives first.'

'Who elects the Chief Minister?'

'MLAs of the party.'

'For how much time?'

'For five years.'

'Then why don't they go with the Chief Minister for five years? Why this groupism?'

'Because they all want to progress.'

'Where and which way?'

'Every MLA wants to be a Minister and every Minister wants to become the Chief Minister.'

'But there can be only one Chief Minister at a time.'

'Yes but who can stop people from dreaming to be the Chief Minister.'

'But after five years?'

'No, one is ready to wait here.'

'Now, which group you have joined?'

'I am in Sharma's camp. But now Sharma is not in Chief Minister's group.'

'So, you also...'

'I have also joined the other group along with Mr. Sharma.'

'Who heads that group?'

'Prandhir Singh.'

'Who is he?'

'The Education Minister.'

'So Mr. Sharma and Prandhir Singh, both...'

'Yes, both have joined hands. They have decided between themselves that Vishal Singh would be ousted and one of them would take over as Chief Minister and the other would become Deputy Chief Minister. They have promised Ministership to me. Now you will also have to help us in this effort. We cannot wait any longer.'

'For what?'

Thakur was a bit silent now.

'You cannot tolerate Vishal Singh as the Chief Minister or you cannot stay with Ministership any longer?'

'Both are related issues.'

'But what for is your restlessness?'

'Leave it all. You have unnecessarily started a wrong issue. When you are with me, why this dry discussion. No, Rita. Don't be so unkind to me. I have brought you along so that I can release my political tension.' Saying this Thakur placed his hand on her shoulder... He pressed her shoulder hard as if to demonstrate his power. Rita suddenly jumped.

'What are you doing? My shoulder is not made of stone.'

'No, it is as soft as butter. But it was indicative of my strong love for you.'

'Keep the jerk to yourself. I only expect love. That too slowly.'

'Forgive me.'

'Forgiven.' Rita posed to be authoritative and laughed. Thakur also joined her laughter.

The bus reached Pathankot. Passing through narrow roads of the bazar, it made its way to the bus stand. The passengers were in readiness to get down. They collected their luggage. Pathankot was relatively less cold. It was a bit cold in the mornings and evenings but hot during the day. This bus had come from the hills. All the passengers belonged to the hills. They all were wearing warm clothes.

It was a strange scene at the bus stand. Most of the people were in pants and shirts or in kurta-pyjama but the passengers from the hills were in coats and sweaters. Some of them were wearing colourful Kullu caps. A few of them had woolen blankets also. Some women were dressed up in clothes made of blankets. The passengers of the hill bus were conspicuous in the crowd. It appeared as if muddy water from the hills was intermingling with the deep blue waters of the sea. It took sufficient time for the muddy water to lose its identity in the sea water.

The bus conductor called a coolie. Thakur and Rita's luggage was kept aside first of all. The conductor took the coolie to Mr. Thakur.

'Your luggage, Thakur Sir.'

'All the luggage?'

'Yes, Sir.'

'Here's also.'

'The attache belongs to her.'

'Yes, it is mine.' Rita confirmed it.

'Please check if anything has been left out.' Thakur said looking into the eyes of Rita.

'No, everything is here.' Rita said and then she spoke to the bus conductor, 'Thanks a lot.'

But Thakur did not say a single word of thanks to him.

They hired a rickshaw and reached the Jallandhar Bus Stand. A bus bound for Jallandhar was ready to leave. Thakur asked Rita to board the bus. He went to the booking window for tickets. After buying the tickets, he also got into the bus. Soon after the bus left for its destination.

It was a bigger bus in comparison to the hill bus. The road was also broader and cleaner. The bus was moving at a high speed. Thakur was also fast in smoking. Rita was travelling with Thakur for the first time. The cigarette smoke irritated her. She had often picked up a quarrel with her husband over this issue. The very sight of a cigarette would provoke her anger. She was unable to tolerate the smoke.

But she had to accept smoke along with Thakur. He asked her once or twice formally. 'Rita, smoke does not bother you?' Rita just said out of courtesy no, no. It does not bother me. You can smoke freely.' She wanted to please Thakur.

'Rita, you have to do a big job.'

'I do not know anything of politics.'

'You will be taught all the nuances of politics.'

'Shall I be able to perform the job assigned to me within time?'

'Surely.' Thakur tucked the burnt cigarette to let the ash fall.

'But what shall I have to do?'

'We shall all unite to oust Vishal Singh from the Chief Minister's post. Then Sharma or Prandhir Singh will become Chief Minister. I shall be inducted in the Cabinet to represent the hilly area.'

'And?' Rita was listening to Mr. Thakur intently. She moved closer to him.

'And you will also be alloted a ticket from somewhere to get you elected as an MLA.'

'Truly? Is that possible?' Rita was extremely happy. She had a hearty laugh. She moved still closer to Mr. Thakur. Thakur placed his hand behind Rita. Then moved his hand to her shoulder to fondle her.

'Rita, everything will be possible.'

'But the people here in the hills are orthodox. How will they accept me? Moreover I belong to Punjab. Even if your party allots me a ticket, the village folk will not vote for me.' Rita expressed her apprehension.

'You are right, Rita but...' Thakur was in a thinking posture.

'But what?'

'But we shall manage. Hilly area is quite widespread. If our candidate takes over as the Chief Minister, we shall create an extra Assembly seat. And that seat will have more of urban voters rather than the villagers. Moreover, the Congress ticket is in itself a guarantee of win. Who knew me in this area? It is not like that now in my case but there was a time. He lit his cigarette again.'

'What kind of time it was?'

'There was a time when if the Congress ticket was pasted on a pole even, it was a sure win. The electorate had such a confidence in Congress that the voters even did not bother to know the name of the candidate. It was only Congress and Congress and nothing else.'

'And now?'

'Now the situation is different.' It is true that there is no other party as yet to throw a challenge to the Congress. Yes, only a few comrades and a few members of Jan Sangh are there to oppose.'

They sometimes make their presence felt. But no party can compare with us.'

'Can I also win if I fight election on its ticket.'

'When even poles have been winning on Congress ticket, why not you, who is extremely beautiful.' Thakur fastened his grip on Rita.

The bus was moving at a fast speed. Occasionally, the bus stopped to pick up passengers standing on the road-side. Or the bus sometimes halted to let the passengers get down at their destinations. Thakur and Rita were lost in their own world unaware of other passengers. There bus of conversation was moving at its own speed.

'No, no, it is your greatness. I don't have any capability in me.' Rita said surrendering herself under his hand.

'You just watch my dear Rita through my eyes.'

There was a glimmer in Rita's eyes.

'Rita, what is that you don't possess? You are young and beautiful. You have capability and a will to serve the people. You will turn out to be a high-class leader. Alas! you were identified much earlier, you would have been a very senior leader by this time.'

'Why did you not invite me earlier?'

'Why did you not meet me earlier?'

'How could I see you? I did not know you.'

'Listen, I had identified you in the first meeting. All are not experts.'

'That is true.' Rita laughed.

'I recognized the talent in you at first sight.'

'Yes. You had come closer to me at the first sight. You continued watching me for sometime. In the beginning, I felt bad about it. Then you talked to me. You enquired about me. But I could not ask anything about you. Later I asked someone and knew that you are a heavy-weight leader.'

'How did you feel then?'

'Very nice.'

'Why?'

'Truly speaking, I do not have a good personal life. You know my marriage has not been successful. He is always drowned in liquor.'

'Wine and women both. As if he is the only handsome youngman in the valley.'

'Yes, he is of that sort. I live with him under one roof but just like co-passengers in a railway compartment. The co-passengers may share their views sometimes but we both live in a suffocating atmosphere with high-volt tension. Liquor helps him to forget everything for long periods but I am put to frustration. I don't have anyone of mine. No independent existence. I don't have anything to do. No one requires me. My life is like a pitcher with a hole which cannot hold water. I found a shelter when I came to you.' Rita had water in her eyes. She came close to Thakur. He was smoking.

She had also many friends. She is sighted with new faces daily. Her husband is also of the same character. But what could he do? When she started flirting here and there, he started drinking... But now she is in my fold. She is so young, so beautiful, so educated...that one likes to love her. Moreover, she will be quite helpful to me in politics. Thakur was lost in his thoughts but was smoking heavily at the same time.

'Rita forget all that. Your new personality has been unfolded now. You have a mission in life. You have reserves of efficiency. You can lead lakhs of people. How does it matter if you are a bit late in life. It often happens that gems are identified late.'

'I depend upon your support.'

'And I depend upon you, my Rita.'

'Sincerely yours.'

'Yes, take care. You are mine only. Your friendship with others should now be only a formality, the only relationship will be between you and me.'

'Agreed.'

'Yes, if I get a ticket for you, you can surely win the election. And if it does not happen, there are other alternatives. If you do not want to contest, you can be nominated to Legislative Council. You can be sent to Rajya Sabha. You can be a Chairman of a Corporation. Let us hope that we have a Chief Minister from our group, then anything is possible.' Thakur said looking at Rita. They looked into each other's eyes with warmth.

'Mr. Thakur, the journey is almost over. We talked so much. But you have not told what is my role in this drama?'

'I shall tell you everything. You have to do all the things.'

'What is all the things after all?'

'Rita, in a democracy all the decisions are dependent on the support of MLAs. Vishal Singh is the Chief Minister today because he enjoys the support of majority. If we can encourage his supporters to join our group, we can have our Chief Minister. We have to win over the MLAs. You can do all this for us.'

Rita was serious now. Then she suddenly laughed.

'So Rita we have reached Jallandhar now. I used to be dead tired when I travelled all alone earlier. But you are with me this time, I feel fresh even after so long a journey.'

The bus stopped at the bus stand. Coolies came to the bus. They both took a rickshaw and went away.

□

16

'Ranjit, this is my personal work. You have to do it.'

'Shankar, I shall be happy if I can do anything for you but I have not followed you.'

'You will understand.'

'Make me understand.' Ranjit said and extended his glass towards Shankar. Shankar was pouring liquor from the bottle. Both of them were under mild influence of liquor. The glass was full but liquor overflowed.

'Shankar, the glass is already full.'

'Let it be filled.'

'Oh, it is being wasted.'

'Let it be.'

'You are a strange fellow.'

'As long as you don't promise that you would trace her, I shall not stop pouring liquor.'

'But the bottle is empty.'

'Oh, is it? empty?' He threw the bottle away.

'Shankar, I am your friend. I shall do whatever you ask me to do. But tell me what will you do of that girl. How shall we locate her. Neither her name is known nor her whereabouts. Even her village or her parents are not known.'

'You were on the wheel with Pramod that day. You must be aware of the spot where those girls had got down.'

'First tell me why do you want to trace her now?'

'There is something special.'

'It is not related to Pramod, I think.'

'Yes, yes. You are very clever. You have guessed it right.' Shankar was silent for a few moments. Ranjit drank a bit from the glass. He poured some water in the glass. And he was enjoying his drink now.

'Pramod? He posed himself as a big officer. My friend Khushal was put behind bars by him. All of them advised him to behave but he did not listen to any one. Now he has been despatched to Keylong. He will remember the incident for ever and will forget idealism but what is his relation with those girls.'

'You want to know all the things just now. You just collect the information. Then we shall arrange to get him thrown even beyond Keylong.'

'Truly.'

'That will be nice.'

'He will have to continue there life long.'

'So we should take Khushal also with us?'

'Not at all. It will upset our plan. You and me, we both have to do it secretly. No one should even know about it.'

'O.K. my dear friend.'

'When do we go?'

'It is Sunday tomorrow. I shall come to you early tomorrow and then we go on the hunt. But you should have collected information about her name and address. I did not see her face even. They got into the jeep from behind and got down the same way. I could not see anything in darkness.'

'Ranjit when you were face to face on the road, the headlights must have been on then.'

'It was dark night. Moreover, it was raining. It was a little foggy. I had to be focussed on driving. Shankar I am fond of drinking but I am not fond of staring at the girls.'

'That is why you married thrice.'

'Gone are those days of youth. Ranjit had indulged in many adventures then.'

'All right, you don't remember anything.'

'A bunch of colourful girls was walking on the road-side trying to save themselves from the rains. They were talking to each other and making jokes. Someone would talk of someone's love, trying to befool her. They were reminded of the presence of Pramod. He looked impressive and dominating. I shifted my look to some other things. Pramod saw them and asked me to halt the vehicle. He asked them to board the jeep from its rear entry. Joyfully, they entered the jeep. One of them said, 'You have saved us, Sir. Neither

Pramod nor I answered back. They requested to drop them at a spot after covering some distance. That's all.'

'Ranjit, you belong to the police department. Can you define the identity of any one of them?'

'The girl who was sighted in the lights of the jeep was middle statured but very beautiful. She had tried to save herself from the glare by covering one of her eyes with her palm. She appeared very charming in the sparkle of light and fog. If the officer with me, I would have made her sit in the front seat beside me. And I would have seen her to my fill.'

'Can you recognise her?'

'It's difficult because I had not seen her complete face but I can try. But Shankar, Pramod did not talk to her. He did not enquire anything from her. What can be common between the two?'

'Where did you go after that?'

'Mandi.'

'Then?'

'Yes. I recollect. There is something.'

'What?'

'Sir did not return with me. He returned in another jeep with someone. I returned the next morning with the big boss.'

'When and with whom Pramod came back?'

'I don't know.'

'This is the point. You have been befooled. He dropped her at a point. And on return, he must have gone to her.'

'Well done Pramod. You advise others but what about yourself? Shankar we shall trace that girl and compel Pramod to leave the place.'

'He has been sent to Keylong.'

'We shall oust him from the state. He had arrested my chum, Khushal. I shall avenge it on him.'

'All right, then, we meet tomorrow morning.'

'Agreed.'

Ranjit got up tottering and moved to the door. Shankar escorted him to the door. He sat on his bed. He was happy that he could entice Ranjit, who was the only person who knew about the girl. He felt delighted and proud over his success.

Shankar wanted to go to bed but was not sleepy as yet. He was happy that he could win over Ranjit. He was worried about tomorrow. What and how the things will progress? He was feeling restive. He had high esteem for Pramod. Pramod had been sinned against. So Shankar was all the more sympathetic towards him. They were now friends. He earnestly desired to trace that girl so that Pramod could be relieved of his tension.'

He could not sleep as he was disturbed in mind. Shankar got up, opened the door and straightaway went to Pramod's place.

'Come in Shankar. You are here at this time?'

'Yes, I could not sleep. So I come here.'

'You did well.'

'Why?'

'I was also not feeling sleepy.'

'So we are in the same situation.'

'It appears like that.'

'But there is one difference at least.'

'What is that?'

'You are lost in a girl and I am lost in a friend who is infatuated by a girl.'

Both of them laughed. Shankar sat in a chair lying closeby. Pramod reclined in his bed.

'Why did you not get sleep?' Pramod asked Shankar.

'Because of anxiety and also because of happiness.'

'Happiness? What for?'

'I just narrate.' Shankar sat erect.

'Have you got her? Have you come to know about her whereabouts? Shankar tell me, I am very much perturbed.

'Destination is yet far off. We have not got the path even but we have a man in our fold who knows the path.'

'Who is he?'

'Ranjit.'

'How?'

'I had called him her for drinks. I made him drink to his fill. He is convinced now and will go to the spot with me tomorrow morning. He will try to tell all the details.'

'Well done, my friend. But how was he persuaded?'

Shankar narrated the whole story to him. They kept on laughing. Pramod was appreciative of Shankar's success. He felt relieved and thanked Shankar. He made tea himself and they took tea.

'I shall go with you tomorrow.'

'No, you will not.'

'Not me?'

'Yes not you. I and Ranjit will go. I have not told the entire story to Ranjit.' I have just told him that Pramod has some affair with that girl. We shall enquire about that girl and report it to the higher authorities. Ranjit is ready not to help you positively but he is up against you. He is a close friend of Khushal. That is why he is very angry with you. He should not know anything about this. We shall not be able to trace anything without his help.' Shankar said while sipping tea.

'O.K. As you wish I shall stay here.'

'Exactly. Pray for our success.'

'Does Ranjit know anything?'

'He belongs to this place and knows the spot where they had got down. He remembers the face of one of them. But the difficulty is how shall we enquire without telling the name? We shall have no answer to the question – why do you ask? It is a ticklish matter. Since it is related to the heart beats of a friend, we shall try every method.'

'Shankar, I have to leave Kullu now. I wish to see her once before leaving.'

'May I ask you one thing, Pramod?'

'Do ask.'

'What will you do if she is traced?'

'I just...shall talk.' Pramod felt uneasy. He himelf was not aware what would he do in case he met her.

'Yes, you will talk. But what after that?'

'After that?'

'Pramod, I know your emotions. I respect your feelings. But I have been stuck with a thought since that day. You will talk but she may not reciprocate with the same warmth. And in case, she turns out to be a married one?'

'No, she is not married.'

'Did you ask her about it?'

'Shankar if I had the courage to ask her. I would not have been in this uncertain position at this moment.'

'Then how do you know she is unmarried?'

'There was no bindi on her face nor she had red powder in her hair.'

'Did you take notice of all these things when she came to say "Thank you" for the first time?'

'No, I thought it afterwards. But I have her total image in my mind. I now can recognise her even in a crowd of the fair.'

'Agreed, she is not married. May be she is engaged. She may not talk to you.'

'She will.'

'How?'

'She came and thanked me that day. She was hesitant and shy. I was engaged in conversation with Prakash Verma at that time. She stood by me silent. She made an effort to initiate conversation but was silent again. She moved forward and then retraced her steps. I viewed her once and then shifted my gaze. Prakash Verma was discussing some serious issue. I continued to listen to him. I thought she had come to Mr. Prakash Verma. When she approached me to thank, I was alarmed.'

'Why were you alarmed?'

'Shankar, she was very charming.'

'Not was, she is.'

'Yes, certainly.'

'But why did you feel alarmed?'

'Her arrival before me and to present thanks was all unexpected. She was very attractive in her fair colour. It appeared as if a rose drenched in dew stood before me. Her eyes were as deep as a sea. Shankar, I was surprised. Something had happened to me at her sight. What happened, I did not know. But it had happened never before.'

'Not even at the sight of Rita?' Shankar said in jest. Pramod had told Shankar about his introduction with Rita. His bus journey with Rita from Dharamshala to Mandi, he had shared all those details with Shankar. He had none else of his own. He would feel relieved after talking to Shankar.

'No, Shankar, how does Rita figure here in our talks?'

'Why?'

'Rita is a saleable commodity.'

'And she?'

'She is different.'

'What do you mean?'

'I had felt something in my body when I met Rita. That was momentry stir. And when I knew about her that she was a call girl-type woman, I developed hatred for her. I did not agree to her recommendation in Khushal's case. I travelled in her company.

We walked on foot near Dhauladhar. She sat close to me for hours. I felt her warmth. But Shankar she could not leave any imprint on my mind. I have the least fascination for her. She had invited me on my arrival here. She had a liking for me. But I do not have any relationship with those butterflies who move from flower to flower.'

'And that girl? She became known in one meeting.'

'Yes, only one glimpse made her known to me. Prakash Verma left when she started talking to me near Raghu Nath's tent. We were all alone. She waited for sometime after thanking me but I could not say anything to her. I almost became a statue at her sight. My past collided with the present and my present was lost in my future. I could have asked her name and about her village. I had forgotten myself. She wanted to talk to me. That is why she stood waiting. She must have something in her mind for me that enabled the village girl to come to a police officer. But when I did not engage her in conversation, she said namastey with folded hands and went away.'

'And you watched her going?'

'Yes, I continued watching her. She looked back once after covering some distance.'

'What emotion she carried in her eyes when she thanked you with folded hands?'

'Expression of love, a desire unfulfilled.'

'You should have called for a dialogue.'

'I wish I had done it.'

'Did you not feel like that?'

'I had a burning desire but I could not summon courage to talk to her. She had come to thank me. I should have extended the conversation further.'

'So you are sure that she is unmarried and is also in love with you...?'

'Yes, I am confident.'

'But both the aspects do not sound true.'

'Why?'

'If she was equally restless for you, she could have found you. She knows your address. At least she knows that you are in the police department here.'

'That's right, Shankar. Then...' Pramod was now downspsrited. His excitement was gone. He looked pale.

'How could a simple village girl could find out a police officer? She came once, came closer, talked to me but the police officer missed the chance, why and how will she now come? I shall have to go to her now.'

'Shankar, its all right. She must be thinking the same way but how can she come? I had read a lot for me in her eyes that day.'

'Pramod, there must be fire on both sides. And it should be, well I take your leave now. Please take rest. I shall come to you tomorrow evening.'

'Right Shankar. I shall never forget your obligation.' Pramod escorted Shankar to the door. He stood there for some time. Then he came out with him. Both of them walked on a deserted road. It was pitch dark at night. Lights flashed in darkness like thin rays. Shankar stopped after covering some distance. He requested Pramod to go back. They saluted each other and departed.

□

17

The rickshaw reached a segregated place after crossing through a number of lanes. Thakur Budh Singh told the address to the rickshaw puller after consulting his diary. The rickshaw puller was moving ahead as directed.

'Is there some one's home'. Rita asked.

'Yes'. Thakur repplied.

'Totally out of the city.'

'Yes.'

'Mr. Sharma is a Minister. You had told that he belonged to Jallandhar. Are we going to his residence? Hearing Sharma's reference from Rita, Thakur was reminded of an old incident. He recollected that a party was arranged at his residence in Kullu when Sharma had visited the town. They had started taking drinks after the dinner was over. Rita was serving drinks to them. When the party concluded late at night, Sharma had taken Rita along with in his car. Sharma had told that he would drop Rita at her home. Thakur made an enquiry next day and was told that Sharma took Rita to the rest house where she had stayed for the night. Remembering this episode, Thakur felt uneasy.

'Why? You have remembered Sharma just after entering his city.'

'Since he is a very close friend of yours.'

'And yours?'

Rita kept silent. She was not prepared for this question. She looked at him. He was boiling with rage but smiled when Rita looked at him.

'Rita, you had gone with Sharma in his car that night.' Thakur said although he did not want to touch this topic. His intellect controlled him but his emotions overpowered him.

'Yes, you had sent me with him.' Rita said indifferently.

'I never wanted to send you.'

'Then why did you ask me?'

'In fact, Sharma wanted to take you along.'

'And you sent me finding him fond of my company.'

'Yes. I thought it was right.'

'And you ask me today as if you did not like it.'

'I was reminded, so...'

'What so?'

'So I remembered my angry mood also.'

'You called me yourself. You made me sit all alone in your house. When all the guest's left after dinner, the actual party of your friend Mr. Sharma started. You had asked me to serve the drinks. I did as you directed. Later on Sharma said that I should sit with him in his car. You asked me to sit with him in the car. So why should you be unhappy and angry with me?'

'It is not for that.'

'Then what for?'

'I sent you with him so that he could drop you at your residence.'

'Then?' Rita was alarmed.

'You tell where did you go with him?'

'To my home.' Rita wanted to read Thakur's mind.

'To your home? Thakur repeated sarcastically.

'Yes, to my home.'

'To your home...to our home.' Thakur said in low voice. He continued smoking looking towards the skies. He would light another one when the first cigarette ended.

The rickshaw puller stopped at a point and went to a house to require the address.

'How did you enjoy at your own house that night?' Thakur said drawing a deep puff.

'I do not understand what you want to say or what you want to know. When I am so close to you, why all these riddles? Be frank and ask boldly whatever is in your mind.'

'Did you really go to your home that night?'

'Don't you believe me?'

'Since when the rest house is your home? Thakur's clever watch was an attempt to read Rita's emotions.'

'Mr. Thakur, I am Rita in the true sense. May be you know the real meaning of this word. I don't know what prompted my parents to christen me as 'Rita'. It has come true now. I left my parents' house after marriage. I wanted to live in my husband's house but neither I got my husband nor his house. Yes, it is but a dilapidated house with walls made of bricks. I do live in that house but that is not mine. I feel at my own house wherever night falls or wherever I am wanted. No one likes or longs for me in my dilapidated house. No one is happy when I go there. If I don't go, no one is angry with me. No one ever waits for me. You call it my house. It means you don't understand me. You called me affectionately. You introduced me to the Minister. He talked with me pleasingly. I felt his attraction and desire for me quite positive. For me that rest house was my home for that night.' Rita spoke at length and was silent now. There were tears in her eyes. She tried to hide her tears in her 'anchal.'

Thakur was dumb founded. He felt the tables turned upon him. He did not want to torture Rita that way. Rita was invaluable to him because he could use her for achieving his ends. At the same time, he felt attached to her also. And she had accepted his love in the true spirit. But he did not like it when Rita sat in Sharma's car. He felt envious when he came to know that Rita had stayed with Sharma in the rest house. He had pent up anger in his mind. Today it came out like lava.

'Rita, excuse me. I never meant it.'

Rita silently wiped her eyes.

'You have rightly pointed out that I did not try to understand you fully. I have been unsuccessful that way.

Rita sat on the other side of rickshaw. It was her way of expression of anger. She had her gaze downwards. Neither she looked upwards nor she answered any question.

'Will you not talk to me now? I have begged pardon from you. Will you not pardon your Thakur.' His muscular hand was now on her shoulder.

'It is not a matter of pardon but I did not relish it.'

'Please leave it now... How far is the destination?' Thakur asked the rickshaw puller.

'It is nearby. That is Kapoor's building with a sign of fish. They are called Machchi wala because of the fish drawn on it. We would have reached much earlier if you had told the real name. I know him very well. You said Prem Kapoor but he is Machchi wala Kapoor.' Rickshaw puller said with his heartbeat raised.

Rita thought in her mind, Thakur wants full control on me. He did not like my going with Sharma that night. He had this complaint in his mind. If I had to be tied to one person for the life, I would have continued with my husband. I was formally married to him. Everything was there. But it is no life. Nothing new. The same thing repeated. I would have been suffocated there. I don't know why crores of ladies have tolerated all this since centuries.

I wish I could strike at all these bindings. I need Thakur's support to achieve my ambition in politics. So I shall have to spend some time with him as per his wishes. I can review it later. I should not have spoken so much. I could have apologised for the mistake. I could assume that I would not go with any one in future now. Thakur did not show continued resentment. On the other hand, he apologised.

'Here it is Sir, Kapoor's house.' The rickshaw puller said and stopped. He stood on one side.

'Come on Thakur, I have been waiting for you so long.'

'Kapoor, you should have told me your complete address.'

'I had dictated the complete address.'

'You are Machchiwale Kapoor. You did not say anything about fish.'

'Yes, people know me here with that name.'

A servant came out of the house. He took the luggage and went inside. The rickshaw puller got his money and went back.

'Thakur, you should have brought Mrs. Thakur....'

'Be silent.' Thakur kept his hand or Kapoor's mouth. Rita was following him. She could not hear Kapoor's comment.

'Who is she?'

'An influential new Congress worker.'

'Yes.' There were changing emotions on Kapoor's face.

'Thakur, why influence me with her presence?' I thought you are with your wife. Anyhow, but what has she to do in so important meeting?' Kapoor laughed.

'Sharma knows her. It is his selection. He has invited her specially.' Thakur revealed.

'O.K. That's the point. Why did you not disclose it earlier?'

'Come this way, please.' Kapoor turned back. He went to Rita and said while escorting her.

'You had difficulty in locating my residence? He asked Rita moving closer to her.

'No, not at all. Thakur had told rickshawala about the address.'

'We have constructed new house. It is a new colony.'

'It is a good site.'

'Yes'.

A few persons were already sitting in a room. Thakur and Rita also joined them.

'Would you like to use the bathroom? It is this way. Kapoor guided Rita.

'Thanks. I was just feeling like that.' Rita accompanied Kapoor.

'The construction is new. It's not complete as yet. It is not fully furnished also. Moreover, no one lives here as yet.' Kapoor spoke while accompanying Rita to a corner of the house.

'So you don't live here?'

'No, my village is in this district. I represent the area in the State Assembly. I had purchased this land earlier. I have built a house. My family lives in the village.'

'Really. That's why bachelordom is visible here.' Rita said pointing out towards the disorderly things lying here and there. Both of them laughed.

'Here is the bathroom. Let me see if the servant has kept a towel and soap here or not? Kapoor entered the bathroom.'

'Yes, everything is O.K.' Kapoor said and came out.

The political gettogether was going on in the room. The cigaratte smoke was in the room. Serious political discussions made it all the more hot.

Mr. Dhanwant Rai Sharma occupied the main chair. He was conducting the entire proceedings. Prandhir Singh sat close to him. Thakur Budh Singh joined them.

'How far has our objective has been? I am a bit late in coming.' Thakur said while taking a chair.

'Because you were coming with a commodity.' Sharma was satirical.

'Really Thakur! You have enticed a rare beauty.' Prandhir saw towards her with tempted eyes.

'Prandhir, it is something rare, indeed.'

'She is a combination of youth and beauty.'

'And the natural beauty of the hills has been given a spectaculor look. Kamdev, the god of love may faint at her sight.'

'What will be our reaction?'

'I am noticing your reaction.'

'What?'

'You are losing your control over yourself.'

'She has not sat among us yet. Nor she has spoken. What will happen to you when she mixes up with us.'

'The same fate will be mine as yours.'

'Oh. Thakur sits silent.'

Sharma and Prandhir were busy talking to each other. Thakur sat silent. He was busy smoking and pushing the smoke upwards. Sharma and Prandhir were Cabinet Ministers. They were old friends. But for a brief political interval, they had been together in politics. Both of them were reputed leaders in their respective areas. They both had their graphs of MLAs. Since Sharma had deserted Vishal Singh and joined the Prandhir Singh group, a spark in Punjab's politics was simmering. Sharma was with Prandhir a year ago also. Then he joined the Chief Minister's camp. Now again he was with Prandhir. They were friends in personal life also. They had now joined hands in politics also. Both of them were fond of wine and women also.

'Hello Mr. Thakur. Please say something.'

'I am listening to both of you.'

'Silently?'

'He is Thakur, the original Thakur. He does not gossip like us. He believes in practical.' Both of them laughed. Thakur was a bit serious. He also laughed.

'That is why Sharmaji...Remember that night? Instead of dropping Rita at her residence, you took her along...'

'Speak out Thakur. Why have you stopped. Instead of dropping at her residences...' Prandhir was curious to know.

'There is nothing behind it. Thakur is unnecessarily talking useless.' Sharma was a bit hesitant.

'Tell me the whole truth, Thakur.'

'Sharma had taken her straight to the rest house.'

'After that?'

'Ask him what happened after that.'

'The same that happens. She was recruited an active Congress worker.' Sharma dispensed their curiosity himself and laughed. They all joined him in laughter.

'Would you all like to take tea first?' Kapoor asked.

'Yes, Yes. You arrange for the tea,' Prandhir said.

Kapoor went away. Rita came after a short while and seated herself. Thakur introduced her to Prandhir. In the meanwhile Kapoor came. All of them went with him to the adjoining room. There were chairs around a table. The room had been turned into a dining room. They all enjoyed tea and eatables. Thereafter, they went to the other room.

'Tell me, Mr. Sharma, what is your plan? I have come as per your instructions.' Thakur said.

'Prandhir, take out that list. Prandhir opened his briefcase as asked by Sharma. He took out a file from beneath and came to Sharma. He opened the file and placed it before Sharma. He said, 'Mr. Sharma, the list is ready. There are eighty MLAs in all in the party. Here is the list of these thirty-five who are with the Chief Minister. These twenty-five are with us. There are the committed people on either side. It is difficult to win over any one of these. Here are the remaining twenty MLAs.'

'Prandhir, nothing is ever permanent in politics. Never take it like that. The point is to ascertain whom and how to win him for how much and our capability to pay for it.' Sharma looked around. Kapoor had also come and sat close to them.

'The only difference is that of value. All are saleable but at different prices.' Thakur said while having a puff of cigarette.

'Yes, it exists. And your comment has a truth in it. But I do not believe that it is the only truth.' Kapoor joined the discussion.

'What do you mean?' Thakur looked askance at Kapoor.

'There are some MLAs who cannot be bought at any cost. You make the plan keeping them aside.'

'Exceptions are always there.'

'Not exception only. Will you include people like me in the seleable list?' Kapoor was fuming with rage.

'No, no, Kapoor. We do not mean it like that. You are right. Those who are our hardline followers, they are rock solid in loyalty. It will be a futile excercise to win them over.'

'Sharma, I had already pointed it out. You did not listen to me wholly.' Prandhir opened the file again and lent towards Sharma.

'Yes, yes. You show me your list and also tell me about your plan.'

'Let us first listen that. Then we discuss it. Yes, Rita, I hope you are not feeling bored.' Sharma asked Rita with penetrating eyes.

'No, no, why should I feel bored. Your conversation is all very interesting and hot. Moreover, I am new to all these things. I shall learn from you talks.' Rita said while taking care of saree.

'You have called her for this purpose. She is an influential lady of Kullu. She has joined our party and she is fully prepared to help our group.' Thakur said while introducing her in detail.

'So Prandhir, you were right. The entire game depends upon those twenty. What is their position.' Sharma said trying to make a meaning of it.

'Here is the list of those twenty.' Prandhir took out the four lists from his file and kept them on the table. They picked a copy each and started reading it.

'Well done. The analysis is very scientific. There are details about every one.' Kapoor said.

'Prandhir is a veteran player in politics,' Sharma commented.

'The poor Chief Minister will continue no more,' Thakur said while viewing the list.

'So this is the position of these twenty. You will have to plan keeping them in mind. If these twenty join us, we shall be forty-five.' Prandhir told his calculations.

'We can win over a few from the forty-five.' Thakur said having a deep puff of cigarette.

'Yes.' Sharma did not comment more.

'Yes, start from the top. Prandhir you discuss one by one.'

Look Mr. Sharma, I have categorized these twenty into separate groups, to understand them and to motivate them to break away. The first group consists of these three. No temptation can break them. They do not drink and they are not greedy for money. They will have to be committed ministerial berths. They are men of principles. Once they agree, they will keep their word.'

'Prandhir seems right. What do you say Thakur?,' Sharma asked.

'I do not know them intimately. They belong to districts close to Kapoor's area. He can tell it better?'

'I have my doubt about Rama Shankar. He is right about the other two,' Kapoor said.

'Why do you doubt him?'

'He is caught in a case. The Chief Minister is protecting him. He may not be prepared to desert the Chief Minister's camp at this juncture?'

'What is the case?'

'His brother Vinod Shankar had been arrested a few months ago in an opium case. Opium worth one lakh was caught from one place. When the enquiry was conducted, his brother's name also figured in it. The enquiry officer was the brother of a Jan Sanghi MLA. He arranged a number of witnesses against him. I learnt that he took Vinod Shankar in confidence and suggested that if he could drag his brother's name also in the case, the case may be settled. He agreed to it. The police had made arrangements to arrest Rama Shankar but he got a tip about it. The matter reached the Chief Minister. Rama Shankar pleaded for help. The whole case is now being dropped. So you exclude Rama Shankar from the list. He cannot leave the Chief Ministers camp.' Kapoor made it clear.

'Has that case been brushed aside totally?' Prandhir asked Kapoor.

'No, it has not been closed as yet.'

'Then he can be pursuaded to cross over.'

'How?'

'By assuring him that once we have our own Chief Minister, the case would be closed finally.' Sharma said confidently.

'And he can be made to understand that if the Chief Minister wishes the case can be dropped forever. But the sword of Damocles has been kept hanging on his head. He can be nabbed any time. He is a man who is of doubtful nature. Once he understands your logic, he will join you whole heartedly.

Prandhir explained his argument further.

'Will our Chief Minister drop such a serious case?' Kapoor could not digest the argument.

'Why not?' Sharma said.

'But why?,' Kapoor almost shouted.

'Why not Kapoor?' Prandhir also spoke loud.

'Will the same persons let off the accused and the smuggler who in fact have the responsibility of nabbing them?' Kapoor was outragious.

'Kapoor, it is politics. All is fair here. It is not a child's play to persuade an MLA to cross over to your side. We must compensate him for it.' Sharma tried to make him understand the point.

'And moreover, what is wrong in it? It becomes our duty to help our MLA or his brother if he is involved in a case like that. After all what for is our own government?' Prandhir explained Sharma's comment.

'It is one thing to help but it is quite another thing to hush up the crime committed by someone. Are all not equal in the eyes of justice? Joining our party does not mean that he has an immunity against law. This will encourage crimes and our party will become a group of criminals.' Kapoor's anguish was visible now.

'You are a raw youngman. You have only read books and listened the speeches of leaders. You have neither lived the real politics nor you have witnessed it as yet.' Thakur said while throwing the smoke upwards.

'Anyhow, it is beyond my comprehension. But one thing...' He was thoughtful.

'Yes, speak out please.' Sharma became alert.

'It is O.K. if you have simply to make a promise to Rama Shankar that in case we have our Chief Minister, his case would be dropped but if the promise has to be carried out also, then...' Kapoor looked towards Prandhir.

'We shall fulfil it also. We have been doing it,' Prandir said forcefully.

'Please go ahead. You have just started the list.' Kapoor expressed his disappointment.

'Kapoor, you are being sentimental. You cannot go by emotions. Politics is a game. And everything is fair in it. Power cannot be attained just by singing hymns. We shall have to play the game to get power,' Sharma said.

Kapoor was silent.

'Prandhir, go ahead. This assurance should be given to Rama Shankar. You talk to him yourself. And if you feel, I can also talk to him. To discuss the issue of dropping this case and to induct him as a Minister. So he will surely join us. Now what next?' Sharma said announcing his decision.

'The next cluster is of nine MLAs. They can be allured by money alone. They have different price tags. They can be won over by lakhs or thousands but money they must get. They are always eager to make money. Seven of them are those who have joined Congress after leaving the opposition parties. Even then we had coerced them with money. They continued making money in

Congress regime also. Last time, when the Cabinet was being formed, they frequently changed their loyalty,' Prandhir continued.

'They changed their loyalties as many times as they got price for it. I remember Prandhir that majoirity of MLAs in this list are Harijans,' Sharma interrupted.

'Yes, Mr. Sharma, majority of them but three are others too. The top five are Harijans and they are very poor. They were elected on Congress ticket. Two of them are cobblers. One of them is who used to carry shit on his head. The other two used to sell the polished leather of the dead animals. They had no status. They earned both ends meals with difficulty. Now they are leaders. They have their bungalows. They have purchased lands. They have got an element of sophistication and adamance also. But Mr. Sharma...'

'Yes, Yes, go on,' Sharma said.

'But their mindset has not changed. The more they get, the more hungry they become. The poor souls sell themselves time and again.'

'Could they have been saleable commodities even before their joining the politics?,' Kapoor asked.

'No, not then.' Sharma said.

'Yes, even a poor man in a village has his dignity.' Thakur blurted.

'No, they sell themselves also but they have some scruples too. Once they commit themselves to someone, they fulfil it. They are friends of friends. It is true poverty makes them weaker at certain moments but they stand unmoved at least for sometime. I can say that majority of poor people are not saleable,' Prandhir said.

'And these MLAs?' Kapoor inquired.

'They are prone to barter.'

'Because the big leaders who are eager to grab power indulge in buying them. If there are no buyers, how will they sell themselves. One who mended shoes till yesterday, is a member of the legislature assembly today. One who lived in a small hut, is housed in a hotel today. When people offer lakhs of rupees to buy him, he cannot restrain himself from being sold. If they were given training in clean cultural practices, they would have served the society better because they had seen poverty. They could have been made instrumental in abolishing poverty.' Kapoor's eyes were red.

'Kapoor, I do not follow what you say. We are here to plan something big here. You are delivering a futile lecture. Don't you want to change the present Chief Minister?' Sharma said angrily.

'I do want to change him and will rest only after ousting him. That is why I have joined all your hateful and mean activities only because had the Chief Minister not insulted me that day, I would never have joined you. But now I am with you and shall remain so. If that is the way to the destination, Kapoor is very much with you.'

'Well said.' They all cheered him with clapping.

'Now your plan will be successful. Kapoor is a very useful person who is clear at heart.' Rita broke her silence. She had been listening to all of them so far.

Sharma saw Rita with sharp eyes. In turn, Thakur looked at Sharma. Prandhir was silent. Kapoor looked back to have a glimpse of Rita.

'Thank you Rita,' Kapoor said smilingly.

'Proceed further,' Sharma asked Prandhir.

'I hope food is ready. We may discuss the rest after taking food.'

'No, Kapoor. I have to immediately go to Chandigarh. I have called some prominent leaders there also for the same purpose. Prandhir will also accompany me. We shall take meals after completing the issue. Sharma pointed out, 'O.K. I ask them to lay the tables a bit late.' Kapoor went the other side and returned after a few moments.

'Yes, Prandhir.'

'So these five are the Harijans. And one is Pandit Vikal Narayan among the rest four. He is as big a liar and a crook as big the 'Tilak' he pastes on his forehead. Even if we pay the price for him, we cannot be sure of his loyalty. But he is an avaricious man, always looking for money. We should manage him in such a way that the money is not lost. We shall have to entrust this job to Kapoor. He is close to him and he can manage also.'

'Sharmaji, agreed. Once I have accepted you as my leader, it is my duty to carry out your orders. But Thakur will also help me.'

'Yes, I shall be with you. We shall avail Rita's services also.'

'No, we have a bigger assignment for Rita. I shall tell her,' Sharma promptly said and kept Rita at hand. Thakur looked at Sharma with harsh eyes. Rita smiled in her thoughts.

'You may have as much money as you require. I shall hand it over before going. Yes, Prandhir, what next?'

'Now there remain eight MLAs. Three of them are from the hilly region. They own allegiance to crorepati. Jagbir who is king of illegal felling of forests. He makes them fight elections. He bears their election expenses. They follow him. We shall have to rope in Jagbir for these three MLAs.'

'Prandhir is perfectly right. Jagbir is a king of the hills. He earns crores of rupees by illegally felling trees in the forests every year. He controls all three of them. He is also annoyed with the Chief Minister these days,' Thakur revealed.

'Why is he annoyed?,' Sharma asked.

'He was the biggest timber contractor in the hills so far. No one ever challenged him. And if any one came, he could not survive. Last year the brother of Minister Dilbagh participated in the forest bid. He was in competition with Jagbir. The bid was high. Both of them quarrelled. A case is going on. It is a matter of lakhs of rupees. The officers favoured Jagbir but Dilbagh made it a prestige issue. Now the Chief Minister is helping Dilbagh's brother under his pressure. His monoply is being destroyed. He is disturbed. He can be motivated to join our camp.' Thakur finished his comment, took out a cigarette and lit it.

'Kapoor, call my P.A.,' Sharma asked.

'The signs are favourable,' Prandhir said.

'Sir,' P.A. was before Mr. Sharma.

'Just ring up Chandigarh. Jagbir is a hill contractor. A meeting between him and me should be arranged tomorrow positively. But no one else should know it.'

'All right, Sir.'

'These three have to be tackled. Go ahead.'

'These two are from the liquor fraternity. They serve them liquor and make them dance to their tunes also. We need not contact these two straightway. It will not be beneficial too. We should talk to the liquor kings. But for these two, the others are with the Chief Minister.'

'Promise them lowering of tax. If the tax is reduced, the smuggling will increase on the border. They indulge in large-scale smuggling also. They will benefit both ways.' They were surprised at Sharma's comment.

'Sharmaji, it is a ticklish path.' Kapoor heaved a deep sigh.

'I have not followed you.'

'We shall have to promote smuggling also to oust the Chief Minister?'

'Ask what we shall not do and shall not get done for it?'

'O.K. Prandhir will do it. He is on good terms with some of them. You immediately invite them for talks,' Sharma suggested.

'Now what about these three?; they are young and fond of colourful life. They are fond of drinking and dining. Think about them. We shall have to fondle them from all sides.' All were silent on Prandhir's comment.

Sharma looked at Rita. Thakur also looked at her. Rita cast her eyes downward.

'Sharmaji, why do you talk indirect. Just say, Rita will capture three of them,' Thakur said.

'Why veil yourself once you have decided to dance.' Thakur said while looking at Rita.

'Perfectly right. I was also thinking on these lines. The three of them should be introduced to Rita. They should be paid money also. And a few boxes of liquor be despatched to their houses. Rita will takecare of the rest. Will that be all right, Rita?,' Sharma looked at Rita.

'As you wish.' Rita laughed.

'After doing all this, we shall assemble again in Chandigarh. We shall have to go to the High Command at Delhi after assuring ourselves of the majority support. And much more will have to be done. Prandhir and Kapoor will shoulder responsibility here. Thakur and Rita will accompany me to Chandigarh.' Sharma got up. Kapoor went to the other room and came back after some minutes. He asked all of them to go for lunch. They all sat for lunch.

'Sir, one thing...' P.A. said appearing before him.

'Yes, say.' Sharma asked.

'Sir, there are two programmes scheduled on way to Chandigarh.'

'Yes, oh. I forgot. What are they about?'

'Sir, you have to deliver a lecture at Rotary club, Ludhiana and you have a public meeting in a poor Harijan colony.'

'O.K. We leave just after the lunch.

They all took their meals quickly. Sharma took their leave. The car was at the door with a national flag on it. Sharma asked

Thakur to sit beside him. Rita stood closeby. The luggage had been kept in the car.

'Mr. Sharma, you and Rita, go by this car. I come in another.' Thakur said looking towards Mr. Sharma.

'Yes, what did you say?,' Sharma was thinking.

'No, not like that. You all come in another car. Thakur, you sit with me. You will go with me. Sharma asked the driver to open the front seat gate. Thakur understood his intentions. He sat in the front seat. Sharma called Rita to the back seat. The car started. The people standing their said namastey with folded hands. The incumbants in the car waived their hands.

Kapoor kept watching Rita and Sharma. The car disappeared soon.

□

18

'Thanks, Sharmaji. You are welcome....' A sea of humanity converged to welcome Mr. Sharma as soon as his car reached near a big hall in Ludhiana. A large number of people with garlands in their hands stepped forward. Mr. Gupta, President of the Rotary Club himself opened the door of the car and Mr. Sharma came out. He welcomed him with a garland of flowers. With garland around his neck, Mr. Sharma moved towards the hall. Mr. Thakur and Rita followed him. The elite citizens of Ludhiana standing on both sides of the path loaded Mr. Sharma with garlands. A few ladies presented bouquets to Rita also.

It was a new experience for Rita. She had never accompanied a chief guest in a welcome function. She felt very happy to be one of the guests in the welcome function. All eyes were fixed on the Minister and Rita. Rita was delighted beyond expectation when she was presented bouquets by the women present there.

Mr. Sharma occupied the highest seat on the stage. The Rotary President, Mr. Gupta sat next to him. Mr. Thakur and Rita were also requested to sit on the dias. In a short while all the persons present took their seats. Secretary Rotary began the proceedings. The influential people from the city welcomed the Minister with garlands once again. The representatives of different organizations also greeted the Minister with flowers. A welcome song was also presented. Thereafter, the Secretary of the Rotary Club invited the President Mr. Gupta on the podium.

'We the people of Ludhiana are delighted to have honourable Minister Mr. Sharma here today. We have been thinking for quite some time to organize a function to honour the distinguished Minister Mr. Sharma and to seek his blessings. Mr. Sharma is a towering leader of our state. He is one of the most effective

Ministers in the Cabinet. He is a veteran freedom fighter. He has devoted his life to the cause of the nation and the society from his childhood. He is known for his integrity and clean image. He has never indulged in coercive politics.

'The Rotary Club is alive to the needs of the weaker sections of society and is engaged in serving them to its best ability. But sir, the most important requirements of our times is to revive the good old moral values in our behaviour. The masses are losing their faith in the persons holding high offices. There was a time when the masses responded to the dictates of the politicians spontaneously. The majority of the people believed in their leaders and leaders also maintained their credibility. But I am sorry to point out that after Independence, there is fast erosion in our moral values and we are no more eager to maintain the scruples.

'The Rotary Club organized a meeting earlier to ponder over the same problem. It was decided that a competent speaker may be invited to deliver a lecture on the topic "Relevance of Moral Values in the Social Life". We surveyed the people around. I have no hesitation in saying that it took a long time in finding out the right choice. But I am happy to say that even today there are distinguished persons like you who can speak on the topic with authority. It is the land of Lala Lajpat Rai. The state is proud of you as you have steadfastly maintained the traditions set by Lala Lajpat Rai.

'We shall organize seminars for the common masses after your key lecture. It will be our attempt to educate them about the moral values. This is the only project that we have identified for this year. Now I request the honourable guest to address the audience on the topic.' Mr. Sharma got up from his seat, kept the garlands on the table and slowly moved towards the podium. The hall once again resounded with the clapping noise.

'At the very outset, I want to compliment the Rotary Club for having chosen a topic of national significance for my speech. I am grateful to you for having invited me to deliberate on this topic. It is a basic problem that is being faced today by our country. Before Independence we all had a greater objective confronting us. Mahatma Gandhi had invested politics with morality and religious fervour. We followed him in letter and spirit. In fact, there was a need to tread on the same path after we attained freedom but unfortunately we failed to hold the tradition There is a visible erosion in our moral values.

'Riches and the economic propensity is not the only index of greatness of a country. India was a rich and prosperous country before it fell to the invaders. In fact, loss of our national character and erosion in moral values led us to our downfall. We were subjected to slavery for thousands of years. The nations survive because of their moral fibre. If we lose our moral strength today, our liberty will be at stake once again.

'Politics in post-independent India has been infested with selfishness and conspiracies. Everyone of us wants to grab property, power and position by hook or by crook. Moral values have been left far behind in the race for power and pelf. Before freedom, our destination was India and we were devoted to its welfare only. But today, it appears that our destination is power and pelf only and not the nation.' There was a huge applause for the sentiments of the Minister. Tears trickled down the eyes of some of the spectators even. The audience felt that the Minister had revealed a great truth and was a true coterie of it.

'I have no hesitation in holding leading personalities responsible for degradation in social and moral values. The impact percolates from the top to bottom. Our target is not power and position, it is the means to attain our objective. Mahatma Gandhi had advocated that we could not achieve our right cause by wrong means. I have always tried to follow the principles propagated by Mahatma Gandhi in my long political career. My aim in life has been to serve the people. I may or may not be in power and position but I am committed to the cause of the people.' The hall once again resounded with the clapping of the audience.

'Unfortunately, a new philosophy has emerged these days. The new culture advocates, one may adopt any means to get one's work done. Money and other temptations may be used to get the favours. They use even nefarious means to strengthen their positions. We must take a pledge today that we shall not use any wrong or illegal means to achieve our objects even if we lose our power and position or if we are not able to get our personal works done.' Rita had been listening to the comments of Mr. Sharma intently and was surprised to hear all those lofty ideals. She was reminded what had happened at Mr. Kapoor's residence in Jallandhar. Mr. Sharma had vociferously advocated the policy of inducing defection and dissidence to oust the Chief Minister. In that very meeting, when Kapoor had opposed the use of unfair means to oust the CM, Mr. Sharma had said, 'All is fair in love and war.' Rita had now two images of Mr. Sharma in her mind, one the Sharma that justified any kind of fair or foul means to oust the CM and the other who was advocating the ideals in morality in his speech at the Rotary function. She was not able to decide who was the real one of the two images. She was amazed at the transformation of ideas of Mr. Sharma in such a short span of time.

'If we could swear not to use unfair or immoral means to get our work done, India would emerge stronger and stronger. I am sorry that majority of the people talk about moral values and deliver ideal lectures but no one follows the tenets in practice'. Some youths sitting in the back seats of the hall cheered him with clapping. Rita again focused her attention on what Mr. Sharma was saying in his speech.

'I had started my political career under the patronage of Mahatma Gandhi. I have seen many ups and downs in my life. I have passed through adversity and prosperity in my life but I never compromised on moral grounds. May be it is the reason that you have invited me to sermonize on this topic.'

The leading personalities of Ludhiana were present in the audience and they all listened the lecture attentively. There was a strange kind of smile on some of the faces. Perhaps they had known Mr. Sharma closely.

In the end, a vote of thanks was presented. 'We are obliged to Mr. Sharma for having taken out some time from his busy schedule to deliver a lecture on this particular topic. His meaningful advice on moral values will show us the right path. Mr. Sharma is a seasoned political leader of the state. He has upheld the traditions set by Mahatma Gandhi. I on behalf of the Rotary Club thank him from the core of my heart.' After going through the club formalities, all the guests assembled in the lawn close to the hall for light refreshment. Mr. Sharma was surrounded by known and unknown people. They were all talking to him, giving their reactions and appreciations. Some leaders of the party were introducing some important people to Mr. Sharma. Mr. Sharma felt happy when someone said, 'Never ever I heard such a meaningful speech'. A few of the persons were meeting him for personal works. They were now enjoying the snacks. Some of the ladies were discussing things with Rita. Some persons were talking to Mr. Thakur also.

Mr. Prem Kapoor joined them in the tea party. He took Mr. Sharma aside and whispered something in his ears. Mr. Sharma called Thakur and asked him to talk to Mr. Kapoor in privacy. With cups in their hands. Mr. Thakur and Mr. Kapoor moved to a corner.

'I have come to know from a source that the Chief Minister is also wooing some of the MLAs. He has invited them to Chandigarh and has made special arrangements for their transportation. It is also learnt that he is tipping some MLAs by offering them different positions.' Mr. Kapoor shared his information while sipping tea.

'But how could the Chief Minister know about all this? We had confined the entire information to us.' Thakur said expressing his surprise.

'Don't forget he is the Chief Minister. He has his men every where. And CID people also work for him.'

'That is right.'

'How should we go ahead?'

'You need not worry. The Chief Minister will come to know that we are trying to oust him. He will also try to counter our move.'

'I am reminded of one thing.'

'What?'

'Mr. Sharma had asked for raising funds to win some MLAs. I don't know if he remembers it. If the Chief Minister is also making efforts to woo MLAs, we shall have to try harder. We shall require more money. Money can be arranged from Ludhiana. We should remind him about this.'

'All right.' Kapoor did not evince keenness in the proposal. Mr. Thakur went to Mr. Sharma and brought him to the exclusive corner. Apprising him of the latest developments, he said, 'Do you know what Kapoor has said? The Chief Minister has come to know about our plan. He has also started to mobilize MLAs in his favour. We shall have to put in extra effort now. And we require relatively bigger amount of money. You once pointed out that you had granted permission to some new industries. It's better if you can talk to them immediately.'

'That's good. You have reminded me at the right time.' Mr. Sharma moved in another direction with his cup of tea in his hands. He was looking with searching eyes. He moved forward and called someone to come to him. He went along with him in a lonely corner.

'Yash, we are facing a great problem these days. We need your help.'

'You need not worry Mr. Sharma. You have established me. I am at your back and call. You just order what you want.'

'The present Chief Minister is not performing well. Majority of the MLAs want me to be the Chief Minister. Since all of them wish to install me at the helm of affairs, I feel I should accept their desire. But we shall have to work very hard. And to mobilize MLAs in our favour, we require huge amount of money.' Mr. Sharma whispered in Yash's ears.

'How much do you need?' Yash asked in a low tone.

'How much can you contribute?'

'Whatever you require?'

'Well said. I am proud of you. You arrange ₹ 2 Lakhs for the time being.'

'Where should I hand it over?'

'You bring it to me at Chandigarh.'

'All right.'

Mr. Sharma moved in another direction. He identified two three more persons and told them to contribute for the purpose. Later he called Thakur and told him that he had arranged for ` Eight Lakh. And asked him if that was sufficient amount for the purpose.

'Eight means...eight?'

'Yes, exactly eight.'

'Thousands?'

'No. Thakur, no. Thousands cannot topple governments. It requires lakhs of rupees.' Mr. Sharma whispered into Thakur's ears.

Thakur blushed at the news. A person came to Mr. Sharma, took his empty cup of tea and brought another cup for him.

A group of youth was busy taking tea in one corner. They were discussing something and would burst into laughter occasionally. None of them came to the Minister. There were other MLAs also but the young brigade was least worried about them. Probably, they did comment about the Minister or the MLAs but they appeared to be enjoying their own fraternity.

'They chose such a Minister for deliberating on moral values who is totally bereft of the same,' one of the youth commented.

'Sharma has his shares in many industries located in Ludhiana and he gets his share monthly.'

The owner of Swadesh Industries not only obliges Mr. Sharma monetarily but arranges so many other things for him. Whenever Mr. Sharma comes to Ludhiana, he does not stay in the circuit house but prefers to stay in the guest house of Swadesh Industries where he is served with women and wine'.

'They say Mr. Sharma is not on good terms with the Chief Minister these days.'

'It is heard that Mr. Sharma has formed a dissident group of his own and is trying to oust the Chief Minister and to occupy the coveted post himself.'

'And he is trying hard to mobilize MLAs in his favour.'

'Both the groups are very active these days. To keep the MLAs with their groups, both sides are collecting money for horse trading.'

'And interestingly, our Rotary Club has invited Mr. Sharma to deliver a sermon on moral values.' Hearing this all the young boys burst into laughter and attracted the attention of the gathering there.

They all came out after the tea session was over. The office-bearers of the Rotary Club were escorting Mr. Sharma to his car. They all bade him good-bye. Thakur occupied a seat in the front and Rita sat in one of the back seats. The youths were watching all this. One of them asked his friend. 'Who is the lady accompanying Mr. Sharma?'

"I don't know.'

'Is she Mr. Sharma's wife?'

'No, not at all. I have seen his wife. It is not she.'

'Then who is she?'

'May be someone who shares moral values with him.' They all laughed loudly.

Mr. Sharma noticed their laughter while sitting in the car. The car started and left the place for its destination.

□

19

There was a Harijan colony adjacent to a village located on the Chandigarh-Ludhiana Highway. There were colourful buntings on the way from the metalled road towards the colony. The kachcha road had been repaired. Gates had been erected at two points. The poor Harijan colony normally presented a gloomy outlook but it was vibrant with life today. A few government officers and employees were already present in the area. There was also a movement of the vehicles. A stage had also come up in the ground adjoining the colony. The news of the arrival of the Minister was being announced on the public address system. Some tents close to the dias had also sprung up. Plates had been arranged on the tables already. Cooking was going on nearby. Its fragrance had engulfed the entire populace.

The villagers dressed neatly were coming out of their homes. The children were already roaming about the function pandal. They would run from one place to the other in a jovial mood or they would reach the stage close to the mike. The organizers stopped the children from making noise. The village women in their colourful attires were marching towards the ground. With wrinkles on their faces, the old men were also walking towards the stage. All eyes were on the road.

'He has come... the Minister has come,' this course was now audible from all sides. A few officers moved forward. They asked the people to stand in lines on both sides of the road. Efforts were being made to seat the children on the carpets.

With his hands folded, the Minister was heading towards the stage. A few partymen along with some officers were with him. Rita followed him. Some persons garlanded the Minister. the women showered flowers on him. Slogans such as 'zindabad' were raised with enthusiasm. The Minister occupied a chair on the stage.

A young man clad in khaddar clothes came to the mike and welcomed the chief guest. He called some persons who came to the stage and garlanded the Minister.

'It is a matter of great pride for us that a senior Minister has come to the Harijan colony. No one believed me when I told the poor people about the programme of the Minister to visit this place. They retorted that how and why should such a senior Minister could come to our village. But I was confident that Mr. Sharma would certainly visit us. On behalf of the poor populace of this village, I welcome Mr. Sharma, the honourable Minister, from the core of my heart.'

The village Pradhan read a citation in honour of the Minister wherein he was compared with Lala Lajpat Rai and Mahatma Gandhi. Specific words had been chosen to eulogise him. Mr. Sharma was described as a great leader and a messiah of the poor. Seasoned party workers had been seated among the crowd at different places so that they would induce the spectators for clapping intermittently. Whenever any speaker showered praise on Mr. Sharma, clapping would start from one corner or the other and rest of the audience followed suit. Sometimes the enthusiastic party workers gave a big hand without any spur also. The Pradhan presented the framed citation to the Minister which was gleefully accepted in a bowed manner by the chief guest. The audience once again clapped vigorously.

'It will go as a historic day in the history of our village. We the Harijans can never forget this moment. The Congress not only obtained freedom for the country but for the Harijans also. The party has given a new lease of life to the Harijans, who have been treated as downtrodden for centuries together. Our party is marching ahead on the new path of socialism. The coming of Mr. Sharma here is indicative of the fact that our party is the party of the poor and the Harijans.' One of the leaders from the area concluded his speech with these words and earned a great applause from the audience. More speakers came on the stage one after the other. They all showered praise on the party, its policies and Mr. Sharma.

In the end Mr. Sharma took the podium. He said, 'My dear Harijan brethren. I am happy to be amongst you. The local MLA had been requesting me time and again to visit your village but my engagements delayed the programme. I am sorry I could not come earlier. My party has launched a number of welfare schemes for the poor and the Harijans. We are following the ideals set by Mahatma Gandhi. Mahatma Gandhi had said, 'The true India lives in the villages. If we want to uplift our country, we shall have to work for the upliftment of the villages. The poor live in the villages. As long as we do not uplift the poor, freedom is meaningless."

'Brothers and sisters, we attained political freedom in 1947 but this is not the end. The departure of the Englishmen has not set all things right. We must remove poverty, unemployment and backwardness. You will be delighted to know that our party is devoted to this cause. We have to transform India into a welfare state. We have recently announced socialism as our objective. Our government is working for the common poor man.

'I want to caution all my poor fellows against one thing. It is a fact that Congress achieved freedom for India but many other parties are vying these days to attain power. Some parties are guided by the foreign powers and others by the capitalists. They are least bothered for the country. Our party is the only party that is committed to the welfare of the poor community. You should not be taken in by the false propaganda of these parties. They dance to the tunes of the rich people. If they grab power, they will make life miserable for the poor masses.'

The audience clapped at regular intervals to appreciate the sentiments of the Minister. Zindabad slogans were also raised at times. The veteran party workers of the village presented a vote of thanks in the end. The function was followed by sumptuous tea party. Sweets and snacks were laid on the tables. The children were trying to slouch in. They were tempted by the sweets but the persons on duty pushed them out. The poor villagers were talking to each other standing out of the tent arena. Some ladies were also trying to peep in. They were least worried about the Minister or the guests there. They were looking at the plates full of sweets and snacks. The tea was over, the Minister came out and proceeded towards his car.

'Sir, I have to make a request,' the old man said with folded hands.

'Yes, do tell me your tale.' The Minister stopped.

'I am a poor helpless man. I don't have any offspring. I am all alone in this world. I do not have any source of income. I had a small hut to live in. It was blown away by the storm recently. I don't have a shelter now. I am staying with a neighbour these days. I am too old to work. Kindly help me.' He touched the feet of the Minister with his folded hands and bowed his head at his feet.

'All right. Send your request in writing. The government will surely help you.'

'Sir, I also want to make a point,' a woman said moving closer to the Minister. She was an old woman wrapped in rags. She was trembling. May be she was speaking to a Minister for the first time.

'Yes. yes.'

'My husband is dead. I don't have a source of income. The land where I live in a hut belongs to the Pradhan of the village. The person who read the citation in your honour wants to eject me out. I pray the government makes arrangement for my shelter and also helps me financially so that I can perform the marriage ceremony of my daughter.'

It's O.K. Give an application in writing, ' the Minister moved forward.

'There is no light in our village even today.'

'The village road is kachcha so far. It is difficult to move on it during rains.'

'Even the drinking water is not available to us. The villagers are compelled to take water from the pond which is not potable.'

The village needs a high school too.'

'Agreed but all the facilities cannot be provided simultaneously. It requires a huge amount. The government will solve the problems one by one gradually.' The Minister said in an exhausted tone.

'Sir, you are right. We do not want all the demands to be translated into action in one stroke. But I must request you for tarring the road and to make provision for drinking water in the first instance. The department has told us that there is provision of, rupees five thousand only in the budget but they require rupees fifty thousand for the target. If this is the way of the department, the road will take ten years to be rendered pucca,' a young man said confidently.

'And same is the case with the drinking water scheme. The scheme was conceived many years ago. It is projected in the budget every year. It requires rupees two lakh in all but this year only fifteen thousand rupee has been allocated. It means we shall have to wait for many years before we get the potable water. The government has extended facilities of pucca roads, drinking water and electricity, etc. to the cities but the villages are sans these facilities,' another youngman said.

'I have listened to your demands intently. The developmental scemes require huge amounts. The allocations for different schemes are made by the government on the basis of money available in the public coffers. I shall try at my level that more money is allocated for the development of your village,' the Minister assured the people around and stepped towards his car. The villagers were also moving forward. They wanted to present their demands. The local MLA did not allow them to go closer to the Minister. He himself accompanied the Minister to his car. The sky resounded with the slogans of zindabad. The villagers looked at the caravan of cars curiously. There was dust and dust all around.

□

20

The political activities had intensified in the capital. The Chief Minister Mr. Vishal Singh was in constant touch with his supporters. He was told by some MLAs that Dhanwant Sharma was trying to win over the dissident MLAs to his side. The Chief Minister had asked his confidant Mr. Pawan Lal to keep a watch on the activities. Pawan enquired from all sources. He talked to some CID officers who were close to him. He consulted some journalists also. Pawan then told the Chief Minister that efforts were afoot to oust him.

The Cabinet meeting was scheduled that day. One hour before the meeting, the Chief Minister called Mr. Sharma to his office. Mr. Sharma responded to the call immediately and was soon with the Chief Minister in a jovial mood.

'Mr. Sharma, you are one of my old friends. You are one of my confidant supporters in the Cabinet. I have been watching you for quite some days that you do not seem to be yourself. If there is anything wrong, please do share it with me. I have called you individually for the purpose.' The Chief Minister initiated the dialogue.

'I also have been thinking of meeting you. I have learnt that you have some misconception about me. Mr. Vishal Singh, you should not forget that there are some persons who do not relish our closeness. They are jealous of us. They want us to fall apart. They want to create differences between us. They are backbiters. I have accepted you as my leader. Trust me, I am your faithful soldier.' While expressing his viewpoint, Mr. Sharma looked downwards and could look upwards only effortfully. He was respectful to the Chief Minister.

'I also felt the same way. I can never be doubtful about you. But I am not able to understand why such rumours are floated about you again and again? Why some persons discuss all these things?'

'Can I know about such people?'

'Some ministers and some MLAs.'

'Such persons are neither your friends nor mine.'

The Chief Minister looked at Mr. Sharma in a hush hush manner. Sharma's gaze was not consistent. He kept silent for some time. After a pause, Mr. Sharma said, 'Such persons are enemies of our party also. Our party is so big and old. You have been chosen as the Chief Minister. Delhi High Command is happy with you. So why should we think of dislodging you? And even if someone tried to act that way, he would not be successful.'

'But Mr. Sharma, why such reports are emerging from the CID sources also?'

'What kind of report?'

'It is reported that a meeting was held at Jallandhar wherein you and some MLAs participated. A list of MLAs was drawn there. It was discussed how the MLAs could be won over. And a woman from the hills had also come specially.'

Hearing this, Mr. Sharma felt uneasy. There was strange sort of expression on his face. He responded cautiously, 'I feel there are our enemies in the CID also. If such reports continue, there will be a split in the party. They will create something out of nothing. It will have to be investigated how and from where the report originated.'

'I was also perturbed to read this report. I could not believe it. I thought someone sitting in Chandigarh must have made this mischievous report. I called the IG and enquired about the same. He told me that the report had been received from Jallandhar itself.'

'No, Mr. Chief Minister, this report is totally false. No such meeting was held there. Neither it could have been thought of. I can assure you of my support and shall ask you to continue as the Chief Minister. No one can harm you. You leave it to me, I have never deceived anyone in my life. I shall prefer to die rather than deceive my leader.'

'O.K. Sharmaji. I expect the same sentiments from you. I shall get it examined who is behind this conspiracy. We shall have to be cautious against such elements. You have now assured me, I am rid of the anxiety now. I am grateful to you.' The Chief Minister got up from his chair. Mr. Sharma shook hands with him warmly. They exchanged pleasant smiles and Mr. Sharma came out of the office.

The Chief Minister asked his PA to send Pawan Lal to him. After a few minutes, Pawan Lal came to the Chief Minister.

'Pawan, I have discussed the entire issue with Mr. Sharma. Your information is totally wrong. CID report is also not true. Sharma is totally loyal to me. I feel someone is playing mischief to create a wedge in the party.'

'Mr. Chief Minister, you are so simple; Pawan's report cannot be wrong. I do not want to say anything on the basis of CID report. There can be a scope for error but my sources cannot be wrong. Did you ask Sharma about the Jallandhar meeting?'

'Yes, I did ask.'

'What did Mr. Sharma say?'

'He bluntly refused and said no such meeting had been held there.'

'Sharma is misleading you then.'

'What do you mean?'

'The meeting had definitely been held there. I have got a detailed report about it. The meeting was held in the newly built house of Prem Kapoor located on the outskirts of Jallandhar. Sharma, Prem Kapoor and Thakur were present in the meeting. A lady named Rita had come there with Thakur. She has been newly inducted in our party. The meeting lasted for full five hours, all of them took their meals together. Separate lists of MLAs were drawn. It was discussed who and how they could be won over by coercing them. I can prove it that the meeting had been held and Mr. Sharma was present there.'

'What is the source of your information?'

'I have my confidant CID officer there. He had deputed a person to have vigil on Kapoor. He pays monthly allowance to one of the Kapoor's servants. The same servant gave all the information. He is the confidant of Kapoor. He attended the members for serving water and tea, etc. He sat outside the meeting room also. Not only this, he has passed on a chit written by Prandhir Singh's hand also, wherein he has written the names of MLAs.'

'Was Prandhir also in that meeting?'

'Yes, he was also there, I forgot to tell you his name.'

'I am unable to understand whom should I believe. Sharma was just discussing his faithfulness and you say he is the person causing dissidence.'

'Mr. Chief Minister, the rebel will never accept before you that he is trying for a rift in the party. He can form a splinter group only by keeping you in the dark. You need not worry. I have come across many Sharma-brand people. I am making all the arrangements, I have talked to a large number of MLAs. I shall arrange their meeting with you very soon. You need not to worry as long as Pawan is there.'

The Chief Minister was silent for a few moments. He rubbed his eyes with his fingers and looked at Pawan intently.

'All right. I trust your ability fully.'

Pawan stood up, shook his hands and came out of the room.

The Chief Minister talked to his PA on phone and then relaxed into his chair with closed eyes.

'You appear to be somewhat tired,' Harijan Minister Darshan Singh said to him after entering the office.

'No, I was just waiting for you. Did you enquire about that?'

'Yes, I have enquired. The meeting was held at Jallandhar. Since Mr. Sharma has arrived in Chandigarh, his activities have spurred up. Efforts are afoot to win over our MLAs. My supporter Harijan MLA is being allured with money. They promised Pyar Singh a sum of ` Twenty-Five Thousand yesterday. They also gave an understanding that in case Mr. Sharma becomes the Chief Minister, Pyar Singh would replace me as Minister.'

'Pawan Lal also told similar things.'

'Mr. Chief Minister, you should be cautious against Pawan Lal also.'

'What do you mean?'

'I mean what I say. Pawan Lal is a liar of the first order and a manipulator. He is working for you these days but in fact, he is moulding things for himself. Taking advantage of the tussle between you and the dissidents, he wants to be decorated as the Chief Minister. Beware of him fully.'

'But he expressed complete loyalty to me today.'

'Sharma might have also expressed his loyalty to you.'

'Yes, I had called Sharma also today. We discussed things at length. He even said that he would prefer to die rather than sabotage my chief ministership.'

'How great of Sharma? Ignoring his Ministry, he is busy sabotaging you day and night. He already thinks himself to be the Chief Minister and has allocated the different portfolios to his friends. And he is swearing commitment to you.'

'Darshan Singh, I am unable to make out. Whom should I trust and whom I should not.'

'Why can't we make it out. There is need to read the faces in their true colour. They are not the same inside and outside. Leave it to me. I am an illiterate, poor Harijan but I have seen the times. I am watching their movements minutely. I shall not allow them to harm you in any way. You should not do any thing visible but keep a watch on Pawan Lal.'

'All right. You please keep a vigil.'

Both of them got up.

□

21

The sky was overcaste with clouds for many days. It had rained intermittently. The chill was on the increase. It was a bright day today after many days. It was a sunny day. Some of the people were roaming about in their lawns and talking to each other. Children were playing at some of the places. Sitting in the Sun, a few students were reading their books.

The morning today in Kullu was very pleasant. The small Kullu valley was surrounded by mountains on three sides. On the right side, the murmuring waters of Beas river flowed down. There was a hillock on one side of the Beas river with steep slopes. The birds were also chirping in the sun.

Unaware of all these activities, Ranjit and Shankar were moving farther away from Kullu town. They talked to each other at moments in between and would continue to walk ahead. A bus came from behind. Shankar raised his hand, the bus stopped and they boarded it. The conductor asked Shankar about their destination. He pointed his finger towards Ranjit.

'Just a little distance farther.' Ranjit said.

'Please tell me the name of the place so that I issue tickets accordingly.'

'If we had known the name of the place, we would not have been confused.' Ranjit said in an irritated tone.

'Where for should I issue the ticket?'

'For anywhere.'

'What do you mean!'

'In fact, we do not know the place where we have to go. We recognize the place but do not know its name. Now please decide yourself where for the ticket is to be booked.'

The conductor stared at them.

'Please keep this note with you and you issue us the ticket when the spot comes.' Shankar gave a five rupee note to the conductor.

The conductor passed by them.

'It is just the beginning.'

'Let us see what happens next. . .'

Shankar was in a thoughtful mood and Ranjit had his eyes on the road. He was searching the place where he had stopped the jeep to drop the girl on the evening of Dussehra. He tried to recollect the spot. The bus was running at a high speed but his mind was even faster in thought. At times he felt, he was at the spot. Then he would think that that was not the same place.

'This is the place where she had met.' Suddenly, Ranjit spoke aloud.

'Really! Here?'

'Yes, exactly at the same place. I remember it. I had seen these boulders at the same place in the light when the jeep had stopped. They were walking on foot on the left side of the road. I had stopped the jeep near this boulder as desired by Pramod and they had got in here.'

'Ranjit, now be alert. If we have located this spot, we shall be able to spot that place also where they had got down.'

'Why not, Shankar! Ranjit will not rest till she is located.'

The bus stopped after covering some distance. A few passengers got down and a few others, boarded the bus. Ranjit Singh with his head out of the window looked watchfully all around.

'That appeared to be the similar place.' Ranjit said looking at Shankar.

'Watch it seriously. We must locate the particular place.'

'I am trying my best. I am not able to recollect. No, this is not the same place. May be it is farther away.' Ranjit was not looking out now.

The bus moved on. Shankar was looking intently on Ranjit's face. Ranjit peeped out of the window and fixed his gaze on the road passing by.

'The turn ahead—there was also a turn. May be this is the place we are looking for. There was a big tree before the turn. Some stones were lying under the tree. They had got down there. Shankar I think we are nearing the place we are trying to locate.'

Shankar looked at Ranjit anxiously and at other times, he looked at the bus passengers. Then he fixed his eyes on the road ahead. Pramod flashed in his imagination.

'Yes, please. Stop the bus here.' Ranjit requested the conductor. Ranjit got down and Shankar followed him.

'Please take your remainder.'

'No please. You keep it. We have found the place.' Shankar moved on.

The bus went on its way.

There was a tree on the road side and some boulders were also lying there. Ranjit did not find any other sign there. They looked around but there was no house nearby. There was no way in any direction. Ranjit sat on a boulder. He kept his hands on his head and said, 'It's a strange case. We have made it to this place. Where next we should go? Neither the name is known nor there is any way to anywhere from here.'

'Are you sure that you are not mistaken? This does not appear to be the place. She must have landed at a spot from where some path emerged. There must be a village nearby. Neither any village nor any path is visible here.'

'I am also thinking the same way. But Shankar, this appears to be the desired spot.'

'Let us go further and find it out.' Both of them moved onwards. They met some boys coming there way. Both of them were walking silently. They stopped when they reached those boys. Shankar said, 'Ranjit, ask these boys. They appear to hail from this place.'

'What should I ask? You tell me what should I ask?'

'You are right in your statement. What can be asked? We don't have any knowledge.'

'Oh children, please come here. Is there any village on the left side of the road?'

'Yes, there is. You go further some distance. There is a way towards the left. That way will take you straight to that village.'

'Thank you.'

'Shankar, this is the place. We were going in the same direction that day. They had turned the left side after getting down the jeep. I feel we are gradually heading towards our destination.'

'My god! We reach the desired spot or I am...' Shankar was reminded that he had brought Ranjit on some other pretext. They both went on silently. It was a sunny day after many days. The sun provided comfort in the chilly weather. However, they were not worried about the weather. Shankar was worried.

'Look here Shankar. Here is the way to the village.' Ranjit jumped with joy.

'Agreed, let us go this way.' Both of them left the main road and took the bylane.

'Shankar, tell me what shall we enquire in the village?'

'I am also not able to make it out.'

'When we are not clear, how we shall proceed in the matter! How will we enquire about her?'

'I have been thinking since last night. What and how we shall seek the information? I am at a loss to decide. It is a ticklish job.' Shankar heaved a deep sigh.

'Don't worry. We are from the police department. We shall find out some way before we reach the village.'

'But Shankar, you will kindly do this job. You have come to the village often for investigations. You are experienced. I am just a driver. I have located the spot. And I shall reach you the village also. Rest is your job.'

'You had seen her. Your job does not end by taking me to the village. You will have to arrange her meeting with me.'

'I shall do that provided I recognize her. But Shankar I had only a sudden glimpse of her and that too stands very dim in my imagination. It will be difficult for me to identify the picture in my mind on seeing the actual one.'

They were happy to find that they were close to the village now. On reaching the village, they contacted the Nambardar.

'Sir, he is Mr. Shankar Lal. He has come from the Kullu Police Station for some investigation.' The Nambardar became a bit cautious finding that they were from the police department. He greeted them with folded hands. He asked them to sit on the cot. He went into his house and came out with a dari. He put it on the floor and sat on it. He said, 'Kindly tell me what investigation you have to do?'

'Some of the girls were walking on the road on Dussehra evening. The police has learnt that some one teased them that day'. Shankar initiated the conversation.

'No. Nothing of the sort happened. Had there been any such incident with the girls of our village, they must had told me.

Moreover, there is no such culture of the plains rampant in the villages close to our village. The girls continued to reach their homes on Dussehra night but no one registered any complaint.' Nambardar said in a surprised tone.

'Nambardarji, police is always aware of all the incidents and Mr. Shankar Lal is a senior officer in the police. May be the girls did not report to you just out of modesty. If such incidents are allowed to happen without a check, the miscreants will feel encouraged. Don't feel embarrassed. You tell us the truth.' Ranjit tried to handle the situation wisely.

'You are right. I would have myself reported the matter to the police in case any such thing had happened but nothing happened. No girl said to me anything. Moreover, none else discussed it with me. So how can we bring it to your notice after so many days that such kind of incident happened.'

'That would be commendable if no such thing occurred. You appear to be hesitant in revealing the truth. This is not good on your part. We are responsible for maintaining law and order. We exist for this purpose. We are worried since we came to know that the incident happened in your village. We shall not allow such incidents to happen in our area.'

'It's all right. But when no one has reported it to me, how can I tell about it to you?'

'Can you arrange our meeting with those girls?' Shankar Lal meekly said.

'Which girls?'

'The same girls!'

The same girls, I am not able to follow you. When no incident happened in my village and no one reported it to me, with whom should I arrange your meeting?'

'You arrange our conference with all those girls.' Ranjit suggested.

'This does not make any sense.' The irritated Nambardar blurted.

'You can do one thing. It had rained on one of the Dussehra days. Some of the girls who had gone to see Dussehra had returned in the evening. You may call a few of those girls. They had come across a jeep. The occupants of the jeep had given them a lift and had dropped the girls in your village. Kindly find out those girls and arrange our meeting with them,' Ranjit said to the Nambardar.

This is just like a riddle. You know all our girls go to Kullu daily during Dussehra festival. Whom should I call? Should I call the entire village?'

'We have come from the police station. The government has ordered us to investigate. If you cannot arrange our meeting with those girls, you accompany us to the police station.'

On hearing this, a chill went down the spinal chord of the Nambardar. He felt uneasy at the thought of the police station.

'I do not mean that. I just enquire about them. Why go to the police station. I arrange your meeting with them here itself,' said the Nambardar. Then he went in and came out with two glasses of tea. He served the tea to them. And then he went into the houses that stood opposite to his residence. They started sipping tea.

'Your plan has worked. Let us see now if we get at anything.' Ranjit commented while taking tea.

'Let us hope we are successful in our mission otherwise it would be discouraging for us. I am feeling bad to think about all this,' Shankar said woefully.

'Shankar, why worry so much? If we cannot find her, it's O.K. Pramod has gone to Keylong. He has been punished much. He was not that bad. He commited only one blunder. He picked a quarrel with Khushal otherwise he was a nice man. Neither he took liquor nor he ate meat. He was unlike a policeman. I felt pity on him many a time. Shankar, he has been punished sufficiently,' Said Ranjit while keeping his empty glass on the table.

'No, no, Ranjit, he has not been punished as yet. We think when we unravel this episode, we shall be able to pay back Khushal thereafter.'

Nambardar came to them with three girls. These are the three girls who had gone to Kullu on the rainy day. You can ask them whatever you want.'

'Please come and sit here. When did you return from Dussehra on that rainy day?' Shankar asked them in a serious tone.

'In the evening.'

'Where did it rain on your way?'

'Almost halfway through.'

'How did you reach home, then?'

'Drenched in rain.'

'Did you come across any jeep on the way?'

There were many vehicles going and coming.'

'Did any jeep stop for you and you came by it to your village'

'No. Neither any jeep stopped for us nor we came to the village in it. We walked the entire distance on foot. We were all drenched badly on that day.'

'How many girls had gone to Kullu?'

'We were ten to twelve girls in all and eight to ten boys who had gone to Kullu.'

'O.K. You may go.' Shankar said pessimistically. Ranjit looked at Shankar.

'Mr. Nambardar, which is the other village adjacent to this village? Had the girls from those villages also gone to Kullu?'

'Girls from all the villages had gone to Kullu.'

'Please try to understand that the issue is very serious. We have instructions from our high ups that the names of those girls who boarded the jeep that night must be communicated to them. Kindly help us wholeheartedly.'

'I am ready to help you but there should be some information. They were the only girls from my village, others belonged to nearby villages. But these girls never got into the jeep. Where should I locate the girls who actually boarded the jeep?'

'You accompany us to the nearby village.'

'All right, I am ready to go.'

Ranjit and Shankar made their way to another village along with the Nambardar. There were small villages located on the way with short distance from each other. They enquired in all the villages. The villagers reacted astonishingly at the query. They were not even ready to talk on the issue initially but the police tag made them cooperate. Even after investigations in all the villages, they could not find any such girl who had boarded the jeep. Meanwhile some of the girls had gone out and a few of them lived in the city for their studies. They had come home during Dussehra holidays but now had gone back to their places. Two or three girls were employed outside the village. They were also not at home at this time. Leaving those girls, Shankar enquired from all other girls but could not find out the desired one.

Tired and exhausted completely Shankar and Ranjit reached the road in the evening. They had been on the move for the whole of the day. They had not taken their meals. They are tired in body and mind because they had not been successful in their mission. Ranjit stopped a truck coming from the opposite direction. Both of them came to Kullu by it.

□

22

Shankar went straight to his lodge, tired and tense. He was unsuccessful in helping his friend Pramod. He was so depressed that he forgot to go to his friend's place even. He was going through the hassle once again. Ranjit was the only person who could have helped to trace her but even he failed in his attempt. Shankar was worried about Pramod's reaction. He knew well that he was obsessed with the girl. It bordered infatuation. Pramod will not be satisfied until and unless she was located. Shankar's efforts had proved futile.

Shankar got up after a nap. It was deep dark outside. Pramod might have been waiting for him, he thought. If I do not go to him just now, he may be frustrated. It would be difficult to face him. What and how he will explain the failure of the campaign to him, he felt uneasy at this thought. He got up from his bed in a huff and was on his way to Pramod's place.

Pramod was roaming to and fro outside his room. Shankar saw him and stopped for a moment. He was a bit confused to decide how to handle the situation. However, he summoned courage and went to Pramod for the disclosure.

'Shankar, I have been madly waiting for you. Welcome, my dear friend,' Pramod's heartbeat had increased. He was perspiring profusely. Anxiety was writ large on his face.

'Pardon me Pramod, I am late in coming to you. Let us go in.' He caught Pramod's hand and they both walked in.

'Pramod, I am sorry I could not do any thing for you. We tried our best throughout the day to locate her but to no avail. Ranjit helped me earnestly but nonetheless we failed in our mission. I can understand your feelings but what cannot be cured must be endured,' Shankar consoled him. Tears rolled down the eyes of Pramod.

'Shankar, please tell me the story in detail. Also suggest the alternative,' Pramod urged him.

'Be bold, my friend. Face the situation calmly. Who never had any relation with you and was not even known to you, why wail for him. Youth is a gift. Don't waste it. The only alternative is to forget her.' Shankar delivered the sermon.

'No Shankar, I can forget any thing but not her. My intellect does advise me to forget her but my heart jumps in protest.'

'What do you plan next?'

'I shall wait.'

'How long?'

'As long as I can't find her.'

'Pramod, you will never find her. We do not know her whereabouts. Only Ranjit knew where she had got down the jeep on the road side. He identified the place and we followed the route to the village. Surveyed all the possibilities. We went there on the pretext of police investigation in the case. The Nambardar and others helped us in our queries but the entire exercise proved futile. We could not find her. There is no ray of hope at the moment. You intend to wait for her endlessly. That is ridiculous. You won't be able to trace her. I shall never allow you to waste time and your vibrant youth. The flicker has gone out. Take heart and breed new hopes in life.' Shankar went on to console him.

'Shankar, may be you are right. Sometimes I also think the same way. I understand I shall not be able to mould things my way.'

'You need not worry. Time is the greatest healer. You will have new ideas and new hopes emerging. That will make you forget her.'

'You may be right. But it is not that easy to forget her. It is the place where I fell in love with her at the first sight. It is the land of beauty and charms. However, I am destined to leave it as I am transferred to Keylong.' Pramod was emotional in his speech.

'That's the true spirit. If you continue to stay here, she will haunt you but once you leave the place, you will gradually phase her out from your memory.

'All right, Shankar. I am prepared to accept the verdict of the time. I shall try to be myself. I have to look after my family also. I must leave for Keylong very soon, may be tomorrow.'

'That is nice. You should not stay put here any more. You have your detractor in Khushal. And someone told Prakash Verma yesterday that you had not left for Kullu as yet. Thank god Thakur is not here these days. He would have forced you to leave immediately. So it would be in your interest that you proceed to Keylong to join your duty there.'

'I wish there was a Shankar in Keylong also with me.' Pramod looked at Shankar affectionately.

'Yes, Pramod. There is a friend of mine in the forest department. He has also been transferred to Lahaul-Spiti. His name is Hari. You will have to walk on foot the entire distance beyond Manali. You will find it difficult to walk it alone. Hari is a perfect gentleman. He is my childhood friend. If you wish I can introduce you to him. You can chalk out your programme with him.'

'No matter, you could not arrange my meeting with her but you should surely introduce me to your friend Hari.'

'Let us go to Hari just now.'

Shankar introduced Pramod to Hari. He had been staying with one of his relatives at Kullu. Shankar asked Hari to take care of Pramod who was passing through a tough time. Pramod was equally happy to be introduced to Hari. Keylong being a new place for him, Hari would certainly make it comfortable for him. He found a lovely companion in Hari.

They decided to start their journey to Keylong the very next day. Pramod was busy packing up for the journey.

□

23

'Is it the temple you talked about?'

'Yes.'

'What is its name that you told me?'

'It is called the Hidimba temple. Pandvas had come here after the great war of Mahabharta. Hidimba was a native of this place. Bhima married her. The temple is after her name. It looks very old,' Hari said while looking at the temple.

'It does not look like a temple at all.'

'Yes, but the temples here are of this type.'

Pramod and Hari walked towards the temple steadily. Passing through the huge sized deodars, the path led to Hidimba temple. The temple was almost invisible among the big trees. The temple was made of thick wooden sleepers. The atmosphere was calm. Rustling leaves of deodars were musical and evoked the poet in Pramod.

Shankar had accompanied Pramod and Hari to Manali. They had to start from Manali the next day. Pramod had chalked out his programme after a meeting with the police officers. They had warned that only two of them should not go to Keylong. More people were also bound for Keylong. They had been contacted. Rohtang Pass was situated at a height of thirteen thousand feet. Harsh winds blew there. The Pass had to be crossed at a particular time. The next day programme was decided accordingly. Pramod and Hari had stayed in the police station for the night. Pramod wanted to see Manali after lunch. So Hari took him to Hidimba temple.

Both of them entered the temple. They offered flowers and coins as offerings, stood there for a few moments. Hari came out of the temple but Pramod remained inside. Hari kept loitering here and there but Pramod did not come out for quite some time. Exhausted Hari went inside. He saw Pramod sitting silent in one corner with his eyes closed. Hari came to him, saw him sitting in a stance and came back. He thought Pramod was praying in a worshipping mood to propitiate his gods. Hari kept moving around the temple and then sat on a big boulder under a deodar tree. Time went by. But Pramod had not yet come out. He felt tired. He went inside again and called Pramod. Pramod woke up from his slumber.

'Pramod, you were lost in your meditation.'

'No meditation. I just made a request, I begged some thing.'

'What did you beg for?'

'I shall have to tell you since I have to travel a long way with you. Moreover, I can't keep it to my heart. You are my friend's friend, hence my friend also. I cannot hide anything from you.' Pramod kept sitting there in the same posture. Hari watched him curiously.

'Your wish has been granted or I wait for some time more?'

'It is granted for the moment. I had heard Hidimba's name in my childhood but never thought that there was a temple after her name. I do not know who and what for this temple was made after Hidimba's name? Hidimba had met Bhima here. I have also expressed a wish. If that is granted, I shall come again here to pay my offerings, ' saying all this Pramod came out.

They kept wandering close to the temple for some time. Then they made their way to Manali. Pramod heard the violently flowing waters on the other side of Manali. He was fascinated by the sound of water and enquired what it was? Hari told him that it was the Beas river flowing boisterously. It was a new experience for Pramod to watch a hilly river from so close a range. The pure and transparent waters flowed in a frolic mood. There was music in its waves. He sat on a boulder, took out a paper and scribbled some thing on it. He was singing to himself.

Hari Singh could make out that Pramod wanted to be left alone for some time. So he came out leaving Pramod behind.

Hari kept wandering aimlessly just to pass time. He returned to Pramod a number of times but found him engaged in writing something. He never wanted to disturb him. He walked back stealthily. It was growing dark now. The rays of the Sun had disappeared. It was getting cold. Moreover, Hari was now tired to the bones.

He said to Pramod, 'What's the programme? Shall we have our dinner here?'

'No, my dear. I have finished it. Now we can go.' Pramod got up.

'What have you finished?'

The poem I was writing.'

'So you are a poet too,' surprised Hari said.

'I am not a writer but poetry emerges spontaneously at times. You know this place is extremely beautiful. The tall deodar trees are charming. They appear to have been waiting for someone. The rustling leaves are musical. The murmur of Beas, its transparent waters, the artistic white pebbles present a charming view. That is why the valley is called the abode of gods.'

'You are a poet in the true spirit. Its getting dark. So let us go now and take our meals and go to bed early so that we can take up our journey early tomorrow.'

They were soon walking on the banks of the Beas river.

They took their dinner and went to sleep early.

'Pramod, you kept sitting in the temple with your eyes closed for long. I wandered during that period here and there. I was tired to the bones. Then you sat on a boulder and kept writing something on the paper. You seem to be worried. Please share your anxiety with me,' said Hari tossing in his bed.

'Yes, Hari. There is a storm in my mind. I wish I could forget my past as suggested by Shankar but there is a conflict in mind and heart.'

'And now you have the poem with you?'

'The poem is not a burden on my mind. It comes as a relief. The turmoil finds expression in words and acts as catharsis.'

'What makes you to be in the police department. Police and poetry are two different worlds.'

'I am not in police department by choice. It is because of sheer coincidence.'

'Will you recite the poem?'

'Do you really want to hear it?'

'Truly speaking, I don't have any interest in poetry and I have never read a poem except the poems in the syllabi. Once I joined the forest department, I have been dealing with the forests, trees, boulders and files only. I feel curious to listen to you as it is you who has written a poem. I must listen to you.'

Enthused Pramod got up, took out the piece of paper on which the poem was written from his pocket to recite it for Hari.

O, currents of Beas
Why are you so musical in your noise
Why do you prick my anguish
Are you also in search of someone
'Who had met you once
You knew him
Advanced closer to him
Talked to him
But the poor fellow
Missed the opportunity
Lost his way
You are passing this way
But no one knows
Where and in which direction
He is exhausting himself
To find you.
O, currents of Beas
You are flowing so hastily
Striking against the boulders
Making way
Pleasantly
You are marching ahead
I wish
You are destined to meet
Your beloved one
And if you come across
My beloved.
Oh, currents of Beas
You will communicate to me surely
Through a drop of water
Or through a messenger in the shape of wind.

'You seem to have been stung deeply. Pramod, you have not revealed your story to me but your poem is quite explicit. Let us sleep now.'

'Now we are co-travellers.'

'And soon we shall be confidants of each other. I am by your side now. You need not worry. I shall assist you.'

They were soon snoring.

They started their onward journey next morning in the company of many other persons bound for Keylong. They had hired coolies to carry their luggage.

Manali is situated at a height of seven thousand feet. After crossing the Beas bridge, they were on their way to Rohtang. At the start, the road was smooth and wide but gradually it became narrower and narrower. It was a zig-zag way going up and down frequently. It was a new experience for Pramod to walk on foot in a hilly area. On the other hand, Hari was accustomed to such marches as he belonged to Kullu and secondly he was in the forest department where he often walked the distances on foot. Pramod was often left behind but Hari would stop at some point to wait for Pramod. The caravan reached Rohtang Pass after a few hours.

Situated at a height of thirteen thousand feet, Rohtang is the gateway to Lahaul and Spiti. Sharp winds rattled the place. Pramod had difficulty in standing erect even. Though Pramod was clad in woolen clothes, he felt the biting chill.

'Hari, the journey is very tough. Shall I be able to reach my destination or I stagger on the way itself,' Pramod said laughingly.

'You don't worry at all. There is no ascent ahead, it is descent onwards. It was only tough up to Rohtang Pass,' Hari consoled him.

'Thank god. I thought I would not be able to walk any further. I cannot tread the ascending road at all. I feel exhausted. I have never climbed up the mountain earlier.'

The caravan had reached the stone cave. One of the groups called both of them and asked them to join at the spot. Both of them reached the spot and entered the stone cave. It was a tea shop. Here the atmosphere was warm because of fire. Pramod felt relieved. He was happy to know that they would get tea there. Tea break over, they all came out and started their onward journey.

'Pramod, look at that huge boulder.'

'Yes, I am looking at it.

'There is Vyas Kund' (Vyas reservoir) under it. Maharishi Vyas had done his penance here. At a height of fifteen thousand feet, water oozes out of this kund (reservoir). Look at the thin current of water. This takes the shape of Beas river after covering some distance.

'Beas river? That is a big river but here it is only a thin layer of water flowing. How can such a small quantity of water turn into a huge river?' Pramod was surprised.

'Vyas Kund is the origin of Beas river. The small spring of water releases a little quantity of water which flows down. Many other rivulets join it on its way. The snow on high mountains melts and the water flows down and merges in the Beas river. By the time the river reaches Manali, it becomes a huge river. And at Kullu, it swells like anything.'

'It's wonderful. Every big thing exists in its tiny form in the beginning. To this small current of water at the Vyas Kund, no one can believe that it is the source from where Vyas originates.'

'Please hurry up. The velocity of the wind is increasing. It is not safe to stay here any more. We should leave this zone as early as possible.

They started walking fast. The road descended down after the Rohtang Pass. As they went down, the impact of winds decreased. There was decline in cold as well. While walking down, Pramod felt less of fatigue. They reached Koksar after getting down three thousand feet. They had to stay there for the night. It was already evening. Chandra river was flowing by. The same Chandra river flows down from Koksar and joins Bhaga river near Keylong and is called Chandra Bhaga thereafter. And it takes the shape of Chenab river.

'Hari, this place is also very beautiful. It appears that after crossing Rohtang we have entered a new world, entirely different.'

'As we go deeper into this part of Lahaul, the same feeling will get intensified. It is a wonderland. Two worlds exist on either side of Rohtang Pass.'

'Hari, have you been to this place earlier?'

'Yes, it is for the second time that I am here.'

'How did you come last time?'

'The cause is the same this time, as it was for the first time,' Hari said.

'What do you mean?'

'Pramod, I have been sent to this place twice just to punish me.'

'What bungling you have done?'

'No bungling at all. I have one weakness, i.e. I am fond of liquor.' What weakness? Everyone takes it.

But for the last four years, there is an officer in Kulu who is averse to liquor. I drink heavily. I have consumed liquor many a time while on duty. He has not tolerated it. Last time I had been sent to Kaza. I stayed there for one year. With great difficulty, I got myself transferred to Kullu. I tried to avoid drinking after coming to Kullu. I could avoid it for a few days. Then I came across my old friends. They made me drunk during day time. Everyone noticed me. So I stand transferred.'

'Hari, you are very weak. Why can't you restrain yourself?

'It was to be and it happened. If I had not repeated my blunder, how could I meet a friend like you. Have you liked this place?' Hari tried to change the topic.

'How far is Keylong from this place?'

'Around 120 kilometers from Manali.'

'How many days will it take to reach Keylong from here?'

'At least three days more.'

'We shall be walking on foot all these days?'

'Life goes on foot in the hills. It flies and floats in the plains. But here is neither of the options.'

There were only two or three shops in Koksar. There was a forest building nearby. The other members of the caravan stayed in the shops and Hari and Pramod stayed in the forest building. Meals were cooked in one of the shops. They went to bed after taking their meals.

The caravan started again next morning for Keylong. There was no ascent like Rohtang Pass. Even then the path was quite difficult. It was a small pedestrian path. At places they had to tread over the small or big boulders. It was the maiden experience for Pramod. The caravan had to move at a slower pace to keep Pramod with it. Since Pramod was not accustomed to walk on foot for long distances, he had developed abscesses under his feet. He however tried to keep pace with the caravan.

The stopovers on the way had been identified in advance. Arrangements for the stay of members were either made in the shops or in the homes they would get meals at their places of stay. With the melting of snow at the Rohtang Pass, Lahaul-Spiti was again connected with the rest of the country. The movement of the people would start both ways. But this phenomenon remained only for a few months. With the fall of snow, Rohtang Pass was closed and Lahaul-Spiti remained cut-off.

After a continuous tourney of two days, they were now close to Keylong. When they started for the onward journey on the third day, there was a reflection of fatigue and satisfaction both on the face of Pramod and Hari. He was happy because it was the last day of the journey and that he would be in Keylong soon. During the three day tough tourney, Hari was a great relief to Pramod. The journey was arduous indeed. But Pramod was heavy in heart and mind alike because he had her in mind. She had neither met him nor the efforts of Shankar to trace her were sussessful. He was haunted by the incident. He felt the pangs of separation and often there were tears in his eyes. He tolerated the torture for two days and kept it to himself. Later on when Hari asked him about the matter, he could not resist the revelation. He told it to Hari. He had felt relieved and he got Hari's sympathy also. Hari advised him almost in similar manner as Shankar had done to him but Pramod was all the more emotional for the girl.

'We shall reach Keylong today.'

'I shall be happier than you. I was worried about you from the very first day. I thought it would be difficult for you to walk the arduous distance on foot. I never believed that you could undertake the journey.'

'I have not covered the distance myself.'

'Then who has covered it?'

'Hari, truly speaking, if you were not with me, I would have staggered on the way. It is a rocky path. I would have died on the way. Moreover, her memory would have killed me. I am not walking, it is your affection that makes me to go on and on.'

'Don't say like that. After all we all help each other. Moreover you are my friend now, a very close friend.'

'I am thankful to you from the core of my heart. I shall expect similar attention from you.'

'Do not worry at all. I shall see that you don't have any difficulty there.'

'What kind of city Keylong is?'

'It's not a city. It is a small hilly village.' Hari laughed at Pramod's comment.

It was a clear day. The sun was shining. The warmth gave a pleasant relief from the chill. The caravan was going at its speed. They both were following it while enjoying their conversation.

'So the biggest place of Lahaul-Spiti is a small village?'

'Yes, a typical village.'

'What is its population?'

'Approximately five hundred in all.'

'What is there in Keylong?'

'Nothing. There are only small houses of the people. There are a few government offices. Keylong is encircled by high mountains on all sides. Rocks and flowing rivulets add to the charm. Snow-clad high mountains.'

'Any important place, any temple worth visiting?,' Pramod asked.

'Yes there are some Budhistic monasteries here and there. They are also situated on high hills. Yes there is another place of interest.'

'What is that?,' Pramod asked curiously.

'During my last posting here, I had stayed there in a house. The owner of the house had told me that one of the great freedom fighters Ras Behari Bose had stayed in Lahaul and Spiti during freedom struggle.'

'Ras Behari Bose? In Keylong? He must have made the story.'

'No, not the least. It has now been confirmed. The government is planning to install a statue of Ras Behari Bose in Keylong.'

'How could Ras Behari Bose of Bengal reach Keylong on foot? And why? What for?'

'Pramod, may be you do not know that Ras Behari Bose was a great revolutionary. The revolutionaries had thrown a bomb at Lord Harding in Delhi. The entire plan had been drafted by Ras Behari Bose. The revolutionaries had gone underground after the incident. The British Government had laid police traps to nab the freedom fighters. Ras Behari Bose was planning to intensify the struggle for freedom from the foreign lands. He came to Keylong in 1913 disguised as a sadhu. Keylong was the safest place in those days. The Britishers had no direct control on this area. No big officer was stationed at Keylong. Ras Behari Bose stayed with a person named Tooktook who was employed in a post-office. It is said that he stayed in Keylong till the winter was over. He received his letters there. The government became suspicious on the basis of a letter. The rumour spread in Keylong that some senior police officer was coming to the place. As soon as he learnt it, Ras Behari Bose disappeared from the place. Tooktook received a letter from Ras Behari wherein he had thanked his host for the shelter and his hospitality. There was something written in Bengali at the end of the letter which could not be deciphered by anyone. Tooktook kept the letter with him. After many months, a Bengali was posted in the post-office. Tooktook showed that letter to him. It was then found that the sadhu was in fact Ras Behari Bose, who had left India and had gone abroad.'

'Keylong is indeed a historic place. You have told a very good story. Had any one else also seen that letter?' Pramod stopped for a moment.

'Yes, a Naib Tehsildar when learnt about it, he verified it. Tooktook's son Tanjin is the Nambardar there. This incident had been told to me by him. It was widely discussed. Some of the people had expressed the desire that the incident should be made known to the entire world. And a few persons had also suggested that a befitting memorial be erected in the memory of Ras Behari Bose.'

'I shall love to visit that house where the revolutionary Ras Behari Bose had stayed.'

'I shall surely take you there. Tanjin is my friend. If his house is not occupied, we shall hire the same for our stay. Look there, that is Keylong, Pramod.' Hearing the name of Keylong, Pramod felt as if all his fatigue had been taken away. He saw beautiful houses on the hills of Keylong.

They were now in Keylong. There was a small police post. Everyone there welcomed him. Pramod and Hari stayed there for the night.

Pramod took over the charge the next day. Hari also reported at his office. Pramod had difficulty in breathing at night. He got up once or twice and sat up in his bed. Hari had told him that sometimes one felt suffocated because of deficiency of oxygen in air. When one feels suffocation, one should sit up in the bed. Pramod had got up many a time. He felt restlessness.

There were high mountains all around. The biting cold was intolerable. The winter was not at its zenith in Keylong as yet but it was very harsh for Pramod. The cold winds affected his face. His lips dried up. There were some spots on his face because of the hot sun. He was feeling very strange. The short-statured persons with lovely eyes were clad in heavy woolens. Pramod felt strange that the local people smelled strangely. They did not take bath regularly. May be it was because of extreme cold that they did not feel like taking bath daily nor was it a practice there. The stink of different persons made one averse to them. Pramod talked to some employees from outside. They told that in the beginning they also felt the same way but gradually got accustomed to it.

Since Hari had old acquaintances here, he managed a house on rent. Pramod and Hari both lived together in the house. Hari knew cooking, so Pramod had no difficulty as far as food was concerned. There was no hotel in Keylong. Employees who came from outside had to cook meals for themselves. Pramod was surprised to find that cooking of dal took one and an half hour to two hours what could easily be cooked in half an hour at his home.

Hari found it difficult to enjoy liquor freely because of Pramod's stay. He was not happy during his three days journey in Pramod's company. Once Pramod felt that he was drunk. Pramod had asked him regarding the same but Hari warded off the discussion somehow. Hari found some of his old friends fond of drinking in Keylong but his greatest problem was that he could not consume liquor at home in the presence of Pramod. He used to take drinks outside and it was difficult for him to come home drunken. He was in a great fix. He could neither leave drinks nor could he ignore his friend Pramod. He requested Pramod once or twice to allow him to take his drink at home but Pramod always persuaded him to leave drinking because addiction of liquor is a bad habit.

It went on the same way for a few days. Many months elapsed. Pramod gradually adjusted himself to the conditions. There was not much of police engagements as the people were peace loving. Crimes were a rare thing. Pramod found it difficult to pass his time. Soon he was introduced to the local people and he found some friends in them. It became easy to pass time in their company. Dak used to reach Keylong after big intervals and the newspaper from Manali arrived through dak.

It was a Sunday today. The weather was clear after many a days. There was a little snowfall. The snow glittered in the sun shine. Pramod and Hari along with their friends went to a Budhistic monastery to enjoy the holiday.

Pramod was astonished to see the Buddha temple. It was centuries old temple. A large number of lamas lived there even today. The chief lama took them to the main hall of the temple. Fine daris and druggets were laid on the floor. They all sat on them. The chief lama joined them. Small tables were kept in front of them. Then the cups were placed and hot tea was poured into them. This was saltish tea. A person who had come with the group told Pramod that namkeen tea was a normal thing there. And it is prepared in a special way. Even the tea leaves used are a different sort of material. Then tea is poured into a hollow bamboo piece. butter is added to it and is churned to mix it properly. It is heated again. Pramod liked the saltish tea. Saltish tea was followed by a cold drink. Hari was watching Pramod's reaction mischievously and Pramod was watching activities of other people. His fellows picked up their cups and started to drink. Hari finished his cup in just one sip. Pramod attempted the drink. As soon as he tasted it, he felt surprised. He kept his cup on the table. Hari could not restrain himself but laugh.

'What is it, It smells foul'. Hari asked astonishingly.

'It is called chhang,' one of his companions said.

'Chhang? It stinks.'

'This helps us tolerate the severity of winter here.'

'What do you mean?'

'It is a light beverage prepared from barley. It is called chhang. All the people in Lahaul and Spiti take it. It is not high in degree. So it is not a hard intoxicant.'

'Chhang or liquor and that too in the temple?'asked Pramod.

'Yes, in the temple. Liquor is an integral part of life here. It is consumed in temples and homes alike. But in temples only chhang is served, not ara.'

'What is ara?'

'Finished alcohol. People distill liquor in their homes here. Ara is kept for years at home. It is high density liquor. In some of the homes, fifty-year old ara drink is available. The older the ara is in a home, the greater the esteem for the family in society.'

'But the liquor is being served in the temple and you are all taking it. I cannot make it out.' The bewildered Pramod asked.

'Pramod, it is Lahaul and Spiti and not the plains. It is a different world all together. In many of our festivals, we worship our gods with liquor. Chhang is offered to the deities. Hindus and the Buddhist people recognize the importance of chhang alike. You are new to this place. Stay here for some time. Let the snowfall start. Everything will be frozen. You will not see anything else but snow and snow all around. People will close themselves in the four walls of their homes. They will not come out for many days. They open their doors only when it stops snowing and the sun is shining. They spend months together closed in their homes. The blood starts freezing. At such a time, this chhang and ara come to their rescue. Pramod, you are showing your aversion to these beverages but they in fact are the life blood of our survival. That is why our deities also drink chhang.' The local fellow accompanying them said. He picked up his tumbler of chhang and drank it in one go. Chhang had been served three or four times by this time. They were sipping the beverage and the lama standing close to them would fill up the emptied bowls. Pramod enjoyed the scene silently.

'Pramod, you should also take a little bit.'

'Me? I have never touched it even.'

'You had never been to Keylong too.'

'I have come to Keylong but this does not mean that I shall follow whatever you do.'

'If you have to stay here, you will have to change yourself a little.'

'Hari, you are sitting silent. You are enjoying the party. You are taking drinks one after the other on the pretext of the temple.' Looking at Hari, Pramod commented after a long gap.

'Pramod, Chhang is in Budhistic monasteries what holy water is in the Hindu temples. If you don't take it, they will feel bad. It is considered a disrespect to the gods. May be you take a little bit of it but you will have to accept it.' The local employee whispered to him in a serious tone.

'Does he mean it?,' Pramod asked another person standing next to him.

'That is the truth. When I was new to the place, I had the similar feelings. Later on I got accustomed to it. You need not worry. It is very light. It won't affect you. As you have come here, you will have to take the holy Prasad.'

'Hurry up Pramod. It is getting dark and we have to go home.'

Pramod was in a fix. He hesitated for some time. They all insisted on him. The chief lama looked at him astonishingly. Pramod took his bowl hesitatingly. He sipped just a drop from it and kept it on the table.

'A little more, try it once more.'

Pramod drank a few more drops with difficulty. He witnessed dance of the lamas after some time. A few lamas played on the musical instruments. Shortly afterwards they all went to Keylong.

Pramod tried his best to adapt himself to the Keylong life. Hari helped him a lot. He thought that he was gradually forgetting the girl just as he was forgetting about Kullu. But he found it to be his misconception. He became more and more enamoured of that girl as the days went on, Pramod wrote letters to Shankar. He asked Shankar to try once again to locate the girl with the help of Ranjit. Shankar made efforts to dissuade Pramod by putting forth his arguments in the letters but to no avail. He became all the more depressed. Hari was his only consolation. Hari loved Pramod. The only obstacle between the two was the liquor. Hari attempted gradually and was successful in inducing Pramod to take chhang. Pramod liked the drink. They now would take chhang daily in the evening. It was light intoxication. And Pramod would feel relieved of his anxiety. It was growing colder in Lahaul and Spiti. Chhang gave him relief from the cold to some extent. Pramod had often said that he would take chhang only but never would he consume hard liquor. They kept their word. After a few months, Pramod tasted ara too in the company of his friends but he never allowed any other liquor in his home except chhang.

□

24

It was a common talk in the villages where Shankar and Ranjit had gone to locate the particular girl under the garb of investigation that someone had misbehaved with the village girls while they were returning home after the Dussehra festival. The news spread like wildfire in the adjoining villages. It was a hot topic. The village elders were trying to identify the girls and to trace the eveteasers. This became the talk of the villages but no one could find out who the girls were and who were the culprits.

The village Panchayat held its meeting one day. The Numberdar enquired about the same topic. The Numberdar said, 'It is a matter of great concern for our village that someone should tease our girls. And all the more worrisome is the fact that the girls did not report it to the village elders. It is a matter of shame that the police came to our village for the same and stayed here throughout the day to find the facts. I fear the police may come again for the same purpose. We may not be summoned to the police station.'

'Your apprehension is right but no one has talked about the issue so far in the village. Had the incident taken place, the girls must have had reported it to their parents and they would have talked to us surely. And even if the girls had not talked about the matter for one reason or the other, it would have come to light after police investigation. If it had happened in reality, there would have been indicators by this time,' The village Pradhan said.

'I am surprised at the fact that no girl reported about the incident and no one else knows anything about the happening. Then how could the police know that someone had teased the village girls on their return from Dussehra festival. Some one might have told the police, he could have told the names of the girls also.

If he did not want to disclose the identity of the girls, he could have told the names of the persons who misbehaved with the girls. It is beyond our comprehension. It amounts to a riddle almost,' One of the Panchayat members Hari Singh said.

'Hari Singh, we have to sort out this problem. A few of us should go to Kullu police station to enquire about the person who had lodged a complaint there and also to know the progress in police investigation so far. This involves the dignity of the village as well as its girls. The police can come again to investigate and that will be a nuisance for us.' The Panchayat Pradhan put his viewpoint before the gathering.

The Panchayat decided that the Namberdar and Hari Singh, Panch will go to Kullu Thana and enquire about the whole episode. Both of them went to Kullu the next day. They talked to the Station House Officer. The SHO called the Munshi. He checked it in the register and confirmed that no complaint was ever lodged from that village.

'Why the police had come to our village to investigate then?,' the puzzled Numberdar wondered.

'They might have gone to investigate something else,' the Munshi said.

Two policemen had come to the village a week ago. They came straight to my home. They had narrated the incident like this. Some girls were returning to the village after visiting the Dussehra festival in the evening when it was raining. Someone had gave them a lift in his jeep and had dropped them in the village. Some unknown person had teased them. The police wanted to enquire about the incident by consulting the girls,' the Numberdar said.

'Munshiji scan the entire register and find out if anyone was sent for investigation to the village?'

'No Sir. I have checked it thoroughly. I remember the persons by rote who are sent for investigation. No one has been sent to their village for investigation during the last two years,' Munshi said confidently.

'Then what is all this fuss about?' The police officer said in a surprised tone.

'Sir, they were men in khaki. I told them that no girl had complained about it to me. They took me along and surveyed the entire village. They enquired from the Panchayat Pradhan and asked other persons also. I was with them for the whole day enquiring about the girls in all the villages. We had a Panchayat meeting yesterday. The members expressed concern over the incident. No girl had lodged any complaint whatsoever. Then who lodged the complaint with you and why? We have come to you to know about the facts.' The Numberdar explained the purpose of visit.

'Sir, the police has never been to our village. There are no strifes. It is the first time in my life that the police had come to the village.' Hari Singh said with a pinch of grief.

'Can you tell me the names of those policemen? The thanedar asked.

'No, Sir. We did not ask their names.'

'How were they dressed?'

'They were not in uniform.'

'If they were not in uniform, then it could have been anyone. May be it is a local problem of your village. The neighbouring villagers might have played a trick with you. The police does not go to a village without a complaint. Unless we send the police, we have nothing to do with such incidents.' The Station House Officer said.

'All right, Sir. We just wanted to know the facts. If it is a village matter, we shall solve it at our own level. We shall try to find out those persons. If there is something unruly, we shall seek your help,' Hari Singh said.

The Numberdar and Hari Singh returned to their village fully satisfied.

'Khushal, what are you doing these days?,' the Munshi inquired of him. 'Mr. Thakur has returned yesterday. I shall be with him for a few days. I have been free these days,' Khushal said while occupying a chair.

'You are very lucky. You get your salary from the government. And you enjoy life, courtesy Mr. Thakur. We are bored to death here. We are awfully busy the whole day and you enjoy throughout the day. No one can question you.'

'It is one's own luck. But I help him in winning his assembly seat. I work day and night for him when it is election time. He simply addresses the public meetings. I muster votes for him by all methods, fair and foul. That's right that I enjoy life to the brim for five years after the elections.'

'There cropped up a peculiar problem today. No incident took place. No one reported anything. How strange someone in the garb of police makes enquiries and investigations.' Munshi said while lighting a bidi. He gave one bidi to Khushal also. Khushal asked for a match box and the Munshi obliged him.

'What was the matter? Who had gone for investigation and where had he gone?'

Munshi repeated the entire episode as was told by the Numberdar and Panch Hari Singh.

'Oh, yes. I know it. Ranjit had come to my home day before yesterday. We consumed liquor. He was saying something when he was over drunk.'

'What did he say?'

'Ranjit told that Shankar had taken him to the village. They kept wandering in the village throughout the day. They searched for the girl who had been misbehaved by someone on the Dussehra festival.'

'Then the Numberdar was right. But what was the problem?'

'Ranjit had revealed that Pramod had an affair with one of those girls. Shankar and Ranjit had gone there to trace the girl. Ranjit is a friend of mine. Ranjit wanted to take vengeance on Pramod for what he had done to me. He had accompanied Shankar to the village They wanted to unearth the Pramod affair so that he was punished further and sent beyond Keylong even,' Khushal said while enjoying the bidi.

'Khushal, I know you are very clever but in this case you will be at the receiving end,' Munshi retorted.

'I have not followed you.'

'You will learn only then when some Pramod pushes you behind the bars. You know, Shankar is Pramod's man. He is his bosom friend. He had gone to see him off at the bus stand. Shankar has a friend named Hari who was also going to Keylong. He had made both of them know each other. They went to Keylong together from Manali. Shankar is in touch with Pramod through letters. How can Shankar go against Pramod?'

'You are absolutely right. I can't understand the problem.'

'It may be a conspiracy of Shankar and Pramod to deceive you and Ranjit. You and Ranjit have been instrumental in getting Pramod transferred to Keylong. You should be cautious.'

'May I call Ranjit?'

'Yes. Do call him. I talk to him just now.'

Khushal went outside and Munshi started writing something in the register.

'Ranjit, narrate the entire incident. Why did you go with Shankar to the village.'

Ranjit narrated the whole incident in detail.

'So it is true that you were driving the jeep that night and Pramod was on his way to Manali with you,' Munshi enquired.

'Yes, that is true.'

'And it was raining that night. You met the girls on way. They were given a lift and dropped after covering some distance.'

'Yes, that is also right.'

'Do you know those girls?'

'No, not at all.'

'Did Pramod talk to any of the girls?

'No, he did not talk to any of those girls. Yes, he stayed away from me in Manali. He returned in another jeep.'

'How does it matter?' All the three kept talking for long. They reviewed all the possibilities. However, they could not reach to any conclusion. They were at their wit's loss.

It is a fact that Shankar is Pramod's friend. It was Shankar who told Ranjit the entire story and both of them wandered in the village. There must be something deep in it. May be they are trying to trap me and Ranjit,' Khushal said.

'I have my doubts too. Shankar had invited me to drinks once. He had elicited a commitment from me that I would do it for him. You are right. We should remain cautious,' Ranjit expressed his apprehension.

'You don't worry at all. Thakur has come. I shall talk to him just today. He has been shifted to Keylong but now he will have to be pushed to Kaza. He will never forget me.'

Khushal went straight to the bazaar. He kept wandering here and there. He shared his problem with some of his other friends and then came back to the police station. He looked for Shankar as he urgently wanted to talk to him. But he was not available immediately as he was out of station.

Khushal went to Mr. Thakur in the evening and told him in detail. He said that Pramod was trying to trap him and Ranjit even after having been transferred to Keylong. He added that Shankar was assisting him in the matter. He suggested that Pramod should be transferred to Kaza and Shankar may be shifted to Keylong. Mr. Thakur could not refuse the suggestion. He called Prakash Verma the next day. Prakash Verma showed his reluctance in the matter. He told that Pramod had already been suspended and then transferred. There was no reason for his suspension. So the department will have to revoke his suspension after a few days. There is no reason to transfer him to Kaza from Keylong. Mr. Thakur gave no credence to Prakash Verma's argument. Instead, he asked him to do as Khushal wanted him to do.

A few days later, Pramod was transferred to Kaza and Shankar was shifted to Keylong.

□

25

The bus was overcrowded. This bus from Kullu to Manali was scheduled in such a way that the school children and the commuters from offices travelled by it. The bus was crowded daily. Savitri and Kamla found it difficult to stand in the bus. There was no seat available. They daily travelled in it after the school and office hours were over. The bus had gone only a little distance that a passenger got up from his seat and asked them to occupy the same. The passengers in the bus were talking to each other. Kamla and Savitri were also in conversation. Suddenly, Savitri heard the chit chat of those people.

'Unexpected things have started to happen. Do you know what happened in the village adjacent to our village.'

'The incident related to the policemen?'

'Yes, the same one. But what is that episode? It is turning out to be something strange.'

'What is the story?'

'It was raining on the Dussehra evening. Some girls were returning home after a visit to the Dussehra. The rain drenched them. A jeep came from behind. The jeep gave them lift. They got down near the village. They went to their homes. Later on, the police came to investigate. The policemen said they wanted to meet those girls because someone had teased them on that day. But none of the girls had reported any such thing. When the villagers went to the police station to enquire about the complaint, the police showed its ignorance. Neither anyone lodged a complaint with the police station nor anyone was sent for investigation. It is a peculiar case.'

'The times have changed. Old practices are yielding place to new. Why should we bother?

Savitri looked at Kamla and Kamla wanted to know Savitri's reaction. They had a silent conversation. Both of them got down from the bus at a particular point. They started for their village on foot.

'Kamla, did you listen to what they were saying?,' Savitri asked in a worried tone.

'Yes, I did listen to them. Even the Namberdar had enquired it from me.'

'When did he ask you?'

'The day the police men had come to the village.'

'Is it true that the police had come to our village to investigate the matter?,' astonished Savitri asked her.

'Yes, they had come. The whole village knows it.' Kamla confirmed it.

'You did not share it with me?'

'You were not here those days. You had gone to attend a marriage ceremony of your aunt's son. You returned on the day before yesterday. So I did not have a chance to share it with you.'

'What did the Namberdar ask you?'

'He asked if any jeep owner had given us a lift and if any one had misbehaved with the girls?'

'What did you say?'

'I refuted the charge. No one had misbehaved with us. The police officer sitting in the jeep had not even looked at us. How gentle people they were. We were almost badly drenched in that rain. We had not even raised our hand to halt the jeep. We could not dare it. They had stopped the jeep themselves when they found us drenching. Then how could I say that someone had misbehaved with us.'

'Did you see those policemen who had come on enquiry?,' Savitri said heaving a deep sigh.

'No, I did not see them.'

'Did you enquire?'

'Yes, I did but he had been transferred, You have not forgotten him as yet.'

'No, Kamla. I don't know what has happened to me since that day. You know we had occupied the rear seats and had got down unnoticed. I saw him for a moment. Next day, he stood near Raghu Nath's tent. I recognized him instantly. I had seen him that night but he had not seen me. I kept standing near Raghu Nath's tent for long. I don't know why I felt intensely to talk to him at that moment.

I could not understand what I should say to him. Then an idea flashed in my mind. I decided to thank him for the help he had rendered the earlier evening. I summoned courage and went to him. It took me much time to go to him. Some other police officer was in conversation with him at that time. I moved forward twice or thrice and retraced my steps every time. But something haunted me and dragged me to him I could not restrain myself. Ultimately, I was with him. I thanked him. He could not make it out. He was alert now. The other police officer left the place. I stood there for some time. I felt like talking to him but I could not. And since that day something has happened to me.'

'Did he talk to you?'

'No. he simply said that he had performed his duty. There was no reason to thank for the act. He did not talk anything else.'

'Did you want to say something more to him?'

'I wanted to say so many things to him.'

'Then why did you not avail the opportunity?'

'I don't know why I could not speak my heart out.'

'Neither you said anything nor he spoke out. The incident is over. He is no more in Kullu. He has gone on transfer. What goes on in your mind?'

'Kamla,' Savitri caught her hand and both of them stopped on the way. She was driven into her past. Savitri blushed at his thought. Something was going on in the mind of Savitri and she was haunted by it. They stood there holding each other's hand. Savitri looked into Kamla's eyes.

'Why don't you speak? You cannot hide anything from me.' Kamla was now wiping tears trickling down from the eyes of Savitri.

'Kamla, I am unable to forget him. You had discussed once. I wanted to forget him but could not. I got information about him through someone from the police station. I came to know his name and also learnt that he had been transferred. I tried to contain myself. I wanted to forget him but more I tried, more he has stuck in my heart. Tell me what shouid I do.'

'Savitri, I have been watching it for many days now. You are my intimate friend. You made his reference only once but I have been reading the storm in your eyes. I heard all your conversation when you were trying to know his name through Bimla. But now he stands transferred. What can be done? Moreover, we do not know who he is. And where does he belong to? Nothing is known about his family.'

'I have not given a thought to this aspect. So I have decided to throw it all into oblivion but I cannot, Kamla, may be he sent the policemen to the village to collect information about me.' There was a satisfaction on Savitri's face now. They started moving onwards.

'If it was that way, why should the police talk about the misbehaviour?'

'He does not even know either my name or the name of the village. When I went to thank him, I had immediately come back. If he had a desire to enquire about me after that meeting, how could he locate me.'

'If he wanted to meet me, there could have been other ways too.' Both of them kept on walking. Savitri taught in a Kullu school. She was the daughter of a poor Brahmin who was no more. Her mother got her educated up to matriculation and she got a job after teachers' training.

Her family members included her mother, two brothers and a sister. They had some farming land but it was not sufficient to sustain them. The family depended on Savitri's salary. Savitri was the most beautiful woman of the village. She was beauty incarnate. It appeared that the nature's beauty had been epitomized in her figure. She was quite serious in nature. No one could tease her. She only walked up to the road. Kamla lived in her neighbourhood. She also worked in an office in Kullu. They both took the bus from the road touching their village.

'Come on Savitri. Let us sit together for some time.' Kamla requested her when they reached near Kamla's house. Savitri's house was on the right side. They daily bifurcated from this point.

'Thanks Kamla. I want to go to my home as I feel very sad.'

'Don't be a fool. Life is a long journey. We meet so many people on our way and many more will come across in life. Don't strain youself. Forget him.'

'No, Kamla, I feel that there is some relationship of the earlier life.'

'You are an ardent fool. Have you read some novel? You had gone to Mandi. You might have seen a movie.'

'The incidents narrated in the novels and the pictures are based on imagination. They are not the truths of life.'

'O.K. I take your leave.'

Both of them went their way. □

26

'Pramod, don't take it to heart. They could only get you transferred. It was Keylong earlier, now it is Kaza. There is no tougher place beyond Kaza. This is the maximum their government could do.' Hari consoled him.

'Transfer does not frighten me. In Keylong too, I am far away from my home place. Kaza is equally good as far as distance is concerned. I shall get a chance to see a new place. But I cannot understand their attitude. What kind of government is it in India? I should have been told about the crime I have committed for which I have been punished. Why I am being kicked like a lifeless stone from one place to the other.' Pramod said anxiously while keeping his hand on his head.

'It has started happening this way since politics has intruded upon administration. Pramod, the British rule was much better as compared to it. All things happened in a systematic manner and not haphazardly. Only defaulters were punished and defaulters could never go unpunished. And these days, if you have a political connection, you can go scot free even if you have committed a crime. They punish the honest people instead.'

'Hari, the British rule was not good but those were the days of slavery. Slavery is a curse. Our country is free today and we have our own government.'

'And Khushal is making merry in Kullu and Pramod has been flung in Kaza. The policeman who is always drunk during the day is considered as the saviour of the department and an honest officer of the stature of Pramod has been made a rolling stone. Is it freedom? Did we wage a war for freedom only for such acts?' Hari looked askance at Pramod.

'That is a separate issue. We cannot denounce the importance of freedom only because of the weaknesses of the administration. We cannot call the British regime days as glorious days. Yes, I have been sinned against without reason. I am sorry to think that there was none who could deliver justice to me. How strange?'

'If it were the British rule days, such officers would have been shunted out. Now we are free, free to drink and indulge in unwanted acts. It's all right Pramod. Sing songs of freedom and be lost in Kaza.'

'You were here with me in Keylong and I had good time here. What shall I do in Kaza, and how shall I go alone to such a far-off place. I learn that there are low and high mountains on the way and the track is very arduous. I am thinking on resigning from my job. I would arrange some petty business near my home. I have to fend for my family. My parents have high hopes of me. I have three sisters to marry off. I shall have to bear it all. I cannot leave my job.'

'Pramod, don't be disheartened. Hari knows how to live up to friendship. I have made all the arrangements. I have found out my departmental job there. I shall go to Kaza with you.'

'Really? I bow before you. A person who has friends like Shankar and Hari need not to worry!' Pramod was not worried now. Both of them left the room and were walking on the road. They talked to people who met them on the way. Pramod cleared his backlog with the shopkeeper. Thereafter they met some of their friends.

The next morning, Pramod and Hari left Keylong for Koksar. Before leaving Hari told Pramod that Shankar's transfer had been cancelled. Pramod was worried because he felt that Shankar was penalized because of him. Shankar belonged to Kullu district. He was neither interested in politics nor in political engagements. But after a short while in service he could understand that poltical support was necessary to carry on with the job. So he had made friends with some of the party workers of his village. When he came to know about his transfer, he contacted those party workers. It is a fact that he had to organize a drink party at his residence for some of them. But they completely compensated him for his expenses. All of them went to Mr. Thaur, the MLA. They requested him to get his transfer orders cancelled. The MLA asked them to convince Khushal. They became adamant and said that it were they who got him all the votes from that area. A few of them were devoted workers of Mr. Thakur. On hearing about the vote factor, Thakur felt uneasy. He accepted their demand and Shankar's transfer was cancelled. Hari's friend who had come to Keylong from Kulle the earlier day had carried this news.

'Hari, you have told me a very good news. I was worried about Shankar. Now I feel relieved. Shankar remains in Kullu, and you are accompanying me to Kaza, I have no concerns now.'

'And there is no place beyond Kaza where you can be transferred.'

'What is beyond that?'

'The China border. Even Khushal and Thakur cannot get you transferred there.'

'They hired coolies for luggage and started their journey. Stopping over thrice on their way, they reached Koksar. Pramod had stayed at Koksar after crossing Rohtang Pass. Koksar is the point from where two ways diverged, one to Keylong and the other to Kaza. Both of them had stayed in Koksar for the night. They started their journey to Kaza next morning. Some other people joined them for Kaza.

The road wound itself to Spiti via Gramchu on the banks of Chandra river. The journey from Kokksar to Kaza was very tough. We reached Kunzam Pass after many hours journey. This pass was the gateway to Spiti valley. Its height was greater than Rohtang Pass. Pramod felt difficulty in breathing when he reached at a height of fifteen thousand five hundred feet with the caravan. He sat down. He was tired to the bones and found it difficult to breathe because of low oxygen. Hari had made all the arrangements. He gave water to Pramod followed by hot cup of tea from his thermose. But they could not stay at Kunjam Pass for a longer period as it was neither possible nor bereft of danger. Sharp winds were blowing. The winds could take a dangerous turn any moment. So they crossed the Kunjam Pass swiftly. They halted for the overnight stay on their way and started the onward journey the next morning.

'That is the Shigri glacier,' Hari told Pramod by pointing to it by his finger.

'Glacier? You mean a mountain of snow.' Pramod expressed his surprise.

'Yes, yes, that is the glacier. It is the biggest glacier in Asia and the second biggest in the world. It is twenty to thirty miles in length. Centuries old frozen mountain of snow. It slides only a few inches annually. Chandra river receives the water flow from it.' Pramod was surprised at Hari's comment. He stopped suddenly and looked at the mountain keenly. It was bright sun shine now. The glare was intolerable. Pramod went closer to the glacier in the company of a few of his co-travellers and stood there for quite sometime

'We don't have much of time here. You cannot stop to write a poem on the spot. Hurry up. The next stoppage is quite far off.' Hari caught Pramod's hand and dragged him almost.

While travelling from Koksar to Keylong, Pramod had felt the peculiarity of the land. It was a different world altogether. But the journey from Koksar to Kaza was all the more distinctive. The height of the entire area ranged from ten thousand to twelve thousand feet. Some part of it was like desert. There was sand in the air. And mounds of sand stood there just like the ones in Rajasthan. Pramod was haunted by the novel and strange scenes of Nature. The bright rays of the Sun had turned the high mountains red in reflection. The impact of the sun rays, snow and the ferocious winds eroded the mountains continuously. There was no greenery for miles together. Pramod would stop intermittently on his way to have a look at the wonderful mountains that surprised him.

'I could never imagine that a desert was located at such a height.' Pramod said to Hari.

'It does not rain here. It simply receives snowfall. The sun is always scorching. And the winds are invariably harsh. No bud or leaf grows here. And even if it sprouts, the sun rays or the snow burns it. Even the stones on the mounts have been burnt and rendered red. Everything is converted into sand which flies in the air.

'Where the snow water flows down, why they have not planted trees there?'

'They are trying to grow some these days.'

'But why did they not think of plantation earlier?'

'There is a strange belief among people here. How did it crop up, no body knows. They have a false superstition. It says whosoever would plant a tree, he would die. The forest department planned many tree plantation programmes for this place but we could not get labour for the purpose. The locals opposed any plantations. They have been convinced now but it took a long time. To start with, labour was brought from Kullu. Now the trees have been planted on the banks of the river but their number is very small.'

'Isn't it that the plants grow naturally on the mountains?'

'It rains a little bit upto a height of nine thousand feet. The atmosphere and the environment is favourable for natural growth but beyond a height of nine thousand feet, the plants do not grow automatically. This is the natural phenomenon.'

'It is a stange world. There is no greenery for miles together. You cannot come across a green leaf even. The sand blows as it blows in a desert. Nobody knows for how long these red mountains have existed under the blaze of the Sun. As if to narrate their agony,' Pramod said.

'May be it is for the first time that a poet has reacted to the mountains' fate.'

'How do the people live here without trees, and greenery?,' Pramod said astonishingly.

'There is no population here. You will not come across any village for miles together. There is only sand, mountains and the river flowing downwards. There is no forest abutting the villages. There may be some bushes here and there. The locals gather them and use it as firewood. Another wonder is that the people dig some spots to find out the logs of wood buried underneath. That is also used as fuel.'

'When there are no trees, how do they get heavy old roots of trees?'

'The forest department has conducted researches on this aspect. One of our officers is of the opinion that there might have been a huge forest here in this area. It might have been destroyed one way or the other. And as a result people find big, heavy roots of trees under the ground.'

'Your department should conduct research on the food these people eat.'

'They only grow one crop annually. Barley is the only crop here. They use it for loaves and brew whiskey from it.'

'Hari, there are big plain areas. Cannot they cultivate the land?'

'Yes, the farming can be done. Some people are of the opinion that if the river water is tapped for irrigation, this barren land can be rendered fertile in no time. There arc many big grounds touching the Spiti river bank.'

'Has no plan been formulated by the government?'

'The government has so many other businesses to perform.'

'What do you mean?'

'As a stooge of politics, the government has to fight elections, has to transfer its employees from this place to that and vice versa.' Both of them laughed at this comment.

'The names here are quite interesting. It appears that Shaivism was prevalent here at one time or the other but you said that all people here believe in Buddhism.'

'There is a famous Hindu temple on way from Keylong to Udaipur. It is called Trilokinath temple. But in Spiti valley it is Buddhism only. They are followers of Mahatma Buddha. But you have rightly said that majority of the names are influenced by Shaivism. The Siva lingam is related to Hinduism. Here the word ling is part of many names. You go on counting the names. Shichling is the name of a place near Kaza. It is the distortion of Shivling. In the local language, the sounds ch and sh are prominent. This place might have been originally called shivling which later came to be called Shichling.'

'Hari, you seem to be a linguist. How long you have stayed in this area?'

'I have stayed in Kaza twice. I know the entire area. May I enumerate all those names? Listen—Shichling, Hurling, Murang, Shamling, Baaring, Choking, Darling, Sabling, Naing, Quling, Lingti and many more.'

There is no spot worth seeing in Kaza.' Pramod broke the silence after some time.

There is a village located ten miles away from Kaza named Kibbar. This is the highest village at a height of fifteen thousand feet.'

'I must visit Kaza, then. It will be a delight to be in Kaza, at a place which is the highest in the world.'

'You will call her loudly. She may listen to you,' Hari said.

'Hari, why do you remind me of her? Don't make my wounds fresh again. Yes, tell me what more is there to see?'

'There is a high hillock seven kilometers from Kaza. There is a famous Buddha monastery. The minarets of the monastery have golden pitchers on them. Around two hundred lamas live in it. Many old books are preserved there. The monastery is five hundred years old. The pictures are embroidered golden on the clothes. It is astonishing that even after centuries the glitter of the paintings embroidered has maintained its original lustre. In the hierarchy of Buddha monastries, Key monastery of Kaza is only third in ranking following the one in Lhasa and the second one in Leh. Dankar monastery is situated five kilometers upwards from Shichling. This ranked fifth in the world in hierarchy. Forty lamas live here. The Head Lama is elected through election for a period of three years. It is said that the election tradition has been in vogue successfully in the monastery for hundreds of years.'

'I am surprised to hear that in this desert there are monasteries. As old as five hundred years. What prompted people to come to such difficult inaccessible places that too five hundred years ago,' Pramod asked curiously.

'You are right. Life is very difficult here. No modern age comforts exist here. It is covered with snow for almost eight months in a year. The people are closeted in their homes. They are cut-off from the rest of the world. Nothing to eat and nothing to view. But hundreds of lamas live in these monasteries and they are absorbed in their penance. '

'What kinds of social life is here?'

'The people here are contented. They don't have the modern comforts but they do not rue the unavailable. They have their own social beliefs, their own values and guidelines. Dancing and singing are the great reliefs in life here which is hard. Women are very hard working. They dance and sing profusely but they do not believe in ostentation and pretensions. Like the nature of the mountains, their dances open up gradually with silence and depth overpowering the activity. The songs are melodious and catching. Most of them are related to God Buddha. They harvest only one crop in a year. Some folk rear milch animals. They don't have activity to do at home throughout the year. They enjoy chhang and ara and keep busy dancing. Their world is restricted to this side of Kunjam Pass. Modernism has not reached them, they have no regrets for it. May be this is the reason that crimes are not committed here. Pramod, you will be alarmed to know that the residents here never lock their houses. Many of the villages are not even aware of the locks. No one lifts or steals anything belonging to some one else.'

'It is heaven, then.'

'Horses of this place are very famous. They are able to run fast on narrow tracks of the mountains. Once I met a school teacher. He told that Spiti horses had been sent in the Mahabharata war also. The word Spiti means the owner of the horses. With the passage of time, the word changed from Ashavpati to Shivapati and then it transformed into Spiti.'

'Hari, you have done a lot for me. If you had arranged a horse, I would have escaped the fatigue.'

'Yes, I missed it. If I had said it to someone in my department, we could have got a horse. You have reminded me of the possible facility, I shall try to arrange one for you from the next village.

They went on and on. There were many stopovers on the way. Pramod had different kind of eatables on the way. They reached Kaza after many days. Hari stayed there for a few days. He made all the arrangements for the stay of Pramod. Pramod was now busy with his job. He made friends with his acquaintances. Life went on.

□

27

The weather at Kaza was slowly changing. It was growing colder and colder. There was a thin layer of snow on the mountains. It had started snowing heavily for the last few days. Kunzam Pass had been closed. The Spiti valley was segregated from the rest of the world. The people confined themselves to their homes. There was no life visible on the roads. It was clear weather when it stopped snowing. The movement of the folk started when the snow melted. Pramod was sick of loneliness. The engagements were almost negligible. He had not sufficient material with him for reading. He would get the four to five days old newspaper only when the Kunzam Pass opened. They got the newspaper only when the pass opened and not otherwise.

Pramod was happy that he got a letter from his home before the Kunzam Pass was closed and he had immediately replied it also. The dak bag carrying his letter had crossed Kunzam and Rohtang Pass, That dak was the last dak of this season.

Pramod adapted himself to the Kaza conditions gradually. He had some friends there. He now enjoyed taking a little bit of liquor in the company of Hari. He now started consuming more quantity of liquor. The conditions here were different. It was harsh cold here which made even the breath freeze, The sun was not visible for days together. No other eatables except flour, pulses and rice were available. Vegetables and fruits were rarities. There was no work at all. Under such circumstances, Pramod spent most of his time in the company of his friends enjoying liquor.

Pramod thought of his father and sisters. Were he in Kullu, he would have gone home to meet his family. He was often restless to remember the Kullu girl. He would then remember Hari. All these memories made him impatient. Drinks came as a consolation at such moments.

He often thought that all this misfortune had fallen upon him because of his own actions. He should not have confronted Khushal.

He alone had taken the responsibility of setting his department right. Why did he bother for his department when his officers, the local MLA and even the Minister were little interested in its welfare. Pramod now realized that he had committed a blunder. He should have remained silent and let the things go on as they went. If he had acted that way, he would have continued at Kullu. He got up at this thought. He thought, 'If he was in Kullu, he would have come across her one day or the other. Why did I create all this for myself.? I wanted to set the government right. I wanted to punish Khushal for his miscreations but I fell into the trap myself. I committed a blunder. One man alone cannot change the world. And what necessitated me to change the world? The huge world has not been created by me! May the creator change it. I am a small fry. I made a mistake. I should have flattered Mr. Thakur and could have lived like Khushal. My transfer could have been made nearer my home rather than at Kullu. It would have been quite comfortable. Is it me who has invited all this adversity?' Pramod would go on thinking for hours together. There was no work at all. Pramod was not interested in what was demanded of him in the office. His devotion to duty was decreasing gradually. Greater consumption of whiskey showed adverse signs on his body and mind.

It was snowing all the time. There were heaps of snow on the mountains. Only snow was visible all around and nothing else. Life had become almost snow. Nothing was known of the rest of the world. There was no contact with the outside world. Days and months passed by. With the melting of snow, there was a ray of hope that the roads would open for traffic and they would be connected again with the country.

□

28

It was open weather now. The snow was melting slowly. The interior paths in Spiti valley were opened to traffic. People started moving on foot. After some days, Kunzam Pass was also opened for traffic. Dak held for months together reached Kaza. Pramod received letters from his home and from his friends after a gap of many months. And now he could know what activities had been going on in India during that period.

Pramod had never gone home since he joined his job. His father and sisters repeatedly asked him to visit his home. Pramod applied for one month's leave. He reached Kullu after many days journey. He stayed with Shankar. He tried to locate the girl once again in the company of Shankar. He had no whereabouts of her. He wandered here and there aimlessly. He went to his home and joined back at Kaza after spending his vacation.

Time went on. The winter started again. Pramod prepared himself for the winters. He had sufficient experience of the previous year now. One had to confine oneself to the four walls of the house when it snowed. He had to store the ration before time. Pramod had brought a large number of books from home. He had brought some papers also. He thought he would read and write when snowfall would restrict him to the four walls. He was trying to forget the girl whom he had met near the Raghu Nath's tent on the day of Dussehra. He consoled himself by arguing to himself why remember who has not been located despite efforts? He now felt that his meeting with her was momentary. Sufficient time had passed by now. Who knows where she is? God knows where has she reached in her journey of life. Pramod tried his best to adapt himself to the new circumstances. All said and done, he occasionally felt the anguish of the meeting he had again with her near the Raghu Nath's tent. Emotions overpowered him keeping aside the logic. He still felt the sting of separation.

One evening he was engrossed in the same thoughts. He lamented the missed chance. He could not sleep. It often happened that he would invite his friends over drinks or would go to them for the purpose. It was just a routine now. Her thought haunted him and he could not have a wink of sleep. He tossed in the bed, and then got up and kept loitering in the room. He stood close to the window. He switched on the light. He turned the books, took a piece of paper and sat by the table.

There were tears in his eyes which soon dried up. He was no more remorseful now. He kept on writing something on the paper and then got up. He looked satisfied and happy.

Let it be that way. I shall write something keeping her in the centre of the story. May be a poem, no, no that will not do. I may not be able to put my emotions in a poem that requires certain technical restraints. A story can be a better option but it will also have a shorter space. Isn't the subject matter too small? She just came, thanked me, stopped for a while and went away. It is not worth a short story even. But I must write something bigger. I had read an English novel *Thelma*. *Thelma* stood in a boat near the bank of the river and from there itself.... Yes, I shall also scribble a novel. May be destiny had sent her to me at that moment to inspire me to write a novel. Pramod came to his bed with all these thoughts in his mind. He had felt relieved. He was soon fast asleep.

Pramod was absorbed in his official work. He would meet his friends and read books as well. He was preparing himself for writing a novel. He often felt bad that he had fallen a prey to the habit of drinking. Then he would console himself by saying that it was not possible to pass time had he not indulged in drinking. But now he had realized that he must leave drinking. He had friends who joined him in drink parties. Neither his friends nor the habit of liquor made him avoid the parties. He made deliberate efforts to say goodbye to drinks but simultaneously he continued with it.

It was the evening time. He had finished his official work. The dak had not reached that day. He sent his peon to the post-office. The peon came with the information that the person responsible for bringing the dak had come late. The dak has reached just now and will be delivered shortly. Pramod kept waiting for the dak in his office.

The dak arrived after some time. He kept the newspapers aside and started reading the letters. There was his personal letter also. He opened it, read it and then closed it in his pocket. He screened the other letters and then kept them there in the office. He came out of his office. He was just to leave the place when his peon brought the newspapers. Pramod often carried the newspapers home but had forgotten today and the peon made for the lapse.

He was reading *Thelma* these days. The novel had engrossed his attention so much so that he would take on to it as soon as he reached home after the office hours. Now the newspapers did not bind him as much as the novel did. He took the papers in his hand and reached home. He put the newspapers on the table, took his tea and then started reading the novel. *Thelma's* character haunted him. As the story of the novel was progressing, Pramod was returning to his past. While reading *Thelma*, he became enamoured of the girl whom he had met near Raghu Nath's temple. Many a time he was emotionally disturbed.

After a little while, his friends came. They took drinks followed by dinner. They left Pramod's residence late at night. Pramod went to his bed with a newspaper in his hand.

He scanned the news of different places for some time but was astonished to see a picture on the third page. He saw it intently and felt an electric shock. He rubbed his eyes, took the picture close to the lamp and watched it searchingly. He got up from his bed, loitered here and there restlessly and again saw the picture in the light. He was sweating now and his heartbeat had increased. Wonder and surprise was writ large on his face The caption under the picture read—Miss Savitri, the Kullu government school teacher, who has been selected for the Best Teacher Award of the state for the year.

'I have found her at last. I have recognized her right. Her eyes, her face, this is she exactly. I shall surely meet her. Definitely, I shall see her.' Pramod was moving to and fro in his room. He was almost mad with joy. He had shut all the windows to guard himself against cold but now he opened all the windows one by one. He moved the curtains aside. A cool breeze entered the room. He was roaming inside his room. He would stand close to the window and would catch hold of the iron grills of the window. He touched the grills with his forehead. He was in a thoughtful mood. The picture in the newspaper caught his attention. He relived the moment when she had met him. There were tears in his eyes. He tried to control himself. He was walking restlessly in his room. He went to his bed but he was not comfortable. He felt pricks in his soul. Sleep eluded him. He cut out that picture from the newspaper and kept it in the inner fold of his purse. He was now roaming in the room.

'How should I go ahead now. I cannot forget her. I must meet her at least once. There is some secret behind the incident. A momentary meeting has left its impact on me. It is so intense and so fresh in memory. May be we have some connection of the previous life. Even passage of time has not decreased the intensity of feelings. And when I was trying to forget her, why did her photo appear in a newspaper? Why did the same paper reach me? It has certainly a divine scheme behind it. May be we are made for each other. May be God wants to unite us in marriage.' Time went on and Pramod continued walking in the room. It was mid-night. Pamod could not sleep. There was a chain of thought in his mind. The Sun rose. Pramod felt irritation in his eyes. He felt tired. The body ache made him uneasy. He lay on his bed and was soon asleep.

When he woke up in the morning, sun rays welcomed him through the open windows. The room was cool. Pramod closed the windows. He took out his purse and viewed the photograph once again. He wanted to confirm it. But he rightly recognized the photograph of Savitri in the sun that she was the same girl who had met him near Raghu Nath's tent.

He kept thinking for long. How should he go ahead and by what means. He was late for the office, so he made haste for office. He was not at home there even. He was restless. At last, he applied for leave and made his way to his residence. He thought for a moment and then scribbled a letter to Shankar, 'My dear friend Shankar, the last night was the golden night of my life. You cannot even imagine what happened yesterday. Come on and hug me and load me with congratulations. You will ask why? Shankar, I have found her. But I have a grudge. She is in Kullu. You are in the police department in Kullu. She lives there and you could not find her. I live hundreds of mile away in Kaza but I have found her.

Anyhow, I cannot claim the credit of her discovery as it truly belongs to The *Tribune* newspaper that carried her photograph on the right top on page 3. You will kindly get the newspaper and see it. I got only one copy of the paper and I have taken out the cutting and have kept the photo with me. I am not sending it to you. Her name is Savitri and she teaches in Govt. High School, Kullu. The state government has selected her for the best teacher award. I have examined the photo minutely. I am hundred per cent sure that she is the same person. Shankar, I wish to meet-her at Kullu immediately. But it will take two days before I can leave Kaza. A person of our department is going to Kullu today with the dak. I am sending this letter to you through him. I have written a letter to Savitri also. You will please meet her as soon as you get my letter. You convey her my message and deliver this letter also. I am coming to you very soon and shall then meet her.

'Shankar, I am extremely happy today but I am afraid I may not go mad with happiness. I wish you were with me today so that I could share my joy with you. I don't have any of my Shankar in Kaza. There are friends who enjoy drink parties with me and vice versa but no Shankar in them.'

'You will not delay. You will go to her promptly. No work is more important than this. Leaving aside all your other engagements, you will kindly contact her. I am already too much late in this direction. Don't delay it any more. I shall reach Kullu very soon so that I can meet her immediately. - Yours Pramod.'

Pramod kept the letter on the table. He took an envelope and wrote Shankar's address on it. Then he took another paper. He wanted to write a letter to Savitri. He could not make out what should be the content. How, what and with what salutation, he should start the letter. He was a bit confused. He kept on thinking over the issue. He got up abruptly, closed his room and marched to his office. He asked one of his colleagues to despatch the important dak to be sent to Kullu next morning. After giving instructions to the concerned person, he came home again. He had not eaten anything since morning except only a cup of tea. In between he felt hungry but could not eat anything.

He loitred in the room with a pen is his hand. He would sit in the chair to write some thing but again stopped confused. He spent almost one hour in this frame of mind. He thought the office dak must be ready by now. Now he was determined to write a letter to her.

'Dear Savita,

I saw you once in Kullu Dussehra near Raghunath temple.

That was a short meeting. You had come to thank me. I had never imagined that one of the girls who had been extended lift in the jeep night before because of rain would come to thank me. I was surprised to see you. You stood there for some time. I saw you wholeheartedly only once. Your eyes spoke some thing which I thought was directed towards me. But I could not understand all this at that time. You waited there. I wanted to say something but I could not summon courage. And in the meanwhile you left the place.

'After that I made frantic efforts to locate you. I saw your photograph in the newspaper yesterday and the previous meeting came afresh before my eyes. My emotions are once again aroused for you and my eyes are flooded with water.

'I do not know where do you belong to, who you are and how you look? I do not know how do you feel about me? But believe me I cannot live without you.

'If you feel offended by my expressions, I shall tender my apology.

'I am sending this letter through my friend Shankar. I am trying for leave. It may take two days. I shall start from Kaza as soon as my leave is granted. One has to travel on foot upto Manali. I shall reach within three to four days. On reaching Kullu, I would like to meet you without delay. You will please tell Shankar how and where you would like to meet me. And what after meeting, that will depend upon your decision. I had made my mind the moment you left me after conveying your thanks. I don't have to make any other decision. Moreover, emotional decisions are not taken by viewing pros and cons. Relations are not made. They just happen. The relation has happened. It now depends upon you. It has happened in my case and I am committed to it.

Eager to meet you.

Yours

Pramod

Pramod had hesitated for hours together before writing the letter but once he started it, he finished it in one go. Tears from his eyes had fallen on the letter while he was writing and he encircled the drops with his pen. He wrote Savita on the envelope. He put Shankar's letter also in it. He put the envelope with in envelope and put Shankar's name on it. He went to his office with the envelope. The employee was ready with the dak. He called the man and told him Shankar's address. He also made him understand that the letter was to be delivered to Shankar only. And if Shankar is not available at that time, he should keep the letter with himself and deliver it personally to Shankar when he is available. The messenger went away. Pramod left his office after some time. He invited his friends to dinner that night and had special food made. They enjoyed the drinks and the dinner festively.

□

29

Shankar was just in the mode of retiring to bed when someone knocked at his door. He got up and opened the door.

'Here is a letter for you,' the visitor said while handing over a bulky envelope. Shankar looked at the visitor inquisitively and received the letter.

'Where from have you come? Who has given you this letter?' Shankar asked with his searching eyes on the letter.

'I have come from the Police Chauki Kaza to deliver the special dak. This letter has been sent by the big boss.'

'Mr. Pramod?'

'Yes, Sir.'

'Thanks. Come on have a cup of tea.'

'No, thanks. The officer had instructed me to hand over the letter to you only. I was in a hurry to hand it over to you. I searched for you during the day. You had already left when I reached your office. I came here also twice or thrice. I take your leave Sir.'

Shankar sat on his bed, opened the letter and moved closer to the lamp. There was an envelope inside with Savita inscribed on it. Shankar was surprised. He thought a wrong letter had been delivered to him. Who is this Savita? Why her letter has been sent to me? Who is the sender?'

He once again read the address on the outer cover. It was his name and his address. But the inner envelope was for Savita. He found another envelope inside which was for him. He took it out and read the letter. He was astonished. He read Pramod's letter again and again. He took Savita's letter in his hands. There were tears of joy in his eyes.

'Well done, Pramod. At last, your penance is complete. In fact, strange are the ways of love. But what about that Savita. May be she has something for him in her heart? And if she is married? At least Pramod will have the consolation that she has been located and his efforts have not gone futile. Shankar kept the letter for Savita carefully and went to sleep.

Next morning Shankar was ready for the task. He kept the letter in the inner pocket of his coat and started for the government school. He recalled that he knew some of the teachers there. He sent a message to his acquaintance through a boy requesting her to make arrangement for a meeting with the teacher who had been declared the Best Teacher of the State. Tell her that I had a special message for her. Shankar stood there and she went inside.

After a while Shankar saw a girl coming out. She was blooming like a rose. She was a combination of beauty and politeness. She walked slowly. Her eyes were on the earth. She was simply dressed but looked very beautiful rather extraordinary.

Shankar saw her from a distance. He was reminded of his friend Pramod. He heaved a sigh and said, were he present here? Pramod was right, Shankar thought. The beautiful woman had come to thank Pramod herself and the attraction both ways was not unusual. Shankar looked at the girl and was praying to his gods to enable a meeting between the two.

'Namaskar.' She said with folded hands. Shankar kept silent. He could not say anything.

'You have called me?' She said with her eyes fixed on the ground.

'Yes, I did. Sorry for the inconvenience.'

'No, it has not been inconvenient for me. Tell me what can I do for you?'

'Your name is Savita?'

'Savita? No. I am not Savita.' Shankar was confused to hear it.

'You have been declared the best teacher this year?' Shankar asked.

'Yes, yes. I am that fortunate teacher but my name is not Savita.'

'May I know your name please?'

'Yes, why not. I am known by the name Savitri.' She blushd for a moment and kept her eyes down.

'Yes, yes, Savitri. May be he has the right to call her as Savita.' Shankar muttered.

'What did you say, Sir?'

'No, nothing. I have to make a point with you.'

'Please do speak out.'

'Pramod is my friend who worked in the police department in Kullu. One day he was going to Manali in a jeep. You were walking with your friends along the road. You were being drenched by the rain. He asked the driver to halt the jeep to provide a lift to you and your friends. You travelled in the jeep some distance.'

Some reactions appeared on Savitri's face. She had something else in her mind when she came to him. May be there was a message from someone. May be there was the father of some girl. But she felt uneasy when an old episode was unfolded. She stood holding the support of the tree.

'You had come to Kullu to see the Dussehra fair. You went to the Raghu Nath's tent and thanked Pramod for the courtesy. Then you went away. Your thanks have taken away our friend from us. He is yours since then. He remained disturbed and tense. He has been transferred to Lahaul and Spiti for one reason or the other. He had an earnest desire to meet you before going to Lahaul.

'Then, why did he not meet me?' She said suddenly but later on felt a bit hesitant and fixed her eyes on the earth.

'How could he meet you? He did not know your whereabouts. We made all out efforts. We took the jeep driver with us and went to the place. We spent full one day in the village trying to locate you on one pretext or the other but all in vain. And how could we find you.'

'I remember there was common talk about the police investigation regarding eve teasing of the girls,' she said pressing her teeth forcibly.

'No one had misbehaved with the girls. But one of the girls had certainly teased my friend and now that girl has been caught. She stands before me.' Both of them laughed.

'I had gone to those villages with the driver. We came back after wandering for whole of the day. Pramod was disappointed. The poor soul left for Lahaul. He was further transferred from Lahaul to Kaza. He had gone home recently on leave. He stayed with me for two days. We wandered in Kullu and its surrounding villages searching for you but could not find you anywhere. Disappointed Pramod went back. Last week your photo was published in *The Tribune*. The paper reached Kaza after three days.

Pramod recognized you. He sent a letter to me through a special messenger. Pramod is coming soon to Kullu on leave. He wants to meet you.' Shankar became silent and looked at her. There were emotions visible on her face. She was happy and surprised simultaneously. She was also excited. Perhaps she was not able to control herself and stood holding the tree.

'Are you also eager to meet my friend?'

She felt shy and hesitant to hear these words. She hid her face smilingly.

'I have understood it. I am very very happy. I was afraid that you may or may not meet but the greater apprehension was whether you would like to see Pramod or not. Here is a letter for you that Pramod has sent. And it is Pramod who has turned you in Savita from Savitri not I.' Shankar handed over Pramod's letter. Tears of joy fell on her hands stretched for receiving the letter. She took the letter abruptly and then turned the other way.

'Pramod will come to me straight. You just tell when and where I should arrange your meeting?'

'This job is neither mine nor his now. You have to do whatever you want.'

'Shankar laughed at her comment and said, 'All right. I shall come here to fix the time with you and accordingly I shall arrange your meeting.' She said Namastey to Shankar with folded hands. Shankar was about to go back, when he heard, 'I am highly grateful to you. I will not forget the favour throughout my life.'

'So you have also been waiting eagerly for Pramod,' hearing these words she went to her school pleased.

Savitri had been selected as the best teacher of the state but she was not in her spirits today. Neither she was a teacher any more nor the best one. She had Pramod's letter in her purse and she was impatient to read it. There was no privacy in the school where she could open the letter. Without having read the letter, she could not say anything. She feigned to be suffering from headache and sat in one of the rooms. The pretext of headache also did not help her. She went to the headmaster, applied for leave and left for home. She came to the bus stand, boarded the bus and got down at the spot where Pramod had dropped her one and half years ago. She was now on the village road. Everything appeared changed. The school, the travel in the bus and the path everything looked new. She was accustomed to walk on the road daily but today she felt as if she was also a changed person. She looked on both sides. She had taken out Pramod's letter. There was no one visible around. It was a lonely place. She hung her purse on one of her shoulders, opened the letter and was about to read it when she heard a sound from the bushes closeby. She was alarmed and immediately put the letter in her purse. She looked around. There was none. She sat on a boulder, took out the letter and started reading it. She blushed while reading it. Tears of happiness trickled down from her eyes. She read the letter repeatedly. She would close her eyes. went into a thoughtful gesture. There were tears in her eyes. She was quite emotional. She sighted circle in one corner of the letter. She saw it attentively and found that there was a sign of drop in it. She could imagine that it was a trickle from Pramod's eyes while he wrote the letter. She could not hold herself and in excitement, kissed the sign made in the circle.

Time had stopped for her. She did not know how long she kept sitting there. She got up only when she found some persons coming on the way. She kept the letter carefully in her purse. She wiped her eyes with her hanky and was now on her way to her home. She told at home that she did not feel well, so she had come on leave.

Savitri was held in high esteem by the villagers once they knew that she had been declared the best teacher of the state. Many people thronged her home to congratulate her. His relations from the surrounding areas also came to compliment her for the achievement. She was happy at the developments. And now after getting Pramod's letter, her joy knew no bounds. Family members thought she was extremely happy because of the prize. She went to school the next day. Her friends could discern that something special had happened to make Savitri delighted. They asked her the secret. They commented sarcastically also but Savitri maintained her normal posture. She felt as if the time had stopped. An hour passed. She felt happy and relieved. The wait was tortuous. One day, two days and then three days passed but she did not receive any message from any quarter. She was however aware that it took three to four days from Kaza to Manali. She went on with her routine work, though there was anxiety and joy in her mind.

□

30

Pramod finished his office work. He packed his luggage and arranged for leave. The weather had changed. It was about to snow. The last caravan from Kaza to Manali was already on the move. Some people at Kaza advised Pramod not to leave now. Bad weather could create problems for him. But Pramod knew that if he missed the chance now, he may have to stay here for six-seven months at a stretch. Pramod could not stay back so long now.

On enquiry, he found three persons who wanted to embark upon the journey. So he left with them.

Pramod was flying on the wings of imagination. There was a tinge of fastness in his pace. He felt as if some force was dragging him on. While walking he was drowned in his thoughts. The photo he had seen in the newspaper was conjured before his eyes. He wished to reach Kullu in no time. Shankar must have met her. She might have read his letter. He was a bit scared when he thought she might have reacted the other way.

Suppose she takes it negatively. May be Shankar has not delivered the letter. May be she has refused to receive the letter. May be she does not have a similar feeling for Pramod. He would halt at this thought. He would gaze at the red mountains and feel disheartened. 'No, it cannot be that way', he thought in turn. So intense and so pure feelings could not be one sided. 'She must also have similar favourable feelings for me,' he thought. He would then look at the snowy mountains with a soothing feeling. Occasionally, he talked to his fellow travellers and tried to forget the stress.

The first day of journey was over. They stopped for the night. The caravan moved on the next morning. Pramod did not feel any kind of fatigue this time. The weather was a bit bad since the last day. The sky was overcast with clouds. The cold whiffs of air made one think that the mountains had fresh snow fall. He thought if it started snowing, they would not be able to march on. If the road closed, they would not be able to move either. Rocked between hope and disappointment, Pramod went on covering the distance.

It was mid-day now. They stopped at one place, took the food they had brought with themselves. They drank water and moved on again. The winds started blowing after they had covered only a small stretch. The compatriots told Pramod that their journey was endangered, they should go back. There is a village nearby. Pramod said he could not retrace his steps. They discussed the matter among themselves. And by the time, the winds stopped and they moved again. The sky was loaded with clouds. One of their fellows stopped suddenly. He saw the snowfall on the mountains and said, 'It will not be wise to continue our journey. There is a village behind. We can stay there. There is no place for shelter for miles together if we continue our journey. If the storm starts blowing, and the snowfalls, we shall be stuck in between.'

'Then what?' Pramod asked.

'We shall freeze in snow.' They all were disturbed to hear it.

'We shall not move further. The storm is at hand. We can reach the village left behind.' The travellers started backwards. Pramod stood there. He saw the snowfall and the thundering clouds. He looked at his co-travellers then, closed his eyes and thought, if she has received my letter, she must be waiting for me. If I stop here now, I shall have to stay for six months. No, no, I must cross this storm just now. I must go on.'

They marched back but Pramod stood there. Pramod started his journey after a few moments. He was happy that the harshness of winds had receded. There was a small room on one side of the road. He thought if the winds were harsh, he would stop over there for some time. He felt the sharp winds lose their velocity just because of his determination. He now started his onward journey.

He had gone only a few furlongs that the sharp winds started again. It soon turned into a storm. The snow started and it became difficult for Pramod to walk. The cold winds from the opposite direction affected Pramod's eyes and the snow fall on his body made his march difficult. It was now impossible to walk. Pramod was writhing with pain. The storm was fierce now. The sound of winds was harsh for his ears. Disgusted he turned back and ran. It was chill cold. He slowed down after some time as he was tired to the bones. He reached the small room. He stood in its veranda and set his clothes right. He removed the snow from his mouth and clothes. He saw this way and that way. His companions must have reached the village in time. Pramod was all alone in the fierce storm. He kept his bag down and took out a warm sheet and a towel. He put off his coat and cleared it of the snow inside. He cleaned all the clothes with his towel. He wrapped himself in the woolen sheet and sat on his bag.

It was snowing heavily now and the storm was at its height. In no time the mountains of snow appeared there. The path was covered with snow both ways. The stones had covered themselves with snow. There was snow and snow all around. The high red mountains had also turned white. He was worried now. Where will he go? There was no way visible. How far the small room could provide him shelter. Time went on. It was now getting dark. Pramod got up and had a round in the veranda. He approached the door. It was locked. He was shivering badly. He thought he will have to spend the night there. He took a stone and tried to open the lock with it. He could not break the lock but the chain gave way and he entered the room. There was a bed on a cot. Utensils were also kept there. Firewood was also there. He felt relieved to see all this. He wanted to kindle the fire. The wooden sticks were there but nothing to light it. He searched around. He found a match box. He lit the fire and warmed himself. He felt sleepy after some time. He had closed the door from inside. He could hear the harsh sounds of the wind. He had no hunger. He extinguished the fire and went to sleep.

□

31

Eight days passed. Pramod did not reach Kullu. Shankar was concerned about him. 'He might have started late,' Shankar thought. He got all the more anxious thinking that Savitri might be worried to think about the non-arrival of Pramod. He thought once or twice to go to her in the school to console her but his shyness kept him away. He had just come from his office when Savitri reached his residence with one of the friends. Savitri had come along with the same teacher who was an acquaintance of Shankar and through whom he had sent the message to her. Shankar received them in the room and said, 'I can understand your concern. I am also worried about him. But since Pramod has started his journey, he will reach sooner or later.'

'She is very much upset for the last three, four days,' the teacher accompanying Savitri said.

'She is right. I have also found it difficult to pass the days.'

'Did you enquire from somewhere?,' Savitri spoke slowly.

'I was just waiting for him as yet. But I shall get enquired tomorrow through my office.'

'May be the roads are open to traffic?'

'Yes, yes. A party arrived here just day before yesterday. Yes, the weather is getting worse but the road remains open for many days.'

'Please get it enquired in detail. You will kindly inform me as well. I find it difficult every moment. It hangs heavy on me. I don't know why and where he is stuck?' Tears rolled down from Savitri's eyes and fell on her clothes.

'I understand your concern. I wanted to come to you to discuss the same issue. I also love my friend very much. I am also worried. He has written that he would come here. Come he must. He is always firm on his stand. It is official work. May be he has been delayed because of some official delay. The weather is inclement. May be he has been compelled to stay on his way. Don't be perturbed. God will be kind to him.' Shankar advised Savitri to be patient. Shankar served them tea. After taking tea Savitri left with her friend.

Shankar discussed it with his friends in the police station and came to know that Rohtang Pass had received heavy snow. Kunzam Pass was also closed. No movement was possible. May be Pramod had crossed the Rohtang Pass before the snowfall. In that case, he must be either at Manali or close to Kullu. Shankar was impatient. He applied for leave and went to Manali. He enquired from the police station. No one had any information about Pramod. He talked to people around. Someone who had come from Kaza told him that the weather had changed there suddenly a few days ago. The area faced fierce storm. And experienced heavy snow fall closing all the traffic. Shankar was apprehensive about the safety of Pramod. May be Pramod had started from Kaza and the storm blew fiercely, he might have been trapped in adverse weather. He prayed to God that Pramod may be safe wherever he is. Shankar came back to Kullu. Worried as he was, he spent two three days restlessly.

Shankar expressed concern about Pramod in his department. Kaza was contacted through wireless. After three days, it was known from there that Pramod had left Kaza for Manali before the storm but did not return to Kaza. Shankar feared something unwanted. He also gathered information that the persons who had embarked on journey to Manali with Pramod had returned to Kaza before the storm. They also told that Pramod had not agreed to their insistence to retrace his steps and marched ahead to Manali instead. Shankar got all the more worried about Pramod.

Heavy snowfall continued and all the mountains were white with snow. One could not go beyond Manali. Shankar had no means to know about the welfare of Pramod. He was at a loss to decide what and how should he tell it to Savitri?

Savitri came to him at his residence another day.

'I am sorry I have not been able to gather information about Pramod,' Shankar said in a worried tone.

'Had he started from Kaza?' Shankar remained silent on this point.

'Please tell me in detail. Don't try to hide anything. It is a question of life and death for me.' Savitri tried to wipe her tears.

'Yes, I have got all the information about him. Pramod had started from Kaza with a few companions. They witnessed a fierce storm on the way. His companions returned to the base but Pramod did not go back despite their repeated requests. They reached Kaza after a few days but nothing was known of Pramod.'

'What has happened all this? The story has worsened instead of being having a happy ending. I never thought of it this way.'

'Pramod is one of my those friends without whom I can not live. I understand your feelings also. He was so impatient to meet you that he affronted the fierce storm even. So many days have passed. God knows what has happened.'

'I am on this side of Rohtang and he is on the other side. What a tragedy?' Tears flowed down her cheeks.

'Don't be sad. Life has its own ways even in the storms that rock us. Sometimes the wait is prolonged beyond expectation. You both have intense feelings of love for each other, I feel even God cannot scuttle it. This is the only hope. I cannot think of any thing else.' There were tears in Shankar's eyes too.

'There is nothing beyond Manali and also on this side of Kaza. There are no signs of life. There is snow and snow around and everything is covered under snow there.' Savitri burst in to tears.

'Yes everything there freezes but no such snow has evolved as yet which can freeze love.'

'Has anyone ever survived the heavy snowfall and the fierce storm?', Savitri asked.

'I do not know but I certainly know that my friend Pramod will survive all such storms and reach Manali one day.'

They remained silent for some time. Their eyes were wet. They did not know what to talk. There was grave silence. Only voice of sipping tea disturbed the silence.

'What should I do now?,' Savitri said with tears in her eyes.

'I also wanted to ask the same question.'

'If both of us ask this question, who will answer us.'

'Have faith in God. There is no alternative. We shall have to wait and pray. I remember I had sent Pramod to Keylong in the company of Hari when he went there for the first time. He had gone to Hidimba temple at Manali with Hari and had spent lot of time sitting inside. Hari had been loitering outside the temple. Hari had written to me in detail. May be Pramod was remembering you while sitting in the temple. He had gone a frustrated man from here. You had not met him by that time. He must have prayed in Hidimba temple for you. I am confident that Hidimba will certainly protect Pramod.'

They were again silent for some time.

'Will you go with me to Hidimba temple some day?,' Savitri said cautiously.

'Why not? But what will you do there?'

'The mountains are covered with snow. And my hopes are buried under snow. Now Hidimba's blessings are the only hope. Please do come with me to Hidimba temple.'

'All right. When do you want to go?'

'Tomorrow afternoon. I shall have half day's leave. I shall go home after the visit to the temple,' Savitri said and went away.

□

32

'May be it is the place where Pramod had been sitting for quite sometime.' Shankar said pointing a finger towards a spot inside the Hidimba temple. Savitri moved forward, saw the spot watchfully. She kept her palms there and then sat down. She closed her eyes. Shankar came out of the temple. He relived in imagination the moments Pramod had spent inside the temple and Hari had kept wandering here and there under the pine trees. Hari had to wait for Pramod for a long time. Today Savitri was praying for Pramod as he had prayed for her the other day. What a strange coincidence? When Pramod was here Savitri was not and now she is present, he is not. Savitri was not known then. Now Pramod is known but no one knows where he is lost.

After wandering for sufficient time, Shankar stood at the gate of the temple. He peeped inside, she was sitting still at the spot as if it was Pramod. Her eyes were shut as if in a trance. Shankar did not want to disturb her. He retraced his steps silently and was under the pine trees once again. He felt exhausted. He was also aware that Savitri had to catch a bus for her village from Manali. He again came to the gate and coughed to attract Savitri's attention. She noticed his arrival and got up.

'Mother Hidimba will certainly accept your prayers. May be it is the result of Pramod's prayer that we have found you. You have been praying for Pramod sitting at the same place where he had prayed for you.'

Savitri got up slowly. She came before the temple. She had brought flowers, etc. from Kullu. She put her offerings before goddess Hidimba. She offered some coins also. Then she got up. She gave some Prasad to Shankar. He was watching Savitri. He smiled for a moment but then tears rolled down his eyes just as lightening is followed by heavy downpour. Savitri also could not restrain her tears. Both of them came out of the temple.

'I am confident that Pramod is safe and will reach this place soon.'

'I have also faith in your trust. Moreover, we cannot do anything except keeping faith.'

'Trust is something big. Trust is God.'

'When will Rohtang Pass open?' Savitri's words disturbed Shankar. He was on the earth now.

'Only after a few months.'

'After months?'

'Yes, but Pramod must be having a safe stay somewhere.'

'There may be many villages in between.'

'Yes, there are many villages on the way at short distances. People live there. He might have stopped somewhere.' Shankar's voice was trembling. He knew for miles together there was no village on the way. He had learnt after enquiries that there was no village situated for a stretch of 30 miles from the point from where Pramod's fellow travellers had gone back. How could he tell it to Savitri but his tongue faltered while speaking this lie.

'You will kindly meet me occasionally. You are his friend. I cannot share this with any one at home. And even if I tell, what should I say? You are my only support as long as he does not return.'

'You need not worry. I am at your beck and call. I shall be happy to do anything for you. You are my friend's belonging. I shall have to take care of you till my friend comes.' They had covered some distance from the temple. Savitri had controlled her emotions now. She had wiped her eyes but the eyes spoke the entire story.

'I once again request you not to torture yourself by thinking about the possibilities. We must be patient and courageous for the time being. I shall inform you as soon as I get some information.'

'Will he come?,' Savitri asked him.

'Yes, he will definitely come. I have full faith.' Temple bells rang when Shankar said it. Some devotee must have rung the bell before offering prayers. Savitri was pleased to hear the sound of the bells. Shankar also smiled.

'How wonderful. Even the temple has stamped our decision and determination with the ringing of the bells. They were now at the bus stand. They boarded a bus bound for Kullu. Savitri got down at the particular point. Shankar went to Kullu.

□

33

One after the other many days passed. Pramod was restless in the beginning but gradually he compromised with the prevalent situation and conditions. It was crystal clear to him that he was fully entrapped. There was no way out on either side. It will take six months before the roads were opened for traffic. He will have to live all alone for six months in the same room.

That room was in fact the office of the forest department. The employee had gone to Manali after the snowfall. He would come back only when the roads opened. Pramod inspected the material lying in the room. There were some rice, flour, pulses, ghee, etc. It was the kitchen material which was now so important for him. His first reaction was positive and he was naturally happy as all things required for sustaining life were lying in the room. But soon he could feel that the ration was not sufficient if he was made to stay there for six months. He felt frustrated and disappointed. Once the ration is exhausted, how will he survive, what will he eat? He was anxious and worried.

Gradually, he was stable. He kept Savitri's photo under his pillow. There was a calendar bearing the photo of God. He also hung it on the wall. He would take some snow, put the rice in it and keep it on the stove for cooking. It took much longer than it takes in the plains. He would drink the beverage made of rice or sometimes he cooked chapaties. He knew he had to sustain with the ration for six months. So he used the little quantity and often drank the liquid made of flour or the rice.

After a few days, the weather changed. The snowfall stopped. The sun shone. He removed the snow from the veranda. He moved forward but could not see any thing. He could not see any stone that were visible before the snowfall. It had been snowing heavily.

It was many feet deep. He looked around for a long time. The sun rays were bright now and the reflection of the same in the snow blinded him almost. He went in to his room.

It was a strange experience in Pramod's life. All alone, he was closed in a small room, and he was destined to stay there for months together. He changed his clothes when he felt that the dress had gone dirty. He had clothes in his bag. What next? He did not have soap, water available for the purpose. His beard and nails were also growing. He had carried only a few clothes with him. He thought he would get the required things from Shankar. Thoughts thronged his mind. He thought whatever he could imagine. He had nothing to do except thinking. What more could he think. He felt his head heavy. He passed his time in praying to God and seeking his blessings.

He would watch the photo published in the newspaper. He would see Savitri's picture. After having continuously watched her, he would now talk to her also. He would say something and then would wait for an answer. He heard the voice of Savitri resounding in his ears. He would keep sitting for hours together thinking and talking. He would get up from the cot, open the door and come out in the veranda. He was fed up with the whiteness of the snow. He again entered his room to find the same calendar, the same photo of Savitri. Pramod thought how small this world had become. Many a time the weather was inclement. Fierce storm would blow. The walls of his room were shaken. He was frightened. He felt the sharp winds were uprooting his room. He occasionally heard the sound of moving glaciers. He had heard that in such a weather the snow mountains flow like boulders in the stream. Whatever was on the way, it was dislocated and flowed with the glaciers. Whenever he heard such a voice, he sat cautiously. He would keep Savitri's photo published in the newspaper carefully in his pocket. If the glacier swept away this room, he must at least have Savitri's photo intact. On thinking this way, Pramod comforted himself. He would stroll in the veranda when the weather was clear. She viewed around. He could see nothing else but the snow all around.

Once or twice, he noticed some birds in the veranda. Pramod was almost eccentric. He started talking to them. He spoke loudly. Probably, the birds were also astonished to see a man there which earlier they never had seen.

Pramod would talk to himself. Once he thought he should go on speaking lest he forgets to speak after living for months together in such an atmosphere. He longed for going back to his world, his home. He wished to meet his father and his sisters. And he had to complete his journey that he started from Kaza. Just now, he was on his way. Kullu is his destination. Thinking all this, he would feel his head heavy. There is a limit to thinking also. To think and to sleep, this was his routine.

□

34

The phone bell rang. Mr. Sharma who was loitering in the veranda took it himself.

'Yes, who is speaking? Yes, I am Sharma speaking,' Sharma said looking around.

'Thakur speaking. The meeting is slated for today afternoon.'

'No, no. Nothing is audible on phone. Leave the phone and you come here positively.' Sharma closed the phone. He called someone after a few minutes and asked him to bring a cup of tea. He sipped tea and was lost in his thoughts. About half an hour passed.

'Sir, Mr. Thakur has come.'

'Please bring him here.'

'Namaskar Sharmaji, why are you off colour today morning? I had to inform everyone about today's meeting,' Thakur said while occupying the chair.

'Thakur, we must be vey careful now. The Chief Minister is in the know of all the happenings. The midday meeting will not be held at my residence. We shall not discuss anything on phone. All the details reach the Chief Minister. And if our plan also reaches him, we shall be undone. That will be an end of our story.' Sharma rang the bell. He asked his attendant to bring tea and sat in the chair worried.

'But what has happened Sharmaji?'

'Whatever transpired at Jallandhar is known to the Chief Minister. I fail to understand who passed it on to him. We were only a select few. Moreover, we held the meeting out of city. No government officer was with us. Only my personal staff was present. 'Whatever we discussed in camera, even that is known to the Chief Minister.'

'This is strange. How could it happen?'

'Who can it be?'

'Thakur, what about Rita?'

'Not at all. The question does not arise. She does not know any one. I have full confidence in her,' Thakur said confidently.

'I also trust her.'

'It may have added to your trust. I have not seen her since she has come to the capital. We learn that she spends most of her time with you. It is O.K. We have to make her a full time party worker,' Thakur laughed mischievously.

'Thakur, we cannot humour it away.'

'Excuse me, Mr. Sharma.'

'Thakur, you do one thing. Meet individually all those persons whom you had to invite in today's meeting. Don't use the phone. You consult Prandhir and Kapoor. Decide some outside place for meeting. Make all of them reach there. No one else except you three should know that place. They should only know that they were going to attend an important meeting. Don't disclose the place of meeting even to them. You will inform me and I shall reach the spot.'

'It is perfectly all right. We shall have to act calendestinely now. You might have been successful in the mission that was entrusted to Rita.'

'Yes, not three but she has won over five MLAs. She had told that she had severed them from the Chief Minister's group. You have misgivings that Rita has been with me for these days. I am busy in this job. I have been asked to break these MLAs, and I am doing it. You are unnecessarily jealous. And she was with you day before yesterday. You are not aware of yourself.'

'And before two days?'

Let us leave this issue. We can make the best as per availability. You go ahead with the job and send Prandhir to me.' Both of them got up. Thakur shook hands with him and went out. Sharma kept loitering in the room, noticed the time and then sat in the chair. He opened his briefcase, took out a file and started reading it.

Prandhir entered the room after some time.

'Did Thakur meet you?'

'Yes, he met me and has briefed me in detail. You have done the right thing by changing the venue of the meeting. I was also doubtful. Moreover, we should not hold meetings here in the capital and that too in our bungalows. The secret may slip away. And as long as we do not talk with the High Command in the capital, we should keep things secret,' Prandhir said while occupying the chair.

'We should have kept it secret but we could not. The whole issue has reached the Chief Minister. We shall have to manage it now.'

'You need not worry. I know the weakness of Vishal Singh. I meet him just today. I shall convince him in such a manner that he will not believe in any thing said to him after that.'

'How?'

'I and Vishal Singh belong to the same caste and community. Swearing on caste, I shall convince him that I could never side with Mr. Sharma. I shall also make him understand that we cannot befool ourselves by making a Brahmin Chief Minister in place of a Rajput. I shall take along with me some more Rajput MLAs. Whatever has reached the Chief Minister, I shall get it washed. But Mr. Sharma, we must finalise our programme in today's meeting and should go to Delhi to meet the High Command. It cannot be delayed any more. We must hurry up.'

'Your proposal is right. Confuse the Chief Minister and in the meanwhile, we should equip ourselves. What about Darshan?'

'We have discussed with him in detail. He is already a Minister but his status is of Minister of State. I promised him a Cabinet beth but he has not agreed as yet. He is a poor Harijan. If we offer him fifty thousand, he will defect. I am also in touch with him. I learn that a PWD contractor in his area is his close friend. He gives financial help to him during elections and also lends his jeep free of charges. I have called for him. I have entrusted this job to the Chief Engineer. He will ask the contractor to pay rupees fifty thousand or even up to one lakh to Darshan Singh to make him quit the Chief Minister's camp. There is a proposal to construct a bridge in that area worth rupees fifty lakh and I have suggested that the contract be given to the same contractor. I am confident that tempted by this offer, he will ensure Darshan Singh's departure from the Chief Minister's camp.' Prandhir was full of confidence. The door opened and the attendant brought tea. They were now taking tea.

'Prandhir, how do you rate our position at this time?,' Mr. Sharma asked him while sipping tea.

'Our position is good. We are in majority now. If Rita's claim about the win over of those two persons is right, then we are in a comfortable majority. We must calculate in today's meeting and then we should go to Delhi for talks.'

'What is the venue of the meeting?'

'The Canal Rest House.'

'It must be kept a secret. Do not take many cars. All should be accommodated in two or three cars. You should sit silently in the room. The entry should be in neither person's name. You should post your confidant outside the rest house to have a watch.'

'You need not worry. I have told everything in detail to Mr. Thakur. He is experienced in such matters. Yes, Rita is also coming.'

'Why not. After all she has managed five MLAs. She has done a greater job than the Ministers even.'

'She will come with you?'

'Or will she come with you?'

'She looks comfortable with you, Mr. Sharma.'

'You are normally very serious but it appears you are also enjoying jokes today.'

They both laughed. Prandhir shook hands with him and went out. Sharma came to the veranda and kept walking to and fro for a few minutes. And then he moved to the dining hall. His wife and children were waiting for him at the breakfast table. He joined them. The children were busy talking to each other. His wife tried to initiate conversation but Sharma was silent, in haste to finish his breakfast.

'Dear father, you are always worried. You should talk to us at least on the dining table,' the elder daughter said to him.

'I don't know why people want to become Ministers. They are not free for a moment, always busy. It never gives a feeling of home. It is home as long as the children are there. That too because of children. Rest everything happens like a machine,' Mrs. Sharma said while pasting butter on the roasted bread pieces.

'So you are buttering the children today?,' Sharma tried to release the tension.

'Father, what is the problem. You were receiving so many phone calls yesterday. Horse trading is going on. Who is in whose favour and who is in the opposite camp. I learn you are holding a meeting today,' the elder son of Mr. Sharma said.

'And there is a news in the paper also.'

'What is the news?'

'There is a divide in the party. The dissidents are bent upon changing the Chief Minister and that the leader of the dissidents is Mr. Sharma.'

'And my father will replace Mr. Vishal Singh as the Chief Minister.' The younger girl started clapping after placing the toasts in the plate. The other children also clapped with her.

'Kudos to Chief Minister, Mr. Sharma.' The younger girl raised the slogan. They were all in a jovial mood now. Sharma was serious since morning but now he became jubilant.

'Do not believe in the stories of the newspapers. There is no such movement. You should not discuss these things,' Sharma said in a serious tone.

'We should not discuss. May be something is going on silently and secretively.'

'Yes, there is simmering. Most of the MLAs want me to be the Chief Minister. Majority is with us now but this should not be leaked out,' Sharma said it in a low voice.'

'It will be great fun then.'

'My father will be the Chief Minister.'

'There are only two cars at his disposal as yet. Sometimes my friends come and there is no car outside. And once my father becomes the Chief Minister, there will be many cars here.'

'I shall leave my college studies. I shall establish a big industry in partnership with my maternal uncle at Ludhiana. My father will be the Chief Minister and the whole government will be at my beck and call,' the elder son said.

'Yes, all things will happen then.' Sharma stood up after watching the time. The children sat at the table but Mr. Sharma went inside his room. His wife followed him.

'Is that true?' His wife asked him getting closer to him.

'Sharma never plays half heartedly. Just wait for some time.'

'So, you will occupy the Chief Minister's chair.'

'It looks like that.'

'Truly. It will be a big news. You are fully competent to be the Chief Minister. God knows who made Vishal Singh the Chief Minister. You are a veteran leader, much older than him. You are not only better qualified than him but more capable also. You should decorate the Chief Minister's chair. I had shown your horoscope to an astrologer last month. He had told me that your stars are very favourable after two months. And success will be at your doors.'

'So you do all these things without my knowledge.' Sharma kept his hand on her wife's shoulder and drew her closer to himself.

'As advised by the astrologer, I arranged prayers also. He had pointed out that one of the planets had ill-effects.'

'Who is that astrologer?'

'He is the greatest astrologer and tantric in the Capital.'

'You call him. I want to talk to him personally.'

'All right. I shall call him today evening.'

After sometime Mr. Sharma left for his office.

□

35

'We have not met for many days,' Vishal Singh said to Prandhir while shaking hands with him.

'In fact, I was out of station for some time. I had not been to my area. I spent a few days there and then attended a couple of marriages. I felt I had not met you for many days, so I came to see you.'

'You are welcome. I want to discuss something important with you.'

'Yes, Yes, please do tell me.'

'I learn that activities have increased these days. A group of disidents is gaining momentum against me. They are planning to oust me from Chief Minister's post.'

Prandhir tried to laugh at the comment.

'What is the matter? You are laughing?,' the Chief Minister asked.

'You are very simple and credulous. Such rumours are a common thing in power politics. There cannot be any truth in it,' Prandhir said looking into the Chief Minister's eyes.

'Is that a lie?'

'Yes, it is a lie, rather a white lie.'

'So many persons have told me. A few Ministers and MLAs have also talked to me about it. Yesterday a journalist confirmed it. The newspapers have also been carrying such news for some days.'

'How does it matter? It is being spread. Our enemies are involved in it. I fear the opposition party is planting such stories. They don't have anything on their side. They were badly beaten in the elections. They don't have any hope to win elections in future as well. They want to break our party from within.

'Then what is the problem?'

'No problem. You are the Chief Minister and you will continue as such. I also wield my influence,' Prandhir said raising his head.

'The gossip mongers spread rumours like anything. Prandhir, it is also being said that you are helping Sharma to become the Chief Minister. But I did not trust this report.'

'How can you trust it? How can I be against you? How can I make efforts to install Sharma as the Chief Minister? Listen to me Chief Minister. Let us have politics. Caste is definitely an issue. Being a Rajput; how can I go against a Rajput Chief Minister? I shall not be able to face my community. I cannot be a *gaddar* (betrayer). It is after many many years that the Chief Minister is from our community. All others also think about this community, so how can I betray a Chief Minister who comes from my caste. This can never happen. I shall never commit this crime.' Prandhir said quite confidently.

'I expected the same response from you. I was worried when I learnt that you along with a few other Rajput MLAs were also a part of this conspiracy. If my own people stand up against me, how can we dissuade others. Prandhir, you handle all the Rajput MLAs. If anyone is angry or has a misunderstanding, you arrange his meeting with me. If any one has a issue or wants to get some work done, I shall do it.'

'You are unnecessarily anxious. What is Sharma's stature?

'Yes, Sharma has no standing of himself.'

'And Sharma is my friend too. Many MLAs talk what suits them. Some are angry with you and comment whatever they feel in anger. This does not mean that they are planning to oust you as Chief Minister. And Sharma cannot do anything without my support. And if Sharma has anything in his mind, he will talk to me first. I shall never support any move that aims at ousting a Rajput Chief Minister. Even if god comes to replace you. I won't support the move.' The Chief Minister felt relieved after having talked to Prandhir. He rang the bell. The peon brought tea. They were sipping it.

'Please do not worry at all as long as Prandhir is there. But you should take care of Pawan Lal. He is a very tricky fellow. He keeps track of all the activities. He has his connections with Delhi also. He has his control over a few High Command members. He swears to become a confidant of you but that is all selfish.'

'But he gave me an assurance that he was working in my favour and is taking to all.'

'May be he is honest so far in his loyalty to you but he can prove a betrayer any moment. His track record confirms his vulnerability. He has been making and breaking Chief Ministers. He may create a rift among all and may aspire to become the Chief Minister himself.'

'Any evidence?'

'There are no evidences for some moves but his activities smack of it. His hold over Delhi is stronger than before. His acquaintance with an influential leader of Delhi has matured into friendship. They enjoy drinks together.'

'So he should also be watched.'

'You need not worry. Leave it to me. After all it is a matter of our own community.' Prandhir got up shook hands and left the place.

A few minutes later, the Secretary of the Chief Minister came with files. The Chief Minister started signing the files. The Secretary would open the file for the CM and he would sign it. After one lot of files was over, the peon kept the other lot for signatures. The process continued. The third lot was there now.

'Mr. Gupta, you see I am putting my signatures only. I am not reading anything. I believe that you will not get wrong thing done.'

'Sir, you need not worry. But you seem to be disturbed these days. The Secretary said after keeping the file before him.'

'Nothing very serious. It all goes on in power politics,' the Chief Minister said while signing the papers.

'Sir, there are lots of rumours these days.'

'So, you also know something.' The Chief Minister kept the pen and looked towards Gupta.

'The dissidents are very active these days. CID has also filed various reports containing lots of information. The dinner parties have come a common sight in the Capital. The different groups are busy with dinner diplomacy. The rumours are very hot. It is being circulated that Mr. Sharma heads the dissidents. He wants to topple you to become the Chief Minister himself,' Gupta said while moving the file forward.

'Yes, I also heard it. But when I asked them, they swore by my loyalty.'

'Excuse me, Sir. Politics and loyalty?'

'May be you are right. Loyalty is only a show-piece sometimes.' The Chief Minister was now silently signing the files.

'Sir, you did not complete your comment.'

'It does not need to be completed.'

'But it can be guessed.'

'You have understood it?'

'Leave it, Sir. It will add to your anxiety.'

'Yes, Gupta. I am very much perturbed. I just wanted to say that only dogs are faithful these days. I had read a philosopher saying this long before. It said, 'The more I think about man, the more I am bound to praise the dogs.' It had appeared very bad to me at that time. I thought the philosopher was wrong. All human beings are not alike. Not about all the people, but my opinion about all the politicians is now on those lines.'

'Sir, I cannot say anything.'

The phone bell rang. The Chief Minister picked up the phone. 'Yes, I am busy at the moment. Who is it?'

'Pawan Lal wants to meet you urgently. PA informed the Chief Minister on plone.'

'Yes, send him immediately.' The Secretary could understand. He kept the files aside and went out. The peon picked up files from one heap and came out.

'Yes, come in Pawan Lalji. What is the news?'

'Some dissident MLAs are holding a meeting today now at Sharma's residence. I have come to know it from one of my sources.' A lady has come from Kullu along with Thakur. She is new to politics but she is very beautiful and young. She is a frequent visitor to MLAs hostel these days. A few of the MLAs have become friends with her. She seems dangerous in my opinion. I learn she will also attend the meeting today at mid-noon.'

'What is her name?'

'Rita.'

'She accompained Sharma to the Rotary Club and later also, she was with him when he addressed a public meeting in the Harijan Colony. She is prominent in the Capital these days.'

'All right. You collect the details of today's meeting that is scheduled at Sharma's place at midday.'

'I just came to inform you. We are fully cautious. We shall not let them do anything. You will please call and talk to Darshan Singh.' Pawan Lal left the office.

The Chief Minister asked his PA not to allow anyone to come to his room.

Vishal Singh kept sitting silent for long. Then he got up and started moving to and fro. Anxiety was writ large over his face. He felt exhausted. He was looking at the chair. He came close to it. He shook the chair with his hand. The chair revolved round.

It was at its original position after the round. He was roaming in the room with his hands in his pocket. He now only stood near the window looking outside but saw the Assemby building beyond. Then he shifted his gaze to the room inside. When he felt tired, he sat in the adjoining room.

The phone bell rang. The PA informed him that some people from far-off places had come to meet him. The Chief Minister occupied his chair.

'There was fire in our village. About 50 houses were gutted. We have not received any compensation from the govt. so far.' The poor people from the village told the CM.'

'Have you brought it in writing?'

'Yes, Sir.'

'Give it to me. We shall try to help you.'

'Hail storm has destroyed the crops in our area. We don't have any other source of livelihood. We shall not be able to recover even the cost of seed. What shall we eat? How shall we survive. The government should come to our rescue.'

'I have kept your application for help. I shall examine it.'

'Sir, you will examine it, but hunger does not wait for anyone. We are totally undone.'

'All right. You go please.'

'A water supply project for our village has been in news for the last five years. You had laid its foundation stone. You had announced that the scheme would be completed within one year. Five years have elapsed. It is not even half way through.'

Our village folk climb up a distance of 5 km to fetch water. The summers have been harsh this year and all water sources have gone dry. In some of the villages, people are consuming unhygienic water containing worms. We have come to request you that the project may be completed immediately to enable us to have potable water.' A villager pleaded with folded hands.

'The govt. has lots of businesses. The govt. coffers have less of money and more of works.'

'But Sir, you had promised to complete the scheme in one year.' A youngman from the deputation reminded the Chief Minister.

'Have you come to teach me? You should behave yourself. If I had announced it, I got it started too. Only five years have elapsed. The work will be executed in proportion to the finances available. The govt. has so many other responsibilities to perform.' The Chief Minister said in an unpleasant mood and asked them to leave.

For many days now, the Chief Minister was not able to give full time to the persons who came to meet him. So there was a huge rush of visitors today. The deputations were explaining their difficulties before the Chief Minister. Some of the visitors had come to get their individual problems solved. The Chief Minister was listening to all of them but his mind was focussed on the activities of dissidents. The Chief Minister was not attentive to the problems of the poeple, their difficulties, etc. He listened the prayers of the people in a mechanical manner, took the applications and sent them. It appeared as if a machine installed in the chair was working automatically. The Chief Minister was busy rebutting the dissidents. After sometime the Chief Minister asked his PA not to send any more visitors to him. And he sat in his chair silently.

'Sir, this is a very important file. Please pass your orders. I shall bring rest of the files afterwards.'

'Please bring it.' The Chief Minister had his pen in his hand. The Secretary opened the file and kept it before him.

'We are going for one only.'

'Yes, Sir, just one at present.'

'How much will it cost?'

'We are purchasing a small aircraft but this will also cost at least one crore rupees.'

'O.K. we need it. We cannot run the govt. travelling in cars. Moreover, some other state govts. have also purchased small aircrafts. The Chief Ministers of those states go to Delhi to attend meetings in their own planes. We feel bad at such occasions.' After all it is a matter of State's honour. One crore is not a big amount. Bring this file in the Cabinet meeting to be held day after tomorrow. I have discussed it with all the Ministers. It is a formality to get the nod of the Cabinet. We should have the aircraft on priority.

'All right, Sir.' The Secretary went out with the file.

'Sir, you have to attend a meeting of Board of Directors of Tourism Corporation,' the PA said while entering the office.

'Yes, I know it. So we go now.'

'Yes, Sir.'

The Chief Minister left his office.

'Sir, here are members of a deputation, who have been waiting for the last three days to meet you. You may talk to them while walking,' the Secretary said coming close to him.

'Yes, please say what is your problem?'

'We represent the State Primary School Teachers Union. We had held a meeting in the Capital. We had gone to meet the Education Minister day before yesterday. We have other demands too but the most important point is that the primary schools in the state do not have sufficient buildings nor they have the required staff. The govt. has opened single teacher schools. Each school has four classes. There is no peon also to serve water. The teacher opens the school, the children clean it and there are four classes to be taught. How can one teacher teach four classes? We are ready to do it also. There are many schools where the students don't have mats to sit on. Despite our repeated requests, the department does not supply the mats. Where should we seat the children? The children sit on dirty ground. How can they study?' A young teacher from the deputation told the Chief Minister.

'What do you want?' The Chief Minister asked angrily.

'We do not demand anything for ourselves. The govt. should at least make mats available for the school kids.'

'There are thouands of schools. It is not a child's play to buy mats for so many schools. It will require money. The govt. does not have money. We shall purchase mats when we have funds. You talk to the Diretor of Education and the Minister for Education.' The Chief Minister said moving on.

'We have met them, Sir. They have said that shortage of funds is the reason for not purchasing the mats. The Chief Minister will arrange for the finances, they have said.' One of the teachers said while walking behind.

'Will the Chief Minister give money from his pocket? You are talking trash. Go and teach children in your schools. Don't indulge in leadership.'

The irritated Chief Minister said and moved on. A person stood there after opening the door of the car. The Chief Minister was soon in the car.

The car with a flag fluttering sped away.

The car was going at a high speed. The wind struck the ears of the Chief Minister as if it said... The houses of the poor people have been gutted, the crops have been destroyed but the govt. coffers are empty for them. There is no money to complete the water supply schemes. There is no money to buy mats for school children but the govt. will purchase an aircraft worth rupees one crore for visits of the Chief Minister.

The Chief Minister shook his head as if to get rid of these thoughts that worried him.

□

36

There was great hustle and bustle in the Canal Rest House situated not far away from the Capital. People were coming and going. There were a few persons at the entrance who watched every visitor with questioning eyes. All of them reached the spot in time in three different cars. The time and place of meeting had been changed. It was evening time. And it was getting dark. They all sat in an innerroom. Mr. Sharma arrived in due course of time. The room was locked from inside. Some people stood at different places outside to keep a strict vigil.

Sharma, Prandhir, Thakur, Kapoor were the main leaders of the dissidents. Some ten prominent MLAs had also come to attend this meeting. Only Rita was a non-MLA invitee.

'We have to conclude this meeting quickly. The Chief Minister must be having an eye on our activities. We must leave this place before he sights our meeting,' Sharma said at the outset.

'We need not linger on now. We are in majority. We should decide about the next step,' Mr. Prandhir said.

'We have already decided. All these efforts are a sequel to it. We don't have to have a new decision.' Kapoor expressed his opinion quickly.

'I mean, the decision about the next step. Our decision is final to change the Chief Minister Vishal Singh,' Prandhir said.

'Mr. Sharma will replace him. I just want to make it clear that we have taken these two decisions in the beginning itself. And we must fulfil both of them. There are different opinions sometimes. I am a hill man. I abide by the decision once I have taken it. I make it clear that I am with you to oust Vishal Singh provided we agree to install Mr. Sharma as the Chief Minister,' Thakur asserted forcefully.

'There is no doubt in it. Decisions cannot be changed frequently. If we try to change them, we shall achieve nothing. As far as I know no one has said anything against it. Only some MLAs of the other groups when we are trying to woo raise these questions but the final decision has to be taken by us. It has already been settled. There is no need at all to discuss this aspect again.' Kapoor made his point.

'Yes, Yes, it is right. Mr. Sharma is our leader. Let us discuss the next step.' Prandhir said categorically.

'Take out the list.'

Prandhir opened his briefcase, took out the file and placed some papers before them.

'So what is the situation Mr. Prandhir? Please explain it.'

'We have won over more MLAs than we tried to wio. All of us have tried our best. The greatest wonder is that Rita has won over five MLAs.'

'What an achievement? A woman has conquered five MLAs.' All of them laughed at this comment of Mr. Thakur.

'After all, she is a hill woman.'

'Not only of hills...'

'May be the capability of both the sides is harmonised.'

'Yes, Prandhir, please go ahead.' Sharma avoided the witty comments.

'Here is the list with me. We have clear majority now. We have promised Cabinet berth to some of them, after discussion with Mr. Sharma. We have paid money also to some of them. Half of the promised money has been paid, the rest half will be paid after the job is done. Some of them have been served drinks and a few others have been promised withdrawals of cases they are ttrapped in. How Rita has managed five MLAs, only she knows. We only know the five are under her command. Now the question is what is our next step. I suggest that some of us should meet the High Command at Delhi. But we should not go emptyhanded to Delhi.'

'We must have something in both of our hands.'

'In both the hands?'

'Yes, in both the hands. I know the Delhi High Command. We should have a complaint against the Chief Minister in one hand with signatures of all MLAs who belong to our group and sizeable money bag in the other hand. Four-five members of High

Command are very powerful. They take the final decision. No one will listen to us unless we have any of them as our well-wisher. One of them has been won over by Pawan Lal. And another is a friend of the Chief Minister. We must take at least two of the rest three with us.' Sharma said seriously.

'This is exactly true.'

'So we have two tasks in hand.'

'No, three. To draft a complaint, to get it signed by all the members of our group and to arrange for a money bag. Please decide who will do what?'

'Kapoor and Thakur will draft the complaint by 10 a.m. tomorrow. Prandhir will help them in getting signatures of all. I shall arrange for money.' Sharma conveyed his decision. They all nodded their heads in agreement.

'Who will go to Delhi?'

'Prandhir and Sharma should go.' Thakur said.

'Two are not sufficient; one more must accompany there.'

'The third one is Rita. She must go with them. She will be required in Delhi also.' Hearing this, some of them were alarmed, a few smiled and a few nodded in favour.

'Yes, yes. Rita is doing a lot for us. She will be useful in Delhi also.' Sharma said while looking at Rita.

They took tea in haste and came out. They went away in their cars. The rest house was calm once again.

□

37

They got signatures of all the MLAs on the representation next day. Kapoor and Thakur faced a lot of difficulty in drafting the complaint document. They did not have any solid point against the Chief Minister. Not even any evidence of corruption. It was necessary to level some serious charges in the complaint that was to be submitted to the High Command. It included a charge that the functioning of the Chief Minister was not right. He did not take the Ministers and MLAs into his confidence. They were feeling suffocation. The party workers are getting disappointed because they are unable to get their works done. The Chief Minister has almost lost control over the administration. Another charge levelled against the Chief Minister was that he connived with the Opposition secretly. He even attended the marriage caremony of the son of an opposition MLA whereas he never cared to attend such functions of Congress MLAs. The complaint document concluded with the assertion that he had lost the support of majority MLAs of his party and the MLAs cannot tolerate him any more. So they should be allowed to change the Chief Minister.

Prandhir, Kapoor and Thakur went to Mr. Sharma at his residence. They handed over the chargesheet to him.

'So all have signed it?,' Sharma asked Prandhir.

'Only one remains.'

'Who is he?'

'Balbir.'

'He was quite committed to us. He met me twice. What has happened to him?'

'He has sold himself,' Thakur said frowningly.

'How?'

'We had paid him twenty thousand. He has been with us for the last ten days. Pawan Lal took him along for two-three days. It is learnt they have paid thirty thousand and he had joined the Chief Minister's camp.

'Why did he sell himself? We had purchased him. They paid higher amount, so he crossed over. He is not to be blamed. If one has decided to sell oneself, he must try to get the maximum possible.' Kapoor said in a disappointed tone.

'How does it matter? We have a clear majority.'

'I endorse your viewpoint, Mr. Sharma but at times I feel distasteful. We are buying MLAs. We are coercing them. Balbir took twenty thousand from us and thirty thousand from them. It is a mockery. And are we not deceiving ourselves, our democracy and even our country?' Kapoor poured forth his hurt feelings.

You are again in your spirit. Kapoor your sentiments were true in bygone days and we live in Kalyug of politics. All is and will be fair here. Don't moralize again and again.' Thakur looked at Kapoor with burning eyes.

'O.K. do whatever you like. Indulge in any sort of activity that helps change the Chief Minister. I stand by you.' Kapoor tried to console himself also.

'The things are very favourable this time,' Sharma said.

'How?'

'You have got the paper signed by so many MLAs in a very short time. I have enacted this game many a time in the party. It is not easy to get signatures against the Chief Minister. No body dares. And the stars are too favourable this time.' Sharma said bubbling with confidence.

'Mr. Sharma, since when you have become an astrologer?'

'I am not an astrologer but an eminent astrologer has told me.'

'What has he told?'

'My wife met an astrologer. She showed my horoscope. He immediately said that the man of this horoscope will soon ascend to a very high position. I had invited the astrologer to my home. I talked to him at length. He read my forehead and told many things. He asserted it with confidence that my efforts this time will be successful. The Chief Minister will be changed and I shall succeed. He is a *tantrik* too. He revealed many things to me about Tantra. He will perform Path (worship) for me next week. He told that

Vishal Singh's stars are not favourable. Moreover, he will invoke tantra against Vishal Singh. I have paid him rupees ten thousand for the same.'

'Then you are through.'

'I have planned a tour to Delhi just within a day or two. I shall not disclose that I go to Delhi straight from here. As soon as the programme is over, I shall leave for Delhi on one pretext or the other. Prandhir you also reach Delhi by making some excuse. I arrange for a meeting there and send a message to someone for the purpose,' Sharma said.

'And Rita?'

'Yes, Rita will not acompany us right from here. She will reach the appointed place in Delhi. We should work in such a manner that no one doubts us.'

They all got up. Sharma bade good-bye at the door.

□

38

'Pawan, no meeting was held at Sharma's place yesterday noon.' The Chief Minister said looking at him with searching eyes, 'must have been held. I learn from reliable sources.'

'So your reliable source has been proved wrong. No meeting was held yesterday noon at Sharma's place. Sharma was all alone at home and then in his office till evening. I had a strict vigil. Your information was totally wrong.'

'Now they are also very alert. May be they changed the time and venue at the eleventh hour.'

'Yes, it is possible. But may be someone is passing on misleading information to us.'

'No, Mr. Chief Minister, they are certainly hatching a conspiracy against you. I discussed it in detail with Balbir yesterday. If there was no conspiracy, why would they pay rupees twenty thousand to him to win over?'

'Twenty thousand? Who gave it?' The Chief Minister asked with a surprise.

'Thakur and Prandhir made the payment. They had won him to their side by paying rupees twenty thousand. He remained with them day and night. He attended two of their meetings also.'

'It is strange. He was one of our most reliable MLAs.'

'You need not worry. He is with us now.'

'He received twenty thousand from them. How can he be with us?'

'We did a tit for tat.'

'What do you mean?'

'They had paid him Twenty Thousand. I paid him Thirty Thousand,' Pawan said with a pride.

'So you gave a higher bid.'

'Yes, you may say like that.' Both of them laughed.

'What more did Balbir reveal?' The Chief Minister was now curious to know more.

'Sharma is leader of the dissidents. They have conducted many meetings. As soon as they are sure of majority, they will ask the High Command to remove you. I had a detailed chat with Balbir. He had been assured Ministership also by them. I explained to him that he got twenty thousand from them and thirty thousand from us. Why should he hanker after Ministership now? He was happy and is with us now.'

'How many people are with them?'

'At present the majority is with us. But you will have to be active and alert.'

'You tell me, what should I do and how?'

'You call five to seven MLAs one by one. Promise them a berth in the Cabinet. Some are hungry for money. Get the permits for them. We shall have to keep the MLAs with us by hook or by crook. The Opposition attack is severe. We cannot sit idle. You be in constant touch with Delhi also. If the High Command is satisfied with you, there hulla-gulla will not matter. But you should do all that will please the High Command.

'You have your deep links too there.'

'I am trying at my level. One of the leaders is my friend. I can get anything done from him. I did talk to him. He said he would not allow anyone to harm you. He has talked to the party President and the Prime Minister also. Next time when you go to Delhi. you must meet them. He is a very influential leader.'

'You mean Kedar Lal?'

'Yes, the same fellow. He is in-charge of an important Ministry. He holds his influence in the party as well. He is also a member of Central Parliamentary Board. He got me party ticket.'

'O.K. I shall talk to him on phone today and meet him whenever. I go to Delhi. You will take care of me, Pawan. I depend upon you. The manipulators have joined hands against me. I feel Sharma has his eye on the Chief Minister's post only. He made a bluff to me by saying that he is loyal to me and on the other hand, he is trying his best to dislodge me.'

'Vishal Singhji, only Pawan Lal is faithful to you. There are some others too but I stand by the person whom I am committed. I won't change come what may.'

'Very nice. You are my main support.' The Chief Minister patted Pawan Lal. Both of them got up. The Chief Minister went up to the door to see Pawan off. The Chief Minister occupied his chair again and talked to his P.A., Darshan Singh entered the room after some time.

'What happened about the yesterday meeting?,' The Chief Minister asked Darshan Singh.

'Pawan's information was right. They had rescheduled their meeting yesterday. It was to be at Sharma's residence but they changed the venue. They held a meeting last night out of the Capital. You confirm it from CID.'

'I thought Pawan's information was wrong. He had come just now. I said to him but your comment makes me believe that he was right.'

'They all had gone somewhere yesterday. Someone told me. I rang them up at their homes. No one was available and the family members did not disclose about the places they had gone to. It means none of them was at his home last night and that they were at one place together.'

'You are correct. You and Pawan Lal will keep a strict vigil on their activity. They are all dangerous people.'

'Even Pawan is also not trustworthy.'

'No, Darshan don't say that.'

'I doubt him absolutely. He is winning MLAs for our group but he treats them in his individual manner. He settles the things for himself. He does not make a mention of you. He is very close to Kedar Lal in Delhi. May be he is trying for himself.'

'Sharma told me that he is loyal to me. Prandhir said he belongs to my community. So he will not tolerate any damage to me. Pawan Lal is also hobnobbing in my favour. Whom should I trust?'

'Most of your supporters are working against you.'

'Most of or all?'

'Not all.'

'Darshan Singh, I am perturbed.' The Chief Minister stood up looking at him while trying to dust his pant.'

'What are you doing all this?'

'Darshan, I feel as if my own pant is also dragging my feet. Doubts all around. Disloyalty hovering everywhere. Loyalty turning trecherous and treachery wearing a garb of loyalty. What kind of India it has come to be. Whither is politics moving?' The Chief Minister said gloomily.

'You are getting emotional. What exists is before us. Politics has its way. We shall work accordingly. Why are you disappointed. We are here to assist you.' Both of them were silent for some time. Then Darshan Singh stood up, folded his hands in salutation and left the room.

□

39

'Hello Sharmaji. You have come to Delhi after many day's. Is everything O.K. in your state?' Radhakrishen got up to welcome Mr. Sharma and Prandhir.

'It's O.K. but the State is not in good condition. That is why we have come to you.' Sharma said while occupying a chair.

'And Mr. Prandhir, you have also come after a long gap.

'Yes, there is lot of work to be done in the State. We don't get free time. But we had to dish out time. The situation in our state is very bad. The party is totally shattered. The legislators are frustrated beyond repair. If we do not get your blessings, the party will lose its credibility in the state and will suffer humiliation in the coming elections.' Prandhir came to the point straight.

Radhakrishen looked askance.

Radhakrishen was All India Party Secretary. Heavily built, he had a bulging belly. The blackish complexion made a contrast with his white dress. It was a deep contrast between the white clothes and his dark complexion. He had a longish white cap on his head. He looked bulky even in his Jawahar jacket. He commanded special status in the party. Although Prime Minister's will was supreme yet he also gave credence to Radhakrishen's suggestions. All problems relating to the party were initially referred to Radhakrishen. He looked at them searchingly, then rang the bell and asked the attendant to bring tea for all. He took out a cigarette from the pack lying on the table. While taking the lighter, he extended the cigarette pack to both of them. Both of them thanked him for the offer. Radhakrishen lit his cigarette, had a deep puff and then looked upwards.

'I thought there was no problem within the party in your state. Anyhow, tell me, what's the problem?,' Radhakrishen asked them while enjoying his smoke.

'The Chief Minister, Vishal Singh is playing in the hands of wrong people. His style of functioning is not good. MLAs are dissatisfied with his working. Corruption is on the increase. The Chief Minister has no hold over the bureacracy. The common Indians are getting angry with the party. The people who do not like the Chief Minister are hobnobbing with the Opposition. His continuation as Chief Minister will harm the prospects of the party.' He said in a serious tone.

'What do the MLAs want?,' Radhakrishen asked Prandhir trying to read his eyes.

'Change in leadership.'

'Whom do they want to elect their new leader?'

'Here is it. MLAs have sent their demand to the High Command in detail.' Prandhir said while putting forth a bundle of papers. Radhakrishen placed his cigarette on the ash tray, put on his spectacles and started perusing the papers. There was silence in the room for a few minutes. After some time, the door opened and the attendant brought tea. Radhakrishen picked up his cigarette and enjoyed a deep puff. The dying cigarettes was aglow once again. Sharma and Prandhir enjoyed sipping tea. And Radhakrishen continued to examine the papers.

'So you are fully prepared this time.' Radhakrishan commented while taking tea.

'It is our compulsion. We cannot let the party be destroyed.' Prandhir said proudly.

'Prandhir, leave aside the party. The party does not gain strength if we change the leader midway. If you want to protect the interest of the party you should allow the chosen Chief Minister his full term for five years. If there is any flaw in his functioning, we and you can collectively rectify. Change in leadership should be affected only under extraordinary circumstances. Your chargesheet does not strengthen the view that there in dire emergency to change the leadership. The fact is..., Radhakrishen stopped to have their reaction.

'No, Radhakrishen, Sir, that's not the truth. We are not doing all this to become the Chief Minister. We simply want to save the image of the party. You know I am a very old worker of the party. I am a Minister today. And if you ask me tomorrow to leave Ministership and to work for the party organisation, I shall happily accept it. But Vishal Singh, the Chief Minister has annoyed all the legislators. Now the majority of MLAs are not in a mood to accept him as the leader.' Sharma said while keeping his cup on the table.

'O.K. the majority wants to change the leader, Mr. Prandhir, but whom do you want to be the Chief Minister?'

'Mr. Sharma, Radhakrishen was surprised to keep his opinion. Mr. Sharma looked downwards in humility.

'So that is the truth. Whom does Pawan Lal favours these days,' Radhakrishen asked.

'Pawan has no permanent sides. He moves with the changing mind. But he is the right hand of the Chief Minister these days.'

'All right. You meet the Prime Minister. You talk to other members of the Parliamentary Board also. The Central Parliamentary Board will meet one day after tomorrow. I shall put up your chargesheet in that meeting. The decision will rest with the Parliamentary Board. But I personally do not feel good about all these things.' Radhakrishen said after lighting his second cigarette.

'We cannot sit idle when the situation has worsened beyond repair. We have been in line with the Chief Minister completely. We never uttered even a single word against him. We have been making efforts to build his image in the state. But he does not give us any weightage. He does not seek our advice, suggestions even. Corrupt people have surrounded him.' Prandhir carried his argument further.

'Look Prandhir. One thing is very clear. You don't have any solid thing against him. Much is happening in our party now. Before 1947, we had made sacrifices to the utmost but after Independence we do not lag behind in corruption. Some of our leaders have excelled the Britishers also in this field. I have a picture of our party in different states before me. You don't have anything against your Chief Minister. No one has ever complained against his honesty and gentlemanliness. So I don't appreciate your attempt to oust him. You should keep in mind one thing, i.e. we have drifted apart from Gandhi's way. I don't know where shall hunger for power will take us. There is no end to power warfare. There is only one post of Chief Minister but the aspirants are many. We shall have to contain ourself at a certain point. When you all have elected Vishal Singh as your Chief Minister, he should be allowed to continue his term for five years. The tussle has started in some States. There is no end to it. Once the people know that the Chief

Minister can be changed, the game will start immediately. All will be involved in the excercise. It is happening in many states. It is in the interest of the party that you abandon your effort to change the leader. I can call senior leaders from both the camps to Delhi and can arrange your meeting. I can get the shortcomings removed that you find in the funding of the Chief Minister. But you have brought a chargesheet and also the signatures of the MLAs. The majority is bent upon ousting the Chief Minister. This is a serious matter. All right, I shall put it on the agenda of the Parliamentary Board meeting.'

'Please, Radhakrishen, majority has to be listened to in democracy. The MLAs have compelled us to move forward and there is party's interest also if the leader is changed. We don't have any other link in Delhi. We deem you as the greatest and our closest leader. Moreover, Vishal Singh does not have deep regards for you. If Mr. Sharma takes over as the Chief Minister of the state, you can think you are the Chief Minister. We pray that you help us in accomplishing the end result of our move. We should get instructions from the High Command. Majority is with us.' Prandhir said while getting up from his seat. Radhakrishen escorted both of them to the door, with a cigaratte in his hands. They saluted him and came out and boarded their car.

Radhakrishen went to his chamber. He examined those papers once again with intent. He read the list of MLAs and saw their signatures. After a little while, he asked his PA to connect him to the Prime Minister. He discussed the entire issue in detail with the Prime Minister. The Prime Minister instructed him not to include it in the agenda of the Central Parliamentary Board meeting scheduled for day after tomorrow. The Prime Minister asked him to show all the papers to him.

Prandhir and Sharma moved to their place of stay.

'Radhakrishen appears to be a toughman,' Sharma said looking towards Prandhir.

'Not very tough. The party leader should talk the way he talked in the first meeting. We have just submitted the papers. Did you notice one thing? How happy he was when I said you would virtually be the Chief Minister of our state. I have uttered only one sentence as yet. I know him well. He will change altogether once we hand over a money containing envelope followed by a hint to him by Rita.'

'There seems exaggeration in what you say. It can't be that way to that extent.'

'Sharmaji, you have not experienced such a situation earlier. I have passed through such conditions many a time. I know about these leaders in detail.'

'Whom else we have to meet in Delhi?'

'We must control Kedar Lal, Roshan Singh and Dalbir Singh before we see the Chief Minister. They are members of the Parliamentary Board and they have a say in the High Command.'

'Kedar Lal is very close to Pawan Lal. He will make every effort to save the Chief Minister.'

'Yes, I have heard it that way. They all meet the leaders. We shall also meet Kedar Lal and try to win him over to our side. We shall have to find out someone close to him.'

'Banwari Lal, MLA from Uttar Pradesh is a friend of mine. I obliged him once. He is Kedar Lal's son-in-law. If you wish, may we cantact him?'

'Wonderful. Nothing can be more effective than what you have said. If we can woo the son-in-law, the father-in-law cannot escape our net. Call him on phone immediately.'

Both of them reached their residence. Prandhir booked a call for Lucknow. He waited for some time and then enquired about the call. Even after enquiring repeatedly, the call did not mature. Prandhir converted his ordinary call into an urgent one. When it also did not mature even after one hour, he converted it into a lightning call. After a while, he talked to Banwari Lal. Banwari Lal promised to reach Delhi, the very next day.

□

40

As soon as the train from Lucknow reached Delhi, Hari Shankar was searching Banwari Lal intently. Banwari Lal had informed Hari Shankar also telegraphically of his programme.

Hari Shankar was a leading businessman of Delhi. He had the biggest steal business house in North India and had a great say in the political circles of Delhi also. One of his political friends had told him a few months ago that the government proposed to leavy a new tax on steel. He got the information confirmed and then discussed it with his industralist friends. They planned to import steel in bulk before the tax was levied. This could earn a profit of many crores for them. Hari Shankar and his fellow industrialists sent their men to foreign countries and ordered purchase of steel. The ships carrying steel were on their way to India but the government imposed tax on steel before the consignments reached India. They had not expected it. they had transacted the business on old rates. With the new taxes imposed, they were perturbed. Some of the industrialists got the delivery of their consignments somehow or the other but many others could not get their consignments released because of the increased tax rates. In the absence of steel availability, many industries were closed. Others were on the verge of closure. All the industrialists held a meeting together and thought over the problem. The importers of steel were losing fifty crores in all. It was not possible to bear such a huge loss for a few industrialists. They decided to find out someone big in position who could get the tax proposal dropped. Someone arranged Hari Shankar's meeting with Banwari Lal. They tried to get the needful done with the help of Banwari Lal.

Banwari Lal clearly told Hari Shankar that it would require a huge sum to get the unusual work done. Many meetings were held between Hari Shankar and Banwari Lal. Hari Shankar called all his fellow industrialists and apprised them about the talks that were held between him and Banwari Lal. They all decided that the increased tax must be waived off because a loss of fifty crore would destroy their establishments. The industrialists authorised Hari Shankar to strike the deal as he thought fit. Hari Shankar talked to Banwari Lal. Banwari Lal went to Kedar Lal. After a detailed discussion, Banwari Lal told Hari Shankar that they would have to pay thirty lakh to get this tax waived off. Banwari Lal also asked for two lakh rupees for himself for settling such a big deal.

Hari Shankar went with this proposal to his fellow industrialists. They all arranged another meeting in Delhi. After great deliberations they decided to arrange thirty-two lakhs to save their fifty crore damage. They decided to collect the amount from different industrialists in proportion to the size of their consignments.

Hari Shankar was surprised while collecting this amount. One of the industrialists in that meeting was the President of Congress Party of a State. He was also present in the meeting. Rest of the industrialists had requested him many a time to use his influence in Delhi to solve the problem. He had made all his efforts. He had met the leaders in Delhi and had also met the concerned Minister but to no avail. He was also asked to contribute one lakh to the pool and he happily agreed to pay it. Hari Shankar had asked him, 'You are state party president and it is your government at the centre. We the industrialists are compelled to present a graft of thirty-two lakhs to get our work done and the amount includes one lakh as your contribution also. Don't you feel it absurd?' On hearing Hari Shankar's comments, he felt a bit slighted but said, 'Delhi has developed a culture of its own. It has its own rules and practices. A new culture of corrupt behaviour has emerged over the years which has dwarfed the walls of the party. I could not get this work done in my party. It is the only way left to get the work done. I have also to save my industry. So I am contributing as you have decided for all.'

They collected thirty-two lakh rupees. Hari Shankar handed over the entire amount to Banwari Lal. Banwari Lal went straight to Kedar Lal. Hari Shankar was satisfied now. The industrialists went to their homes. They were now confident that the government would soon withdraw the new taxes.

One after the other, three months elapsed but the government did not revoke the taxes. The industrialists were now restless. They spoke ill of Hari Shankar. Doubts arose in their mind about Hari Shankar. Hari Shankar went to Lucknow and discussed it with Banwari Lal. Banwari Lal told him that he had a clear commitment from Kedar Lal. It was after talks with his leaders that Kedar Lal had settled the amount at thirty lakh. As asked by Hari Shankar, Banwari Lal had gone to Delhi. After meeting Kedar Lal, he had met Hari Shankar. He had been assured that the work would be done shortly. Then and only then Hari Shankar had assured all the industrialists.

One more month passed. Their demand was not fulfilled. All the industrialists had assembled in Delhi. Hari Shankar was perplexed. He had talked to Banwari Lal in Lucknow the previous day. Banwari Lal had informed him of his arrival in Delhi today.

Hari Shankar rushed to the First Class compartment of the train. He was looking for Banwari Lal. A few other people were also waiting outside the compartment. They were watching the passengers who got out of the compartment.

'Namaskar Banwari Lalji,' Hari Shankar said as soon as he saw him. 'I am in a predicament these days,' he added.

'I understand your anxiety. I am also worried very much. But don't be disheartened. I am here now. We shall talk to them.' Banwari Lal said while shaking hands with him.

'Namastey. Another man greeted Banwari Lal with folded hands.

'Hello, Sir. How do you do? When did you reach?'

'Prandhir had called me here day before yesterday. He has sent me to receive you there. Mr. Sharma has also come with him and he is eager to meet you. He has desired that you straightaway go to him from the station. He has invited you for breakfast there,' Suresh said moving forward.

'No, Mr. Banwari Lal, you will have to accompany us first. All my companions are here for the last three days. They have been waiting for you,' Hari Shankar said expressing his concern.

'Mr. Sharma wants to meet the Prime Minister. He has requested for the time but he wants to have a word with you before meeting the Prime Minister,' Suresh implored.

'Sharma used to be totally calm. Why this turbulence now?'

'There is a great upheaval there these days. The MLAs have signed a memorandam to replace the Chief Minister. Now Vishal Singh will not remain the Chief Minister of the State. Will they elect the new Chief Minister? Most of the MLAs want Mr. Sharma to be the Chief Minister. Sharma is eager to meet you. Kindly accompany me immediatety to have a meeting with Mr. Sharma.' Suresh finished his statement and held him with his hand.

'No, no Mr. Banwari Lal first you come along with me for just ten minutes. You talk to him first and then meet Mr. Sharma. I shall also accompany you. I have a very old acquaintance with Mr. Sharma. I shall tell him that I had taken you with me first. He will not mind my insistance.' Hari Shankar said emphatically.

Banwari Lal suddenly stopped. The coolie was following him with the luggage. Banwari Lal could not make out with whom he should go first. On one side, it was his friend Suresh's request and on the other side, the message of future Chief Minister was also important. He knew that many under-currents were active in politics. The game to oust a Chief Minister and to instal a new one is always very interesting and tempting. Banwari Lal wanted to enjoy the game fully. He could sense when he received a message from Mr. Sharma in Lucknow. He understood his role fully well and wanted to play it whole-heartedly. He was not able to say no to Hari Shankar's request either. After all he had taken thirty-two lakh from Hari Shankar and had failed to get his work done. Banwari Lal was in a fix. When he saw Suresh, he felt he should first go with him to meet Mr. Sharma and the moment he looked at Hari Shankar, he thought he should first go with him.

'I am not able to decide where should I go first. Both the requests are important for me. Now you both decide,' Fed up Banwari Lal said.

Suresh and Hari Shankar talked to each other. Banwari Lal purchased a few newspapers from the nearby stall and started scanning them.

'Banwari Lal, Sir. We have made a compromise. Hari Shankar will go with us to Mr. Sharma's residence. You first talk there and then leave with Hari Shankar from there.'

Two cars were waiting outside the railway station. They sat in them and made their way to Sharma's place.

□

41

'What a surprise? Hari Shankar, you are here, with them?' Sharma was surprised when he saw Hari Shankar.

'I had some urgent work with Mr. Banwari Lal. I had gone to the railway station to receive him. I met your messenger Suresh there. I thought I should also pay my regards to you before I go for my assignment.'

'That is very good. We have not met for long.'

'I am worried for sometime now.'

'You are a big man. You have huge industry. May be there are problems and hindrances but you can brave all such oddities. I know.'

'It's not like that, Mr. Sharma. The problem this time has broken us.'

'Tell me if I can do anything?'

'I shall meet you today evening.'

'All right. You wait here. I talk to Mr. Banwari Lal.' Sharma went to another room with Mr. Banwari Lal. Prandhir joined them there. Suresh introduced Banwari Lal to them. Sharma said he knew about Banwari Lal for long. He had met him also but had never close-door party with him. They discussed general things for a few minutes. Then tea was served.

'Let us come to the point.' Prandhir started the dialogue.

'Right. Hari Shankar is waiting for me outside. I have to accompany him after talking to you.'

Mr. Banwari Lal, we need your help. Mr Vishal Singh is the Chief Minister of our state. The majority of our legislators has decided to remove him. They have signed the memorandom. We now want Mr. Sharma to be installed as the Chief Minister. It will be against the party interest if Vishal Singh continues as the Chief

Minister. We cannot tolerate damage to the party anymore. We have come to know that the Prime Minister gives weightage to what Mr. Keder Lal suggests. Mr. Kedar Lal is your father-in-law and is very close to you. You kindly arrange our meeting with him, may not the meeting only but get the things settled as we have told. We shall do as you direct us. But we want Kedar Lal's all out blessings in installing Mr. Sharma as the Chief Minister.' Prandhir made his point briefly.

'We shall be extremely obliged to you. To be frank, I am not tempted by the Chief Minister's post. I am an old servant of the party. But Mr. Banwari Lal, the party's status in our state is going from bad to worse day by day. We cannot tolerate it anymore. I never wanted to be the Chief Minister but all the legislators want me to accept the responsibility. So how can I escape it. You know it well how the things work in Delhi. It requires hobnobbing. We are not expert in this field. Who and how should one be contacted and at what time, they say Delhi is special in this culture. I know Kedar Lal. We have met him number of times. Pawan Lal from our state is very close to him. He is helping Chief Minister Vishal Singh. I am afraid Mr. Kedar Lal may go against us on the behest of Pawan Lal. We seek your all out help in this effort.' Sharma concluded his statement and looked towards Banwari Lal.

'Sharma is a close friend of mine and you are also one of my friends. I am asking my friend to help my friend. Banwari Lal, you will have to oblige me. We shall rest only when we see Mr. Sharma becoming the Chief Minister,' Suresh said enthusiastically.

'Please listen, it is not so easy. The High Command does not like to change the Chief Minister time and again. Moreover, it generates instability in the state. The High Command is not happy with the activities of dissidents in many states. Dissidents in different states are trying to change the Chief Ministers. The Central Parliamentary Board discussed this issue in detail recently. It was decided that the activities of the dissidents should not be encouraged. It creates instability. Dissidents in politics hinder the developmental work. I agree that the majority is with you in the state but that is not the only deciding factor. As long as you don't have members supporting you in the Parliamentary Board, your point will not be accepted. You need first of all the party Secretary Radhakrishen to be on your side. He should then convince the Prime Minister.' Banwari Lal looked at Prandhir and Sharma.

Sharma looked at Prandhir and Prandhir at Sharma. It was all silence for some time.

'We agree with you. But please tell us how can it be accomplished.' Prandhir broke the silence.

'You can talk to me. Kedar Lal is not only my father-in-law but he is my political guru also. He gives weightage to my askings. If you talk to me specifically, I can guarantee his help,' Banwari Lal said.

'Yes, we expect the same thing from you. We are in touch with the other members of the Parlimentary Board. Some friends are engaged in this. If you can win Kedar Lal to our side, we shall be successful in our mission.'

'Yes, you tell me.' Banwari Lal looked in Sharma's eyes.

'No, no, you just say.' Sharma searched Banwari Lal.

'Don't hesitate. Whatever you want, you say it frankly,' Prandhir said plainly.

'It is a gigantic task. You can judge it yourself. For such a big task,' Banwari Lal felt shy in spelling out his conditions.

'Come with me.' Sharma took Banwari Lal to another room.

'This is a wise step, Mr. Sharma. We cannot have such deals before everyone.' Banwari Lal said while occupying a chair in the corner.

'I understand your point. I have met you so many times. You had once come to our state also. Banwari Lal, I am just a Minister today. And if you favour me, I can become the Chief Minister. I and my government will virtually be your government. You tell me for the time being.'

'Mr. Sharma, you know such tasks are not accomplished in Delhi without money. Many people have to be roped in. Politics has become a very dirty activity. Elections require lakhs of rupees. I shall mould Kedar Lal fully to your advantage but that will require...'

'Please don't hesitate. Say it frankly. But keep it in mind that our friendship should be permanent. Promises must be kept.'

'Banwari Lal does not believe in half-hearted promises.'

'But what about Kedar Lal?'

'Banwari Lal has not only held the hand of Kedar Lal's daughter but he is responsible for his political manifestations also. Sharmaji, you speak out. You leave the rest to me.'

'Now you tell it please.'

'Five lakh. Kedar Lal will go to the Party Secretary Radhakrishen for you, and then he will go to the Prime Minister. Kedar Lal will advocate your point in the Board meeting.'

'It is difficult for me but I shall arrange it somehow. You come here at six in the evening and you will get half the amount today and the other half afterwards.'

'No, Mr. Sharma. It is not a business of that type. The promise will be kept but you will have to give the amount in one installment only.'

'O.K. as you wish. The deal will remain between you and me. You please come in the evening.' Both of them came into the room outside. The breakfast was laid in the adjoining room. They all sat on the breakfast table. They discussed a number of things. Sharma would go serious while talking. And then again would start the conversation. Hari Shankar had also been invited to join the breakfast. Breakfast over, Hari Shankar took Sharma aside and whispered into his ears.

□

42

The industrialists sitting in the room had mixed reaction on the sight of Banwari Lal. They greeted Banwari Lal by standing up. They shook hands with him. A few of them were happy to see him but simultaneously they could not hide their anger also.

'Mr. Banwari Lal is an MLA from the state but he has his say in the circles of Delhi. He is called for big tasks. A few persons had reached the station to receive him. But he was compelled to go there first. I had also gone there with him. So this is the reason for delay. I had sent a message to you otherwise.' Hari Shankar explained while taking his seat.

'The delay does not matter. But please Banwari Lal, save us from being wiped out. You are also short of time and we too have been waiting for long. When we had struck the deal with you, we were losing fifty crores. We gave thirty-two lakhs to save our fifty crores. Many months have gone by. Even an amount of thirty-two lakhs has not done our job. And the loss of fifty crores has now grown into hundred crores. Our industrial units have been closed. We shall be totally ruined. We shall have nowhere to go. You can save us, only you can.' An aged industrialist gave vent to his anguish.

'I understand your anxiety. I am more worried than you. I promised you and received thirty-two lakhs but your work has not been done so far. I am sorry for it. I beg your pardon. But I am not to be blamed for it. This department is with Kedar Lal. I had handed over thirty lakh rupees to him. He had drafted a note and sent it to the Prime Minister. He had personally met the Prime Minister also. I understand he had done his work. Now I have come here. I just enquire about it in detail.' Banwari Lal had sensed the anger of all.

'It is not a question of sending a note by the Minister to the Prime Minister. We had struck a deal with you. Who had to send a note and to whom, was your business and none of our concern. We had given thirty lakh rupees to see the tax withdrawn. You had to get it done. It was not an easy job to raise thirty-two lakh rupees. You don't know how we collected the amount. We had raised this money at your motivation to see that our fifty crore was saved. Mr. Banwari Lal, my predicament is that I had collected this amount from my fellow industrialists for you. I had initiated the talks with you. You promised me and in turn I assured my colleagues. And now they show their anger on me and moreover they doubt my integrity. You please make it clear that I had given you thirty lakh rupees.' Anger and anxiety was apparent on Hari Shankar's face.

'Yes, yes. There is no doubt in it. You had handed over a complete sum of rupees thirty-two lakhs. Not even a single penny less.' Banwari Lal addressed all of them.

'We also don't have any doubts about it.' A young industrialist sitting in one corner said.

'Why no doubts? Many of you have said like that about me. On one side, our work has not been done and I have been suspected unnecessarily. I have been very anxions because of it. I was thinking of a meeting of all of you with Mr. Banwari Lal to make the matter clear,' Hari Shankar said confidently.

'Banwari Lal, please tell us, what will happen next?'

'I have done what I could do.'

'Yes, you have done nothing so far. Yes, we had done our part. It was decided that we would pay rupees thirty-two lakh rupees and that you would get the increased tax withdrawn.' The elderly industrialist spoke angrily.

'You kept your promise and I also fulfilled my promise. I gave thirty lakh to Kedar Lal. His Ministry sent a note. I did not do any dishonesty. I had told you that. I would charge rupees two lakh for this job. I retained only two lakh. I am honest to the core in such deals. I do not like bungling of even a single paisa. Only the government or Kedar Lal can withdraw the tax. I just arranged a contact between both of you. The deal was sealed perfectly. Your money was made to reach the concerned quarter. My job finishes here.' Banwari Lal said in a harsh tone.

'No, Mr. Banwari Lal, it is not so simple. Any one could have given the money. Your promise was to get the work done. I make it clear that we have been completely shattered. Hundred crore rupees have bean lost. We gave thirty-two lakhs to you. If you don't get our work done, we shall not allow you live in peace. I do not believe in oily talks like others. Either you get our work done or you return our thirty-two lakhs otherwise.' A young industrialist was furious now.

'What otherwise? You have called me for talks or for threats?' Banwari Lal also flew into rage.

'It is not a threat but we cannot let it go silently. Even after taking such a huge amount, if you and Kedar Lal do not get the needful done, how can we sit silent? Banwari Lal please listen, others can be silent and may bear the losses but I cannot. I shall tell the whole world about this happening and expose you and Mr. Kedar Lal. You are dishonest to the core. You receive huge amounts in the name of top leaders and in turn you do not keep your word. I am telling you in plain words, I shall not tolerate it.'

'No please. Anger will not solve any problem. Don't feel slighted Mr. Banwari Lal. Our talks will not be leaked. You just get our work done.' Hari Shankar intervened to soften the heat.

'Hari Shankar, I appreciate your anxiety but you should also feel my difficulty. Such missions are not achieved through anger and threats. I facilitated your dialogue. Rest of the work was to be done by him. I still assure you that I shall try my best. But the action has to be taken by the government. I can simply convey.'

Banwari Lal was a bit softened. Hari Shankar and some other members pacified the situation. The young industrialist sat silently on his seat. The atmosphere was still tense. Banwari Lal asked Hari Shankar to meet him again the same day and left the place. The industrialists continued the discussions for long. One of them suggested that they should find out some other source to get their work done. That they should not depend upon Banwari Lal alone. Hari Shankar told that the Department was with Kedar Lal. Kedar Lal will play the vital role in accomplishing their work and no one could be dearer to him than Banwari Lal. Some others suggested that they should try to find out a link with the Prime Minister. It is a matter of crores. It is just possible that the Minister is helpless to settle it at his level. They all decided that the Prime Minister would settle this problem. May be both the Lals are not competent to help us. We may be wandering in the dark aimlessly. Hari Shankar revealed that Sharma was trying to become the Chief Minister of his state. Majority of MLAs are with him. We can find out a stronger link in Prime Minister's residence through Mr. Sharma. Hari Shankar also told about his scheduled meeting with Sharma the same evening. All the industrialists decided to meet again that evening to discuss it further.

□

43

There were two more leaders in Delhi in addition to party Secretary Radhakrishen and Kedar Lal, whom it was necessary to woo. Sharma and Prandhir were busy in this plan. Mr. Roshan Singh and Mr. Dalbir Gupta were members of the Central Parliamentary Board, who commanded respect in Delhi's politics. Sharma knew well all of them but he tried to have an inside view of them so that he could effectively use them. He took Rita along when he went to see Roshan Singh. They discussed the things at length. Roshan Singh also said what had been said by Radhakrishen. The High Command did not have a favourable opinion to change the leadership. Sharma and Prandhir pleaded emphatically. Roshan Singh was talking to Sharma and Prandhir, but his eyes were fixed on Rita. He tried to drag Rita into the discussions but she was a novice in the field. She was unable to understand the top level intricacies of Delhi politics.

'I have understood your point. It's a difficult job but I shall make all out efforts. It will need to persuade the Prime Minister. After all he will take the final decision.'

'Agreed that we all give our opinion but ultimately the Prime Minister takes the decision... There is sufficient substance in your proposal. The state leadership should not be changed time and again. Agreed. But when the existence of party is at stake in a state, there is no alternative but to have a change in leadership,' Roshan Singh said while looking at Rita.

'Yes, yes, that is the crux of the matter. You have rightly understood the context. We wish you make the High Command understand it. Please get this work done. We shall do whatever you ask,' Sharma said in an encouraged voice.

'You need not oblige me. You are our old friend. I shall be the happiest man if you become the Chief Minister. I shall talk to Mr. Radhakrishen and the Prime Minister today itself. But you should take care of one thing.'

'What to that?'

'The activities have increased about your state in Delhi. Pawan Lal reached Delhi yesterday. Your Chief Minister is also to be in Delhi soon. You will have to keep your mission a secret. All the people will come to see us. You both will not visit us repeatedly. You send Rita here in the evening. Once I talk to the Prime Minister and the Party Chief, I shall send message through her.' Roshan Singh's voluptuous eyes were searching Rita. Rita felt a bit shy. Sharma and Prandhir were happy to find Rita's use successful.

'Yes, surely. You have said it right. Now Rita will be the link between us,' Sharma said confidently.

'Mr. Roshan Singh, we are fully assured of your help now. It is your responsibility to install Sharma as the Chief Minister. Your blessings will certainly see us through in the mission,' Prandhir said while looking into Roshan Singh's eyes.

'You need not worry. I shall help you to the maximum.'

All three of them returned after the parleys. Rita had no part to play since she came to Delhi with them. She could not have discussions with the top leaders. Sharma and Prandhir were the main actors so far. Roshan Singh assigned a new job to Rita.

Roshan Singh's car reached Rita's place before time to fetch her. She was sitting with Mr. Sharma at that time. Sharma had asked his PA to send Rita there in his car. He laughed when he was told that Roshan Singh had sent his car for Rita.

'It appears we have hit the right spot.' Sharma looked at Rita mysteriously.

'I have not followed you.'

'You are making big ones understood now. That is something special. Those who do not understand themselves, make others understand.'

'I can understand the puzzle.'

'You had gone to see Roshan Singh with us. We carried out the conversation but he understood you. Now he has sent his vechicle to ferry you. Rita now your real task starts. You have to win over Roshan Singh as you had done in the case of five MLAs. Banwari Lal will take care of Kedar Lal and you will manage

Roshan Singh. We had taken you along purposely. We had gathered complete information about him. Delhi's politics has become very ticklish. I cannot become Chief Minister without your help.'

'I shall never backtrack. You be assured. I hope you won't forget me after taking over as Chief Minister.'

'Rita, I shall not forget you even after my death.'

'I am talking about the period before death.'

'What do you mean?'

'I am talking about the life not about after life.'

'You need not worry Rita. I can't forget you. Once I became the Chief Minister, I shall get you nominated to the Rajya Sabha or I shall appoint you Chairman of some Board in the state. I shall get you appointed to a high post in the party organization as well.'

After a while, Rita left for Roshan Singh in the car. Rita talked to Sharma on phone and told that she would have to stay there for sometime more to obtain some more information. Sharma was told at night that she had gone with Roshan Singh to meet someone for the purpose. Rita did not return that night. Next day she met Sharma and Prandhir. She divulged some information. She got a message again at noon and she went to meet Roshan Singh. The same evening Roshan Singh went out of Delhi for a couple of days. Rita accompanied him. Before leaving, she told Sharma and Prandhir that Roshan Singh was making all out efforts for them. She also revealed that Roshan Singh had already met the Prime Minister and Radhakishen.

Sharma and Prandhir had met Dalbir Gupta a number of times. Despite their repeated pleading, Gupta had told them that he was not in favour of changing the Chief Minister in the states. Sharma discovered another link. He assured to win Dalbir to their side. He took Sharma's car. He was on the move in Delhi for the whole day. On return, he told Sharma that he had done his job and Dalbir would now support them. But when they met Dalbir again they felt he was unchanged. Both of them were frustrated with Dalbir.

Chief Minister Vishal Singh had reached Delhi. Pawan Lal was also with him. A few Ministers of Vishal Singh's Cabinet too were in Delhi. MLAs from both the groups were also converging in the Capital. The state's guest house in Delhi was rife with political activities. The state govt. was in Delhi virtually.

Hobnobbing was in full swing. Leaders of both the groups were meeting the central leadership to place their respective stands.

There was no focus on administration since the activities of the dissidents had increased. Dissidents were mounting pressure to oust the Chief Minister and the Chief Minister was busy saving his post. The hold over administration was over. It was a common talk in the Secretariat. The discussion revolved round the MLAs who were changing sides. The govt. had come to a standstill. The corrupt forces exploited the situation to the maximum. They got their works done by the Ministers. Both the groups required money. They were collecting huge amounts in the name of politics. Some of them were replenishing their personal pockets. Illegal felling of trees were going on in some parts of the forests. The government tried to check it many a time. Illegal felling increased due to slackness on the part of government. The contractors started bribing both the groups. The politicians ignored the activities going on. The officers and employees had also been influenced by the contractors.

The state administration was being run in a routine manner. The work on projects had come to a standstill. Corruption was at its height. There was none to question anyone. The Chief Minister and other senior Ministers were camping in Delhi. There was anarchy in the state.

Pawan Lal conducted all the activities for the Chief Minister, Vishal Singh. Pawan Lal's main supporter was Kedar Lal. Pawan Lal had made his permanent rapport with Radhakishen as well. The state was in news in the newspapers.

Both the sides submitted written memorandum to the High Command. Sharma had submitted a memorandum containing signatures of MLAs supporting him. Chief Minister, Vishal Singh had also come with a memorandum with signatures of MLAs. There were thirteen MLAs who had signed for both the sides. Some of them had been summoned to Delhi. A few of the MLAs played clever. They would go to one camp in the morning and then join the other group in the evening. Crossing over within the same party was in full swing.

The High Command decided to call a meeting of the Parliamentary Board after three days to decide about the leadership issue. As soon as this decision was taken, the activities increased to the maximum. Almost all the MLAs reached Delhi. Rooms were booked for them in some of the leading hotels. Both the groups avoided to let their supporters staying in the state's guest house. They made all efforts to lodge them separately in different hotels. The representatives of one group tried to locate the MLAs of the other group. If they discovered some MLAs they would take him into their fold. They would discuss the details with him. Promises were made, money was offered and the MLAs would change over.

The Parliamentary Board meeting lasted for six hours. It could not decide about the leadership of the party. It was resolved that the party President should call senior leaders to discuss the issue and to make an assessment. The Parliament Board would meet the next day, it was also decided. The party President held parleys with senior leaders. Leaders of both the groups remained busy in horse trading throughout the night. No one slept that night.

Leaders of both the groups were unable to make out about seventy per cent MLAs regarding their loyalty. Some of them were trying to be on both the sides. And a few of them turned sides. Change or no change in leadership, repeatedly the situation was fluid. And if the change in leadership is effected, who would be the lucky fellow? No body knew. So majority of the MLAs were waiting for the tide. They did not want to commit in advance in any manner.

Sharma and Prandhir had no information about Rita since the last day. Rita was extremely busy and she was in great demand. Apart from both the leaders, she had started meeting second rank leaders also. Rita had made her importance felt. She had called Sharma only once during the last two-three days to inform that she was on her job to win support for him. She also told that the High Command would pick him up for leadership.

Hari Shankar and his industrialist fellows were upset with the uncertainty in political circles. Although Banwari Lal was in Delhi, yet he did not meet them. He had an excuse these days that Kedar Lal was busy. All steel industrialists of India were camping in Delhi. They did not know what to do. Young industrialists suggested that they should tell about the thirty-two lakh episode to the newspapers. Hari Shankar and some of his other fellows advised them to keep restrain. They said such an act would spoil their chance to have a favour from the government and moreover, if the government or its representatives were guilty of receiving graft, those who gave it were equally guilty.

Hari Shankar and two of his allies decided to meet Kedar Lal themselves. They somehow or the other got an appointment with Kedar Lal and reached his residence. The place was crowded. Despite great effort, they could not meet him. Someone introduced them to Pawan Lal then and there. Pawan Lal was freely entering Kedar Lal's room time and again. Hari Shankar made his point briefly to Pawan Lal in private. Pawan Lal took Hari Shankar along and went into an adjoining but small room.

'Mr. Hari Shankar, it is a petty job. Why did you not come to me earlier.' Pawan Lal said and closed the door from inside.

'Petty job? We have already paid thirty-two lakh for it.'

'Thirty-two lakh?' Alarmed Pawan Lal repeated.

Yes, Mr. Pawan Lal. Thirty-two lakh. Kedar Lal's son-in-law is an MLA from U.P. His name is Banwari Lal. Someone introduced us to him. We had discussed our problem with him. He received thirty lakh for Kedar Lal and two lakhs for himself. We arranged for thirty-two lakh rupees with great difficulty. Many months have elapsed. Our interest has not been watched. We are in soup. Please help us.'

'I feel you have been cheated. Banwari Lal is not an upright man. But you need not worry. I shall try to help you.'

'In that case, Sharma will also be a loser,' surprised Hari Shankar said.

'What for? Sharma?'

'Banwari Lal has taken five lakh from him on the plea that he would persuade Kedar Lal to help Sharma become the Chief Minister.'

'So that's the point. Sharma now wants to be the Chief Minister with the help of money.'

'No one succeeds here without spending lakhs.'

'After all it is a question of becoming Chief Minister of a State.'

'Will it also be decided with the help of money bags.'

'Mr. Hari Shankar, it cannot be said whether it would be decided or not that way. The world is changed altogether. And India has changed totally. We must accept what exists. You know what has been happening in Delhi in politics.'

'In Gandhi's land, Chief Ministers are installed with the help of money?'

'You perhaps don't remember. One of our party's senior leaders had publically said that lakhs are required to become Chief

Minister and crores if you want to be the Prime Minister. Prices have gone up. So now crores in place of lakhs and billions instead of crores are required,' Pawan Lal said.

'Leave it. I remember this statement was carried by the newspaper. It was hotly debated. Anyhow, Banwari Lal turned out to be a dangerous man.' Hari Shankar picked up his topic again.

'You are to be blamed for it. You gave such a big amount secretively as if money has no value for you. I don't know who introduced you to Banwari Lal.'

'Please now tell us the way out.'

'I can get your work done hunded per cent but you will have to help me at this juncture.'

'Whom do you support?'

'No one is with anyone. Appearances are often deceptive. Anyhow, I am supporting Chief Minister Vishal Singh. But I can tell you that I have played a trick in the duel of Vishal Singh and Sharma. Anyhow, it will be known tomorrow.'

'Our best wishes are with you. What can we do for you?'

'I don't understand what should I say to you. Banwari Lal has already swindled you. I can simply say that your work will be got done but after tomorrow. The night today is the night of political life and death for me. Do whatever you can do. You need not see Kedar Lal. He will not be able to meet you today. If you wish, I can talk to him just now.'

'All right you please talk to him. I shall consult my fellow industrialists and we shall do today itself what we can for you.'

Both of them came out of the room. Pawan Lal made Hari Shankar sit on a sofa on one side and himself went into the room. He came out shortly afterwards. Hari Shankar got up and went to him enthusiastically. Pawan Lal took Hari Shankar in one corner and told that Kedar Lal had their job in mind. I feel Banwari Lal has discussed your demand with him but has not paid the full amount to him. I have talked to him. Once the state's leadership problem is settled, he will definitely help you. And if I can have my say. You consider your work done. Kedar Lal has promised me. So you need not worry.'

'Many many thanks. When will you reach your residence?'

'I don't have a residence these days. You decide the time and place.'

'You tell us.'

'At 5.00 p.m. in hotel Rajdhani.'

'All right.'

Hari Shankar reached hotel Rajdhani at fixed time along with one of his fellowers. Pawan Lal was waiting for them. They discussed in between themselves. Hari Shankar handed over stuffed briefcase to Pawan Lal. Both of them came out and sped away in their vehicles.

□

44

The meeting of the Parliamentary Board was in progress the next day and the top leaders of both the groups were present in the lawn outside. The meeting continued for two hours. But no decision was taken. Chief Minister Vishal Singh was closeted with his main supporters in one of the rooms of the state's guest house. Sharma and Prandhir were sitting in another room of the same guest house. MLAs of both the camps were roaming about to know the latest information which they passed on to their leaders. Pawan Lal was to be seen no where. He was on the move till night. He met MLAs from different groups in different hotels. He kept meeting central leaders also separately. Vishal Singh called for Pawan Lal a number of times the previous day but Pawan Lal was not available. But he had sent a message through one of the MLAs to Vishal Singh saying that the situation was O.K. and he need not worry. The meeting of the Parliamentary Board lasted for two more hours. The Board decided to remove Vishal Singh and to elect a new leader in a meeting to be held two days later at Delhi. It was told to the newspapers that the leader of the legislature party would be elected by the legislators. At the same time, the leaders of all the groups were told that Pawan Lal would be the next Chief Minister.

Leaders of both the groups felt disappointed. No one had expected that Pawan Lal would become victorious in the duel of Sharma and Vishal Singh. They all were alarmed at this decision. Now the MLAs started aligning with Pawan Lal gradually. Pawan Lal had mustered majority support for himself clandestinely. Kedar Lal helped Pawan Lal whole-heartedly. The Party President was neutral. Pawan Lal had established deep friendship with one of the Prime Minister's sons. The relationship had been kept so secret that no one doubted it even. He had been trying to become the Chief Minister since long. He had cultivated his relationship with Kedar Lal and Prime Minister's son for this purpose.

Roshan Singh wanted to help Sharma completely. Rita had full control over him. Rita had almost started to live at his residence. Pawan Lal had come to know of it. He kept a watch on her activities and called her one day in a lone place. He knew that Rita was very anbitious. He had come to know that Sharma had promised her Rajya Sabha seat. Pawan Lal told Rita that Sharma had in fact made a fool of her by promising her Rajya Sabha nomination. Pawan Lal excessively praised Rita. After long deliberations with her, Pawan Lal said he would induct her as a Minister in his Cabinet. Rita did not believe in what he said initially. Pawan Lal was a master craftsman of conversation. He was unmatched in parleys. He talked in such a manner that no one could distrust him. Rita's frozen ambitions become alive now. She had never thought that she could become a Minister also. Pawan Lal convinced her as if she was already a Minister. Rita had now full faith in his commitments. Pawan Lal told her that the Board was all set to make him the Chief Minister but Roshan Singh was the only obstacle. He said he knew that Roshan Singh had been won over to Sharma by Rita itself. If Rita helped him, Pawan Lal was sure to be the Chief Minister and would certainly induct her as a Minister in his Cabinet.

Rita was greatly impressed with Pawan Lal. She dreamt of a bright political future once she became the Minister. Now the question before both of them was how to win over Roshan Singh. Pawan Lal was a wise man said it would not be possible to turn Roshan Singh against Sharma at this moment. He suggested to Rita that she should somehow or the other stop Roshan Singh attending the meeting. They both planned it and were successful in their mission. Rita did not allow Roshan Singh to participate in the meeting and the Board decided in favour of Pawan Lal.

Now the centre of activities had shifted to the State headquarters from the national capital. All the MLAs and leaders were busy pursuing their interests.

Pawan Lal was ready to leave with his followers from Delhi. It appeared that Hari Shankar congratulated him as soon as he sat in the car.

'Hari Shankar, you don't worry. It is just a matter of two days now. I shall come to Delhi and get your work done.'

'Thanks a lot. I and my fellowers will stay in Delhi. We shall wait for you. We cannot leave Delhi as long as our mission is not successful.'

'O.K. You stay put here. I shall come after two days.'

'Our best wishes. If need be, we can come there.'

'There is no need now. The Centre has decided to see Pawan Lal as the Chief Minister. Now it has to be announced in the state.' One of the Pawan Lal supporters said.

A few leaders in the state had been creating ripples but all big leaders had now calmed down. They knew High Command had ordered that Pawan Lal would be the Chief Minister. They had told that the legislators would elect their leader but it was an eyewash. Almost all the MLAs congratulated Pawan Lal. Many MLAs broke away from the opposition and joined Pawan Lal's camp.

The meeting of the legislators was held on the scheduled day. Two observers of the High Command were also present in the meeting. One of the central leaders had told the MLAs separately that the High Command wanted Pawan Lal to be the Chief Minister. It is the High Command's directive, the MLAs were told. The meeting started. Vishal Singh proposed, Pawan Lal's name and Sharma seconded it. All the MLAs were surprised at this move. They knew that Pawan Lal was to be appointed Chief Minister but they did not know that Vishal Singh and Sharma would propose and second his name; the candidates who were claiming the coveted post. The central leaders had directed Vishal Singh and Sharma to do it that way.

Pawan Lal was unanimously elected leader. The state Governor invited him to form the government. He took the Chief Minister's Oath. He returned to Delhi soon after to finalise the names of his Cabinet.

Pawan Lal met the Prime Minister in Delhi. He met some central leaders also. He finalised the list of his Cabinet after consultations.

'Hari Shankar, be seated please.'

'Congratulations to you from all of us.'

'It could happen only because of your help.'

'No, not because of our support but because of your ability. The High Command has asked you to shoulder this responsibility.'

'Yes, now I have to get your work done.'

'We have come for the same. We feel exhausted now.'

'Right. I just get to the Prime Minister. I meet Kedar Lalji also. You see me in the evening.'

Pawan Lal talked to Kedar Lal. And then he contacted someone special at Prime Minister's residence. Pawan Lal knew that such important decisions were taken at PM's residence through someone special. Hari Shankar came to Pawan Lal's place in the evening with two of his fellows.

'Hari Shankar, your case is spoiled totally.'

'What do you mean? We don't follow you.'

'You had given thirty-two lakh but nothing is known about it at PM's residence. Perhaps you do not know that if any Minister at the Centre receives such a huge amount, a part of it reaches the PM's residence through someone special there. I contacted at the PM's place but there is no sign of it.'

'We are deceived then. But where did thirty lakh go?'

'Has been divided between two Lals.'

'It means Kedar Lal.'

'All Lals are alike here. Banwari Lal says he gave thirty lakh to Kedar Lal. Kedar Lal says he received a few lakh which he submitted to the party. I asked the party office bearers. They did not reveal anything. They said they knew nothing. Anyway if you have to get your work done, you will have to talk at PM's place.'

'But what can we do now. From where shall we get money?'

'Mr. Hari Shankar, you need not worry. I have talked to Kedar Lal. I am arranging his talk at PM's residence. If the previous money is not considered in full, they will have to concede a part of it and you will have to arrange some more money.'

Pawan Lal talked to the concerned person at PM's residence, He summoned Kedar Lal. They discussed it in detail in a closed door meeting. Pawan Lal called Hari Shankar after that he met that special man along with Hari Shankar at a secret place. Hari Shankar had brought two briefcases with himself. Those briefcases were handed over to the concerned man. The government issued a notification about withdrawing the increased tax after 15 days.

□

45

After her visit to Hidimba temple, Savitri was calm and quiet. Shankar told her that Pramod had made prayers at Hidimba temple before leaving for Lahaul and spiti. Savitri saw that place where Pramod had sat for propitiating goddess Hidimba. Savitri had been to the temple a number of times but she felt different this tine. The dilapidated wooden doors and the worn out stones communicated a new message of life to her. Large-sized deoder trees looked fresh to her. She felt that the temple was not the same that she had been visiting since her childhood. She kept sitting for long in the temple. She was in a thoughtful mood and she begged favours from the goddess.

Whenever she was impatient, some unknown power caressed her. Pramod's friend Shankar was also with her. Shankar would also console him. But it was the place where Pramod had wept for her and now she was having similar feelings for him.

She had started her normal life once again. She would go to school. She was happy to be absorbed in teaching. She was normal at home. Kamla mostly lived with her. She could express her concerns to her.

Savitri knew that the mountains would remain covered with snow for almost six months and the roads would be closed to traffic. There could be no information about the well-being of Pramod. Every third or fourth day, Savitri would now go to Shankar after the school hours. Shankar would tell her that there was no message about him from any corner. Shankar's sympathetic words gave her strength. Savitri would retrace her steps. This situation continued for many months. Gradually, Shankar was worried.

Once Shankar called Kamla and said, 'You are Savitri's friend. You should make her understand about the position.'

'Tell me what should I make her understand and how?'

'Now there is no possibility of Pramod's survival. He had started from Kaza. His compatriots went back. He continued to move forward. There was snow-fall afterwards. May be his body is safe in snow but he cannot be alive. And if he is hit by a glacier, we cannot be sure of his body being intact. Such mishaps have happened a number of times. No one has survived in such condition ever. Kamla, this is the stark reality and we cannot overlook it. We must face the reality. You make her understand it.'

'What should I make her understand? She has full faith in goddess Hidimba. And you have also assured her. You had said that no such snow exists that can freeze Pramod. Your those words and her faith in Hidimba are the reality for her. Nobody can make her understand anything. I fear that she would go mad when she faces the truth after six months. But it is difficult to convince her today.'

'Kamla, please do something. Tell her the truth straight away and then discuss it with her family members also. It will be better if she is married off. I want her to forget Pramod. We had only this much relationship. Remembering him means that I get nervous. I feel my heart torn. I dream of snow mountains in sleep. Sometimes I see him covered with snow and at other times I find him flying on the mountains. I feel restless. I am unable to concentrate. I want to be out of this tension. I may be able to forget Pramod slowly but as long as Savitri appears before me, it is impossible to forget him. Both of them liked each other so much that Savitri seems Pramod incarnate and vice versa.'

'But Savitri does not want to listen to anything.'

'Kamla, many things happen in this world. People die daily. Their kith and kin weep for them for a few days and then forget them. We shall have to bring Savitri out of the imaginative world to the hard realities of life.'

'And suppose if her conviction is proved true?'

'It is impossible. Pramod is no more now.'

'Suppose she agrees for marriage at our persuasion. And in case after melting of the snow, Pramod comes alive and asks you... where is my Savitri? What will be your answer? Shankar got upset at the comments of Kamla. He roamed here and there. His eyes had a blurred vision. He kept his palm on his eyes and stood beside the wall. Kamla sat silent. No one broke the silence. Kamla looked at Shanker. Tears rolled down his cheek in abundance.

'Please forgive me. I said what came to my mind.'

'Kamla, you are right. No one has survived in such snow. But if Pramod is alive... then?'

'I thought that way.'

I was also thinking that way but Kamla, it is useless. It is a wishful thinking. It cannot happen. The attrocity of snow makes even the boulders freeze. How can one survive the extremity of cold? Pramod could not break the snow mountains. Let us leave it. We don't have any control over nature. Leave it to fate.

It was customary for Savitri to visit Shankar every week to know about the well-being of Pramod. She knew Shankar's reply also. Even then she came to enquire. Shankar knew he had only one answer. He tried to make her understand that he would not get any news about Pramod for months together. Savitri thought it was futile to come to Shankar. She consoled herself too. But when it happened to be the sixth or seventh day of the week, she would again go to Shankar. She did not get any news about Pramod but he did figure in the talks. He did not know where Pramod was. She could only discuss Pramod with Shankar. May be this was the reason that prompted her to meet Shankar and talk about Pramod.

Almost two months passed. Savitri's anxiety grew. Her faith in Shankar dwindled. She did not attend the school for a few days. Staying at home was all the more painful. She again started to attend the school. She took Kamla along and went to Shankar. She asked him to go to Hidimba temple. Shankar could read her mind. All three of them went to Manali to pay a visit to Hidimba temple. Kamla and Shankar kept roaming outside and Savitri sat in the temple. Kamla went inside the temple twice or thrice to see Savitri. She sat their with her eyes closed. Kamla retraced her steps. Two hours passed by. Shankar and Kamla asked her to get up. Savitri returned with them calmly.

'I now stand by my conviction. I know your mind. You are afraid that Pramod may not have survived the onslaught of snow. I also feel the same way and have no hope. But when I sat in the temple, there was a light before my eyes. I have never experienced such a flash in my life. And I saw him alive in that light. I found him the same Pramod as I had seen him near the Raghū Nath's temple. I am confident, he will certainly come back in flesh and blood,' Savitri said while walking with them. Kamla and Shankar listened to her intently.

'Savitri, it may be your faith,' Shankar said.

'It is not only my faith but it is the assurance given to me by Mother Hidimba.'

'Savitri, wa can live only by accepting the truth and not by avoiding it.'

'I do not follow you.'

'Savitri, I also love my friend as you like him. But the fact is that there is no hope of his survival in the snow mountains. I have talked about it with so many people. Our department has made serious attempts to know about his fate. Such incidents have happened so many times. Never ever has anyone survived. I do not wish that you live on false hopes. If you keep hopes of his survival and in case, it turns out wrong in the end, you will not be able to sustain the pressure. There is no alternative now. We shall cherish Pramod's memory but we shall have to forget him.' Shankar stopped suddenly and summoned courage to say it plain.

'What do you say?' Kamla retorted while looking at Savitri.

'Kamla, he is right.' Savitri said braving his comments.

'Then what?,' Kamla asked Savitri.

'But my faith is stronger than Shankar's comments. As long as there is snow on the mountains, I live with this conviction. And if he is proved correct after melting of snow, I shall have no regrets even then. I shall follow the route to that place to find him. I shall end my life there. I have no other world to live but in Pramod's world. My life has no relevance without him. Don't try to convince me. I cannot learn anything beyond what I have learnt already.'

Shankar did not think it proper to say anything more.

For almost one month more, Savitri was busy actively in her engagement. Four months had elapsed by this time. The weather in Kullu was changing. Savitri was a bit plaintive now. She was reminded of Shankar's comment. She would almost cry when she imagined about Pramod covered under snow. Her intellect preferred to accept. She would feel upset. She felt anguish. She would find the entire world burning. After a few days, she fell ill. She suffered from fever for many days. She got her treatment from the village vaidya. Then Kamla got medicines for her from Kullu doctors. But Savitri did not recover. Her mother was greatly worried. Savitri was taken to Kullu. She was kept in the hospital for a few days. All tests were conducted. She had no major problem but her fever continued.

Savitri was sent to her home. Kamla would procure medicine from Kullu for her. Doctors changed her medicine a number of times but the light fever continued. Kamla talked to Shankar. Shankar suggested that Savitri should forget Pramod to live her normal life. Savitri laughed at his suggestion. She told Shankar that she was steadfast in her conviction. Shankar retorted angrily, 'Pramod went into the snow. Months have gone by. There is no information about him, you have fallen ill. What is the wisdom in getting an ailment. You have been reduced to your half and fever has gripped you. I feel your ailment is not physical but it is mental. You have tolerated a lot. But there is a limit to toleration also. Your feelings have rendered you sick. I shall repeat the same advice that I gave you the other day while returning from the Hidimba temple.

'Hindimba temple? Do you want to see me healthy?'

'Yes, why not,' Kamla and Shankar said simultaneously.

'You take me once gain to Hidimba temple.' There was a flash on Savitri's face.

'You are so weak now. It would not be appropriate to take you to a distant place.'

'So it means you do not want me to be healthy again.'

'What do you say?'

'You try it once, take me to Hidimba temple somehow or the other.'

She closed her eyes saying this and was silent. Kamla and Shankar came out of the room after some time.

Kamla and Shankar later arranged for a palanquin and brought Savitri to the Hidimba temple. Savitri was very weak. Fever had affected her body. The face looked pale. It was difficult for her to walk a few steps but there was unexpected fervour in her when she got to the stairs of the temple. She walked into the temple and sat on the spot where Pramod had sat. Kamla and Shankar made her sit in the temple and came out. They wandered there for sometime and returned with Savitri. They found that Savitri's fever was on the wane from the next morning. She was normal in health very soon.

Shankar was surprised at this development. People at the village and in Shankar's family had faith in the gods. They would go first of all to a god when any illness struck them. Doctors and vaidyas had only a few patients to attend. Shankar did not believe much in the divine powers but he felt it was Mother Hidimba's blessings that rendered Savitri healthy. Savitri again started her normal life. She would go to school and do domestic work also. Savitri's mother tried twice to engage her during this period. Savitri postponed the process through Kamla. When Savitri's mother insisted, Kamla told her the real story. Savitri's mother was perturbed. Even if Pramod had happened to be in Kullu, Savitri's mother would not agree to the proposal. Neither the community was the same, nor it was her home district. But nothing was known about Pramod. Savitri's mother knew that there was no chance of Pramod coming back alive. She tried to convince Savitri but to no avail. Savitri's mother was worried about her daughter.

□

46

Five months had gone by. Pramod had become accustomed to live alone in that room. The ration stored in the room was likely to be exhausted soon. He was worried about it. What would he eat, once the food stuff was over. He would think of the time when the roads would open for traffic. He dreamt meeting Savitri in Kullu. Such a thought refuelled him. May be it takes more months before the route is opened. Only a little quantity of flour and rice was left. He may have to live hungry thereafter. His dreams shattered when he thought that he may not survive hunger for so many days.

Pramod passed his days in a routine manner moving around the space available. He would come in the veranda when he felt the bright sun. He would try to walk on snow and then stop finding mountains of snows before him. He initially enjoyed the tranquility. He felt he was going poetic. He was enchanted by the snow clad mountains. He was happy at the sight of nature. There was an expanse of snow and snow all over. Suddenly, the silence gripped him. He would rush back to his room. He would shut the door. Sometimes he slipped into the bed. He tried to weep but there was no water left in his eyes.

In the beginning, Pramod wrote poems addressed to Savitri. Then his pen went dry. He poured a few drops of water into the tube of the pen. He could write for a few days more but again the ink dried up. He searched the room extensively but there was no ink available. He could not write anymore. Pramod could not talk to anyone. Had he some means to write, he could have spent the time easily.

During the last five months, Pramod felt headache a number of times. He suffered from fever also once or twice. But he was soon cured naturally. He had only one medicine with him.' He would collect snow and melt it into water and take it. It was his doctor, and his medicine too.

He had exhausted all the pulses that he had found stored in the room. He would mix flour in water, cook it to eat. And at other times he ate rice. He made all attempts to consume the minimum quantity of grains but the stored grains were in less quantity. The grains were also on the verge of being exhausted but the snow mountains stood as big as they were before. Pramod was irritated to think about the heaps of snow that stood in the way of the traffic.

He once again tried to search every corner of the room today. He thought he may get something more somewhere like pulses, grains, etc. or something else to eat. There was a corner where faggot of wood was kept. The room was very small. He searched the entire room in a few minutes. He could get no eatable. When he was cleaning the fuel, something struck his hand. He caught it at once. It was an old broken mirror. He picked it up and came out of the room. He could see his figure in it. He was astonished at his image. The broken mirror fell on the ground and was again broken into more pieces. Pramod could not feel satisfied. He stood in one corner frightened by his own image.

Pramod had not seen his figure in the mirror for the last five months. He was astonished to see his image in the broken pieces of glass. He could not immediately recognise himself. It was a weakened face with long black beard. Black dust settled on his face and neck. Disappointment and grief writ large on his face. He kept thinking for long. Pramod then picked up a piece of glass, straightened it and saw his image in the mirror. He had controlled his emotions a bit now. He went inside his room with a piece of glass. He kept that piece under his pillow near the photo there. He said to himself... 'look Savitri. How does my face now look?'

Even I could not recognise my face. You may also refuse to recognise me when the roads open. If it happens so, what will be my fate?' He was lying on his bed with Savitri's photo and the mirror in his hards. He was speaking to himself. He looked at Savitri's photo and said, 'Why don't you speak? Will you be able to recognise me or not?'

Pramod felt as if Savitri had fixed her gaze on him. He saw a glimmer in his eyes. He heard his voice saying, 'No, no, how can it happen? I have loved you not your flesh.'

All eatables were now exhausted at Pramod's place. He braved hunger. He would drink lukewarm water. He did not feel bad for some days. But he could not get up from his bed after ten days. He removed snow at a spot to find if there was any leaf of grass but he could not find it. Pramod thought if he could get grass, he would boil it and eat.

Pramod was going feeble day by day. Physical weakness disheartened him. He apprehended his death. He did not know when the road would open for traffic. He removed the snow to find out the way. He made a guess about the direction he had come from. He tried to move in that direction. He made a path but was confused after some distance. He could not see anything. The weather was becoming normal now. The snow started melting but the mass of snow was huge. Huge mountains of snow stood before him. Pramod was now very sad. Time hung heavy on him. He felt broken in spirit.

It was mid-day. The sun was bright. The rays were shining in the snow. Pramod had been lying in bed since morning. He had stopped thinking now. He could not sleep empty stomach. He got up from the bed slowly. He sat in the veranda resting himself on a plank. He looked around. The sky was clear. It was bright day but the entire nature lay buried under heaps of snow. The high mountains looked white. The snow on the mountains had started melting at some points.

'What is it? What type of sound it is?' Pramod got alarmed. He reacted to it sharply. He tried to listen it. He thought may be it his illusion. But after a few moments, he again heard the voice of the people. He was once again surprised. He stood aloft to look around.

Pramod had heard human voice after many months. He felt strange. He felt a current in his body. He felt his body activated. He made an attempt to have a view around with his mouth raised.

He could feel images of people at a distance. Some persons were proceeding further after removing snow. Pramod felt happy. There was a flash in his eyes. He felt as if his penance had been answered. They were removing snow to clear the way. Pramod picked up his stick and walked slowly but his legs failed him. He stood for a moment, then sat there. He walked a few steps more. He wanted to reach those people immediately. He waited for them patiently. Then he spoke aloud to them but to no avail. Pramod had seen a human figure after many days. He could not speak at the highest pitch. He felt as if he had forgotten to speak. He shouted at the top of his voice once again to make it sure that it was his own voice. Those people were now quite close to him.

Pramod now spoke to them at the highest pitch, asking them 'Come here, come here please.'

The people who were clearing the path heard the voice and stopped there. They looked in the direction of the voice. One of those men shouted, 'There is a ghost, a ghost, he had sighted Pramod. The man retraced his steps and ran swiftly. Others also followed him. They left their belongings there. No one looked at Pramod again. No one responded to his calls. They did not stop to verify the truth. They simply ran away.

Pramod was once again sad. Tears rolled down his eyes. After running breathlessly they all stopped at one point. They all asked the man what he had seen when he shouted. He told that he had seen a black ghost. He had long beard. He had raised one of his hands. The nails were grown. He was wearing black clothes and shouting. 'Come here, come here.' We did the right thing by running back. He said, 'Death was imminent today.'

'No one has ever seen a ghost in snow there,' one of them pointed out.

'You may or may not believe it, I saw him with my own eyes. You all must also have heard his voice.'

'Yes, we did hear his voice.' They all said in one voice.

'We are the first group this season which is traversing the path after the snowfall. For months together, no one walked on this route. No one from the other direction also has tread on this path. Whose voice it could be?' Another fellow asked curiously.

'You all heard his voice but I saw him also. I swear he was a ghost and not a human being.'

'What should we do now? If it was a ghost, it must be following us.' They all felt frightened at this comment. Some of them were trembling. They looked at each other. 'What shall we do here. We must go back.' He said and walked back swiftly. All others followed him.

They had covered only a little distance that a group of Border Security Force confronted them. Their chief asked them swiftly, 'Where are you going?' They said they had seen a ghost. The soldiers laughed at their statement. They tried to convince the soldiers by saying that one of them had seen the ghost with his own eyes. Some soldiers felt frightened but the chief did not believe in the story. He asked them to follow him. He will surely like to meet the ghost.

Pramod went back to his veranda with the support of the stick. He sat on a boulder. He suddenly saw a group of people coming. He was delighted. He again started towards the road. He saw those people and they also noticed him. Pramod stopped after taking a few steps. They also stopped. One of them said, 'He is the same ghost. I had seen him. Can he be a human being? And a human being cannot survive in the snow. See his long beard and black clothes. And notice his long nails.' Saying this, the speaker retreated. A few of his fellows also retraced their steps. A few of the soldiers were also frightened. The chief of the BSF group asked in a raised voice. 'Tell me plainly who are you?' His voice reached sharply.

I am a human being. Don't be scared of me. I had been stuck here.' Hearing his voice, they all looked at him intently.

'How did you survive in such a cold?' They all saw his curiously now.

'See that is the room where I stayed for months together.'

They all looked at the room he had pointed out. The BSF Chief now understood the whole story. He moved forward. The other soldiers also moved forward. The earlier group also followed them.

Pramod stood with the support of the stick. The chief headed towards him. Pramod had seen a human being after many months. He was excited. Tears of joy rolled down his eyes. He tried to utter a few words but he could not. The chief spoke to him but Pramod did not say anything. Pramod greeted him with both his hands folded. When the chief went closer, Pramod hugged him.

Pramod suddenly felt strong. He hugged him with all the renewed strength in him. He sighed for some time. Tears trickled down from Pramod's eyes. He could feel the drench of the tears. All the people were onlookers to the scene.

Pramod held him by his hand and took him to the shelter. He narrated his story to all of them. They all listened to him spellbound. The chief called one of his soldiers. He took out a milk container from his baggage. He prepared milk for Pramod. They made Pramod rest in bed. They made tea for all of them. After taking hot milk, Pramod felt as if he had come out of the storm.

The soldiers gave him some biscuits to eat. They gave medicine to Pramod. Pramod felt active now. Pramod got up from his bed after some time.

'Had you not come here today, my death was imminent because of starvation. You have provided me new life.' Tears again trickled down from Pramod's eyes.

'We are nobody to give you new life. You have survived the storm for so many months. And it is He, the Almighty who protected you and it is He who has sent us to you.'

'No. Earlier there was some foodstuff in the room. It had been exhausted many days before. My body was getting weaker and weaker because of hunger. I cannot forget your obligation,' Pramod said while holding his hand in his own hand.

'I wish you reach me Manali at the earliest possible. I want to go to Kullu from there.' Pramod burst into tears. He was weeping like a child. He tried to wipe his tears but the flow was much more. Weeping Pramod placed his head in his lap.

The chief asked three of his soldiers to stay there. He provided foodstuff also. He consoled Pramod asking him to stay there for one or two days more. He should improve his health by taking proper food. The three soldiers would take him to Kullu afterwards. Pramod was now satisfied. He thanked him. He went forward with his men.

It was a changed world for Pramod now. The small room was now filled with life. He was recovering gradually. The three attendents looked after him. The BSF Commander sent more foodstuff for them. He sent a few medicines also. The policemen from Kaza also reached him to know about Pramod's well-being. It took almost one week for Pramod to recover fully. Pramod thanked the soldiers. He sent back the soliders and started on foot for Manali in the company of two soldiers. The snow on the way had almost melted but it existed in abundance on the hills on both sides. People had started moving on the road.

Pramod reached Koksar one evening with his fellows after having stopovers, rest, etc. on way. They stayed there for the night. Pramod wrote a letter. It was addressed to Shankar. Handing over the letter to one of his companions, he said, 'You move much earlier tomorrow, i.e. before we start. You will catch a bus from Manali for Kullu. Kindly hand over my letter to Shankar there. We shall stay at Manali for rest. Tell Shankar that I would wait for him at the spot hinted at in the letter.'

After handing over the letter, Pramod felt easy. He kept tossing in the bed lost in the memories of days he had spent here earlier. He was drawing closer to his destination. Only one day's journey was left. He felt calm on one front. He tossed in the bed remembering the days he had spent in Koksar. He was now close to his destination. Just one day's journey was left. The storm in him was now getting calm but the second storm made him restless. He thought he had tolerated so much for Savitri. Savitri haunted him. He had survived the snowy storms just keeping her memory fresh. He had embarked on his journey months ago to see her but was stopped on way. He was caught in life and death. Now he is reaching nearer to Savitri. And if Savitri has no fascination for him, if she is already married...' He got up in the bed at this thought. Then he started strolling in the room. He was now perspiring and tears trickled down from his eyes. He came to the window and looked outside. He looked at the mountains. The Chandra river looked beautiful in the moonlight.

It appeared as if someone was meeting his beloved after a long gap. Pramod wiped his eyes. He consoled himself. He lied down on the bed but he could not sleep. He felt aches in his body as he tossed repeatedly. The bedsheet was in bad shape.

The moonlight was charming and the murmur of Chandra was enticing. There was symphony par excellence. Pramod tried to control his emotions while loitering in the room.

□

47

Shankar was in his room. He had almost forgotten Pramod. He was occasionally reminded of Savitri. Rohtang Pass had been opened for traffic. There was no news about Pramod. Shankar was sure that Pramod could not survive the harsh weather. He made attempt to forget all about him. As soon as he had Savitri in his thought, Pramod also appeared in his memory.

'I have brought a letter for you,' a policeman standing near the door said.

'Letter for me? Has it come by post?,' Shankar said while getting up.

'Not by post but I have brought it.'

'From where?'

'From Koksar —whose letter?'

'Your friend Pramod's letter.

'Pramod's?'

Shankar was ecstatic. He sat in his bed again. He was lost in happiness and astonishment. Tears trickled down from his eyes. He was not himself for a long time. The policeman standing at the door watched him in surprise.

'Come in and be seated. Where is the letter?' Shankar got up controlling himself.

'Here is the letter.'

Shankar started reading the letter.

My dear Shankar.

I had sent a letter to you many months ago. May be you got it. The letter might have reached you but I got stuck in between. I hanged between life and death.

I have so much to say that I can't write it at the moment. I am not sure if you got my letter or not.

I even do not know if you met Savitri or not.

I also do not know where is she and how she is?

It is not known to me if she loves me as much as I do love her.

Nothing is known to me...

Shankar, I only know that I had started on my journey from Kaza many months ago to meet Savitri. And after many months, I shall reach Manali tomorrow. I am coming to meet Savitri.

If Savitri has similar feelings for me, you kindly bring her to the Hidimba temple where I had offered my prayers while making my way to Lahaul and Spiti. Meet me in the same temple.

I shall wait for you and Savitri at the temple.

Your Friend

Pramod

Shankar was live with new expectation. He closed his eyes and remembered goddess Hidimba. He felt that there was truth in the belief of gods. He saw the time. He talked to the policeman and got up to be ready for the meeting.

Shankar went straight to the school. The school was already closed and Savitri had left for his home. Shankar caught a bus and reached her home. He saw from distance that Savitri was sitting in the compound of her residence. He went in that direction.

'Savitri. You have won. Your trust is victorious. I accept my defeat.'

Savitri raised her eyes alarmingly. She was surprised to see Shankar. She stood up at onces on hearing him. Savitri could not understand the purpose of Shankar's comment.

'Yes, Savitri, you have won, your goddess Hidimba has won.'

'Has he come?' Savitri asked dancing with joy.

The knitting material fell down from his hands. She looked at Shankar with wide open eyes.

'Yes, Savitri, Pramod is alive. I don't know where and how did he stay to survive. He is reaching Manali today evening. He has sent this letter to me.'

Savitri almost snatched the letter from Shankar's hands. She opened the letter. She blushed. There were pearl-like tears in her eyes. She was charged with emotions at this sudden development. Savitri could not contain herself. She was perspiring and shivering. She sat there. She fixed her eyes on the letter.

She read Pramod's name written at the bottom of the letter. She closed her eyes. She opened her eyes and started reading the letter.

Shankar looked at Savitri. He found Hidimba in Savitri. He felt like falling at the feet of Savitri. He thought, it is her confidence in God that helped Pramod survive the catastrophe. Something impossible was converted into possible. Shankar was remorseful now. Why he had taken it guaranteed that Pramod could never survive. Shankar was now impatient to meet Pramod.

Savitri read the letter and almost kissed it. Her face was covered with the letter. Her tears drenched the letter. The letters ink was wet with her tears and it spread to his hands. Tears were now trickling down to her clothes.

'Savitri, I understand your plight. Now get up. A new hope has emerged. Something unusual has happened today. Pramod has come live from the clutches of death. Your love and devotion has made it possible. Please get up and let us go. He must be waiting for you.'

They reached the main road and caught a bus for Manali.

□

48

After crossing Rohtang Pass, he could have a view of Manali. Pramod would intermittently stop. He tried to see Manali from a distance. He could imagine the location of Hidimba temple among the lofty deodar trees on the higher side of the town. He tried to locate the Hidimba temple. Manali now looked closer and closer as he approached it.

It was all descent from Rohtang to Manali. Pramod was walking briskly getting closer and closer to his destination. 'My letter must have reached Shankar by this time, he thought. And he must have told Savitri also who may be reaching the temple. And if she does not come,' he felt sad at this thought. He fumbled for a moment and felt dejected. Darkness engulfed him. He would stop while walking and would sometimes sit on the road side. Gradually, Pramod was quite close to Manali. The Beas river murmurred the sweat songs. Now his path went by the river. He tried to have a glimpse of Savitri's face in its waters.

'Should we go straight to the Police Station or elsewhere?,' Pramod asked his fellow. They had reached a small bridge of Beas.

'You keep on moving. We go to the Police Station later. We have to reach somewhere else.'

'Where shall we go?'

'From where I had started a few months back.' Pramod kept thinking while saying. They went on walking silently. They crossed a small bridge of Beas. They could see some shops open. Pramod witnessed action after many months. He saw a few children and was reminded of Savitri and his sisters. An old man went that way. Pramod was reminded of his father. There was a small chowk in the market. Pramod turned left.

'Where will you go?'

'Have you been to Manali?'

'I have been to Manali. But there is nothing this side.'

'My everything exists there,' Pramod said and walked silently. His fellow silently followed him. They both passed through the zig-zag way. It was pleasant weather. Pramod was lost in his old memories. He had gone to the temple then following the same path and was full of enthusiam. There is a lot of difference between now and then. Nothing was certain at that time. Nothing is certain even today. His future was uncertain at that time and so is it now.

Pramod stood in front of the temple. He looked around. No one was close around. The musical wind was blowing. When he reached close to the temple, he asked his companion to wait there. He put off his shoes, washed his hands and mouth and went in the temple.

He folded his hands before the goddess and bent his head with reverence. God knows what he thought. He opened his eyes and saw the statue of the goddess. He then suddenly saw the place where he had sat for long in the temple. Pramod went to the spot and sat there. He closed his eyes and was lost in thoughts.

'Oh, mother goddess, I have come back to you. You know what happened to me. May be you have tested me. I have come to you for shelter. Listen it clearly. I shall not get up alone from here. I cannot contain myself now. If I do not get Savitri, I shall strike my head against the statue and die. Neither harsh snow could melt me during the long sojourn, nor hunger could kill me. Now I cannot tolerate separation from Savitri. Either bless me with Savitri, or let me be confined to your feet for ever.' There were tears in Pramod's eyes. He once again had a glimpse of Hidimba's statue. He found the statue all the more fascinating. He stared at it for quite sometime.

Tired, he kept his hands on his knees and rested his face on it.

Pramod's companion came to the temple door. He went back after seeing Pramod sitting silently. He came after some time again and went back. It was growing dark outside the temple. Cool breeze nestled the leaves of Deodar. The birds were going back to their nests. The grazing cattle were also returning to their places. The nature was silent. Only the chirping of the birds disturbed the calm of the evening. A storm inside Pramod was on the rise. He could not understand how to control the storm. He was peaceful extraneously but turbulent inside like the lull before the storm.

□

49

Savitri was not normal. She was unable to contain her happiness. It was a tide of joy. She was in the bus and could not control her tears. Shankar noticed her emotions. Savitri felt everything fresh today. Shankar was a changed person. Earlier he had asked her to forget Pramod but now everything was changed. She felt the path altogether new. She passed through that way daily but today the experience was different. The winds were different today. The mountains looked attractive. The fields appeared soothing. She was flying in thoughts. Shankar tried to talk to her just once. She smiled wholeheartedly. Once she burst into laughter. When the bus stopped at Manali, Savitri was the first to come out. Shankar lagged behind. Both of them started upward from the bus stand.

'You seem flying today,' Shankar said while walking on the road.

'Truly, I am extremely happy today. Just as you thought, I also sometimes felt that he would never come back. But my confidence overruled the doubt,' Savitri said moving at a faster pace.

'There is no doubt in it. Your patience has also contributed to it.'

'I was at home. I don't know how and how he spent so many days.' Savitri had a glimmer of happiness on her face.

'Pramod must have had a tough time. It is a miracle that he has survived the harshness of snowy weather. Your love for him has made it possible.'

'Not my love alone but your friendship has also added to this success.'

'No, I had given up. I had no hopes left for his survival. There was no guarantee of Pramod coming back live. Whomsoever I talked, no one expected Pramod to come back alive. But whenever I met you, my optimism was revived.'

'What shall I say to him and how shall I confront him.' Savitri stopped suddenly.

'Should I tell you that?' Shankar laughed at her comment.

'I am having strange feelings.'

'It happens.'

Savitri was moving forward, engrossed in her thoughts.

'Such a meeting is always romantic. And your encounter with each other is something special. You had met each other by coincidence near Raghu Nath's tent. Just for a few moments. You had no exchange of words. Even the name was not asked. And then an interval of two years. So many things happened during that period but there was no decline in intensity of love for each other. I can understand your plight on such a meeting. Similar will be the fate of my friend.' Shankar looked at Savitri. She increased her speed.

It was getting dark. A soft wind was blowing. The atmosphere was calm and the murmur of waters rustled the winds. The birds were returning to their nests. The shephereds were taking their flocks to their homes.

Savitri stopped in front of the temple. She looked intently at it. A man stood near the stairs of the temple. She opened her eyes. He was not Pramod. She was alarmed at first instance and looked at Shankar enquiringly. She looked all around. She could not find anyone else there.

'Don't worry. He must be sitting in the temple at the same spot.' Shankar said smilingly. Savitri now went forward.

The man standing outside approached Savitri. He saluted her with folded hands and said, 'He is in the temple.' On hearing it, Savitri jumped with joy.

'May I wait outside?,' Shankar asked her.

'No, you first meet your friend,' Savitri said hesitatingly.

'No, friendship afterwards, love first. Go quickly. But remember Pramod's friend waits for both of you out of the temple.' Shankar looked at Savitri and then moved to the man standing outside. Savitri walked hurriedly.

Savitri folded her hands standing before the temple entrance. She bowed her head, spoke to herself silently and then went in slowly.

'Oh, mother goddess, she has come.' Pramod got up.

As soon as Savitri saw Pramod, she felt shy. He was starvation struck, just a skeleton...grown beard...he was not the same Pramod that she had seen a couple of years ago. He was almost changed. Savitri was shocked. She again raised her eyes and viewed Pramod searchingly. Her enthusiasm was gone for the moment. She thought God knows how and where did Pramod live in adverse circumstances. She controlled herself.

'Savitri, may be you have not recognized me. It is my re-birth. I have survived just for you.' Tears flowed unabated from Pramod's eyes. His tears flowed down from his beards. Savitri was already sentimental. Time stopped for them. They were simply releasing tears before each other. Savitri then controlled herself. She wiped her tears and slowly moved towards Pramod. She tried to touch his feet but before she could do it, he took her in his hands.

They had so many things to say. They had a store of memories.

Both of them were overflowing with sentiments since they had an inkling of a meeting. How will each one of them start? What will be the answers? The situation did not arise. No words were needed to express their feelings. The eyes spoke all the things. Years explained the entire story.

'Your friend Shankar is waiting outside.' Savitri tried to be different.

'Oh Shankar, yes, yes.' Pramod held Savitri's hand and came out. Shankar was talking to a man sitting under the deodar tree. Pramod called him loudly and he came running. They hugged each other. They were in tears. Savitri watched both of them with intent.

'Pramod, you have done a miracle. You have indeed, defeated death. But how did it happen? I had lost all hopes. But credit to Savitri. She was confident of your survival. And she has won.' Shankar wiped Pramod's tears with his hands.

'Shankar, now stop rolling down your tears. The adverse time is gone. We have to celebrate now. Come here.' Pramod sat on a boulder outside the temple. Shankar sat on the adjoining stone. Savitri and the other man also sat near Pramod and Shankar. Pramod narrated his story in brief covering his journey right from his start from Kaza. Shankar was surprised to know it. Savitri was once again in tears. They were alarmed to hear Pramod's story but thanked God for his survival.

'God knows what force made me survive. I would have been frozen in snow otherwise.'

'Savitri's love guarded you, in fact.'

'No, your friendship is also invaluable.'

'We are getting late. We should now move on. We shall have to drop Savitri at her residence,' Shankar said.

'Where is Savitri's home?,' Pramod said laughingly. Savitri's eyes were now downward.

'Pramod's home was now Savitri's home. But we shall have to make it. We have to plan it. But it should happen very soon now. We both will plan it tonight.'

They all started for Manali. Savitri walked close to Pramod. Shankar was walking by Pramod's side. They were talking to each other. Savitri was a silent listener. Pramod, Shankar and Savitri caught a bus and got down by the road side. And they went to Savitri's place.

'Shankar, I wait here. You escort Savitri to her home,' Pramod said.

'Your house is so far, and you will wait for him all alone whereas you are quite close to my house.' Savitri whispered.

'But I...'

'Pramod, come along. I shall leave Savitri at her home. You shall wait outside.' Pramod joined them as requested by Shankar. All of them walked on pedestrian's path through the field. It was getting darker and the footpath was not visible properly. Deodar trees looked denser in darkness. Savitri thought she did not find time to talk to him. She had thought of saying so many things but she could not say anything. Pramod also felt hapless. He had also not found time to talk his heart to her. Savitri stopped near her home. She caught Pramod's hand. Shankar left them alone.

'I wanted to say lots of things,' Savitri said in a slow voice.

'And there is a mountain of topics in my mind that I have to share with you.'

'The most important thing is that I can't wait anymore...I have tolerated a lot...and you also.' A few tears from Savitri's eyes fell on Pramod's hands.

'I am also in similar state of mind. I am mentally united to you. We have to perform the ritual of marriage very soon for the world. I united with you long back. Pramod pressed Savitri's hand.

'I don't know anything. Do it early whatever you want to do. I have tolerated enough. Can't tolerate anymore.'

'All right. I discuss it with Shankar and tell you tomorrow.'

'Will you meet me tomorrow?'

'I can't live without you.'

'Where and when?' Savitri held Pramod's hand. No sooner did she feel the warmth of his hand, a sensation ran through his body. It was almost complete dark. They could not see each other closely. However, they felt ecstatic at the touch of hands.

'You come to Shankar's place after the school closed, I shall wait for you there.'

'All right.'

Shankar waited for her at a distance. Savitri went to her residence. Shankar and Pramod went back.

On reaching Kullu, Shankar took Pramod to a barber's shop for a hair cut. He arranged a hot water bath for Pramod at his residence. Then he gave new clothes to Pramod.

Pramod was once again cheerful after his meeting with Savitri. He felt smart after the hair dressing and a bath. He felt strange. He had taken a bath after many months. He had changed his clothes after a long gap. He had last taken a bath when he had started from Kaza. There were layers of dust on his body. He had to rub soap on his body repeatedly. He was himself alarmed to see his body before taking a bath. He felt as if he was a beast and not Pramod. Pramod and Shankar had a long chit-chat after taking meals.

'Pramod, now plan your marriage.'

'No plan but I have to marry her very soon.'

'I also mean it that way.'

'I don't have anyone of my relations here. Only you are here for me. So you have to arrange everything for my marriage.'

'We shall have to talk to Savitri's mother. It may be difficult to persuade her. Don't you want to discuss it at your home?' Shankar spoke in a worried tone.

'Shankar, I have it in my mind, too. If I go to discuss it with my family, it will delay the things. And if I get married without taking my father and sisters in confidence, they may feel offended. I am unable to solve the problem. You advise me.'

'Pramod, marriage is solemnized once in life time. It will not be proper to go for it without taking your father into confidence.

You go home tomorrow. Tell the entire story to your father. He might be worried about you, otherwise too. May be he has also lost hope about your survival. Your sisters may also be waiting for you. Go home and bring them all to Kullu. And I settle it with the Savitri's family in the meantime.'

'Your suggestion is perfectly alright. You are my true friend. You have advised rightly. So I proceed tomorrow morning to my home.'

'Very right.'

'Oh, but one thing.' Pramod said with a surprise.

'What?'

'Savitri will come here tomorrow after the school hours.'

'She has to come now. Probably, you decided it once you sent me away yesterday. I had understood it. But you must visit your family. I shall reveal the things to Savitri.'

Next day, Pramod met his senior officer. He explained the entire issue to him. Pramod had not got his salary for months together. He got some advance. After some formalities, Pramod left for his home by bus.

Shankar briefed Savitri when she came to his residence in the evening. She was a bit disappointed not to find Pramod there but was herself when Shankar explained the matter to her.

'Savitri, who should initiate talks with your mother and how?'

'I am worried about it. It is very difficult to persuade my mom.'

'And if your mother does not agree to the proposal, then?'

'Does not matter. The marriage has to happen whether anyone agrees or not. But I wish my mother agrees to it.'

'You tell, who will talk to your mother?'

'I think it would be right if you talk to her. You have met my mother twice or thrice already. My mother was all praise for you. She was very impressed with your behaviour. May be she agrees if you make her understand.'

'Agreed. When you leave for your school tomorrow, I shall go to your mother at your home to discuss the matter in detail with her in your absence.'

Savitri went back.

Next day, Shankar reached Savitri's home. He told everything about Pramod to Savitri's mother. She listened to the story with awe. A sympathy for Pramod grew in her heart. Shankar had told her all the details in a straight forward manner. He told her that

Pramod had embarked on his journey from Kaza to meet Savitri but was caught in the snowy storm. It was also made clear that both of them loved each other and wanted to be in wedlock. Savitri's mother was alarmed to hear about the likelihood of marriage.

'I cannot marry off my daughter at so distant a place. We belong to the hills whereas he hails from Punjab, i.e. from a distant place. We marry off our daughters in our own community. How can I send my daughter to a far-off place?,' the worried mother said.

'It is not far-off. Both the places are in the same state. Moreover, Pramod is in police services on a high post. If he is married here, he will prefer to be in the hills. Be assured, Pramod is a very good boy. He will become a big police officer. In addition, both of them love each other. You consider this aspect also. Suppose you do not permit them to be united in wedlock, and if they go for marriage despite it, then? Since they want each other and have been in pangs during separation and have decided to solemnize their marriage, I think you should bless the couple. I have sent Pramod to his parents. I have advised him to discuss it with his father. I wish the marriage takes place with the approval of both the families.'

'Are you confident that my daughter will live happily? She looked at Shankar with tears in her eyes.

'Rest assured, Pramod is my friend. There can be no better match than Pramod.'

Savitri's mother went to the kitchen. She brought tea for him. Shankar sat sipping tea. She sat silent before him. After a little wihile, she went inside. Shankar finished his tea and kept the glass on the floor. He looked around. Savitri's mother came back and sat with him.

'So you believe, everything will be alright.'

'You need not worry.'

'It has never happened in our village. Never ever anyone has married his daughter in a stranger family. It will become a talk of the village. They will not appreciate it. And if something goes wrong after the marriage, they will blame me. I understand Savitri's intentions. She has been waiting for him for months together. His return was not evident. You and me, made her to understand but she had faith in her deity. Her faith turned out to be true. And it is neither possible nor right now to dissuade her from that path. I fully understand the situation. But I am afraid of the comments of the people. What will the community say?'

'You cannot stop reactions from the people. Let them say what they want to say. They will cease to repeat the same things after a few days. Moreover, what is bad in it? Both of them love each other and are going to be married after seeking your blessings. You should not worry at all. We are all with you.'

'All right. I agree to the proposal. My whole-hearted blessings are with both of them.' Tears of joy rolled down from Shankar's eyes. Savitri's mother went to the kitchen. She brought jaggery in her hand. He gave it to Shankar and said, 'Please have it as a token of celebration. When will Pramod come?'

'He will reach home by tomorrow. He has gone home after a long gap. It is his second birth, in fact. He may stay for a few days at his home. But he will not be able to stay there for long. I have asked him to bring his father here after consultation so that the date for solemnization of marriage is fixed.'

Shankar ran towards the road with long strides. He wished to share the good news with Savitri before the close of the school. The school bell had gone when Shankar reached near the school. The children were going to their homes with their bags. Shankar went straight to the bus stand. Savitri almost ran towards him.

'Savitri, sweaten your mouth.' Shankar had kept a piece of gur for her. He kept it on Savitri's palm. Savitri looked at him with curiosity.

'I am just coming from your home. It has been discussed with your mother. She has expressed approval for your marriage with Pramod. Her blessings are for both of you. She gave me sweets too as a token of her joy over the union. I have given your share to you. Lots of congratulations to you, Savitri.' Savitri did not say anything. She put the piece of gur in her mouth and looked at Shankar with a smile.

'I shall never forget your obligation throughout my life.'

'What obligation? I have done it for my own happiness. I am happier than both of you.'

□

50

The news that Pramod was missing had reached his home after almost one mouth. Pramod's father had sent one of his relatives to Kullu. He narrated the entire story on his return. The Kullu Police had told him point blank that there was no possibility of Pramod surviving the snowy storm. Pramod's father was greatly shocked. He was not himself for many days. Pramod's sisters also wept bitterly to hear the news of his likely death. Occasionally, Pramod's father had a flash of hope regarding Pramod's survival. Almost three months passed by. Hope was diminished and pessimism surfaced.

After a few days, Pramod's father got sick. His sisters were now all the more worried. The three sisters had Pramod as the only brother. Nothing was known about him for months together. Father's illness continued. No medicine showed any signs of improvement in health. He grew weaker and weaker. He had to be hospitalized ultimately. His sisters looked after their father turn wise. They would arrange meals, etc. for him.

Pramod's father was not only physically wrecked but mentally also. His heart was broken and it showed on his health.

One evening, Pramod suddenly reached home. Sisters were overjoyed to see him. They hugged Pramod. Sheila, the youngest sister wept bitterly. Pramod narrated his story in brief and then looked around.

'Pratibha, where is father?' Pramod asked surprisingly.

'Father is in the hospital.'

'In hospital? Why?' Pramod asked anxiously.

'He kept on waiting for you for months together. He could not bear it and fell ill. Treatmeant showed no results. And for the last one month, he is in the hospital.'

'Let us go. I shall meet my father first of all.' He kept his luggage there.

He went to the hospital with Pratibha. Pramod stood outside the room. Pratibha went in and said, 'There is a news about Pramod's arrival.' He was alarmed at the news. He got up and sat in his bed. His eyes were searching Pramod.

'Why Pratibha? Why do you befool me? I cannot tolerate anything. I have my days numbered. How can Pramod now come?'

'No, father. Our prayers have been heard. Pramod is safe and sound. He is just to arrive.' Pratibha said sitting close to her father.

There was joy in his eyes. A glow appeared on his face. For the last three months, he had lost all hopes about Pramod's survival. He had been in grief totally. Friends and family members had made it clear to him that he could not survive the snow storm.

While on his way from home to the hospital, Pramod had counselled Pratibha that he would not like to suddenly appear before his father. He may not be able to absorb the joy to see him alive. So Pramod waited outside and Pratibha had gone in.

'Dear Pratibha, do you really mean it?,' Pramod's father asked while keeping his hand affectionately on her head.

'Have I ever told a lie to you?,' She said looking into her father's eyes.

'So tell me the whole story. Who has told you? When did he start from Kullu? When is he reaching here.' Having been assured, he hugged his daughter lovingly.

'He is already standing before you,' Pramod said while entering the room.

As soon as he heard Pramod's voice, he felt enthusiastic. He was bedridden for many days. Weakness was writ large on his face. Hearing Pramod's voice, he got up from the bed at once. Pramod touched his father's feet. The father took him in his arms warmly.

Everything stopped for a few moments. There were tears in Pratibha's eyes. Nature was also silent while witnessing father and son's reunion. They were in each other's grasp for long. Then Pramod made his father sit in his bed. Father kept watching Pramod with his eyes wide open. He was watching Pramod intently as he had surfaced suddenly. There were tears in his eyes. Words became meaningless. Eyes expressed everything. Pramod looked at his sister and father alternately.

Pramod got up and took his sister in arms. He wiped her tears with her 'dupatta' and made her sit beside his father. They were silent for sometime. No one spoke anything. The three of them saw each other and tears trickled down from their eyes.

'Pramod, my son, you are before my eyes. Oh, God, you are indeed, very kind. I had lost all hopes.' He once again hugged Pramod. His tears touched Pramod's face.

'My son, what happened? Where were you stuck, for so many months in the desolate snowy atmosphere?'

Pramod told the entire story to his father in brief.

Pramod had written a letter to Shankar telling him that he would have to stay at home for a few days as his father was sick. He wrote a letter to Savitri. Pramod's father recovered within a few days. He brought his father home. There was happiness all around at home. The plaintive atmosphere disappeared.

Pratibha was the eldest daughter in the family. Pramod used to talk to her freely. He had told her everything about Savitri. Pratibha talked to her father. Father was surprised. He called Pramod and discussed the issue with him.

After discussion for a few days, his father agreed to arrange Pramod's marriage with Savitri. All the sisters disucssed it with their father. They said, 'It is Pramod's rebirth. May be he has survived because of Savitri and Pramod's relationship.' After discussing it in detail, the father approved the proposal.

Pramod could not contain himself with joy when he learnt from Shankar that Savitri's mother had also approved the marriage proposal. After one month's stay at home, he took his father and sisters to Kullu along with himself.

The department had transferred Pramod to Kullu. His encounter with snow for many months was the talk of the town for a long time. The newspapers had covered it extensively.

After preparations, Pramod and Savitri's marriage was solemnized. The entire family returned to Ludhiana after the marriage. The family was greatly happy. Savitri won the family within a few days. Pramod spent his days happily with his wife and the family.

Pramod and Savitri returned to Kullu after his leave ended. The storm of life had quietened. Pramod had experienced the climate of Kullu, Keylong and Kaza and the snow storm within a short span of time. He felt extremely happy after having married Savitri.

Savitri found in Pramod exactly the same man that she had imagined and expected. She had seen him only for a few minutes and that too, only once. And that image had been engraved on her mind. During the long interval, she did not get a chance to meet him. Only his memories were fresh in her mind. What kind of man he would be, how would he behave? And what about his nature? She could only create his picture in mind. Her flights of imagination about him started taking a concrete shape when she learnt that he loved her and had embarked on his way from Kaza to Manali to meet her.

Savitri found Pramod the same way as she had fancied. But she had aversion for his one habit. He had taken to drinking. Agreed that he consumed a neglible quantity of liquor and had never behaved abnormal at home. But the picture that she carried in mind was of Pramod who would never drink. She felt uneasy with his drinking habit. She talked to him once or twice in this context. He promised to shun drinking, but could not fulfil his promise.

Many a time, Savitri felt it very bad. Sometimes she was irritated but the way she had won Pramod as her life partner dissuaded her to take any aggressive step. Pramod did want to leave drinking for the sake of Savitri. He made attempts to get rid of this habit but it could only last for two-three days only.

Pramod was now guided by the situation. He had come out of a tough path. It was an easy path for him in life. He adapted himself to an easy way of life. Savitri noticed the change in him. He was all together a different man. He would now ignore many things in the department. His habit to have his own way in his own style stood depleted now. He would finish his office work quickly and make his way to his home.

Both of them felt they had everything in life they had aspired for. Pramod would often take Savitri to the place at Dhalpur ground where they had met for the first time. Savitri felt enthused at that spot. She would hold his hand and say, 'I had come to you here myself. I had seen you. I had lots of ideas in my mind at that time but you...'

'Yes, yes. Speak out please. You want to say that I turned out to be a riff-raff.'

'Is there any doubt in it?'

'But you had also not said anything. You had simply thanked me before moving away.'

'Do you understand only the language of the spoken word?'

'What is the other language?'

'Language of love and silence. All understand the spoken word but it is difficult to understand the language of silence. Alas! You had heard that language at that time. That would have saved us from the prolonged separation.'

'Alas! You had made me understand that language.'

'That language is neither taught nor is made to understand anywhere.'

'But the joy of a long struggle is something unique. We regard those things more useful for which we pay more. We attach no importance to a commdity that we get free of cost. What a long struggle we went through.'

'Only you struggled. You hung between life and death for so many months.'

Pramod went to Manali with Savitri occasionally. They would sit in Hidimba temple for hours together. They would live the old memories. They were reminded of the old days. He would loiter on Manali-Keylong way with Savitri.

Gradually, Savitri compromised with Pramod's habit of consuming liquor. She now believed that he could not leave drinking. She did have a commitment from him that he would consume it only in little quantity. He would never over drink. He kept his promise for long. But the promises of drunkards are always fragile. A new officer had joined the department, who was an addict. He cultivated friendship with him. It naturally increased Pramod's frequency of taking liquor. He would return home very late at night.

Savitri felt bad but their love for each other made her ignore it.

The war erupted on the border. New recruitment to army was being made. There were advertisements for recruitment of some officers also. Pramod consulted Savitri. She resisted in the beginning but at last agreed to it. He joined the army. The war ended soon. After some days, he lived with Savitri on the Rajasthan borders. He was promoted. He became a big officer. He got higher emoluments now. Savitri had left her job.

A few years elapsed. During this period, Pramod's two sisters were married off.

Pramod was transferred to Delhi after a few years.

□

51

Pramod was a senior officer now. The army was in a mood of joy after having won the war. Besides relief, it was a time for celebration. Pramod now had a larger company of people who were fond of liquor. Liquor had started showing its impact on his behaviour also. Savitri no more tried to dissuade him from drinking.

Kishore Gupta, another officer, joined as a colleague of Pramod. He cultivated friendship with him. Kishore was completely a modern man. His wife was also of the same class. When they did not feel satisfied with the mess preparation, they would go to a bigger party. They would spend their days and nights in a club. As advised by Kishore, Pramod also took Savitri to some parties. Savitri could not adjust herself to the drinking parties. Kishore and his wife were bent upon breaking the shackles of Indian behaviour. Kishore would drink heavily in night parties. His wife also consumed liquor excessively. Kishore would find a lady friend and Roopsi, his wife enjoyed with male friends.

Pramod was also attracted to the same practices. He did not want to go that way alone. Instead, he wanted to have Savitri along with to enjoy as Roopsi did. He would deliver a sermon to Savitri. He used to take her to the parties. She was ready to do things that would make Pramod happy but she could not and would not surrender to wrong traditions.

Savitri told Pramod many a time that she did not want to remain an orthodox lady. She was ready to accompany him to any party but she would not fall down from grace. Pramod argued with her, tried to win her over to his ways but she did not give in. Now he started going alone to those kinds of parties. He had now some female friends. He was in intimate relationship with a few of them. His friends often asked him why he did not bring Savitri with him. He avoided the answer but later he told them that she did not approve of such parties.

Savitri's beauty was a talk of the area. It appeared that all that was handsome in the hills was present in Savitri's figure.

Whenever she went, all eyes were fixed on her. A few people looked at her fondly. Savitri never appreciated this kind of their behaviour.

When Pramod behaved without restraints in such parties, his friends felt the absence of Savitri. A few of his friends were very keen to meet Savitri. They insisted that Pramod should bring Savitri with him to the parties.

They were sometimes unhappy with each other but since their love was consistent, such moments would pass away. Months passed. Years elapsed. Savitri had been blessed with two children, Ritu and Surekha. The arrival of two girls heralded a new era in Savitri's life. She was now busy with the domestic chores. Now Pramod did not ask her to join the parties with him. She never appreciated his participation in the parties but now ignored this aspect of life.

Pramod's friendship circle increased. People other than army officers had become his friends. Moreover, he was a changed man now. He was a different person now. He had a large number of friends. He had to deal with them differently. He had greater responsibility towards his women friends. He would attend parties at different places. He could not invite anyone in such parties at his own home. So he would arrange his parties in hotels. By virtue of his promotion, his salary had increased but his expenditure also increased because of liquor parties.

Savitri had compromised over parties and liquor. But it did affect their economy. Savitri was exhausted. She said to Pramod, 'I have tolerated so far but I am sorry to say that you have not relented.'

'What do you mean?,' he asked her.

'You waste your salary on liquor and parties. You refuse to pay for even smaller amounts required for domestic purposes. The household expenses have increased. We have two small girls. The expenses will increase gradually. You will have to realise it.'

'You need not worry. I will take care of the needs. You should not interfere.'

'I find a total change in you. You know how we had discovered each other.'

Pramod was silent now.

'I have not asked anything from you so far. You have changed altogether. I know what goes on in your night parties. I have been tolerating it patiently. But mind you, patience has its limits too. Our girls will grow. We have to arrange for their education and marriages. If you spend your entire salary on parties and alcohol, how shall we manage for all these things.'

Pramod listened to her silently.

'I wonder how alcohol has become an addiction to a man who remained undaunted for months together in snowy mountains. You had reached me after conquering so many storms. I was united to you after great hurdles. You had admitted after marriage that you had got everything in life. I was everything for you but now I am just a household idol. Parties have become the way of your life. I know the path chosen by you will lead to destruction.' Tears rolled down her cheeks. She was sobbing after some time. Pramod did not react. Both the children came in after some time. Ritu went to Pramod's lap and Surekha sat in her mother's lap.

'May not be for me but you must think about the kids. Can't you behave for a few years more like the Pramod who happened to be at Kullu and Kaza?,' Savitri said eagerly looking into Pramod's eyes.

Pramod touched Ritu's face affectionately looking downwards.

He made sincere efforts to control himself but his friends would take him to the parties again. His new lady friends made his reformative efforts futile. He now learnt a new lesson in life. He found honesty, simplicity and politeness as useless. To him, only a person could progress in life who understood realities. He had so many examples before him. He had lived tightly as an honest man. He was tossed like a football from one place to the other. His behaviour was now guided by realism. He enjoyed all the luxuries of life now. Success was at his door. His philosophy had changed altogether. He was not prepared to oppose any injustice now as he had done earlier at Kullu. His friends made him believe the new philosophy of life.

A few more months passed by. Years passed. Savitri was blessed with another daughter. She was named Puneeta.

There was no love lost between two of them over the birth of baby girls. Savitri also desired the birth of a son but if wishes were horses, beggars could ride. It was a girl child the third time also. Pramod now spent most of his time away from home. He remained busy with his parties and was happy with his friends. At home, he performed the formality of being a husband. Savitri was busy with her household responsibilities. The girls were growing. They were going to school. But were able to read into the acts of their father.

Pramod was transferred twice during this period. He came to the same place after spending a few years. Kishore and Pramod did not wish to stay away from each other. They were intimate friends, who were similar in habits. The only difference between the two was that Roopsi accompanied Kishore actively but Savitri refused to participate in celebration with Pramod.

Pramod behaved like Kishore freely and sometimes aggressively like Kishore; he also behaved freely with the wives of his friends. They were agitated sometimes. They believed that Pramod's wife was the most beautiful one but he never brought her with him. Pramod told them that Savitri did not like to attend such parties. A few of his friends had tried to cultivate proximity to Savitri. His romantic friends had an eye on her. One or two of them went to Savitri's home also in Pramod's absence but she never encouraged them and had scolded them even for having such thoughts. She had changed herself. She had stopped going to the parties.

□

52

Pramod had a bigger family now. His daughters were in school. Expenses had increased. There was increase in his cock-tail parties. Kishore was also in similar circumstances. His salary was not compatible with his expenditure. He used to borrow to cope up with the situation. But there is a limit to everything. Gradually, he crossed the limit for borrowing also.

Kishore had made arrangements with an Army contractor, who used to supply sub-standard material and that too, in lesser quantity. He would pay some money to Kishore in the barter. The contractor was quite clever. He was dishonest to the extent which was not exposed. Even under the strict vigilance of Army, the bungling could not be noticed and if anyone knew something about it, he would not reveal it.

Gradually, Kishore made Pramod a party to the deal. Both of them started asking for more money from the contractor. Accordingly, the contractor started supplying material lesser than it was ordered for. The quality of the material was further reduced. Some of the soldiers lodged complaints. The complaint was noticed by the senior Army officers. An enquiry was ordered but it was hushed up somehow.

Savitri came to know of all these things ultimately. She was disturbed. She had compromised with Pramod's club life. She had also ignored Pramod's friendship with other ladies but internally she had to struggle a lot. She was almost broken but she controlled herself. She had made compromises to live. But she was shocked to learn about the financial frauds Pramod had committed.

Savitri took Pramod to a solitary place one day on some pretext. She sat with him. She took his hand in hers and said, 'I want to say one thing to you today.'

'Not one but you may say as many things to me as you want,' Pramod retorted half-heartedly.'

'You do not appear to be in good spirits these days. You do not talk to me warmly. I believe I am losing what I had got in Hidimba temple.' She spoke with her eyes downward.

'No, nothing of that sort.'

'It is that way. I want to discuss it with you frankly. I feel you have deprived me of that Pramod whom I had dreamt for, with whom I had fallen in love at first sight, for whom I had dared the entire world.' Plaintive tears trickled down her eyes.

'Not only you, but I also had suffered a lot. After meeting me near Raghu Nath's temple, you had silently left. Nothing had happened to you. I had realized that you were something special to me. I had to struggle a lot after that. I was suspended and transferred. I was restless to know your whereabouts. The days I spent in Lahul-Spiti were the hardest days. I used to be lost in your dreams. I was almost ecstatic when I saw your photo in the newspaper for the first time at Kaza. And then the dangerous snow storm, mountains laden with snow, the retreat of my compatriots and my decision to stay on in the harsh environment. Savitri I had embarked on the journey that day so that I could meet you. I could have gone back with those travellers to a safer place but I could not live without meeting you. I cannot describe in words the seven months I had to spend in the snow bound hills.' Pramod swayed into emotional feelings holding Savitri's hand in his hands. Savitri gazed at him intently. There was a glimmer of love in her eyes once again. Her face brightened. Both of them were silent for a few moments.

'Why are you silent? Repeat the entire story once again. Please go on.' Savitri kept his hands on her eyes. Her tears embossed her story on Pramod's hands.

'Savitri, I am the same Pramod. You have misunderstood me. Yes, the world is changing very fast.'

'I am not concerned with the world. You are my world.'

'I am perfectly alright.'

'No. Don't deceive yourself. Don't befool yourself. You are changing fast and the change is not pleasant.'

'I live with you at home. I love you. Still you say I have changed.'

'Can't you leave Kishore's company,' Savitri summoned courage to say.

Pramod was surprised at her comment. He liberated his hand from her hold and looked at her astonishingly.

'You have started the same issue once again. What's wrong with Kishore? I now don't believe to live a supressed and oppressed life as I lived at Kullu and Kaza. Yes, I am a changed man from that angle. I had attempted to be ideal. They tossed me from one place to another when I was honest. I was insulted by non-entities. When the world around me needs no honesty, when the God also does not like honest people, why should I be honest? Now there are no such inhibitions in me. Ample money flows to me. We are enjoying a comfortable living. Kishore is my fellow in all this. You need not worry.' Pramod once again held Savitri's hand.

'I mean exactly the same thing. You have snatched my Pramod from me.'

'Your Pramod has not been snatched away by anyone. He has become wiser than before.'

'Do you call it wisdom?'

'Wisdom means the same way in today's dictionaries.'

'You have started consuming excessive alcohol these days. You are not in your senses after consuming overdoses of liquor. Our daughters are growing. It affects them also. You attend the parties where your behaviour is also not praiseworthy. You have cultivated intimacy with a few women which does not augur well. It has become a topic among the people around. Now our children are also in the know of it. Ritu and Surekha's friends talk to them about you. Both of them revealed it to me with tears in their eyes.' Tears once again rolled down from Savitri's eyes.

'The idea is now very old. Man and woman cannot be tied to the same hold these days. What is wrong in meeting people during parties. We exchange our ideas in such encounters and receive new ideas along with entertainment.'

'What kind of entertainment?'

'Human behaviour has some shortcomings. One feels disinteserted if the same things are repeated day in and day out..... So there is nothing wrong in mixing up in the ultra modern society...give and take...what is wrong in it?'

'And if I act the same way, how will you react?'

'That is what I want. I have asked you so many times to attend the parties with me. Behave freely. There is nothing in this world except fun and entertainment. Gentlemanliness, honesty are useless virtues. I am fully convinced of Kishore's philosophy. You also accompany me to the club. Attend the parties. You will meet new people. Your circle will broaden, and you will feel freshness in life.' Savitri looked at Pramod with her widened eyes, widened in surprise.

'Then what is misconduct? Bad character? You and me are husband and wife. Neither I like to look at anyone else, nor can I tolerate anyone else looking at me. This is the reason that I have stopped going to parties with you.'

'These are old things. There is no such thing as misconduct or bad conduct. All people are alike. Man is man and woman is woman. Nature has created them for each other. It is but natural that they attract each other. It is the compulsion of nature. The world will cease to exist, the day this attraction disappears.'

'Pramod, do not try to justify Kishore's philosophy of immoral relationship. You and me also attract each other. Is it not sufficient for the existence of the world. If the flow of a river violates its edges, it is called floods. And the inundation always is destructive. So I say you are a fully changed man.' They were now silent.

'I had compromised with all your activities, Pramod. I am happy with my married life within the walls. I have accepted what you do outside but since you have started bungling of money in connivance with Kishore. I am afraid for you. There is a limit to everything. What will happen if you are caught? Please stop all this for God's sake. Please accept my request.'

'Who will catch me? You are worried unnecessarily. Do you know how much is spent on domestic requirements? And you know my expenses have increased. My salary has become insufficient. Moreover, we do not misappropriate the funds on a large scale. All politicians make money the same way. It all exists in our department from top to bottom. A few unfortunate fools live in penury because of honesty. I do not want to join that company. I and Kishore indulge in the activity very cautiously. There is no evidence of what we do. So you need not worry at all.'

'We have a small family. Can't we live comfortably with the salary you get? You misappropriate the funds. You go to the club and parties where you spend so much that you fall short of money at home. Do you like all this? Don't you feel that all should live peacefully at home with whatever you earn. I beg of you. Please come back. You have gone far ahead. The path you have chosen is not good. God knows where it will lead you. I am here. You have your children. You have to fend for their future. You are not even prepared to think whither are you drifting. May not be for me but you must think about the children.' There were tears once again in her eyes.

'Savitri, you are raising useless issues. I am concerned for the family. I am worried about my daughters also. Also about their future. That is why I am trying to earn more money.'

'But you spend all your income on liquor and parties.'

Pramod got silent. He had no interest in Savitri's arguments. He tried once or twice to get up. He had no answer to Savitri's questions. However, he tried to answer those questions. Pramod cast his eyes downwards when Savitri wanted to look into his eyes. He could not face Savitri and felt himself very small before her. An inferiority complex lurked in him. At times, he felt that Savitri was right. He felt like changing the gears of life but that would be his defeat, he thought. What is wrong in what he did! All the world was moving in the same direction. All were seeking comforts the same way. He also thought that he had done lot of penance in life. He had experienced the lurking death for months together. He had had enough of devotion, sacrifice and honesty. He must spend rest of his life lavishly.

'We have discussed a lot. Let us go home now,' Pramod said while getting up.

'What has been discussed? I am unlucky, may be, Pramod you must give a thought to my points once again. You are treading a dangerous path. The end will not be happy. No body says anything in your presence but they discuss it, i.e. you and Kishore's misappropriation of funds is in bad taste. I feel frightened. I shall have to reconcile by accepting it as my bad luck.' They got up and started walking. They went on silently. Words stuck both of them. Savitri shivered. She would then look at Pramod and feel coldenend. There was no impact on Pramod. May be he was lost in his glittering world that had been created with the help of Kishore. Savitri heaved a sigh. She saw this way and that way and went on.

Life went on. She compromised with every new situation she faced. There was no way out except compromise. Pramod and Kishore looted the govt. money shamelessely. Many complaints were filed against them but nothing happend to them.

□

53

'Oh, my eyes?,' Pramod said looking at one of the persons standing while he entered the restaurant.

'I am not mistaken, I think.' He completed Pramod's incomplete sentence. There was a huge crowd in the restaurant. This newly opened restaurant in Cannaught Place was always full to capacity during mid day. All the tables were occupied. People stood waiting on sides. A few well-dressed persons were trying to adjust people at different tables. They asked everyone about their numbers so that they could find suitable tables for them. It was a strange sight. Some were enjoying their lunch delightfully. Others were waiting impatiently. Customers would stand around the table even before the persons sitting had finished their meals. The waiters were ready to dispose of the customers quickly.

Pramod stood with his friends in one corner and waited for his turn. He found one of his acquantances when he looked behind. He was reminded of old memories.

'Rita, you are here?,' Pramod said moving close to her.

'Thank God, you have recognised me,' Rita said looking intently at Pramod.

'Did you doubt me?'

'Exactly. Such a long period has passed. And the incidents that happened in Kullu those days. You are a duty conscious idealistic police officer and we...' Rita was satirical in her comment.

'Sir, a table for two is available there,' A restaurant employee said.

'Come on Rita, we occupy the table.' Pramod asked his friends to excuse him. He told them that he had met his old friend after many years. He wanted to talk to her. Both of them sat on a corner table.

'Rita, you have met me after so many years but you have not forgotton anything.'

'What do you mean?'

'You are satirical in your conversation.'

'Pramod, do you remember. I had gone to your office in Kullu with a small request. I had full trust in you. But you had not favoured me,' Rita said reminding him of the incident.

'And you had got me transferred from Kullu to Keylong. Rita, just because of my refusal.' Pramod put forth his view.

'It was Thakur who got you transferred.'

'Leave it, Rita. These are stories of the past. I have changed a lot during this period. Hardships have shattered my dreams. You are meeting a different Pramod today. It is not of Kullu brand.'

'Is that right? Really?'

'Yes, I mean what I say.'

'Where are you posted these days?'

'Here, in Delhi.'

'I learnt, you had resigned your police job.'

'Yes, everything is changed. I have changed the place. The job is different. My thoughts and behaviour has undergone a sea-change. Rita, you were not successful in changing me. But the throws of time have changed me. I feel you have not undergone a change. You look the same even after so many years. I am surprised to see you in the same mould. Your age has not made any impact on your body.' Pramod took out a cigarette from his pocket and lit it in style. He placed his order with the waiter.

'Oh, you smoke too?' Rita had a surprise.

'I told you, everything is changed. Why cigarette only... everything is changed...Pramod too. You can talk to the new Pramod in a new way.' Pramod said after having a long puff of cigarette.

'It is wonderful. I can't believe my eyes. Anyhow, what are you doing these days? and where are you?'

'I am here in Delhi in Army. Where are you these days?'

'I am Chairman of a Corporation in my State. I visit Delhi occasionally.'

'So, you are a complete leader. And where is Mr. Thakur?'

'He has lagged much behind.'

'I have not followed you.'

'I had left his company long ago. Earlier I was with him in the fight for power in the state. At the fag end, I felt Pawan Lal could become the Chief Minister in their fight, so I switched over my loyalty to him. Pawan Lal had appointed me Chairman of one of the Corporations.'

'But now...'

'Yes, Pawan Lal was about to go, nay he was being probed against so I left him also.'

'Whom did you join?'

'One who was likely to be the Chief Minister.'

'How did you know the prospective Chief Minister?'

'It is just a matter of co-incidence. My guess is normally right. May be you don't know that Pawan Lal has been succeeded by two Chief Ministers. With the change in Chief Ministers, the chairpersons of the Corporations are also changed. But I was not changed.'

'What is the secret behind it?' Pramod listened to Rita intently. His ears absorbed what Rita said but he had his gaze on Rita's face. And occosionally he shifted his gaze from her face to her body. He was nostalgic now.

'Pramod, I like to live in the present.' They both laughed heartily. The old memory was fresh once again.

'Rita, I bow before you.'

'When someone is about to be ousted, I abandon his company. I shift my loyalty to the likely Chief Minister, likely as per my estimate. Then I help him whole-heartedly. So many Chief Ministers came and went, but I continued in my office.'

'We shall have a nice time together. I also don't believe in past or future but I live in the present. Alas! I had understood it at that time. You tried your best to make me understand. Anyhow, I had been astray as much as was my fortune.'

'How is your Savitri?'

'She is just a slave.'

'Is that alright? Then, indeed, you are a changed man.'

'Why?'

'The tales of your love with Savitri had spread in places beyond Kullu. It was discussed in many magazines. You both were referred as the honest, true lovers. Now you say she is bonded. You will change all together. I had never thought. Even the ever-changing Rita also had not thought of it.'

'Rita, there are certain things in life that one cannot understand. You have to live to understand those realities. I was landed in an idealitic world at that time. My feet are on the earth. I could not understand Rita at that time but life has taught me a lesson.'

'Gurcharan, here I am.' Rita called someone going the other way. The youngman looked behind. Rita signalled him to join them.

The fair-coloured youngman looked curiously towards Pramod and sat beside him. He was a lean fellow but was impressive and attractive. He was wearing white clothes. Pramod could make it out that he was wearing Khaddar. But it was not kurta-payjama but pant and shirt.

'Pramod, meet Mr. Gurcharan. A young leader of our party, a rising star leader of the state. He has been recently elected,' Rita said looking at both of them.

'Hello.'

'Hello.'

'And he is Pramod, an old friend of mine. We have met after a gap of many years. I was waiting for you and in the meanwhile he met me. He is an army officer here in Delhi.

Once Rita introduced them, they started chatting. Gurcharan Singh was a very influential leader. He was son of a rich landlord of the state. His family was in politics for many years now. The family had its impact in state politics which they had now extended to the national politics in Delhi. He was much younger to Rita but had cultivated deep friendship with her. Whenever Rita went to Delhi, she surely met Gurcharan. They usually met in the restaurant.

Gurcharan belonged to a rich family. He had inherited all the bad habits of rich people. Moreover, he was a leader now. And that, too, a leader of the party that was in power in the state. He had a group of friends in Delhi too. He had jolly evenings and every night, he had a new female partner at night. He had no specific interest in Rita. It could not have happened. But Rita was in touch with some big leaders in Delhi. They would often meet Rita. She helped in finding women friends for Gurcharan. Both of them wanted to use each other for their purpose. So the friendship grew deeper and deeper.

They continued talking to each other for quite sometime. Pramod and Gurcharan were now interested in each other. They opened up in the first very meeting. Though they had a gap in age, yet they liked each other and were interested to know more.

Rita noted the complete address of Pramod. He also jotted addresses of both of them. He invited both of them to dinner. All of them got up to move to their places.

□

54

Savitri and Pramod lived under one roof, no doubt, but they had fallen apart otherwise. They rarely talked to each other. For sometime, they did not apparently behave in a manner before their children that would make them understand the differences between the two. They would sometimes talk affectionately about the children. Truly speaking, it was just an enactment of relationship which was otherwise false. Now they stood exposed before their children.

Pramod would return home late at night, badly drunk. If irritated Savitri did not open the door immediately, Pramod would knock at the door violently and try to break it open. He would abuse Savitri from outside even. Then Savitri would start weeping and Ritu, Surekha would open the door. Once it so happened that enraged Pramod pushed her daughter Ritu after entering the door. He thought it was Savitri. Ritu sustained minor injuries also. Shocked Savitri got up. Pramod went to sleep in his bed. Savitri slept with Ritu. She fondled her. Savitri was remorseful once Ritu had slept.

Pramod and Savitri had stopped saying anything to each other. They had realized that their ways were apart. Neither of them was ready to change his or her path. Savitri was not worried about herself but she was concerned with the future of her three daughters. The uncertainty and darkness of future frightened her.

Savitri would share her thoughts with her two elder daughters to release her tension. The third one was a sibling as yet. Ritu was lost in herself. She did not find anything bad in her father's behaviour. She discussed it many a time with Savitri. She maintained that all men are similar in behaviour towards woman. Others are also like her father. Ritu was a darling of Pramod. He had taken her a few times to his parties. Savitri had opposed it tooth and nail. She never wanted her daughter to go to any such party. But Pramod insisted and Ritu agreed to go. Savitri was helpless. Ritu had enjoyed herself in the party that day.

Surekha understood her mother's woe. she would listen to her mother for hours together. She would weep at times. She would console her mother. Savitri would sometimes say that she was all alone in this world. Pramod has almost abandoned her. Ritu also does not talk to her. But Surekha would say lovingly to her mother, 'Mother, I am with you. I shall not let you have any problem.'

Savitri would affectionately place her hand on her forehead and said, 'As if you will live with me for ever.'

'No, mother. I shall not go anywhere leaving you in grief.' Surekha would hug her mother.

'Daughters are just keepsakes. Alas, I had a son. I could spend my entire life with his support,' Savitri would say heaving a deep sigh. Surekha tried to console her mother.

Savitri had moved her bed to their daughters' room. Pramod slept separately in another room. The children viewed it with a surprise when Savitri did it for the first time. They had seen Savitri and Pramod living in one room together always. When she was a small girl, she also used to sleep with her parents. And when the girls grew older, they were moved to a separate room. But the parents lived in one room always. Even when Savitri felt difficulty in sleeping in Pramod's room, she somehow continued. But when it became intolerable, Savitri moved out of the common bedroom.

That night, children were already in sleep. As usual, Pramod came home late at night. Savitri was awake. She opened the door when she heard the sound of foot steps. Pramod entered the room with the stink of liquor. He made to his room falteringly. He was so much under the influence of liquor that he fell on his bed without changing his clothes. Savitri helped him put off his shoes. Tears trickled down from Savitri's eyes while she opened the laces of his shoes.

His hair were disorderly. His dress was unseemly. He appeared to be totally exhausted. The smell of liquor not only oozed from his mouth but from his entire body. Savitri suddenly noticed a red mark on Pramod's face. She was alarmed. Blood...injury...she thought and sat in Pramod's bed.

'Oh, how did you get this injury? Blood spots?' She tried to make Pramod get up.

'Injury? What kind of injury? Let me sleep,' He said and changed his side.

'Please sleep comfortably. When did I stop you from sleeping? I don't come even close to you now. I never disturb your sleep. Who am I, moreover. But I could not resist after observing blood stain on your face. So I came close to you. Turn your face towards me. Let me see. I shall apply some ointment. You may sleep after that.' Savitri tried to turn his face towards her side.

'Why are you disturbing me unncessarily?,' Irritated Pramod said.

'What is this red spot? It is an injury. Apply ointment to it.'

'Injury, blood? Has a murder been committed?' Pramod got up alarmed. He examined his face with his hand. He did not feel any injury on his face.

'Who has been hit? Where has the murder been committed?,' Pramod asked looking at Savitri.

'What is this red spot?,' Savitri said while putting her finger on his face.

'This spot?,' Pramod wondered aloud when he saw his face in the mirror. He laughed vigorously. Savitri was frightened.

'Why? Why do you laugh? How did you get hurt?,' Savitri asked.

'It is not blood.' Pramod said laughingly while touching the red spot on his face.

'Then what is it?'

'She kissed me heavily.' Pramod laughed and retired to bed for sleep.

'Then it is my blood. It is the blood of my husband, Pramod, I know how long you have been indulging in such acts. But you have lost all decency now. You kill me and announce it so shamelessly and proudly. You do not treat me as Savitri but take me as if I am a lifeless object.' Pramod's ears were shut to Savitri's comments. Soon he was snoring in his bed.

'You are asleep so easily. You are sleeping after breaking my heart. What has gone wrong with you Pramod? You had started on a different path but where have you landed yourself? You have spoiled the vermillion on my head even as you are alive.' Savitri tried to shake Pramod. She was weeping bitterly. She found two hairs on his coat. She held the hair in her hand and dragged them. They were long. They could not be Pramod's. The spot on his face had told the story. She looked at those two hairs intently. She saw the spot on his face, the red stain made her restless. Her eyes were full of tears. She felt his snores as if bullets had been fired at her.

She sat beside Pramod for long, who was sleeping soundly.

Then she suddenly got up. She looked at Pramod. Now she was no more imploring. She was full of hatred for him. She came out of the room stealthily. It was tranquil all around. She stood by the side of window. The road lights glittered from a distance. She gazed continuously. It was almost mid-night now.

'Why should one drag on life? I have already been deceived in life. I am moving just like a dead corpse. Why should I not commit suicide? Why should I die every moment?,' She thought and entered the kitchen. She took out the kerosene pot. She shook it to measure its quantity. She picked up the match box. She was thoughtful now. She saw the loaves box. A pratha was in the bread box.' Puneeta, the youngest daughter had cooked it herself last night. Since it was not cooked in a nice way, she ate half of it. Savitri felt a jolt. She stopped at once after seeing the prantha cooked by her daughter. The match box slipped down from her hand. She rushed to the bedroom of her daughters. She showered affection on them. Tears rolled down unchecked when she lovingly kissed Puneeta.

'No, no, I shall not commit suicide. What will happen to my three daughters? I cannot punish my daughters for the crimes of Pramod,' she blurted.

Savitri got up slowly. She went to her room. Pramod was in sound sleep. She collected her things and carried them to another room. She picked up her blanket also. She took the books lying on the back of her bed. She came to her daughter's room. She switched on the smaller light. She put off the light in Pramod's bedroom. Then she slept with Puneeta in her bed.

'No, I shall not terminate my life. I shall live for my three daughters. But I shall never meet Pramod in his room.' She slowly slept.

Since that day, she lived in a separate room. She had put up her and Puneeta's bed in another room. Puneeta was happy at this development. She enjoyed sleeping with her mother. Ritu and Surekha could not believe it. But they could understand the reasons for it. Ritu did not take obvious notice but Surekha had asked about it from her mother, who in turn had told the truth. Savitri now could talk her heart only to Surekha. Gradually, Surekha was just like a friend to Savitri. She shared her mother's anxieties.

□

55

Gurcharan and Pramod started meeting frequently. Pramod was impressed with Gurcharan's political connections in Delhi. He wanted to have an intimate friendship with him. He was often reminded of Savitri's comments. She had pointed out to him several times that he indulged in misappropriation of funds in connivance with Kishore. He could be caught any time. While committing all this, Pramod was often apprehensive of the impending danger. If he was caught, everything would go haywire. He found a future support in Gurcharan. He felt if he ever got caught, Gurcharan's political connections could be helpful in saving him.

Rita was in Delhi for one week. Three of them met twice. Later on Pramod continued meeting Gurcharan. Pramod brought him to his home one day. Pramod rarely visited his home. He had never brought his friends. Savitri's behaviour was now totally indifferent. And if at all someone came with Pramod, Savitri ensured that none of her daughters went to the drawing room. Savitri visualized a scoundrel in every friend of Pramod. But that day, Savitri was not at home. Ritu served them tea. Gurcharan was wonder struck to see Ritu. She was more beautiful than even Savitri. A beautiful bud of a rose. Without letting Pramod beware of it, he repeatedly looked at Ritu. He invited her closer to himself on the pretext of talking. Ritu was soon engrossed in conversation with him like a jovial bird. Pramod felt pleased. He thought if not Savitri, his daughter could take care of visitors at home.

Although Gurcharan left after some time, yet Ritu haunted him badly.

Come what may, Gurcharan was in the habit of getting whatever he fancied for. God had blessed him with bounty. He was the only son of a rich, influential family. He was owner of a huge property. He was youthful and handsome. Many girls had come in his life in a short span. Now he was an influential leader of the area. He had been elected. Not only in the state but he was active in the national politics also. Overtly, he was a public man. He was a leader of the country, a representative of the people. But he spent most of his time in seeking physical gratification. Now girls came in contact every day. They were attracted by his charm. But as they entered his life quickly, they left it soon too. If anyone refused his access, he would compel her one way or the other to surrender.

Gurcharan had no difficutly in drawing Ritu closer to him. She was disgusted with her family. Moreover, family did not exist like an institution there. Pramod lived his own life, luxuriously. But it was beyond home. And within the four walls of the house, Savitri lived in a suffocating environment. Neither Pramod nor Savitri had anything for the lively girls. Once she was intimate with Gurcharan, she was lost. She saw life in Gurcharan. A fellow, a friend, who was rich and full of youth. And a leader too.

He was happy when he learnt it in the beginning. He thought cultivation of relationship will ultimately be useful for him. But when he observed that Ritu was in intense relationship with Gurcharan, he was uneasy. He had enjoyed whatever he did. He used to justify it but on finding her own daughter going the same way, he felt hurt. He made efforts to check her. But by this time Ritu had gone further and further. Gurcharan had stopped meeting Pramod now. He had nothing to gain from Pramod.

Savitri did not know anything about it for days together. Ritu would invent pretexts. Earlier Gurcharan would visit Pramod's place but now he never came to his residence. He did not meet Pramod even. It was Ritu who would go to Gurcharan in one hotel or the other. One night, Ritu did not come home. Savitri was worried. Pramod was also not at home. When he came home late at night, she asked him to enquire about Ritu. But Pramod was drunk. He could not understand what Savitri had told him. She continued talking to him but as usual, he went to sleep after abusing Savitri.

Savitri could not sleep throughout the night. She was tossing helpless in the bed. Ritu returned home next morning. She made lame excuses. But her mother could make out what had been going on after reading her face and the plight of body. She asked her in camera. Then she scolded her angrily. Ritu kept silent for sometime. Later on, she burst out. She told her mother that she was now grown up and that she had the right to live as she decided. On hearing her arguments, Savitri was dumb founded.

It went on for some days. No one said anything to anyone. The incident had become oblivious. But Savitri was restless. One day Savitri called Ritu and talked to her in seclusion.

'Ritu, you know, I am already broken. You father has almost deserted me. My daughters are the only hope for me to live for. Please do not do any such thing that may spoil the fag end of my life,' said Savitri while keeping her hand on Ritu's head.

'I earnestly wish that I arrange your marriage in a suitable family in a decent way. You are eldest of the three. They may also go astray if they follow you.' She tried to make her mind clear.

'Mother, you are unncessarily worried. What have I done that makes you so worried,' she said while getting aside.

'Listen, I am your mother. I want to say plainly. I do not like your meeting with Gurcharan. Where were you that night without telling me? I know you were not with Veena that day. You had told a lie. I had immediately got information from there.'

'My dear mother, I am grown up now. You have given me education upto degree level. The world is changed. It is Delhi and not Kullu of the hills. If I go with my friends to a place, you need not worry. The girls are no more captive birds. Woman has got liberation in free India. It is only because of your orthodox practices that you have a rift with my father.' Ritu started making her mother understand.

'Do you think all that your father is indulging in, is right?'

'Yes, mother. Everything is right. All are leading life the same way these days. The age of bondages is over. It is an era of free indulgence.'

'Do you think it is all right? I remain unnoticed, insulted and rejected. Do you justify it?'

'Oh, mother. You have twisted the discussion. I am also worried for you. But where is papa to be blamed? He wanted to see you walk beside him but you refused. Mother, you go along with papa and let me go... .' She went slient.

'And I may allow you to go with Gurcharan?'

'What is wrong in it? Don't I have the right to choose my friend?'

'Friend? You are a girl, and that too, in an Indian society. India is still India. It is not Paris or London as yet. We have certain traditions and moral values.'

'Mother, values have no significance. Life is to live joyfully. It is not for suffocation. I want to follow in papa's footsteps. Why can't I do what papa can do?,' Ritu said obstinately.

'Alas! Your father had accepted my suggestion a few years earlier. I had warned him that his daughters could also follow in his footstepts. You have proven it true. O.K. I don't wish to say anything more. Please remember, your father is on a suicidal path. He is misappropriating the departmental funds. He is misusing the money. And that money is being used for gala living. The family is on the breaking point. I wished that my three daughters did not go their father's way but Ritu, you have already advanced on the perilous and destructive path adopted by your father. You do not wish to retrace your steps. I had only one difficulty before me earlier, i.e. your father's behaviour. Now you have given me another bother. Your father's behaviour had made me think of terminating my life. I desisted from it only having been concerned for all three of you. My daughters are my stay of life. I live for you. May be God is not kind to me in this direction also.' Savitri heaved a deep sigh and left the room.

Savitri felt suffocated. She apprehended danger ahead for Ritu but she kept mixing up with Gurcharan irrespective of her mother's warning. She was now completely liberated.

One day, Savitri found time to discuss the issue with Pramod.

'You know, Ritu has taken up your route. Have you ever thought about her?'

'Yes, I find, she meets Gurcharan frequently. Did you not stop her?'

'Who listens to me? I made efforts to make her undertand the situation but she did not agree to my suggestions. She feels she is right. She argued that her father also does the same thing.'

'So, she equates herself with me.' Pramod felt a bit disturbed.

'I did apprehend that your way of life would have an impact on children. Pramod I am totally broken from inside. I often feel like committing suicide. Your behaviour has made me a living corpse. I, in fact, die every moment. O.K. you tread your path. But please save Ritu. She is the main stay of my life.' Savitri could not control her tears.

It showed a little impact on Pramod. He stayed at home for the evening. He did not consume liquor also. He talked to Ritu in isolation. He tried to make her understand. He met Gurcharan the next day. He told him clearly that he did not appreciate Ritu's meeting with Gurcharan. Gurcharan remained silent for some time and then he started laughing. Pramod flew into rage at his laughter. When Pramod demonstrated his anger, Gurcharan burst out. He told point blank that it was his and Ritu's problem. No one should intervene. Pramod said since he was Ritu's father, he had every right to interfere. Gurcharan said that other women who are in touch with him are also wives or daughters of others. They never interferred.' Gurcharan spoke to Pramod in bad taste. He made his political clout also felt. Pramod returned badly offended and insulted.

Pramod had reaped only happiness in his new style of life. For the first time today, he was shocked. He had indulged in physical relationship with many girls and women. He had never felt bad in the illegitimate relationship. But when his own daughter went the same way, he felt greatly hurt.

Pramod felt for the first time that he had gone astray. Now he was worried about Surekha and Puneeta. He was totally exhausted by the time he reached home. He was tired mentally and physically too. The man with whom Pramod's daughter was indulging in illigal relationship had not only insulted him but had threatend also. Gurcharan had warned him of dangerous results if he tried to intervene in his relations with Ritu. He has hold on Delhi government and has scoundrels at his back too.

For the first time Pramod thought that he must return to Savitri. He was reminded of Hidimba's temple, his first metting with Savitri near Raghu Nath's tent and his sojourn in deadly snow. He lied down in his bed. Kept on thinking. A strife went on in his mind. Should he continue to tread on the path he had chosen or should he make a comeback to Savitri.

More than this thoughtful strife was his physical compulsions also. It was his drinking time. It was the time when he had friends around while drinking. He pined for drinks. In fact, liquor had become a compulsion with him. He was undone by whisky. After some time Pramod got up and went out. Only liquor was the remedy for Pramod. He drank heavily in the company of his friends and then moved away to some other place.

□

56

'Mother, something unpleasant happened today.' Surekha came running to the kitchen and held her mother in her hands.

'What happend? Tell me. Speak out please.' Savitri was alarmed. She trembled at the thought of some thing happening.

'Mother, Papa's office was raided today. They searched it. Papa and uncle Kishore have been arrested.' Surekha wept. Savitri came to the outer room with her. She made her sit in a chair. Then she went out. A few neighbours had came there. A woman consoled Savitri.

'What has happened? Will someone tell me the entire story?,' Savitri said with tears in her eyes.

'Don't be disturbed. It often happens in the offices. Some one might have lodged a false complaint. That may be the reason of search.' A neighbour tried to console her. The news spread in the entire colony. This became the talk of the area. People in twos and fours were discussing the same issue. Those who knew them came to Savitri and expressed their sympathies. Surekha sat sobbing. Ritu had not come home as yet. Puneeta sat in her room silently.

The bunglings of Pramod and Kishore had been in discussion for many days. But they could not be apprehended. They had started gambling also for some months now and had lost enough money in that. Kishore used to have departmental money in his hands. They started using it for personal ends. It was leaked by someone. The office was searched. Almost one lakh was found short. When they were apprehended, their other acts were also exposed. Some people came openly against them. They were prepared to be witnesses against them. A fraud of many lakhs was discovered. The proceedings started in the court after a few days.

This came as a shock to Savitri, who was almost broken. It was difficult to sustain it. But she summoned courage after a few days. She consulted her relations and friends. Most of Pramod's friends were no more there to help him but a few of them did come to Savitri. They started helping her by all means.

'Mother, if you don't take it otherwise, may I ask Gurcharan to help Papa,' Ritu said to her mother.

'You will ask Gurcharan?' Savitri was undecided on the proposal. She had hatred and anger in her mind for Gurcharan. She had learnt a lot about his free immoral activities. But she knew Gurcharan was an influential leader. His help could be useful in Pramod's court case. For a moment she thought it was not bad to seek anyone's help in a time of adversity. And moreover, the future of the family rests on Pramod. If Pramod is sentenced, the entire family will have to suffer. What will happen if Pramod is lodged in the jail. How will they feed for without his salary. She thought it was but necessary to save Pramod from any kind of action. And only political help could be effective in such a case. But then a thought surfaced in her mind, will she have to pay heavily for the favour? She was alarmed at the idea. She had already lost much, but she did not want to lose everything. Thinking all this, Savitri went into the kitchen and was soon engaged in the household activities.

'Mom, Ritu is right. It is important to save papa. What has happened, it has happened. We know you had asked papa to desist this path. But once papa went astray, he did not relent. But now the present is endangered and the future is at stake. If Gurcharan helps as suggested by Ritu, papa would be saved. If papa is safe, the entire family will be saved,' Surekha said drawing closer to her mother.

'Mother, you are thinking all this unnecessarily. Agreed that he is a big leader but I have heard many bad things about him. I am worried already over Ritu's relations with him. And now my sister loves him. They meet openly. There should not be any hesitation in accepting their relationship. Both of them like each other. It would be improper to create hurdles for them. Moreover, sister will not listen to anyone on this issue. The family is facing a calamity. If we accept their relationship, sister will be happy and papa will be saved with the help of Gurcharan.

'Call Ritu, here,' Savitri said after giving a thought to it, Surekha went to the other room.

'Mother, I am here.' Ritu said coming close to Savitri.

'Do you love Gurcharan?,' she asked straight.

'Yes, mother.'

'And he too?'

'Yes.'

'Do you feel you will have a comfortable married life with him? How far the rumours are true about him regarding his bad character.'

'Mother, he is a progressive man. He talks smilingly with everyone, so people doubt Him. I am confident that I can spend my life happily with him.' Ritu turned her eyes downwards after making the comment.

'O.K. you talk to him today. And then invite him to our place,' Savitri said.

'No, you may not invite him at home. It will not be good to invite him, Surekha, you meet him today. If he is true in his love for Ritu, I shall not heistate in accepting their wedlock. And if it is not like that, Ritu should also stop meeting him.' She went into the kitchen after expressing her views. There was a dream in her eyes. If Gurcharan whole-heartedly loves Ritu, he should marry her. Both should live happily. Pramod's case will be settled with the help of Gurcharan. Throughout the night, there dreams looked in her mind.

Surekha met Gurcharan the next day. She told him what her mother had said. Gurcharan laughed at her propsal. Gurcharan was one of them but there were many Ritus. Surekha seriously presented her point. It was an emotional question for her. But it was just a joke for Gurcharan. He laughed spontaneously at Surekha's comment. Then he controlled himself. He said he would first talk at home. Surekha narrated the entire story to her mother.

'If he is not ready for marriage, why both of them meet unchecked? Ritu, tell me, what's the matter.' She asked Ritu who stood close.

'Mother, why raise the marriage issue at this juncture? We shall seek his help to get papa's case settled. Rest of the things can be taken care of later on,' Ritu pleaded.

'She is right, mother. We should get papa released by using Gurcharan's political influence. Who else is ours here? Since they have collected many evidences against papa, only a heavy political influence can save him,' Surekha said keeping her hand on her mother's shoulder.

'Mom, I go to Gurcharan just today. I shall meet senior officers with him and get papa released,' Ritu said joyfully.

'No, no, it will not happen that way. If Gurcharan is not prepared for marriage, then everything I have heard about him must be true. His love is artificial. If we take his help at a odd time today, it means we sell ourself. People will say I sent Ritu to Gurcharan for getting your papa released. Come what may. I shall not tolerate a taint on my integrity. Your father has destroyed many things. Whatever is left, I shall not allow it to be finished. Ritu, you listen clearly, you will never go to Gurcharan. He was just a paramour finding new preys for satisfaction of his lust. He has betrayed many a girl earlier too.' Savitri's face was glowing with confidence. She refused to bend even while she was passing through a tough time.

'What shall happen to us, mother, if papa is sentenced. He has not saved anything for the rainy days. He has exhausted the money he had.' Surekha expressed her anxiety.

'God gives strength to face the odds even when he creates problems for anyone. You need not worry at all. I am here to look after you. I shall do everything for all of you but I shall not allow my integrity to be tainted.' Both the sisters looked at each other after hearing their mother.

Pramod was kept in jail for a few days. He was then released on bail. He made efforts to seek help from all of his friends. Some of the friends tried their best to save Pramod and Kishore but the evidences against them were so strong, that there was no possibility of their escape. They were under scanner of the public for quite sometimes. It was a common talk that they were misappropriating public funds extensively. They had earned a bad name. Barring a few close friends, no one else was sympathetic to them.

The court proceeding went on for a few months. Pramod had no money with him. He never saved anything. But Kishore had plenty of money. He spent thousands of rupees for his defence. His wife Roopsi adopted all ways and means. She tried even to trap a few enquiry officers also. She used money as well as her glamour for the purpose. A few of them exploited her fully and at the same did not favour her in findings of the enquiry. They had no sympathy for the accused persons. In fact, Pramod and Kishore had done nothing to serve except to make bucks by unfair means. Only Roopsi was fighting their case. Savitri simply prayed to God in the evening before the idol of God at home to help her husband. Neither Roopsi's glamour and money was instrumental in rescuing them nor the prayers offered by Savitri. Pramod and Kishore were sentenced to four years imprisonment.

Savitri burst into tears when she heard about the sentence. She had exerted bravely so far. She had not allowed tears to trickle from her eyes. She thought Pramod and Kishore would be saved as senior advocates were fighting their case and there was no dearth of money as well? She was perturbed to think of a span of four years. Pramod did not leave any savings for them. How will she fend for her family for four years. She felt miserable. The neighbours came to her, expressed their sympathy. A few of them consoled them from their heart, others just did it for formality.

Pramod was taken to the jail from the court premises as soon as the final judgement was announced. Only the news of his being sent to jail had reached them at home. The sympathisers left soon. Savitri sat with her three daughters in a gloomy posture. Her eyes had dried up now. Puneeta had slept in her mother's lap after weeping. Ritu and Surekha sat with her.

'What will happen now, mother? Will Papa stay in prison for four years really?,' Surekha asked keeping her head on her mother's shoulders.

'Mother, you just insisted. One should seek help from any corner during adversity. If we had sought Gurcharan's help, may be Papa would have been a free man today. He has his links even at Prime Minister's place.' There was a glow in Ritu's eyes at the mention of Gurcharan.

'Ritu dear, your mother is the daughter of the hills who has been brought up in tough conditions. Though hill people are poor, yet they never compromise on their integrity. You probably do not know that Gurcharan had sent direct messages to me also. He did not intend to help us just for sympathy. You know how Roopsi presented herself to so many people but to no avail. I shall never follow that track. Ritu, you are my daughter. I have given you birth. Gurcharan does not love you. He is a lusty fellow. I shall prepare to die hundred times rather than barter my daughter for Pramod's release.' Savitri's sorrow now disappeared and she looked like confidence incarate.

'Mother is right. I talked to Gurcharan that day. I also felt the same way as mother has pointed out. Our mother never met him intimately. She did not talk to him so intimately as well. May be he had come with Papa at our home once or twice. But mother's assessment of him is perfectly alright. I had a long conversation with him. He is not an upright man. Neither he is gentlemanly nor a decent fellow. He is a bragging sort of man full of lust. I did not like the way he looked at me. Sister dear, now forget about him. We shall help our mother. We shall face adversity jointly. Mother is already broken. Any wrong move on your part will prove fatal for mom.' While saying all this, Surekha slipped into her mother's hold. Tears trickled down from her eyes.

'Mom we both shall find some employment. We shall work and live with integrity. You do not worry.' Surekha said confidentally to her mother.

'You will find jobs? Alas! I had a son. I don't know why God has punished me? May be it is for the sins committed in previous life.' Savitri wiped tears from Surekha's eyes.

'We are your sons, mother. You have brought us up. You have educated us. We both are degree holders, who have qualified with merit. The calamity has not fallen alone on you, it is on the entire family. You need not worry. We have to look for a suitable job soon. What do you say sister?' Surekha looked towards Ritu. Ritu looked beyond silently.

'Agreed, we shall have to think of livelihood for the family. If need be, you can join jobs. But you will keep in mind that you will not create new problems for me. Leave rest of the things to me. Surekha has rightly said that we shall have to bear adversity collectively. I depend on both of you.' Savitri said specially looking towards Ritu who was silent.

Some of Pramod and Kishore's friends advised them to appeal against the judgement. Savitri also endorsed it. But so much had already been spent on the case that it was not possible to arrange funds for it. Kishore had plenty of funds but it remained in Roopsi's custody. She had got made ornaments of gold. Rest was in cash. Roopsi had asked Kishore to keep the entire embezzlement money with her so that he was not nabbed in the case. There was nothing in Kishore's name. Despite all this arrangement, Kishore's embazzlement could not be kept a secret.

Once Kishore was jailed, Roopsi was all alone, disappointed and dejected at home. There was none else at home except the servant. There was no child in the family. In fact, they did not want to have one as yet. Both of them wanted to enjoy the life without a kid. Children, in fact, become a binding. They decided to amass huge money so that they could start some industry. He would then leave the job. He wanted to grow his family later. Kishore used to spend some time in office. He did little official work but remained busy in planning how to debunk the govt. money. Both of them spent their evenings in the clubs and parties. Sometimes they spent the evenings separately with their friends. They had accepted the lifestyle. Since they were so busy, they had no time for the kids.

It was difficult for Roopsi to spend every evening at home. She was fed up with the routine. Time hung heavy on her. She would go to meet Kishore in the jail during day time or would visit her neighbours. But as the evenings dawned, she felt lonely. She could hardly spend the time. Then she started inviting her friends at home. Her friends had been waiting for the occasion. They feared that Roopsi might stop meeting them once Kishore was jailed. Friends started visiting her. She started moving out, from the second week itself. She started going to clubs and parties and learnt to consume excessive liquor on the pretext of sorrow. She started coming late at night, like her earlier practice.

An old friend of Roopsi came to Delhi from Bombay during those days. He was very close with Roopsi at one time. She had not met him once he went to Bombay. He had started a business in there. The industry roared. An ordinary officer in Delhi had become a leading industrialist now. He was a romantic fellow. He had married but his marriage did not sustain. He would come to meet Roopsi to express sympathy for her. He assured her of all help. They once again renewed their friendship. There was none to hinder in the absence of Kishore.

Roopsi went closer and closer to him. And she distanced away from Kishore. Her friend went to Bombay but came back to Delhi again. Roopsi now visited Kishore in jail rarely.

Roopsi went to Bombay after a few days. She started living with him. She filed divorce papers in the court also. She now wanted to marry someone else after leaving Kishore. She communicated the information to Kishore accordingly. □

57

Pramod and Kishore were allowed to stay together in the jail. So they did not have to undergo the dangerous loneliness of the jail. Though the acute jail suffering was intolerable for them, yet they had the moral support of each other. In the beginning, they remained silent for most of the time. They had never anticipated that the army officers enjoying club life could ever be sent to jail. In fact, the thought of a prison is frightening. They had been lodged in the jail. They faced hard time to begin with. It was an entirely different world of thieves and swindlers. They had a culture of their own. Gradually, they also got accustomed to it. They felt easy when Savitri and Roopsi used to come to meet them.

Kishore was disturbed when he heard that Roopsi had gone to Bombay. Roopsi had not told him anything. He couldn't believe that he got a message regarding divorce notice. Kishore had not believed it. But once he got a notice from the court, he was badly shaken. He had burst into tears. Pramod had seen for the first time in life a man weeping bitterly. He had consoled him for an hour together. He tried to wipe his tears. He did not take his meals that day. Pramod also could not eat. Night fell and passed. Pramod tried to convince him but Kishore was broken. He was sad. He could not finish his meals. Pramod also got disgusted.

They sat in a plaintive mood that day. Kishore now did not expect Roopsi to come but Savitri had also not visited Pramod for many days now. Pramod was worried and sometimes he was doubtful too.

'There are visitors for both of you.' An employee of the jail announced. Both of them jumped with joy. At the announcement of a meeting, a prisoner is as happy as anyone who learns about his one lakh lottery.

'Who has come?,' Kishore asked.

'I do not know. But you both have been called together. Surprised they looked at each other. No one had come earlier to meet them both at the same time.

'Oh, you. Where were you for so many days?' Pramod asked Savitri in a delighted manner.

'Namastey, sister-in-law. You have done me a favour by calling me also. I have no words to thank you. I am undone since Roopsi has deserted me.' Tears trickled down from his eyes. It was difficult for him to control himself.

'Dear brother, do not take it seriously. Forget what has happened. You have lost the job, that way of life and money at the same time. Families have suffered. Please take care of what has been left at your end.' Savitri tried to console Kishore.

'I did not feel vexed when I lost my all but Roopsi... ' He burst into tears once again.

'Dear brother, a butterfly hovers over a flower as long as it is open. Butterflies do not come to a withered flower. Had you ever thought that Roopsi would standby you during adversity. If at all you thought that way, you were totally wrong. She had a different attitude towards life. She was never with you, she was only with you because of your post and money. I was not astonished at all when she left you.' Savitri could not resist saying all this.

'Sister-in-law, you are really great. Pramod, you are lucky indeed.' Kishore was all praise for them.

'I am what I am. He made efforts to convert me also into a butterfly. I could not toe his way, so he chose his own path ignoring me. He would not have fallen low if he had thought of his future also rather than enjoy the golden present. Anyhow, it is destiny that decides. You will excuse me, I have said something spontaneously. Are both of you all right?' I was not well for a few days. So I could not come to meet,' Savitri said having her eyes downcast.

'Sister-in-law, you are right. I and Pramod had taken a wrong path and went on it without relenting. Roopsi encouraged me. No one stopped me ever nor anyone made me understand. If there was someone to warn and hold me, I would not have treaded on the path.' Kishore looked towards Pramod.

'No, brother, you say this today. If Roopsi had tried to stop you, she would also have been deserted like me. What a paradox.

One who was beside you for joy, when you gave lakhs of rupees, has now deserted you in times of adversity and has taken away all the money. She has kicked everything here and left,' Savitri again said.

'And one who was deserted then is trying not only to support her husband but me also. Sister-in-law! You are really great. True Indian woman.' Kishore looked at Pramod.

Pramod was a silent spectator in this conversation. He would occasionally look at Savitri and then saw downwards.

'Savitri, how are the girls? You should bring them along somethimes.' Pramod broke his silence.

'I have nothing. Alas! I had some offspring. That would have been my support.' Kishore spoke spontaneously.

'Daughters are O.K. but there is a bigger problem. How should I arrange money for your appeals. As long as Roopsi was here, she spent the entire money. She had paid some fee also to the advocate. Now she is not here. The advocates are asking for rest of the fee. It will require more money to fight the case. You both tell me what can be done.'

'Sister-in-law, I had no dearth of money but the dishonestly collected money had been put in Roopsi's account. I had purchased gold. That was also kept in Roopsi's locker. I kept nothing with me.. She has gone away with the entire money. She did not even think to leave some money behind for fighting my court case. She made away with all the assets.' Kishore once again burst into tears.

'She was here with you only for wealth and she has bunked away with your money. Don't remember her. Forget her. Imagine that it was just a dream. You dreamt it and it is over.' Savitri tried to console him. Pramod and Kishore looked at each other. They had no answer to Savitri's query.

'I am worried about the money required for pursuing your appeals in the court. Four years time is a long period. I may also not be able to tolerate the circumstances for four years. It will be a great relief if the appeal lets you go free or even if it pardons a part of your term, it will come as a great relief but for the money.

'Dishonest Roopsi has taken away all my money, and I have become a pauper.'

'One who has lakhs of rupees has now been rendered a pauper by Roopsi who has now disappeared.' I am left behind but. I am already a pauper. I never got money in my hands.' Savitri could not contain herself.

'Then what will happen of the appeal?' Kishore said looking at Pramod.

'You had saved lakhs of rupees but now you don't have any penny. And I never saved anything for the rainy days. I even do not know how Savitri will make her both ends meet.' Pramod's head was downwards. All three of them remained silent. They looked at each other intermittently but none of them spoke.

'Savitri, there is no alternative now. I know you don't have anything with you. May be no one helps us now. Withdraw the appeal and do not do anything. We shall undergo four years term in jail.' Pramod looked dejected.

'All right. I do understand the situation. Both of you have nothing at your disposal. Do not worry. But we shall not withdraw the appeal. Come what may. I must fight your case in the court. I thought may be you could make some arrangement. But if it is not possible for you to arrange money, I shall make it possible. Both of you should not worry,' Savitri said confidently.

'But how Savitri?' Pramod asked.

'Not by any foul means. You had not left your incorrect path, I shall also not leave my honest way,' Savitri retorted.

They discussed some other issues also. Then Savitri got up to leave. The visiting time was also over. She forwarded a bag towards Pramod.

'I have brought fruits for both of you. If you need anything, please do tell me. I shall bring it on my next visit,' She said.

'Dear brother, may not be Roopsi but I shall continue to meet you.' Savitri assured looking at Kishore.

Savitri moved towards her home after crossing the big door of the jail. She decided not to make any irritating comment about Pramod also. She had kept her promise so far in her meetings but what happened today. She had uttered hurting words. She felt as if she had hurt Pramod also. Then she heard a voice from inside, Pramod has finished my everything. He has brought me on the road. I have been rendered helpless. This adverse situation has not been created by God but it has been created by us. He has made me a rolling stone. No, no, I shall not think anything of that sort. He is in jail now. There were tears in her eyes, and at other moment, there was fury in her eyes.

□

58

Savitri invited one of her relatives and made arrangements for selling her ornaments. She had no other means to raise money for the court case. She could not find out a customer for ornaments at her own level. One of her cousins lived at Darbala. Savitri trusted him like anything. She discussed the entire issue with him. When the girls knew about this development, they were also worried. Savitri made them understand that if they did not properly monitor the appeal in the court, their fortunes would virtually be locked in jail for four years. There was no other way to raise funds. Gloom lurked large at home for some time. Later on they were all prepared mentally.

Savitri's cousin brought a dealer whom he knew well at home. Savitri got out his ornament box and placed it before them. She watched silently. There was tears in her eyes but a storm raged in her mind. She was reminded of old memories at the sight of ornaments. Decorated with these ornaments, once she had come as the bride at Pramod's home. Her mother had gifted her these ornaments with love. Pramod's father had also got made a few of the ornaments. She was nostalgic to remember that her mother had got new ornaments made after she got her own mother's ornaments melted. These were the blessings of the mother. And she had worn those ornaments with enthusiasm. She was emotional to see a particular ornament. She had worn it on her *Suhag* night. After touching it that night, Pramod had made some memorable comments.

Savitri could not sit for long before those ornaments. She went inside. They looked at each other and did not say anything but they could feel the emotions of Savitri.

'Dear brother, please see the ornaments and fix their price. Savitri summoned courage and came out. They were taken out from the box one by one and were weighed. The weight was recorded on a paper in sequence. Savitri was sitting watchful. She felt her eyes hardened.

'Please leave it.' She got up at once, picked up one of the ornaments and kept it aside.

'I can't sell it,' She said sobbing.

All other ornaments were sold for about twenty thousand rupees. The advocate's fee was paid. They waited for the result of the appeal.

After selling her gold, Savitri could not sleep for many days. She was upset when she went near the almirah where the ornaments used to be kept. She was reminded of each ornament. She remembered the moments of her marriage. The earlier days of love with Pramod also flashed in her mind. Anxiety and grief gripped her. She imagined Pramod closely...but it was just a fancy.

She got Pramod's arrear from his office. One month's salary was also paid. Savitri felt greatly relieved to receive this amount. She needed the money. She had got Pramod's salary in her hands after many years. She remembered that just after her marriage, Pramod used to hand over his salary to Savitri every month. She managed the entire domestic expenses. But once Pramod changed his track, she never got his salary in her hands. Pramod was not before her today when they handed over his one month's salary to Savitri.

The court case went on, date after date was fixed but no results were available. Savitri would send her cousin's acquaintances to the advocate to make it sure that the judgement was delivered quickly.

A few of the well-wishers had told that both of them could be acquitted on appeal but the case was being delayed beyond expectation.

She required more money for the case. A little amount saved from Pramod's arrears was with her. It served the purpose.

After a few days, more money was needed for the case. Savitri tried to borrow money from her acquaintances but in vain. Her Ambala-based brother had given her Rs. One Thousand last time which was spent on household commodities. She hesitated in asking him for money. Pramod's friend, who was looking after the case, said he had already spent money from his pocket. He could not afford to spend anything more. Savitri thought of all the sources but she did not find any way out. The advocate started calling Savitri on phone for money. The phone calls were followed by a letter from the advocate's office.

One day Savitri asked Surekha to accompany her to the bazar.

'Why mother?'

'There is something to be done. Please get ready immediately.' Both of them were on the job. Surekha did not say anything for sometime. Savitri was also silent. Sad too. Surekha wanted to know the fact but hesitated. They were going by a three-wheeler and kept mum. Savitri was lost in old memories. She watched her purse frequently. She had had it in her tight grip.

'Mother where have we to go? You have not told so far.' Surekha asked after getting down the three-wheeler.

'This is the address.' Savitri handed over the paper to her.

'To a jeweller's place?'

'Yes.'

'Why?'

'You just find out and let us go.' Surekha enquired from some one and then they walked on the right side of the road.

'But mother?'

'Don't you follow?'

'Is he the same gold dealer who had brought your ornaments earlier?'

'Yes, the same one.'

'Are you going to receive back those ornaments? Had you mortgaged them? I thought you had sold them that day,' Surekha said.

'Dear daughter, my fortune is being mortgaged now.' Savitri heaved a deep sigh.

'What then?'

'Darling, we have to ensure your Papa's appeal. I attempted to raise money from various sources but to no avail. I had sold all ornaments that day except the 'Chanderhaar'. Selling it looked as if I was selling my soul. I had some special memories associated with it that I could not part away with it. But today it also goes.' Savitri was silent now. Tears rolled down her eyes. Surekha looked at her mother once or twice but did not say anything.

'I have ultimately decided to sell what symbolises my life partner but I part with it today to ensure freedom of my husband,' Savitri said once again after wiping her tears.

They ultimately reached the saraf's shop.

'I had kept this Chanderhaar that day. I did not want to sell it. But compulsion has again pushed me to you.' Savitri said while sitting on the sofa.

'My dear sister, you need not worry. We deal in it daily. Misfortune can fall anybody. I have seen many rich people do it. But all days are not alike. If the ornaments are sold at one time, they can be got made at another time too. This goes on. Don't feel bad.' Hearing his advice, Savitri wiped his eyes.

'It is the same 'Chanderhaar'. I require more money for the court case. Will you...'

'Yes, let me see it.'

'But I have a request to make. I shall seek your favour,' Savitri said while handing over the garland.

'Please do tell.'

'You take it please. You may pay a lesser amount but with a condition. You will keep it safe. I shall like to take it back as and when I have money to pay back. It is my husband's...' Savitri was helpless. Tears flowed from her eyes. Surekha moved forward to wipe her mother's tears.

'You need not worry. I shall keep it that way. But you will have to pay more amount because of interest on it. This is our rule.'

'I agree to it.'

After collecting money, they started back for home. Savitri was feeling heavy and light at the same time. She had a heavy heart because she had to sell her 'Chanderhaar,' and she was light to find that now she could follow the appeal with the money she had arranged for.

'Stop, my daughter.' Savitri stopped in front of her house. She viewed her house seriously.

'Let us go in, mother.'

'Your father is in jail. Ornaments have been sold. I had kept 'Chanderhaar'. That too, I have dispensed with what is there in the house here now?' Savitri wept. Surekha took her mother in caringly.

Advocate's fee was paid. Savitri was satisfied. Days went on. Life went on. It had, of course, changed...of course. Late comer Pramod was not there now. But a disappointment was visible in the entire atmosphere. The youngest daughter, Puneeta, used to go to school. Ritu was silently lost in her thoughts. She would go out for a change on one pretext or the other. At times, she remained away from home for hours together. Surekha stayed at home. She would never leave her mother lonely.

Savitri did not get anything despite her effort to put everything at stake. The appeal was unsuccessful in getting Pramod and Kishore's punishment diluted. Savitri was shocked when she learnt about the judgement. She kept weeping for hours together and felt tortured. Then she engaged herself in the domestic chores.

Savitri called her brother from Ambala and discussed the future of the family. One day she came to Ambala with him. She got a teacher's job in a school. Reaching Delhi, she made preparations for moving to Ambala. All were happy to know that she had got an appointment. They saw a ray of hope in the darkness of future. Ritu felt caught in darkness. She did not want to leave Delhi for any place. But she had no other alternative.

The household luggage was being packed. They applied for Puneeta's certificate from the school and started clearing the payments. One day before leaving Delhi, she went to meet Pramod in the jail. Whenever she used to visit the jail, she would call Kishore also along with Pramod. She felt it odd sometimes but she had nothing special to discuss with Pramod in isolation. She, moreover, did not feel like meeting him alone. At times Pramod wanted to talk to Savitri in loneliness but he never got a chance. And he could not dare to express his desire too.

Puneeta went into Pramod's lap and was sighing. There were tears in Pramod's eyes too. Ritu and Surekha sat beside silent. Pramod talked to Puneeta. Savitri enquired about welfare of both of them.

'Sister-in law, you have done so much to pursue our case that I cannot repay even if I am born life after life seven times. You did not say anything in this respect but our friends who came yesterday told us all about your efforts.' Kishore thanked her.

'I have simply done my duty and nothing else.' Savitri saw with downcast eyes.

'You had had to sell all those ornaments, Savitri. I am sorry, you had disposed of your Chanderhaar too. I have taken you to what destination?' Pramod kept his head on Puneeta's shoulders.

'I have reached the place for which I was destined. I could foresee it much earlier. That path had to lead me there. Why rue this destination? That was bound to reach this spot. And you have led us all to the point,' Savitri said unwittingly. All were silent.

'Oh, please excuse me. I did not mean it. We shall meet you after a long gap. I am leaving Delhi.' She changed the topic.

'Why? Where are you going? If you are going, what about the children?' Pramod was alarmed.

'Four years is a long period. I have found a job in Ambala and have rented a house there. I shall live there. We don't have anything to feed for the family here. I have my brother there, who is my stay and support.'

'Service? In which department?,' Pramod asked Savitri.

'The same old department. I have once again become a teacher in a school. You had asked me to leave the service then. You know what you had said at that time.' She was lost in old memories.

'Savitri, no, you will not join service now,' Pramod had said to her.

'Why?' She had moved closer to him.

'I don't like it. Moreover, what is the necessity now. I get a handsome salary. We can sustain ourselves. How much do we require? You stay at home now onwards. You should look fresh when I come home. Fatigue and engagements of service do not allow us to live comfortably. Henceforth, not for anyone, not for the school even, you will be there only for me, my house and for my children only.'

'Where are the kids?'

'They are on their way.' After uttering there words, Pramod had held Savitri warmly. They had lived moments of love for sometime together and the next very day, she had resigned from the school.'

'In which school, you have got a job?' Pramod's question brought Savitri back on the earth. She sat cautiously.

'My brother has arranged it for me. It is a private school. They will pay a paltry sum to begin with but they have promised to give full salary.'

'All right. We don't have any other alternative before us.'

'Sister, our misdeeds have put you to hardship. Please pardon us for the sin. I am responsible for misleading and provoking Pramod. Pramod is lucky that you are making all efforts for him. And, my Roopsi, I don't know where is she making merry. I hope you will come to see us occasionally.' Kishore was also emotional.

'I shall definitely come to see you both but the visits cannot be so frequent from Ambala.'

'That is true.'

'It is my Ambala address. Do write letters to me.' Savitri gave a piece of paper to Pramod. His fingers touched Savitri's hand while receiving the paper. He was reminded of an old incident long back. A touch of Savitri would make him happy. He thought that Savitri's presence, her touch was something unusually pleasant. But later on he got the same feeling from her female friends. A touch of Savitri's fingers today and that too, after so many years made him feel emotional. Pramod would have fallen on Savitri's feet and asked for pardon if it was not jail. He heaved a sigh of repentance and heard his inner voice which said, 'If you were not in jail, Savitri would have felt uneasy in another room.' Pramod was alarmed at the warning.

While parting, Puneeta started weeping. Ritu was also in tears. Surekha made efforts to take care of Savitri. There was sympathy and pity in the atmosphere. It appeared as if the stones of the jail were also sympathetic.

□

59

'Gurcharan, I can't understand your behaviour. Why did you not behave yourself with Surekha that day? You have created a problem for me,' Ritu said while entering the restaurant. She had come to see Gurcharan after many days. He had sent many messages to her. She did try to go to him but she was afraid of her mother. She did not want to add to her mother's woes. Since Pramod's case started, their meetings had become few and far between. Despite all this, Ritu managed to meet Gurcharan using some pretext. She met him after a long gap. Both of them sat on a corner table.

'It's not like that. I talked to Surekha soberly.'

'Why have you postponed your marriage when you had committed it to me? We love each other. So why did you not agree to it that day? You have missed a golden chance. I was so happy that day. My mother had agreed for our marriage.'

'Just for nothing. I thought why should any one interfere when we both have to marry.'

'She was none else but my real sister Surekha.'

'Ritu, you do not know that politicians have so many pressures and tensions. I was under great tension during those days. You had not met me for many days. I had been waiting for you. When Surekha came, my tension increased. My mood was spoiled.'

'Have you ever imagined about the tension hovering over our family? You did not help us at all.'

'I sent messages many a time. May be you did not need my help.'

'Mother had sent Surekha for the same purpose.'

'What do you mean?'

'Mother said, she would accept your help only if you were prepared to marry me. You evaded the issue. So mother asked me to desist talking to you.'

'Oh, this is the secret. You should have told me earlier. I am sorry I could not help your family. Tell me what happened of the appeal.'

'It has been rejected. Father will stay in prison for full four years.' Ritu was a bit sad. She saw around and controlled her emotions.

'Don't worry. If the government wants, it can reduce the punishment even after the conviction by the court. I shall talk at Prime Minister's residence.' Gurcharan touched Ritu's hand on the table itself.

'Will you do it that way but...'

'What but?'

'Mother won't agree.'

'Why?'

'Yes, tell me when will you marry me? If we are married, she will be happy and you will get Papa released.' Ritu was almost ecstatic. Gurcharan looked in the vacuum. There was a strange smile on his lips. He controlled his smile and kept on sipping tea.

'Why don't you speak? I love you and am mad for you. There is nothing to separate us from each other. Gurcharan, I have totally surrendered myself to you. Simply on this faith that you have decided to make me your life partner.' Ritu had stopped taking tea. She wanted to read into his eyes but Gurcharan was trying to hide his feelings.

'Look here, Ritu. I stand by what I have committed. If Himalaya cannot budge from its place, Gurcharan's promise can also not budge.'

'But there is one thing,' she said interruptingly.

'What is that?'

'I hope this promise is not like election time promises of the politicians?' Both of them laughed heartily. The atmosphere was now pleasant.

'Oh no. There is no relationship here with elections and politics and Ritu...' They looked into each other's eyes.

'Yes, you wanted to say something more.'

'I have won the election but this is not sufficient. All my friends want me to see as a Minister. Many people of our party are trying for it. There is always a great struggle within the party to become a Minister. One has to use all the means. I have decided to become a Minister, come what may. Let me be free from it. And its my earnest desire that I should come to take you as my wife when I am a Minister in the Cabinet.' Ritu was listening to Gurcharan with intent. She was lost in imagination to hear about Gurcharan's Ministership. She was now flying in imagination and found herself flying in the golden sky rather than sitting in her chair. Minister, car with a flag on it, servants and honour, all these things flashed in her mind. She had imagined the same way about Gurcharan many a time. She knew that Gurcharan came of a very rich family. She was confident of his rise in the party. It was berth as a Minister, that was his next stop. He was a young leader and had won the elections. She had listened about all these things today from Gurcharan's mouth.

'Gurcharan, when will all this happen?' Ritu was curious to know.

'I wish it happens tomorrow but truly speaking it will take some time. The Cabinet is likely to be expanded on return of the Prime Minister from abroad. I hope I shall get a chance.'

'What should I tell mother?'

'Maintain silence as yet. Let it all happen. When I am donned a Minister, I shall propose for marriage to your family. Your family, I hope, will accept the proposal from a Minister.'

In the meanwhile, they had two rounds of tea. They ate snacks also along with. That corner was a lovely one. It was morning time. There was no rush. They were engaged in chit-chat for quite sometime. Gurcharan's utterings had made Ritu confident of all these things happening likewise. She was very happy and felt relaxed.

'But Gurcharan. A new development has taken place. I shall not be able to meet you now. I have been worried for it for many days now.'

'Why? You already don't meet me frequently. And now you will not meet me at all. How shall I survive.' There was a glimmer in his eyes.

'My mother has arranged a job for herself at Ambala. The entire family will move to Ambala within a few days now. One of my mother's brothers lives there. He will be our main stay. My maternal uncle is looking after all of us.

'Ambala. That is good. It is all the more good. I pass through Ambala when I go from Delhi. I make it twice or thrice a month.

You need not worry. I shall be coming there to meet you. Anywhere, by any means.'

'Gurcharan, why don't you meet my mother and discuss the issue with her. If mother is convinced that you will marry me once you become a Minister, we shall have her blessings in meeting freely otherwise we shall have to meet secretly.'

'Ritu, secret meetings are all the more joyful. It looks good at this age. It will be a forgotton chapter after marriage. So tell me, when and where shall we meet.' His eyes searched Ritu's figure.

'Gurcharan, it is difficult to meet that way.'

'Why? If your meetings with me become difficult, it will be difficult for me to survive. Ritu, I shall not be able to tolerate such a cruel treatment. You may do anything but you must find out how to meet in isolation. Please don't deprive me of that. I feel relieved. The moments spent with you provide me a unique satisfaction.'

'But what shall I tell my mother?'

'The same old pretext. You have to visit a friend of yours. You will tell her that you would either return late at night or would stay there for the night,' Gurcharan said lustily.

'O.K. I can do anything for you. However, my intellect warns me that we should not meet like that before marriage. Till then such a meeting cannot be held.'

'The same old, orthodox arguments. The world has changed altogether and you...India is free now. So are you and me.'

'All right. At the same place, day after tomorrow. Afterwards, we shall move to Ambala. You will then come there to meet me.'

'At 7.00 p.m.'

Both of them left. Gurcharan dropped her at one of the turns near her home. Ritu reached the destined place on the third day at the appointed time. Gurcharan was already waiting for her. It was a first floor flat of a big bungalow.

Gurcharan had taken it on rent. It looked like a government rest house. Ritu enquired about the owner of the building many a time and who lived there. Gurcharan had told her that one of his friends owned the bungalow, who had gone home these days. But whenever Gurcharan called Ritu there, his friend had invariably gone home.

In fact, Gurcharan had the flat on rent. It was well decorated and furnished. There were proper stay arrangements for the night.

He had reserved this place for spending his time in sojourn. He used to invite her lady friends there. The place was mainly used for this purpose. At a few times, the place was also used for clandestine political activities also. There were a few such clandestine places for political activities in Delhi. Here the politicians thought of the political moves and also used the place for releasing their tension through women and wine.

Ritu spent the whole night there. Gurcharan picked her up in his car and dropped her in the morning near her home. She told her mother that her friend had not allowed her to leave at night. The mother wanted to believe what her daughter had said but the eyes and the face of Ritu made her mother suspicious. She could make out that Ritu was presenting a false story. Since Pramod went to jail, it was for the first time that she had stayed out for the night. As they would soon leave Delhi for Ambala, she did not take Ritu's case seriously. After two days, Savitri caught a bus bound for Ambala with her luggage. Her brother had taken some of her luggage already to Ambala. A part of it had been sent through booking.

The bus left behind the high rise buildings of Delhi. It appeared as if the houses and the colonies were running back. Puneeta was looking outside. Ritu was lost in deep thoughts. She was reliving the moments spent in the company of Gurcharan. Surekha was thinking about her father who was in jail or occasionally looked at her mother. There were tears in Savitri's eyes. She was reminded of her first meeting near Raghu Nath's tent, then, her meeting in Hidimba temple...and then the meetings in jail. The snowy storm that continued for months together had not done damage to Pramod or Savitri. But she was defeated today, though there was no storm at all. Her husband was lodged in jail and she was a pauper. She was compelled to join a job. The span of her life lay open before her eyes like a film.

Her brother Sudesh and his wife had come to the bus stand to receive them. Savitri's family was relieved to see both of them. She thought they were not lonely in times of adversity. There is someone to look after them. Though Sudesh had arranged a house for them but they stayed with him for the next two days. Savitri joined her service in the school. They shifted to their own rented house after a couple of days.

□

60

It became easier for Gurcharan and Ritu to meet. There was a friend of Gurcharan near Ambala. He had reserved one portion of his house for Gurcharan only. He was running a big industry with the help of Gurcharan. Gurcharan was also a partner in it. But nothing existed in writing. He had arranged a special licence from Delhi for his friend. He turned millionaire in no time. Gurcharan's aura made him enjoy all fair and unfair favours from the government. And in turn, he gave a fixed percentage of profit to Gurcharan. At the same time, he made arrangements for his rest house.

Ritu would come out of her home on one pretext or the other. She would know Gurcharan's arrival in advance. Savitri got suspicious at times but neither she asked anything nor she said. Ritu had found a friend of her own sort. They became fast friends. Whenever need be, she took her help. She would go for outing with her and afterwards, she used to reach Gurcharan's place. Her friend would also go to meet her male friend. They would then return together afterwards.

It was difficult for Savitri to run the household. She agreed to the proposal of her two daughters that they should also find out employment. There was a job in a kids' school on a paltry amount. Surekha accepted it but Ritu refused it. Savitri wanted her daughter to have job in the city even if the salary was small. But Ritu was not prepared for a petty job. Gurcharan had raised her hopes sky high.

One day Ritu went out on the pretext that she was going to her friend but she did not come back for long. A teacher of Surekha's school was ill. She had gone to see her in a village nearby. There were other colleagues also with her. When she was waiting for her bus, she saw Gurcharan driving his car. She found that Ritu was also sitting beside him. She was alarmed for a moment but kept her silence. She told her mother about it when she reached home.

'Ritu, where had you gone today? You have returned so late.' Her mother asked Ritu.

'I kept wandering with my friend, mother. I did not feel at home.'

'Tell me the truth. Where had you gone? Whom did you meet? It does not behove you to tell a lie.' Savitri was furious.

'I told you that I was with one of my friends. You can ask her.' Ritu was perplexed a bit.

'You have been telling me lies till today. I had sent Surekha to him only keeping in view your emotions.' He evaded. When he does not want to marry you, why do you run after him? You have seen your Papa's fate, even then you are following the same path. Ritu kept standing.' Savitri held her and made her sit with her.

'Despite my aversion, I had agreed to your marriage with Gurcharan. I had sent Surekha of my own. I did not want to hinder your happiness. But he did not agree. He even did not treat Surekha well. Ritu, what has happened to you? Your father is in jail. Helpless as we are, we are trying to survive as a family. In spite of helping the family, you are behaving oddly.'

'What am I doing? Can't I have the liberty of meeting my friend even?' Ritu was upset.

'Who has stopped you? You can meet anyone of your friends but your meeting with Gurcharan....'

'Mom, friends can be of any sex, boys as well as girls. If Gurcharan is my boy friend, why do you raise an objection?'

'I do not accept it. I had clearly told you at Delhi that if he was not prepared to marry you, you will not have any relationship with him.'

'Mother, I am not a kid. I have the right to shape my life as I wish.'

'But you are not an isolated entity. You are a member of the family too.'

'Mother, he will marry me definitely but after some time. He hopes to be inducted as a Minister within a short span. He has assured me that he would marry me after becoming a Minister.' Surekha heard their conversation in the adjoining room. She had sent Puneeta out of home on some excuse. She could not contain herself on hearing Rita's comment. She also joined them in that room.

'It is totally false. He is betraying you. One of my colleagues saw him with you. The discussion revealed that no doubt he is a high profile leader but at the same time, he is extremely corrupt morally. It is true he has massive wealth and property. He has political influence too but he makes false promises to entire young ladies. His bad character is known to all. I was shocked to see him with you. Thank God, my colleagues did not notice you.'

'Surekha, you need not poke your nose in between. It is sufficient for you that you complained against me to my mother.' Ritu stared at her harshly.

'Family's woes and comforts are common. I have also the right to think and speak. You are on a wrong track.'

'Who are you to show me the way?'

'Your younger sister, Surekha.' She smiled naughtily. But the tension could not be released. The atmosphere remained tense.

'Listen Ritu. I shall not tolerate it all. You will join a job in Surekha's school. They are prepared to take you on staff. You will never meet Gurcharan,' mother said in a serious tone.

'No, mother. I won't accept hundred rupee job and that to care for the nose blowing small kids. I shall not be able to take up this job,' Ritu said in a harsh tone.

'All right. You may not join this service but you must forget Gurcharan.'

'No, mother. I tell it plainly. He is my friend. I must meet him. I do not believe in the old-rotten tradition. If you do not want to enjoy the new light of the new world, you may shut your eyes and ears but I shall enjoy it to the brim,' Ritu said looking staringly at Surekha.

'Has the new civilization confined itself to immorality?'

'We can have our independent opinions. I cannot shut my eyes to the new winds.'

'What kind of light is it?,' Surekha asked.

'Unbridled relationship between man and woman. Freedom from suffocating orthodox ideas. I have faith in it. I like it.'

'Flying as the winds, Papa has landed himself in jail.' Ritu was silent on Surekha's comment.

'Why do you bring Papa in the discussion?'

'The same charms of the new winds had attracted Papa. The entire family has reached a point of brink.' Both the sisters were arguing forcefully. Savitri sat silent in one corner.

'Do you know what happened to Kishore uncle. His wife Roopsi has left him and has taken away his entire money. Papa is passing time in jail somehow but Kishore uncle is heading towards madness. Kishore and Roopsi also hankered after new waves of the changing world.'

'Surekha, you need not sermonise. You are accustomed to speak endlessly in the school classes. Their story is different. We cannot compare all.'

'The way you are following reaches the same point where Kishore and Roopsi have reached...or Papa has reached.'

'Leave it Surekha. Let us go to the kitchen. Ritu will not agree. Not to speak of the family, she is not able to think about her own welfare. My Papa's dark night is likely to be extended more. I thought I shall pass this dark period with your support and would wait for the light of the next morning. I thought I shall restart my family life once he comes out of jail. But it is not in my fate. I know there are no flowers in my life, only thorns ahead. I have difficulties in abundance.' Savitri went away wiping her eyes.

Ritu left for Delhi after some days on the pretext for an interview. Her mother tried to dissuade her. Surekha also opposed her move. Savitri knew she was going to Gurcharan in Delhi. She tried to convince her once again. But Ritu had become blunt in her talks. She did not even show an iota of hesitation. She said bluntly that she would do whatever she thought right for herself. Savitri and Surekha were now speechless.

Ritu stayed in Delhi at Gurcharan's special rest house. He started introducing her to his close friends. She became a known figure in political circles of Delhi. She became all the more ambitious. One day she discussed the woeful pecuniary condition of her family with Gurcharan. She asked him to arrange a job for her so that she could support her family. He took out five thousand rupees from his bag and handed over to her saying, 'Darling, you need not serve anywhere. In fact I am creating a situation where people will be at your service.' Ritu was flattered with such a big amount.

Ritu handed over that money to Savitri. She was quite happy to see it. Surekha felt the glitter of a big amount. Suddenly, Savitri was reminded of something. She asked, 'Where did you get all this money from?'

'Mother, I talked to Gurcharan about our family's condition and he gave this amount at once.' Ritu felt proud.

'So you were with him at Delhi?' Savitri was furious.

'Take this amount. He wants to buy the integrity of our family with this money.' Savitri could not contain her rage. She had used such a derogatory word for her for the first time. She kicked away the amount.

'Mother, what's the harm in taking this money. If a friend of mine helps us in adversity how is it a blemish to our family,' Ritu said in a low voice.

'Don't make a fool of me. I know it well. He does not love us. He has no love for you also. He appeases his lust with you and in exchange he throws this amount at our face. Not even a single penny from this amount should be spent in my household,' Savitri went out wiping her tears.

Ritu was now totally severed from the family. Her mother had stopped reprimanding or dissuading her at all. After a few days, she left for Delhi with her luggage on the pretext of joining service there.

Savitri was chronically sick. Her heart was already broken but now her body was also failing. She made it a point to go to meet Pramod once in a month. She would take dishes of his choice for him. Whenever he needed clothes, she provided that too. She would carry fruits also and took care of his requirements. Whenever she went to jail, she made it a point to have warm conversation with him. She would advise him patience and tolerance. She asked him not to worry about the family. A rebel emerged in her whenever she confronted Pramod. She would try to subside it but it surged ahead like anything. She was not able to talk much with him.

Days and years passed. Pramod had completed two years in jail now.

□

61

Ritu went straight to Gurcharan's place in Delhi. He owned a big house there. No member of his family lived there. He had started a new industry in Delhi. Only the managers of that industry and some other employees lived in a part of it. Gurcharan made arrangements for Ritu in an adjacent room to his place in the corner. Publically too, they had started moving together. Ritu had been entrusted with some party work. On this pretext also, Gurcharan made her move with her. Ritu was not worried about her marriage too. She was a busy bee now and had become friendly with Rita. When Rita happened to be in Delhi, they all three moved together. Occasionally, Rita stayed at Gurcharan's place for the night. They would drink heavily at night, play cards and then Rita would retire to an independent room.

Ritu was now ambitious to become Rita. She felt that Rita's life was very good. She had a car, bungalow, post and reputation. No bindings. No responsibility. Rita was tempted to tread in Rita's footsteps when she heard her adventures of her youthful days. Pramod's life had shown her one direction but Gurcharan and Rita showed her a golden destination.

Now Gurcharan was not her exclusive friend. Her friends circle grew larger like Gurcharan's. Gurcharan had no objection to it. Ritu had provided him delight. She was beautiful. He liked her very much. He was only frightened at times when she proposed to him for marriage. Gurcharan was now assured that Ritu would have understood the uselessness of marriage after having enjoyed the romantic overtures of so many friends.

Gurcharan asked Ritu to accompany him on a foreign tour sponsored by the committee. She jumped with joy at hearing it. She got her passport made. There was no shortage of funds with

Gurcharan. Ritu visited so many countries with Gurcharan in a month before coming back. There were some difficulties during travel. Gurcharan introduced her as his friend. The word lady friend was O.K. as far as foreign assemblies or meetings were concerned but among his Indian friends and fellows, Gurcharan sometimes felt embarrassed. The topic was discussed in hush hush voice behind the curtain. At certain places, he would introduce her as a leading worker of the party. He had an impact on his fellows, so no one made any comment before Gurcharan.

After the foreign tour, Ritu came to Ambala for a few days. She narrated her foreign tour with pride. Puneeta listened to her intently. But when she told she had gone with Gurcharan, Savitri and Surekha got up and went away from her. They had developed hatred for her. Savitri was shocked to learn that Ritu never went to meet her father in jail at Delhi. Though born in that family, Ritu did not belong to the family. She found it all strange. The concept of home, family, atmosphere, thoughts...everything was orthodox. She felt she could no longer live in the suffocating atmosphere of her family. She was haunted by the prestigious Delhi. After her foreign jaunt, Ritu felt as if Savitri and Surekha were the antique things. After completing a formality of meeting her family, she returned to Delhi on the third day itself.

"Women and Wine Honoured in Politics at Delhi – the Capital"

Though women and wine have always been associated with politics, yet its prevalence in the nation of Mahatma Gandhi has broken all its records in the party he led. A senior leader freely moved in public with beautiful women. They had special stay points in the capital. Special people were called there. Under the cover of darkness, these renowned leaders did all that normally happens at prostitution centres. Recently, these leaders took a handsome woman with them when they went for a foreign tour. The leader declared her as his wife whereas they were never married to each other. It is learnt that the exceptional beauty has become very popular in Delhi circles these days. She had been seen with some other prominent leaders also.

It has been revealed that her father was on a top position in the army. He had been caught in a serious embezzlement case. He is in jail these days. The father who embezzled money is in jail and his daughter in politics. It is a talk of the town that she does the same thing by virtue of her beauty and youth what her father did in his days.

Where does that beauty live, what does she do, when does she meet the leaders, who are those leades, wait for this information in the next issue.

Ritu was alarmed to read the news. A worry gripped her. Gurcharan kept thinking for sometime. Then he rang up his personal assistant and he said to him, 'Listen, there is a magazine named *Dhamaka*, call its editor on phone just now. Make it sure he comes to meet me just now. Come what may, he must see me.'

Dhamaka's editor came to meet Gurcharan in the evening.

'So you have published this news?,' He said looking into his eyes harshly.

'Yes, sir. I have published it.' The editor shrank a little bit. He had come to know that Gurcharan was a big leader.

'Who gave the story to you?'

'One of the correspondents has filed it.'

'Do you know that it is baseless and false. Don't you feel shy while mudslinging a popular leader?'

'Look here, Netaji. You need not be annoyed. The news is wholly true. I had got it confirmed before publishing it. Leaders of your party have given this news. They have given some evidences also. You just wait a little, the next issue of the magazine will carry the story in its detail. I am publishing some photographs also.' The editor fired his salvo.

'Photos. Whose photos?' Gurcharan jumped in his chair.

'Of the leader and of the beauty.'

'Who is the leader?'

'That I don't know. Look here. If that politician is a friend of yours and you want to help him, let us talk straight. Threats will prove of no consequence. You cannot gag the free press in free India. Moreover, your party fully endorses freedom of speech. Do you know that leader?' The editor looked at him with a squint.

'Yes, he is a friend of mine. Whatever the story, please don't publish anything more about it,' Gurcharan said a little bit humbled.

'That's right. How can I disagre with so great a politician as you are but you know, Sir, for every action, some.... You understand me, Sir.' Gurcharan had no difficulty in grasping his message that was half spoken. He went to the other room.

'Here are ten thousand rupees for you. I can do anything for my friend. Now this chapter should be closed here. You can come to me any time for any help. I shall get some government advertisement and newsprint for your magazine.' The editor received the envelop carrying the money with enthusiasm. He viewed it greedily and kept it in his pocket.

'Thanks. You need not worry. Nothing will be published against your friend. Not only this, we shall publish contradiction of the news already published. We shall write that someone had provided us with wrong information. Yes, we get rarely government advertisements. Please do get those released to us.'

'You will get, rest assured.'

'Thanks. My good wishes.'

Gurcharan was now relaxed. He told the entire happening to Ritu who was in the adjoining room. They both laughed heartily. Gurcharan held Ritu in his arms.

'Darling, anything can be purchased in this world. Even the partriotism of a politician and the pen of a writer can be purchased. That is why we have hung a photo of Mahatma Gandhi on the wall. Neither he nor his messages carry any weight now,' Gurcharan said looking at Mahatma's photos hanging on the wall.

They had both felt jolted at the publication of the news. As it was being discussed in all circles, Gurcharan's political career was at stake. His opponents in the party were raising the issue vigorously. He had not been donned a Minister as yet. The Cabinet had been expanded once. But another expansion was on the cards. He was once again hopeful but the news published could damage his chances. He felt greatly relaxed after meeting the editor.

□

62

'Sunil, don't publish this news now.' The editor advised Sunil after calling him in his room.

'Why, Sir?' He was surprised.

'There is not truth in it. We do not want to pick up problems for nothing.'

'But I have all the evidences with me.'

'Evidences can be false too.'

'My evidences and proofs are true. Here are the photographs...'

'I do not want to see anything. I have to decide what shall go in our magazine. I have decided that the story will not be published any further as I have ascertained all the truth.'

'Sir, it is no fearless journalism.'

'Shall I learn journalism from you?'

'I do not mean it that way.'

'Then what...' The editor looked at Sunil contemptously.

'Sir, I had worked hard for days together over this story. I took Gurcharan's servant into confidence. I got the entire information from him and got important pictures of Ritu and Gurcharan that were taken in India and abroad. There is a great stir in political circles in the capital by that story. Our magazine is in news everywhere. *Dhamaka* has been sold like hot cakes this time. Why did you decide like that despite its increased sale?'

'Sunil, it is not good to expose personal life of people. Private life differs from public life. Why should we poke our nose if a man and woman develop physical relationship by virtue of their mutual understanding.'

'Sir, it is not so simple a subject. Gurcharan is a popular politician and is in race for a Cabinet berth. He should be clean in his private life. Politicans should have some ideals in their life. He is moving around not only with one woman but has affāir with many more. He has kept Ritu at his place. He has kept another woman in his rest house and he has relations with many more. I have come to know that a girl died under mysterious circumstances last year. She was also Gurcharan's friend. She had stayed at his home for many days. Some people doubt Gurcharan as her killer. If I get a few more leads for the story, our magazine *Dhamaka* will be known in India in no time.' Sunil's eyes glistened with pride.

'What was the name of that girl?'

'What I have come to know so far, her name was Pratibha. She lived in Rajender Nagar. I have collected information about her home.'

'O.K. I shall consult it. You keep the material ready but we don't have to publish it in the next issue.' The editor went away. Sunil entered his office in a thoughtful mood.

The editor disconnected his phone. Gurcharan was at home. He said he wanted to meet him for an urgent work. Gurcharan called him at once.

'Sir, forgive me. I have come to bother you once again.' He sat in a chair.

'No botheration at all. You come and tell me.'

'I have held the next part of the last story. I relaxed after instructing my staff. But in the meanwhile our correspondent collected some more information. It appears that someone within your party is divulging this information.'

'What matter has come to you now?,' alarmed Gurcharan asked.

'Sir, did you know a girl named Pratibha?'

'Pratibha?' Gurcharan spoke promptly. The editor was happy but he did not express his happiness.

'Pratibha, who lived in Rajender Nagar. She had been murdered but later on it was shown as a suicide.' Gurcharan kept silent and was thoughtful now.

'Our correspondent says that she had an affair with some famous leader. She stayed with him at his residence. He has obtained some letters and photographs also. He has the entire story ready. It was being printed. I thought since you are known to me, I should ask you about it.'

'You did well. Thanks. May be some another friend of mine may be in trouble. You fire that staff reporter. He must always be busy in collecting such type of news. If you go like this, your magazine will fall from its grace.'

'No, Sir. Magazines survive because of such type of news. If the news is revealing, they wait for the magazine. Who reads simple news these days. Just as the films are not successful without a touch of sex and crime, similarly magazines...but you....'

'Yes, don't publish this news also.'

'If it was published, our magazine would have earned thousands of rupees for us.'

Gurcharan went to the other room and brought an other envelope.

'Please take ten thousand more.'

'No, Sir. It is too little. Prices have gone very high. Cost of paper and printing is sky high. It was such a spicy news that it would have created ripples. Sir, if he is not a close friend, please keep this money. Let me publish this news. Only one issue will earn this much amount. He wanted to hand over the envelope back to Gurcharan. Gurcharan looked at him staringly. He made another visit to the room.

'Have five thousand more. That's all...No more. Yes, get the entire news destroyed.'

'All right. I get it done.'

Gurcharan wandered in his lawn. He sat in the chair and called his servant to bring tea. He enjoyed his tea. Then he asked for his cigarette case. He lighted a cigarette. He rarely smoked. Whenever he felt tension, he released it through smoking.

On reaching his office, the editor called Sunil. He came immediately excited.

'Be seated Sunil,' he asked Sunil, viewing him intently.

'I have collected information about your second story also. I have discussed it with some of my friends also.'

'That's good, Sir. It will prove *Dhamaka* as a successful enterprise. I have got some more proofs. It was Gurcharan who got Pratibha murdered because if she lived, his popularity was at stake. We may also get some letters written by Pratibha,' Sunil spoke enthusiatically.

'Sunil, listen to me. I wanted to say something esle.' He said in a scolding manner.

'Yes, Sir.'

'We shall not publish any news in this regard. Neither there is any truth in it nor do we want to involve ourselves in it unnecessarily. If he files defamation case, we shall be in soup.'

'But the policy of our magazine...to expose corruption...to publish the true stories honetly...free, fearless journalism,' Sunil muttered.

'That is true. You collect some other material. Even more sensational than that. We shall certainly publish that. Yes, you must have done extra labour to dig out the Pratibha story. May be you might have spent some money also. You will be reimbursed that sum. But no news will ever be published about that politician in our paper.' Sunil looked at him astonishingly.

'It appears money has been received,' Sunil said to himself. Then he left the room in a huff.

Sunil had collected the material for the story painstakingly. He was shocked with the editor's stance. He had been engaged in investigation for days together and had to win over many persons to elicit information. Sunil was a youngman. He had chosen journalism as his career intentionally. He wanted to work hard so that he could find a place in a big newspaper.

The editor of *Dhamaka* settled the deal with Gurcharan but Sunil could not compromise with his editor. He collected the entire material of the story from his office. He talked to the editor of another newspaper of Delhi. He resigned from *Dhamaka* the next day and joined the new newspaper.

The story of foreign tour of Gurcharan and Ritu was carried by the newpaper *Kranti* in its next issue in detail. Pratibha episode was also published. The story of Gurcharan's mystery guest house also appeared in the paper. The paper carried the photograph also. Gurcharan was once again in news now.

Gurcharan discussed it with Ritu and accordingly, she shifted to another house. She could not go to the rest house also as it was also under scanner. Gurcharan hired a house in a new colony.

Ritu did come out of Gurcharan's house but she was not satisfied. She once pleaded with Gurcharan that she wanted to live with him. She said everyone knew about their relationship. So why be afraid even if it was published in a newspaper. But Gurcharan made her understand that if she went away for a few days, everything being circulated would stop. He argued that he did not want to give a chance to his opponents before he is inducted in the Cabinet. Gurcharan understood Ritu's feelings. He lovingly engaged her in conversation and then he took her in her car with her luggage to a new house.

Ritu felt for the first time that she had been rendered powerless and that she was an unwanted belonging in Gurcharan's life.

She felt bored in the new house. She had no acquaintances in neighbourhood. A servant had been kept at her disposal but it was difficult for her to pass time. The facilities that were available at Gurcharan's residence did not exist here.

Just after two days, Rita came to Delhi. On learning about it, she went to her. Ritu stayed with her as long as Rita was in Delhi. Gurcharan used to come there. Rita left Delhi and Ritu had again to move to her new house, where she felt lonely.

Whenever Ritu met Gurcharan, she spoke about her loneliness. She implored him many a time to take her to his place. She said she could not stay away from him. Gurcharan would ask her to wait for some more time. Everything will be in order shortly. On her repeated insistence, Gurcharan started visiting her in the new house every second or the third day. Gurcharan would often say, 'Ritu, in fact, it has happened in good stead. We never got such a secluded place earlier. There is none to disturb, no phones, no acquaintances around to stare.'

Ritu would then say, 'But when I am all alone here, I feel bored. Time hangs heavy on me. Believe me, I cannot live here without you. You forget about your Ministership. You become my husband first. You have just to perform the formalities. I have already surrendered myself before you.'

Gurcharan would put her off. He would indulge in romantic talk. A few months passed by in this manner.

Gurcharan had not come for the last three four days. Ritu was not well. She did not go anywhere but had called her friends once or twice at her new place. Only very close friends of her came there. Her health was worsening now and she was worried. She called Gurcharan through her servant.

'Have you forgotton me?,' Ritu said to Gurcharan as soon as he arrived.

'How can I foget you? I can't survive without you.' He put both his hands around Ritu.

'I have been badly ill. The loneliness makes me uneasy.'

'I had a small problem. Some of the people from my

constituency had come. I had to get a licence for one of my fellows. Anyhow, how are you now? Have you taken any medicine?'

'Now the medicine is with you only.'

'I am here with you.'

'Darling, Gurcharan, no excuses now. Now the time has come.' She sat close to Gurcharan and looked into his eyes.

'I have not followed you.' He said while touching lips of Ritu with his fingers.

'We may not abide by the social regulation but nature does not allow violation of its rules. Now you must marry me. There is no other way out.'

'What do you say?,' Alarmed Gurcharan retraced his steps. Then he controlled himself.

'That is why I am not keeping good health. You just make arrangements for marriage quickly.'

'But, but.... '

'Gurcharan, now no buts and ifs.'

'Listen Ritu. There is a solution to every problem. How can the marriage take place immediately? There can be some other remedy also.'

'The only solution of the problem is that we marry each other before the world. When we have indulged in man woman relationship, why can't we marry?'

'Ritu, there are all kinds of arrangements in Delhi. I talk to some renowned doctor.'

'No, I feel frightened. If we got the doctor, anything can happen. It can be leaked out. If any newspaper gets an inkling, another scandal will be raked up. And if anything happens to me,' Tears appeared in Ritu's eyes.

'Nothing will happen. I arrange for some good doctor.'

'Why don't you marry me? Why do you hesitate? We must accept the result boldly.' Ritu said forecefully and she started looking into his eyes searchingly.

'Mind it Gurcharan. I made true love with you. Leaving behind my family, I came to you. I surrendered myself before you. Whatever a woman could offer to a man, I did. You also reciprocated my love fully. Now our love is bearing fruit. Let it flourish. It cannot be aborted. No, I shall never allow it. You accept me openly before the world.' Ritu wept. Gurcharan kept thinking of a way out.

'What has happened to you all of a sudden? How do you talk? If we are bound by such responsibilities so early, all joys of life will vanish. Who does like that these days? Believe me, anything is possible in Delhi. We should not be bound so easly.'

'Where are we stuck? What do you mean?'

'I mean marriage and that too.'

'Do you call it a binding?'

'Yes, it is a binding, a problem. Life should be like the expanse of the sky. No limits, no bonds. Everything our own all around. Life does not mean binding, it is in action.'

'Gurcharan. Sky also binds itself at horizon. A river also flows within its two edges. When it overlaps the shores, it causes flood which distroys everything that comes its way.'

'You appear to be changed.'

'Yes, there is a life that is taking shape in my womb. I am really changing. I now want certainty of life. I wish to live with you happily. Do not evade the decision. It is the time to decide.'

'Oh, pardon me. I forgot. I have to attend an urgent meeting. The leaders of our state are meeting at Prime Minister's residence. I leave for it. I shall come afterwards.' Gurcharan stood up conscious of the time. He stepped towards Ritu, saw at her lovingly. Then he got out of the door.

Many days went by. Gurcharan did not come. She sent messages but to no avail. She was worried and was now disturbed. One evening, she went to him herself.

'So many days have passed. Neither you came nor you enquired about my welfare.' She spoke to him angrily.

'Please come and be seated.' Gurcharan appeared to be a changed man today. Ritu was agitated to see his cold behaviour. But she did not reflect any emotion on her face.

'Ritu, I am awefully busy. I have to attend to so many important assignments of the party and the country.'

'You may attend to all your assignments but marry me first of all.'

'I understood your problem. I have given a serious thought to it and have sought advice also. You need not worry. I am coming to you tomorrow. I have to go somewhere just now. I know you will not mind it.'

Ritu came back to her place. She could not take anything. She could not sleep at night. She was reminded of Savitri and her sisters.

She kept tossing throughout the night but could not have a wink of sleep. She would go on thinking and then suddenly would feel repentant. There was no one there to care for her restlessness.

Next evening, Gurcharan came to her. Ritu was relaxed at his arrival. Vimal also came with him in the room.

'Ritu, we should not refuse to accept the realities of life.' We come across such points in life where we have to take revolutionary decision,' Gurcharan said while occupying a chiar.

'Why all this lecture just on arrival? Don't you get a chance to deliver your speech these days? Just sit and relax. Vimal, you have also got time to come here today?'

'Vimal wants to come to you completely,' Gurcharan said hesitatingly. Then he waited for Ritu's reaction. All kept silent.

'Ritu, let us be plain and straight in our discussion. There is no use of cryptic talk. Whatever decision you have taken, I know that you will not change. And in the context of your decision, I must also take a decision,' Gurcharan said and was silent now.

'You are not talking straight. Please say clearly what you want to say,' Ritu said trembling. She was sceptic in her comment.

'Ritu, I can't marry you. I have my limitations.'

'What are the limitations?' Ritu was agitated over the comment.

'My lifestyle is different.'

'And marriage have no sanctity in it?'

'Please try to understand me.'

'You try to make me understand.' Ritu was furious. Gurcharan also sat stiff. Vimal watched all this, just sitting in one corner.

'I can't marry you.'

'But why can't you marry me?'

'How many women I shall marry? If I marry all my women friends, it will be a long list. Please forget and....'

'And...? Tell me that also.' Ritu stood up.

'I feel sympathy for you. Your friendship with me will remain everything. Try to understand my compulsious. Vimal is also your friend. He is a simple, honest man. His industry has flourished with my suppport.'

'What do you want to say? Speak out quickly. I don't need a lengthy introduction to it,' Ritu said interruptingly.

'You marry Vimal. He is ready to accept you in wedlock.'

'Gurcharan, you really turned out to be what my mother had said about you. Am I a dumb animal? That may be sold at will.

You had promised to marry me. So I remained with you. I left behind my home, my mother and sisters. I accepted your love. Now when I have your offspring in my womb, you ask me to marry Vimal. How dare you suggest it? And Vimal, you too, have agreed? Don't you feel ashamed over it, you are a coward, silly fellow ready to accept a second-hand woman.' Ritu almost boiled. She roamed around restlessly. There was fire in her eyes instead of tears.

'You are a known leader. You want to serve the entire country. You deliver lectures on morality and character and at the same time, you extend such a treatment....'

'Ritu, please don't prattle. You know your place. What do you possess? You don't have a place to live in. I have provided you a shelter here. I introduced you to political circles respectfully. And now you threaten me? I say you accept your marriage with Vimal. I shall get you a coveted post in party after sometime. Then you spend your life comfortably like Rita,' Gurcharan said and stood up.

'No, Gurcharan, Vimal has also changed. I shall not marry Ritu. You had made me agree somehow or the other but my soul condemns me. I feel I have been tainted just for having agreed to your proposal, may be for a short span. No, I shall not go that way. Ritu is right in her argument. Human beings are human beings. They are not saleable commodities. Don't insult womanhood, Gurcharan...,' Vimal also stood up. Ritu looked at him.

'So you have also started showing your teeth to me?'

'Please take your twenty-five thousand rupees. Tempted by the amount, I had accepted your proposal to marry Ritu. I have committed a sin. Ritu, you will pardon me. I had gone blind to the situation. I admit, Gurcharan, you have lakhs of rupees with you, you are a great politician too but not all things are saleable at all places.'

'O.K. Ritu you find your own way yourself. You vacate this house tomorrow. I forget about you. You also forget me.' Gurcharan walked to the exit.

'You are leaving behind a relationship so easily. Was the relationship spread over just a deception? Was that, in fact, lust only? Those promises were...' Ritu stood before him.

'Ritu, promises made by the politicans are just like the lines drawn in water. They are never permanent,' Vimal said.

'Gurcharan, you go. I shall also go somewhere but remember I shall not forget you so easily. You can go by leaving this room but you can't run away from my life so easily. I shall reveal the story of your betrayal to the entire world. I shall expose your woolfish face that you have hid behind. I do not now crave for anything. Your beastly behaviour has ruined me. I have only one desire that I expose your real face to the public. I want to let the public know the black deeds of the leaders. You have ruined me but you also remain prepared for the destruction. Here is the door, you can go.' She opened the door for him.

'You throw a challenge to me?' Gurcharan looked at her with his burning eyes. Then he went away without talking to Vimal even.

'Vimal! Gurcharan has left leaving me in the lurch. I shall drown in the whirlpool. I had left my mother long back for my love. My father is in jail and I am on family way.' She was weeping now.

'Ritu, I shall feel lucky if I can be of any use to you. You probably do not know that Gurcharan had spoiled the life of so many girls. He is my friend but he is not a decent man. I also did many wrong things in his company but my soul chides me now. I don't know how I agreed just by receiving twenty-five thousand rupees. He said he would give me fifty thousand after the marriage.'

'The whole world is on sale for him. If they could, they would buy God even. They buy and sell themselves. So they think everything is saleable.'

'O.K. Ritu. Pardon me please. I have complete sympathy for you.' Vimal also left the place.

□

63

Savitri was trying to live a peaceful life despite all odds. Ritu's going away had hurt her badly. She was mum for many days when Ritu deserted her. She was bleeding in soul. Gradually, she made a compromise with the circumstances but Ritu's departure from home had always made her sad.

She made it a point to meet Pramod regularly in the jail. Pramod also used to wait for her. Though it was difficult to go from Ambala to Delhi, yet she had made it a habit. Normally, she went all alone but occasionally she took Surekha and Puneeta along. Pramod had gone very weak. The main reason was Kishore's sickness. His illness increased day by day. He was kept in the hospital too but it did not help. He was normally silent. He would not speak for days together. Pramod's loneliness grew all the more intolerable when he saw Kishore.

When Savitri came to meet Pramod this time, he could not contain his tears. He had come alone to see her. He told that Kishore had almost lost his senses. He keeps lying like mad people. He has been shifted to the hospital. Pramod had an intimate fellow in Kishore when they too lived together in jail. In fact, he realized the odds of jail only when he was left alone in his jail cell. Finding tears in Pramod's eyes, Savitri could not control herself. Tears rolled down her eyes. She expressed sympathy for Pramod, but in fact, she could not feel anything for him now. She was just doing her duty. Just like a machine. But he neither enthused her with his presence nor made any impact. He was not the same Pramod for her. At moments, she did think about him, his sojourn in the jail, the hardships he might have been facing. She thought about the food he might be getting. To remain in the company of robbers, cheaters, etc. She would then feel pity for him. Just after that there surged hatred and anger for him in her heart. She thought of her happy married life. God had provided them with the bounty. But Pramod took a wrong way. For no fault of her, she had been put to loneliness whereas he had been confined to jail for his wrongs. Savitri always did her duty. She could not make out why she had been punished by God, why all this torture? If only Pramod had listened to her advice, they would not have had bad days as they were undergoing now.

Savitri had found a friend in Ambala. She was a widow. They both visited each other. She was also living a hard life. They both cultivated love for each other. She had her nephew in Ambala who taught in a school. It was an ordinary poor family. She proposed that her nephew and Surekha could prove to be a good matrimonial match for each other. Savitri found him suitable for Surekha. She was worried about Surekha for sometime. Surekha found a teaching job in the school. She made her presence felt in the school within a few days. Her job was regularised. Savitri discussed the proposal with her, she agreed.

When Savitri went to meet Pramod next month, she talked about it.

'Savitri, your proposal is right. We do not know where and how Ritu is but do arrange Surekha's marriage please. You have enquired about the boy?'

'Yes, I have enquired. Everything is O.K. at this time. Rest depends on luck.' Pramod's eyes went down.

'But how will you manage the finances?'

'I shall arrange. I have talked to them. They will also arrange a simple marriage. We are not in a position to give dowry and they are not asking for it even. I have saved some money from my salary, I shall arrange with that.'

'In our daughter's marriage, I...leave it.' His eyes were wet.

'You can get parole. I have enquired, you submit your application just now. Do write for one month's parole for preparations for the marriage.'

Pramod kept silent.

'Then you will be able to spend a few days with the family. It appears centuries have passed since we separated. Many ideas crop up in mind but it was a stroke of fate. No one is to be blamed.' Pramod had heard such a language from Savitri's mouth for the first time. Normally, either Savitri did not speak at all or she would express her anger against him. Pramod had got sympathatic comment for the first time.

'I shall do as you advise but as a prisoner, I do not want to be out of the prison bars. They will raise fingers at me during Surekha's marriage. I shall be discussed. I shall be an eyesore to many. Whenever I get freedom from this jail, I shall be a citizen first. I wish to spend rest of my life with you. I think about the same Kullu, Hidimba...Raghu Nath ji.' Tears trickled down from his eyes. Savitri could also not contain her tears.

Both of them kept silent for some time.

'I wish my desire is fulfilled.' Savitri heaved a deep sigh.

'Don't you trust me now?'

'I have lost faith in all. Adversity has not been caused on us by any one else. We invited it ourselves. When we had no comfort in our luck, then.... '

'Savitri, believe me I shall come out as the same old Pramod after finishing my term in jail, the same old Pramod that you had seen at first sight.' There was a glimmer in their eyes. Savitri looked at Pramod. They both laughed. They had listened the old symphony after after many years.

'Delhi of our dream is too far as yet.' Savitri again heaved a sigh.

'Those days have ended. These also will pass away. I have decided that I shall repent all my sins that I committed against you.'

'You will simply remain with me. That will be heaven for me.'

'Only a little time is left. I am spending my days dreaming my future.'

'So I make arrangements for Surekha's marriage. I have your consent.'

'Why not? Please, I would like to meet Surekha once before her marriage. I want to see my daughter with my own eyes.'

'So you will not.... '

'No. I don't wish to come there as a prisoner.'

'O.K. you may not come. I shall look after all the arrangements.'

'You have always shouldered all the responsibilities. I have simply wasted everything. I had gone astray and my entire family also has been deceived.'

'Don't think about that now. I feel our days are going to change once Surekha's marriage is solemnized. Since we have decided about her marriage, I feel relaxed. Our woes are on the decrease. I have felt good after many years.'

'That I am witnessing. For the first time, you are so affectionate. I shall sleep happily in the jail today.'

On return home, Savitri was busy with preparations for the marriage. The marriage changed her life all together. Now she wore decent clothes. She would dress up beautifully. She would converse with Surekha and Puneeta smilingly. She would go with them to the market. Her sadness had disappeared. Both the girls were very happy.

'Mother, I am happy for another cause, even more than my marriage.' One day Surekha held her mother in her arms and said.

'What happiness?' Savitri kissed her forehead.

'You are entirely changed since my marriage talks started. There is delight on you face. We were vexed to find you sad.' Surekha smiled once again.

'Yes, mother, sister is right in her statment. It appears happiness is returning to our home.' Puneeta was also ecstatic.

'Mother, had I known the secret of your happiness, I would have arranged my marriage earlier.'

'You also...'?

'No, sister.'

'Really, I have another alibi to live for. Earlier I felt I had lost everthing. Nothing had been left. Now I feel that I must care for what has been left Surekha. Preparations for your marriage have instilled enthusiasm in me. I feel as if my life has come alive. He is very fortunate who will marry you. He has restored our good days before coming himself.' Savitri sat on the bed with both of them.

'Yes, Surekha, you have to go to Delhi for seeing your father before your marriage. He was also very happy to hear the news of your marriage.'

'Will father not be present during my marriage?'

'No, he won't come. Even if he comes on parole, he will be still a prisoner. They will point fingers at him. He does not want to come and I have also refused him. Only a short span of time is left. He will then be released from jail.'

'Sister, I shall also accompany you to Papa for the meet,' Puneeta said holding Surekha's hand.

'Yes, we shall all go together.' They both danced at Savitri's comment.

'And mother, we shall meet Ritu also in Delhi. She has also to be invited to the marriage.'

Savitri was jolted when Puneeta talked about Ritu. She was once again plaintive. She felt as if she had been thrown to the ground from the sky. Surekha understood. She changed the topic.

The three of them came back after meeting Pramod.

The date of marriage was decided. Savitri made all arrangements for the marriage ceremony with the assistance of her brother.

Surekha's marriage was solemnized in a simple manner. She went to her in-laws as a bride.

Now there were only Savitri and Puneeta at home. But Savitri was very happy. Surekha would come to see her after every two or three days. Savitri's son-in-law, Praveen, was a simple and disciplined boy hailing from an ordinary poor family. Savitri used to be extremely happy to see him. She would ask them to stay with her once in a week.

□

64

Ritu could not sleep for whole of the night, once Gurcharan left her alone. She found herself in a dark alley of life. There was no ray of hope around. She had none else in Delhi who knew her. Moreover, she had no means of livelihood. She could not go to her mother also. If it was right, she could have gone to her mother to tender apology. She had no credentials to go to her. While going away, Gurcharan had asked her to vacate the house. Where should she go? Where should she live? These thoughts worried her. She was like a flickering lamp.

The attendant left the next day. Before leaving, he told that his employer had asked him to come back. He also told that he had to go back with all the accessories. She was all alone after he went. She did not know how to cook food or how to keep the house. She could not understand what to do and what not to do. Where should she go? She did not eat throughout the day. She felt hungry at night. She went into the kitchen. Some eggs were lying. She prepared omlette and ate it with the loaves that had been cooked last evening. She went to sleep after eating it.

She made efforts to sleep but she could not. She remembered his father who was lodged in the jail. She thought of her mother. She was also reminded of her sisters, Surekha and Puneeta. She remembered them and burst into tears. When she felt her hand on her belly, she was alarmed. She got up. Uncertain future loomed large before her.

Gurcharan had come to his residence after bidding farewell to Ritu. He tried to sleep after taking his dinner but he could not sleep. One of his friends told him on phone that the Cabinet was likely to be expanded again. The leaders from his state had recommended Gurcharan's name. Gurcharan's image had been tarnished by the recent news that were published against him. His detractors had publicised those negative news but now that chapter was over. Another scandal of a senior Minister was published in a newspaper. It was so largely in news that Gurcharan's episode was forgotten.

Gurcharan was worried on one count. The expansion of the Cabinet was on the cards. His induction was almost certain. His opponents were feeding the High Command against him. This time all leading leaders of his state made efforts to get him installed as a Cabinet Minister. He felt if Ritu issued any statement these days, it could harm him. He was upset with the publication of a news against him in the newspaper and feared that if she openly stood against him, and if by chance some newspaper had an inkling of the episode, he would be ruined. He trembled at this thought. He found his chances of becoming a Minister dashed to the ground.

Ritu had not eaten anything that day also. She wandered here and there throughout the day. She went to her bed in the evening. Her mental anxiety had made her tired physically as well. She could not sleep.

'There was a knock at the door. She felt frightened. The knock appeared known. But she could not believe. She opened the door while rubbing her eyes.

'Oh, you.' She was alarmed. She retraced her steps. She was a bit frightened. Last time when he parted, they were quite bitter that she never expected him to come. She stood away.

'Ritu, I have come to tender my apology,' Gurcharan said.

Ritu looked at him. She could not understand.

'I misbehaved with you that day. Truly speaking, I committed a crime. But my soul snubbed me. I had to come yesterday itself but I could not summon courage. I was afraid of you. I had not the courage to face you.' Gurcharan continued speaking while standing Ritu perspired.

'Will you not ask me to sit inside? Have I committed such a big crime that I cannot seek your pardon even.' Gurcharan folded his hands.

'Please do come in and be seated. I was lost. It is your own house. I am living here unauthorisedly.' Ritu went in. Gurcharan also followed her.

'In fact, I had done something unwanted that day. This all belongs to you, Ritu. He sat in the chair. Ritu sat in front of him.

'I can't believe it. Is that true what I hear. I don't trust anyone now, I doubt my ears even.' Ritu's eyes were glistening.

'Ritu, I have come to tender an apology for my shoddy behaviour on that day. I had been pertubed for some days. The conspiracies within the party are on the increase. Because of that, I was not myself. Please forget all that. I am loyal to you as before and shall remain so.' Gurcharan moved his chair closer to her. Ritu was viewing him with strange eyes. She could not understand why Gurcharan said all that.

'I swear by my love that I shall never repeat such a behaviour. Everything will be done as per your desire. I shall leave what is unwanted. I shall change my life style. You just forgive me once.' Gurcharan held Ritu's hand in his hand. He pressed it forcefully. He looked keenly in her eyes.

'Just laugh as you normally used to laugh. I shall then conclude that you have forgiven me.'

'Gurcharan, I fail to understand anything. My wounds of that day are still fresh. They may not disappear so soon. When a woman is insulted on the pretext of love, she is like a living corpse. I am alive before you...probably.' She wept. Gurcharan consoled her.

He stayed with her for the night. The servant also returned. He cooked special food. They dined together. Gurcharan assured her that he would make arrangements of their marriage within a few days. Ritu was happy to hear it. She felt as if she had been sentenced to death. The butchers had taken her to the gallows. Now she had been called back, she thought.

Ritu once again returned to her fanciful world. They started living together. They wandered around. They would take their dinner in popular restaurants. Now he did not invite his friends. Gurcharan had told her that he wanted to meet her only in lonely conditions. He did not feel good in the company of others. One week elapsed in this manner.

'Ritu, a few of my friends have come from abroad. I want to introduce you to them. I have invited them to dinner today,' Gurcharan said while going inside.

'It's all right you have invited them in a restaurant?'

'No, not at a public place. They will have drinks too.... And I shall also have to take it with them. So I have arranged a secluded place.'

'So that the public does not know how the leaders consume whisky,' she said sitting close to Gurcharan on a sofa. They both laughed.

'You have rightly pointed out. This leadership also is a binding. We have to do some activities in a clandestine manner.'

'Not something but a lot.'

'Yes.'

'But our marriage ceremony will not be performed in a closed door.'

'It will be solemnized with pomp and show public.'

Gurcharan spent the evening there. They kept talking intimately. He went round the house. He advised the servant to set the house in order. After some time, Ritu came to her room to dress up for the evening. He instructed the servant on some counts.

Both of them reached in a small room on the fifth storey of a high rise building in Delhi in time. The dinner was laid on a table. Gurcharan's attendant was looking after all the arrangements. Soon his two friends arrived. They were introduced to Ritu. They had just started talking that Gurcharan asked for serving liquor also. Ritu acted as the host. They both enjoyed drinks. Gurcharan was soon under the influence of liquor. He offered a peg to Ritu. When they clapped, Ritu joined them in drinking.

Ritu consumed equal quantity of whisky as was done by Gurcharan. But for the last few days, she was conscious of her health. She had stopped taking drinks and had reduced smoking as well. Once she had a drink today, she could not refuse them for more and more. Gurcharan also kept offering drink after drink to her. She took it gladly. Her eyes were now red and she fumbled on her feet.

When all of them had taken heavy drinks they came to the dining table. Even after heavy doses of whisky, Gurcharan's friends were in senses. Gurcharan was intoxicated more. Ritu had also consumed excessive liquor. She tried to control herself. They talked extensively while eating. Gurcharan's friends narrated stories about foreign lands. They sat together after the dinner.

Ritu behaved properly with friends of her would-be husband. She talked to them in a fine manner. But she felt that they were somewhat typical. She doubted whether they had ever gone abroad or not. She could make it out that they were not actually what they were posing to be. She secretly asked Gurcharan to go home as it was already very late at night. He asked her to wait as he had met his friends after many years. Those friends also insisted that they would like to celebrate the advance party of their marriage throughout the night. Ritu was tired and exhausted. She did not relish the presence of those friends. But she sat there to observe the formalities.

It was the dead of night. The Delhi noise was on the wane now. They all came out of the room. They stood in the balcony. The moon light was sparkling. They started talking while standing there.

'May I call the vehicles here by sending a message through the servant.' Gurcharan went in. They continued their talks, the three of them. Standing in one corner, Ritu enjoyed the rays of moon and the two friends were talking to each other.

'The thud...'

Both of them picked up Ritu and threw her down.

The moon felt shy. The moon light had gone dim. The winds stopped. The silence of night was ashamed. The moon hid itself in the clouds and disappeared.

'What is it? Who is there? What has fallen,' a watchman on the ground shouted as he ran towards the spot where Ritu had fallen.

'Nothing...the same...the same Sherjung,' Gurcharan said while walking towards him.

'The same...what the same?'

'About whom Ramu had talked to you.'

'Ramu? Who is he?'

'Are you Sherjung?'

'No, Sherjung has fallen ill. He had lost his senses. He is in hospital. I am Bahadur.'

'You are Bahadur?,' Gurcharan muttered. The two friends had come down by that time. Gurcharan signalled out to them and made to his car. The moon had come out of the clouds to be a witness to the incident. Now Ritu's dead body lying on the ground was visible.

'Take it. And be silent. The case has been settled with Sherjung.' One of them handed over an envelope full of notes to the watchman.

'What is it?'

'Five Thousand rupees.'

'Five thousand...five thousand.' The watchman hesitated. He felt as if he was being buried under the earth. His hands trembled. The money envelope fell down.

'Sir, why these five thousand and what for? Whose dead body is it?' He was at a loss to understand.

'The amount is for your silence. You forget you had seen us. Forget it also that a dead body is lying here. Go to your room and sleep. Just say, you had fallen ill.'

'No, Sir.' The watchman held his head trying to think over.

'Take two thousand more.'

'No, Sir. I don't understand. It is a murder. You have killed her. I am a poor man and am afraid of God.... You cannot purchase me.... Just wait.' The watchman ran towards the gate. After starting his car, Gurcharan was coming that way. He was just late for a moment otherwise his car would have gone out of the gate. The watchman closed the door at once and shouted....' They are thieves and robbers...murder... murder....'

Gurcharan's foreign friends jumped over the wall to run away.' Gurcharan came out of his car and tried to open the gate but the watchman caught him.

'You are a thief, a robber. You are running away after killing a woman.' The watchman shouted.

'Leave me. Let me go. I am a rich man of Delhi. We have settled the whole issue with Sherjung,' Gurcharan said trying to escape his grip.

'Foolish man...the rich man? Wants to run away after killing a woman at night. You are a scoundrel.'

'Sherjung knows everything. You may enquire from him. Let me go. I shall give you what you ask for.'

'Sherjung is Sherjung. I am Bahadur. I am not saleable. I do no compromise my integrity for money. I am a God fearing, poor man.' Bahadur held him forcefully. He wanted to move but Bahadur threw him on the ground. Bahadur had been raising his voice at the same time. A few people around had woken up. They came there in a group. The lights were on now.

Gurcharan whispered into a man's ears that he was a big politician. Those who killed her have already run away. He should be allowed to go. But the crowd had gathered there by that time. There was a noise. They all held Gurcharan and took him near the dead body. It was lying senseless. Some of the people had gone to the police checkpost. One of the persons brought a doctor from closeby. The doctor told that Ritu had died a few minutes before.

Soon after the police arrived. Hundreds of people collected there at mid-night. Some youngmen had started raising slogans before the arrival of the police. A few youngmen thrashed Gurcharan.

Gurcharan was taken to the police station. The police cordoned off the entire area. The police guarded the dead body.

Gurcharan said the Station House Officer that he had been misunderstood as the murderer whereas he was a leading politician.

'What's your complete name?'

'Gurcharan... .'

'Really. You have won the recent election.' The thanedar stood alarmed.

'Yes, the same.'

'I also belong to your state. In fact, I am from your election area. Your family is quite rich and renowned. There are discussions about your induction in the Cabinet.'

'I shall become a Minister during the current month.'

'Sir, this way.' The senior police officer of the area had reached on the spot. He had been immediately informed about the incident. Noticing him, the thanedar signalled him the way.

'Have the culprits been caught?,' he asked the thanedar.

'Yes, no, sir, no.'

'Why are you trembling? Was any bullet fired?'

'No, Sir, this way... .' He took him aside.

'Sir, he is not the culprit. He is a senior politician of our state. He is Sh. Gurcharan. He has his access to the Prime Minister also. He is likely to be inducted as a Minister this week.'

'Sh. Gurcharan. I know. But why is he here?'

'Sir, he was present there. The mob had caught him before I reached. The people around said that he has...but it is a lie, Sir.'

'Any eyewitness?'

'Yes, Sir, the watchman is the eyewitness.'

'Call him.' The thanedar went out.

'Pardon me. You are facing inconvenience. The Thanedar has told me all the details. May be there is some misunderstanding. I shall try to solve it in a short time,' The officer said coming closer to Gurcharan.

'The people held me just by misunderstanding. Kindly dispense the case quickly. And no one should know that I was in the police station at night. They will make a mountain of a mole hill. I shall never forget your obligation.' Gurcharan was clearly perplexed. The hang over of liquor had its impact on his face, though the heavy intoxication had gone. He was completely disorderly. Perturbed as he was, he would sit now, and then stand up. The police officer watched him seriously.

'Sir, here is Bahadur.'

'Bahadur, what do you do?'

'Sir. I am a watchman.'

'What did you see?'

'A woman fell from the upper storey and died as soon as she fell down. He came down through stairs. He rushed to his car. I stopped him. He told he had settled it with Sherjung. Be silent. Then two more men got down. I was given five thousand rupees. They asked me to keep my mouth shut. I refused. Then two thousand more was offered to me. In the meanwhile, the man wanted to run away in his car. I hurriedly closed the gate and caught this man. They two ran away but I did not let this man escape.

'Please here are those seven thousand rupees. Sir, I am a poor man, afraid of God.' The police officer was stunned to hear the watchman. The thanedar stood aside, without uttering a word.

'Sir, he said he was a leader of Delhi. He tried to influence me by the stature of his leadership. He wanted to escape by pushing me away. He did push me also. Then I threw him on the ground. He posed as a leader. Sir, may be the leaders are saleable but I am a poor man.'

'Who is Sherjung?'

'Sir, Sherjung is also a watchman. He had to be on duty at night today. He suddenly fell ill. He lost his senses. He has been rushed to the hospital. Some person of the name of Ramu had fixed something with Sherjung. He fell ill. Sir, this man knowns him. That's whay he mentioned his name.'

'Very interesting.' The officer looked at Gurcharan.

'Take him away.' Thanedar took Bahadur out.

'Mr. Gurcharan. There is something fishy. I shall have to register an F.I.R. against you.'

'Case? Against me?' Gurcharan said alarmed.

'No Sir. How can the case be registered against him? He is such a big leader. And leaders never commit a crime,' Thanedar said.

'But Bahadur's statement? He is an illiterate poor man and has spoken the truth. This man mentioned the name of Sherjung. He was asked to shut his mouth. Those two persons and the amount of rupees seven thousand. Arrest him as per law,' the officer said.

'You will arrest me? Are you in senses or not. You non-entity you will arrest me?' Gurcharan was furious.

'You are already in custody.'

'You will repent. I shall not let you serve in peace...you wicked officer.'

'You may abuse as much as you want. I shall perform my duty. Normally, policemen are accused of using abusive language. This is what the leaders attribute to us. And you, see how I am listening patiently to your abuses. But by the way, Mr. Gurcharan, who was that girl whose dead body is lying there.'

'Your mother...you bastard.' Gurcharan was enraged. As if he was drunk again. He had lost his temper.

'I did not want to put you to an awkward position but you do not agree.'

'I ask you for the last time to let me go or just give the phone to me,' Gurcharan said getting up.

'Sir, why do you invoke the wrath. He is a leading politician. The seniors will direct us and then we shall have to free him. We can let him go at our level. He may be of some use to us in future,' The thanedar implored.

'Look here. Register the case. Complete all the papers. Make him sit in the adjoining room. And lock him from outside. Since he is a big leader, don't lodge him in the prison cell.'

The thanedar went to his seat.

'Here is the telephone.' The officer extended the phone towards Gurcharan. He tried to connect at two places.

Soon after, there was a phone from the top senior police officer of Delhi.

'Who is there?'

'Sir, I,' Gurcharan and thanedar looked at the police officer.

He stood up from the chair. He had the phone in his trembling hands.

'Is Mr. Gurcharan there?'

'Yes, Sir.'

'Let him go home immediately. What kind of police officer you are? You don't recognise even. Do you know the result of making such a leader sit in the thana?'

'Sir, a girl has been thrown down from the fifth storey of a building. She has been murdered. The eyewitness is there. The girl is dead. The watchman apprehended Gurcharan while he tried to run away.'

'If she is dead, let her be dead. People die daily. They will die in future also. Big leaders never commit a crime. You don't understand. You have gone mad. I order you.'

'But, Sir, I have already registered a case. I have registered his arrest also. Bahadur's statement has been recorded.'

'Tear all the papers.'

'Sir...'

'You are a silly fellow.' His legs trembled while he listened to the phone. Thanedar and Gurcharan were laughing at him.

'Sir, try to understand the entire situation.'

'You fool. You will make me understand? Shall I conduct Delhi police as per your advice?'

'Sir, I do not mean that. But a murder has been committed. The murderer has been nabbed from the site. Shall the police free the nabbed murderer also?'

'May be the murderer is you father.' Gurcharan slapped the officer.

'What has happened?'

'Sir, encouraged by your telephonic message, the accused has attacked me.'

'Sorry, never mind. Just let him go.'

'Sir, listen to me. I can't do it. The police is meant to nab the culprits and not to let the nabbed ones go away. If you want it, please send the order in writing.' He kept the phone.

'Lodge him in the prison cell.'

'Let us see who is lodged in jail.' Rita and a few more people entered the room from the front door. They all looked to be leaders. They all snubbed the officer. Rita took him aside and told that he was a confidant of Prime Minister. He is likely to be inducted as a Minister during the current week.

'Please believe me, I can't help you any way. A criminal is a criminal. May be a small or big one, may be an ordinary one or a big leader.'

'Are leaders not human beings?,' one of them interjected angrily.

'If they are, why all this pressure? If a poor man had been nabbed here, would the leaders have exerted the same pressure?' The officer sat in his chair.

'Put him behind the bars,' he again commanded.

'I am reminded of an old incident,' Rita said while getting up.

'What incident you are reminded of?'

'Long back, I had gone to a police officer under similar circumstances. There was a small problem. He had refused my request. He posed to be an idealist. After that he had to suffer throughout his life. He himself is in jail now and his daughter's dead body is lying there. Give it a thought, you too.' Rita had seen Ritu's dead body before coming there. She was not surprised as Gurcharan had already given such signals to her. Rita was astonished rather finding Gurcharan on the scene of crime.

'About whom you are talking?'

'About a foolish police officer akin to you.'

'His name?'

'Pramod.'

'Pramod. So she is Pramod's daughter...Ritu dear.' He got up. He saw the dead body of Ritu lying on one side. He placed his hand on Ritu's forehead. Tears trickled down.

'Oh, my friend, Pramod.' He sat in his chair.

'You can all go. I shall get Gurcharan committed and punished. He is the killer of my friend's daughter.'

They all came out. In the meanwhile Rita had called many people on phone. Thanedar went to the lock up with Gurcharan.

The Sun has not risen as yet.

'Sir, someone has come,' a policeman said while entering his room. A police officer went inside in the meanwhile. He handed over an envelope to him and asked another officer to sit in the chair. Rita and all others were also present there now. They were offered chairs to sit.

The officer was suspended. The envelope carried his suspension order. A new officer had been appointed in his place. He examined all the papers promptly. He tore away some papers and changed some others. Soon afterwards, Rita and her companions went away in their cars with Gurcharan.'

□

65

The newspapers extensively carried the death of Ritu. Many theories were discussed. The police drubbed it as a suicide case. The police told the newspapers next day that Ritu had committed suicide for some reasons. They had found some evidences to corroborate that Ritu had been mentally upset for days together before she committed suicide.

Savitri was beyond herself with grief when she learnt about her death. She came to Delhi with her brother. May be just by chance, she met Vimal. Vimal told a few things to her of his last meeting with Ritu. She now believed that Gurcharan was responsible for her murder. Vimal arranged her meeting with Bahadur, the watchman. Savitri was sorrowful to know about such a sad end of Ritu. She had forgotten the living Ritu but once she was dead, Savitri was haunted by it. She met Rita and told her that Gurcharan had killed her daughter. Savitri wanted that Gurcharan should be penalised for his crime. Rita told her that Gurcharan had nothing to do with it. Then she said clearly that Gurcharan was a big leader, no one could harm him. When she did not relent on that too, Rita threatened Savitri. Savitri thought Rita to be Pramod's friend. She was confident that Rita would help in the investigations of the death of her friend's daughter. She was shocked to find that Rita was not at all concerned with Ritu's death.

She advised Savitri to forget such a big crime.

Savitri met some of Pramod's other friends in Delhi but none of them assured her of any help. Pramod's friends had forgotten him. One of his friends even had a bad eye for Savitri. She was sorry to receive such a treatment from him.

Savitri met the suspended police officer. He turned out to be Pramod's old class fellow. He asked Savitri to meet

C. Sundaram, a senior police officer. He was the highest police officer in the Capital. Savitri went to meet him along with Vimal.

'The death mystery after a fall from the fifth storey...?' Sundaram tried to recall the happening when Savitri met him.

'She was my daughter...Ritu.'

'But she had committed suicide. I am so sorry. Please see, we cannot do anything in respect of suicide cases. Tell me if I can do any other service?' He started disposing of the files lying on his table.

'No it was not a suicide. I have met the watchman, Bahadur. He had nabbed Gurcharan. Who was trying to run away in his car. Bahadur rushed to the gate and closed it. The watchman had caught him. He had been kept in the lock up also for some time.'

'What are you saying? Someone has told you the wrong story,' Sundaram said surprisingly.

'No, Sir. I have been told the right story. I myself have met that watchman, Bahadur. He had caught Gurcharan. He was trying to run away in his car. Bahadur closed the gate. There were two more men with him.' Savitri went on saying.

'May be that relates to another Ritu.'

'No, Sir. Ritu, my daughter.'

'Yes, there was a stir in the papers about it. I got it investigated by a special officer. I have gone through the whole file. No such detail has been recorded in it.'

'Sir, she is speaking the truth. I know Gurcharan. He got her killed. He himself was also present. It had been planned in advance. Sherjung watchman had to be on duty that night. They had purchased him.

They had promised him an amout of five thousand rupees. But Sherjung fell ill that night. He was admitted to the hospital. So Bahadur was on duty instead. He raised a hue and cry, then Gurcharan called him. Then they gave five thousand rupees to Bahadur. When he did not agree, they gave him two thousand more. But he refused. He nabbed Gurcharan who tried to escape away. He shouted. People from around gathered there. Those seven thousand rupees were also deposited in the police station.' Vimal told the entire story. Sundaram listened to it intently. He felt bad.

'If you are speaking the truth, I am sorry. I am ashamed on the working of my department. There is no greater crime than making a murder look like a suicide. You need not worry. I shall try to deliver justice to you.'

Savitri felt a little assured after meeting Sundaram. She came back with Vimal.

Sundaram enquired about the whole case from the suspended police officer. He was shocked. A clear-cut murder case had been turned into a suicide case. All papers had been changed. False evidences of new witnesses were recorded. The witnesses present on the crime scene were ignored. They had written Bahadur's statement and got his thumb impression on it.

Sundaram knew that a big leader was a culprit in this case. It had been dropped to save him. For a moment, he thought it would not be proper to start proceedings against so big a leader. Moreover, the matter had been disposed of at lower level without bringing it to his notice. But his soul asked him to take action. Otherwise also Sundaram had never compromised on any basic principle. He was known as an honest, feareless officer. That is why the political circles did not appreciate him. There were so many obstacles in his promotion also. People with lesser years of service had superceded him as they were the henchmen of politicians. But he had never cared for such things. He enjoyed performing his duties.

Sundaram called one of his loyal police officers and discussed the whole case with him. He asked him to investigate and submit his report within a week.

Vimal arranged Savitri's meeting with an opposition Party M.P. She narrated the entire incident to him. The issue was raked up in the Parliament. It was a topic in the newspapers once again. The government assured the House that another investigation into the case would be conducted and action initiated against the culprits. It strengthened Sundaram's hands.

Savitri returned to Ambala after a few days stay at Delhi. Ritu's murder changed her totally. She was badly hurt in spirit. She was already broken but Surekha's marriage had again instilled enthusiasm in her. She waited for Pramod's release. She felt she would spend the rest of the life peacefully with Pramod. She did feel that she had lost a lot but not the whole of it. She had started efforts to use the remainder part of her life to advantage. Anger against Pramod had subsided, instead she had a feeling of sympathy for him.

But Ritu's murder changed everything for Savitri. The optimism was on the wane. And she found the life full of darkness. Now she did not like to hear Pramod's name even. Puneeta started to discuss her father but Savitri did not pay any attention to that. One day Surekha and her husband came. They also enquired about Pramod's welfare but she maintained silence.

She did not go to see Pramod after that day. He waited for her. He wrote a letter too. Savitri did not respond to it. She tore away the letter after reading it and consigued the pieces to fire.

One day Surekha asked, 'Mother, you have not gone to meet Papa for many days, now. I had also gone last month. Papa was waiting for you.'

'You met him,' she said and was silent.

'Mother, you will take me along this time. I remember Papa very much,' Puneeta said. Savitri remained silent and was busy with some other work.

Mother, what is the matter? Ritu's murder is a tragedy for the entire family but what is Papa's fault in it? You neither go to meet him, nor you write a letter. Moreover, you don't talk about him at all. He is a greatly worried man these days. I got a letter from him. He had written a letter to you. You did not reply it,' Surekha said seriously.

'My dear daughter, I shall appreciate if you don't ask anything from me about it. I don't have anything left with me. Neither any question nor any answer.' There were tears in her eyes. Both the daughters sitting beside her were now silent.

'Mother, I find a change in you for somedays now. How will you live with something so heavy on your mind. If you do not share it with us, with whom will you share. We also cannot bear it.'

'Surekha, no one else but your Papa is responsible for Ritu's murder. She was treading on the path her Papa had shown. She went astray. God knows how she has been killed. Your father had brought Gurcharan at our home. He was friendly with such poeple. Our family was a happy family. We had everything. He was a good officer. We had sufficient income. But he started on a wrong track. He rejected me and insulted me. I made efforts to check him but he did not stop. He spoiled the entire family. Even my ornaments were sold. I don't know how and why my daughter Ritu was killed. He eroded the happiness of this family himself.

Now I don't want anything. I don't have any one of mine. I do not wish to live.' Savitri burst into tears. Tears flowed down like a river. Surekha take her in her lap. Savitri was almost senseless. Both the sisters took her to the bed so that she could take some rest.

Savitri was often very sad. She had gone weak. She was on leave from school. She now used to spend her time in isolation.

Pramod was sick in the jail. He wrote a letter to Surekha. Surekha went with her husband to meet Pramod. Pramod asked why Savitri did not come to him. They told she was not keeping good health for the last few days. On her return, Surekha suggested that her mother must go to see her father in jail. On their insistence, Savitri said, 'O.K. I shall go on meeting him as long as he is in jail.' She emphasized on the words 'as long as.'

She started visiting him in jail now. Pramod used to be happy at her sight. But she would not talk much now. She would simply ask about his welfare. She would give him something. She would sit silent. She too would answer Pramod's questions briefly. She just observed it as a formality.

Ritu's murder case investigation was complete now. The report reached Sundaram. He had instruction from the Home Ministry that on receiving the report, he should meet the Home Secretary. Sundaram went to him with the report. The Home Secretary told Sundaram that whatever the findings of investigation, he must cover up the report. Sundaram was shocked and surprised. He opposed it. He pointed out it was a clear case of murder. It has been discussed at various levels. It is not fair to cover it up. The Home Secretary at last told him that the government wanted it that way. Sundaram expressed his desire to meet the Home Minister. He was allowed to meet him.

'Why come to me? The Home Secretary must have told you everything,' the Minister said expressing his anger.

'Sir, it will not be fair. A young girl was put astray. She was assured of marriage. When she conceived, she was compelled to marry someone else. When she did not agree to do so and revealed it to the world, then she was thrown down from the fifth storey of a building and killed. And then it was made to appear as a suicide case. Sir, it has been a big crime and it has been committed by a prominent leader. Kindly issue me orders to arrest him. I have come to you for the purpose.' Sundaram was a bit agitated.

'Be at peace. The government works at its own pace. After all that leader belongs to our party. Do you know it?'

'But, Sir, a criminal does not belong to any party.'

'He does belong to a party. A culprit is also a part of society. And all are equal in a democracy.'

'But injustice...murder.'

'Nothing special. It goes on. Many people die daily. She died, how does it matter? Forget it. Go and be peaceful. Cover it up. Do you understand?'

'But evidences...witnesses...papers... .' He asked in a tone of surprise.

'O.K. you go. I shall see to it.' The Minister got up. Sundaram looked at him with his eyes wide open. Thereafter, he left the place.

On the third day itself, Sundaram was transferred from Delhi to Madras. And Bahadur was found dead after one week at his house. Gurcharan had, somehow or the other, shut Vimal's mouth also.

Savitri came to Delhi a number of times. She met many officers. The hope she had in her mind after meeting Sundaram, gradually disappeared. She had now no hope of justice from any corner. She met a few leaders also. A few of them expressed sympathy with her but no one could help her.

Savitri was restive to get Gurcharan punished who was the main accused. For attaining this objective, she went to every possible officer but she did not get justice anywhere.

One of the persons suggested to her that she should herself meet the Prime Minister. She would definitely get justice at his hands. She tried thrice but she could not meet him.

Ritu's murder case was completely hushed up. The proofs were destroyed. The only eyewitness Bahadur was also dead. The matter was forgotton after a few days.

□

66

Savitri was not enjoying her life. She was simply propelling it towards its termination. Most of the time she remained silent. When she went to school, she simply performed her formal duty. She taught and then returned home. She was not interested in teaching also. It was her compulsion. Surekha would come to her every second or third day. She would console her. Puneeta also tried to please her mother. But she had almost turned into a lifeless stone. She said only one thing. 'Was there anyone who could arrange her meeting with the Prime Minister. She wanted the murderers of Ritu to be punished and penalised.' She said repeatedly.

'I want justice...I want justice.'

It appeared as if she was like a branch of a tree, that is broken but hangs on to it. But she had not abandoned two routines, i.e. teaching in the school and monthly visit to Pramod in jail. Both these jobs were mechanical action for her.

Surekha and Puneeta were happy when they found that Pramod's release from the prison was close at hand. New hopes sprouted. Their father would come home after spending three and half years. They were counting days now. Surekha, her husband and Puneeta one day went to the jail and met Pramod. They thought Savitri would be all right when Pramod comes home. The atmosphere at home was now turning pleasant. Surekha planned a project for her father in consultation with her husband.

'Mother, father will be freed on next Monday from jail,' Surekha told Savitri who was in bed.

'Monday...which Monday...the coming...' Savitri got up at once. Puneeta and Surekha were surprised at her behaviour. Then they thought that it might have been because of sudden joy.

'Yes mother, next Monday.'

'We shall all go there to bring Papa home,' Puneeta said.

'Yes mother. We shall all go together.'

'Next Monday....' Savitri said to herself.

'You will go mother?'

Savitri kept silent. She looked into vacuum. Moments passed by. It was Sunday now. Surekha came and asked her to come to Delhi but she refused. She made the excuse that she was unwell. Savitri stayed at home and they three went to Delhi to bring Pramod.

After their departure, Savitri took a bath. Then she stood before the idol of God and offered prayers. Tears trickled down from her eyes. The flow cotinued. She had made tea for them before they left. She had also taken tea. She neither cooked anything nor did she eat. She did not feel hungry or thirsty. She put the things in order in the rooms.

'Mother, Papa has come.' Puneeta shouted after entering the room.

'Congratulations, mother. Papa has, at last, come out of jail.' Surekha's husband touched Savitri's feet.

'God bless you, son.' She went ahead and touched Pramod's feet. All had wet eyes but there was a glitter in Savitri's eyes. Neither her eyes contained water nor any other emotion.

'Please be seated, I bring tea.' She said and went to the kitchen. They all sat in the room and chatted.

'Savitri brought tea and asked them to enjoy it. She offered a cup of tea to Pramod with her hands. Pramod looked in her eyes, who had her gaze downward. They all started taking tea. Savitri went inside.

As soon as Pramod kept his cup after taking tea, Savitri came there. She had an attache cane in her hands. She stood there. All were surprised to see an attache cane in her hands. No one could make it out. Puneeta's cup fell down and was broken. Surekha stood holding her cup with trembling hands. Praveen was also taken aback. Pramod felt he had been pressed under a mountain of snow. Savitri saw them all with her red eyes. No one dared to ask her anything.

'Mother, what is it? Why this attache cane?' Surekha held her with her hand.

'I am leaving.' There was such a tone in her voice that it could not be recognised. It contained anger, remorse and determination.

'Where, mother?' Puneeta and Surekha hugged their mother. Savitri put both of them aside.

'You are free from the jail. I have served you tea. From today onwards, I don't have any relation with you. I am going.' They all were wiping their eyes.

'Savitri, what are you doing? What a torture I underwent in the jail. I had only one stay after coming out of jail. I thought I would start my life once again with you. I thought you had forgiven me.'

'I have enjoyed the fruit of what I had done. Now you leave me...us all...in this way.' Pramod burst in tears.

'I had completely surrendered everything before you. You did not leave anything of mine. You destroyed it totally. I also had a desire to live. I had also tried to forget everything but Ritu's murder has shaken the lava in me. I performed my duties till today. I fended for my family till you arrived. I cannot stay even for a moment with you.'

'But why?'

'Not all questions have answers to them in life.'

'But there is a question behind every answer.'

'Where the entire life is caught in thorns, there are no answers.'

'Please forgive me once,' Pramod prayed.

'And you forgive me. I have nothing in my possession. Apparently, I exist but I am broken from inside. Everything is burst. Just an appearance. I am a living corpse. Whatever is left in me, that's also not under my control.'

'Savitri, please have some logic.'

'I have lived not by reason but by my heart. And excuse me please. There is nothing for you in my heart. If there is anything, it's anger, irritation. My life, the delicacy, the happy married life, honour and integrity of life...and a beautiful bud like my daughter Ritu...all is lost.' She went on saying.

'I am going to Kullu. You will not ever try to meet me. From now onwards we have no ties with each other. Surekha and Puneeta you will take care of your father.' Savitri walked with her attache cane. Puneeta wept, others also.

'Stop mother. Don't put us to this tragedy,' Surekha shrieked.

'No one should come forward. Don't stop me or I shall commit suicide here before you all by hitting my head. Forget about me Surekha and Puneeta. You will keep my word in mind as a heritage...the glimmer of modernism, the devise to acquire money somehow or the other is just like a mound of sand that fritters away in no time. It glitters from a distance but ultimately, it leads to destruction and death. One loses one's destination. Remember it always 'wrong roads never lead to right places.' My dear daughter, comfort is not only in wealth but it is in satisfaction too.' She moved towards the door swiftly.

'All right, you may do as you wish but I am your son-in-law, nay your son...I have the right to see you off at the bus stand for the last time?' Praveen wiped his tears and held her attache cane in her hands. Savitri kept silent.

'Surekha, I leave Puneeta to your patronage. If you can't take her care, you will send her to me at Kullu.'

Savitri moved forward. She faltered for a moment. Looked around and had tears in her eyes. She controlled herself and walked onwards. All stood silent. They were disturbed. Praveen followed her. He tried to talk but Savitri did not speak. Praveen came back after she boarded a bus for her destination.

She reached Kullu. She kept her head in her old mother's lap and wept endlessly. She felt consoled. She was mentally relaxed now. She felt as if the childhood atmosphere had returned. She kept wandering near Raghu Nath's tent. She would sit near Hidimba temple for hours together. She was often nostaligic.

Ritu's memory once again tortured her. She often saw her daughter's killer before her eyes. She was uneasy when she thought of getting justice for her daughter. The peace she had got after coming to Kullu was disturbed. She went to Delhi.

Pramod could not bear the sudden departure of Savitri. Soon after, he felt exhausted. He had great pressure on his mind. He fell ill. No medicine could cure him. Then he turned almost mad. Praveen was compelled to admit him to a mental hospital. His old friend Kishore was already in the hospital. Both of them met each other frequently, they would look at each other, they were reminded of something and then would forget.

They would neither recognise each other nor talk to each other. One had reached the mental hospital because of his wife's infidelity and the other reached there because of his infidelity towards his wife.

Savitri wandered on the roads of Delhi to seek justice for her daughter.

And one day, they saw Savitri's dead body was lying outside Prime Minister's residence, as if begging for justice.

Only after a few days, Gurcharan had been installed as one of the Ministers.

□